Other Avon Books by
Tom Deitz

tales of David Sullivan

WINDMASTER'S BANE
FIRESHAPER'S DOOM
DARKTHUNDER'S WAY

. . . and don't miss
THE GRYPHON KING

Coming Soon

STONESKIN'S REVENGE

SUNSHAKER'S WAR

a tale of David Sullivan

TOM DEITZ

AVON BOOKS ◆ NEW YORK

AVON BOOKS
A division of
The Hearst Corporation
105 Madison Avenue
New York, New York 10016

Copyright © 1990 by Thomas F. Deitz
Cover illustration by Tim White
Published by arrangement with the author
Library of Congress Catalog Card Number: 89-92494
ISBN: 0-380-76062-2

First Avon Books Printing: July 1990

RA 10 9 8 7 6 5 4 3 2 1

For
Gilbert, Bob, Mike, and Paul:
veterans of the old campaigns
and
A.J., D.J., Buck, and Paul II:
warriors of the new

ACKNOWLEDGMENTS

thanks to:

Boo Alexander
Chris Durance
Ben Hatcher
Christie Johnson
Jim Jones
Adele Leone
Buck Marchinton
Paul Matthews
Chris Miller
Jon Monk
John R. Newell
Vickie Sharp
Kerry Stroud

and a special thanks to

K. Michael Waldrip, for a needed distraction

and to Larry and Betty Marchinton for many others

Prologue I: Time A-wastin'

(Sullivan Cove, Georgia—Saturday, June 7—mid-afternoon)

By the time three o'clock had finally dawdled around, David Kevin Sullivan was getting almighty tired of shoveling gravel and busting up rocks. *And* of getting sunburned and dirty and sweaty and sore—especially on the last Saturday afternoon before high school graduation when there were a lot more interesting things to do than engaging in impromptu slave labor on a certain waterlogged farm in the wild south end of Enotah County. *Especially* when it was the first decent day in over a month.

The mere futility of it made his blood boil: half a precious weekend blown to hell because his pa had finally felt compelled to try to salvage the driveway, when David knew with the absolute conviction of the much-put-upon that just 'cause the sun was shining and the roadbed dry enough for them to haul half a dozen loads of rock and gravel from the county quarry to the steep bit of defunct logging trail that provided access to Sullivan Manor was no guarantee *at all* that the dratted monsoons wouldn't return by nightfall and wash it all away again. After all, why should today be any different from the last thirty-five?

Futility for sure then; and it was all his pa's fault. A whole day gone from his life because Big Billy had decided he was tired of parking at the foot of the hill.

Ha! David snorted to himself as he paused in mid-swing to check his watch. More like the old sot was tired of having to tote his endless six-packs an extra hundred yards. Certainly Big Billy had made no move to fix the drive when the ruts got too bad for either his wife's Crown Victoria or his son's beloved Mustang-of-Death to navigate. But when *he* couldn't get out, *then* it was suddenly a problem. In the meantime, the Vic was becalmed in the backyard until David's ma felt confident her oil pan wouldn't go bye-bye on some rain-exposed rock, and he'd taken to leaving the Mustang at Uncle Dale's for much the same reason, even if it did mean a half-mile jog to fetch it.

"I'm payin' you to work, not lean on that there hammer!" Big Billy's admonition rumbled up to him from where he was shoveling their latest load off the back of his old Ford pickup.

David sighed. *Just like a bleedin' chain-gang,* he thought, once more lofting an impressive sledgehammer above his rapidly reddening shoulders before thunking it angrily into his latest obstacle: a recalcitrant white quartz boulder that dead-centered the miniature Grand Canyon of ruts and bare rocks he was ensconced in. *Just like bleedin' Reidsville State Pen.*

Another blow, and another, but his efforts had little effect except to free a runnel of sweat from under the red bandanna that bound his thick, white-blond hair and send it snaking through black brows and into his bright blue eyes. He blinked at the sudden stinging and let the hammer thud into the ooze by a Reeboked foot. A forearm across his face cleared his vision passably but snagged the headphones of his Walkman. He swore softly and re-adjusted them, then retied the soggy rag tighter, taking special care to secure the controversial mid-back ponytail.

—Controversial, because his ma hated it, his suddenly-balding pa was jealous of it, his kid brother and most of his non-track-team friends loved it (the team, whose emblem it was, went without saying), and his favorite uncle and girlfriend hadn't yet made up their minds. As for himself, he hadn't decided either, because he could not divorce the *fact* of it from its symbolic function as both a gesture of defiance against institutional authority (he fully intended to wear it to deliver his valedictory oration in spite of Principal Taylor's protests), and as a sigil of a goal acquired.

Defiance indeed! What he wanted to do now was defy these blasted boulders—either that, or defy his pa, who had set him at them. Except that he didn't think that Big Billy was in much mood for defiance just then.

A final pause for a swig of Dr Pepper from the can on the grass behind him, and to flip over the Led Zeppelin tape he'd been listening to, and he was at it again: swinging the hammer in long, clean arcs that made his hands throb and the hard, smooth muscles of his bare torso tense and relax in syncopy.

"Don't pick at it, *hit* it," Big Billy admonished grumpily. David glanced up, scowling, to see his pa expertly flip a pile of gray and white granite chips into a particularly muddy depression.

"I'd *like* to hit it—or something," David muttered back. It was bad enough to have his afternoon co-opted, but to have his technique criticized as well—that *really* made him crazy.

As if in sympathy to his sudden burst of mental agitation, "When the Levee Breaks" began on the Walkman, and David swung harder, smiling grimly at the appropriateness of the tune as he let the grinding rhythm add its own energy to his rising spleen.

Thwack—crack, thwack—crack, and by God let Pa call that *tickling! Thwack—crack,* and a section of boulder shattered, leaving one insolent, sharp-edged excrescence that looked to David exactly like the damned thing was giving him the finger. He dealt it a solid one and saw it fly off to the right downhill.

"Incoming," he hollered absently.

"Shit!" Big Billy yelled back, then: *"Damn,* boy, watch what you're doin'! That 'un like to 'uv snagged my eye-ball!''

David didn't bother to look up. "Sorry," he grunted, though he wasn't, much.

"Cut my damned face," Big Billy continued incredulously, and then David did look up, to see his pa lower a hand from a ruddy and mud-spattered cheek and stare at a thin smear of the blood that decorated both it and his left cheekbone an inch below the orbit. The blood was scarcely redder than the hair Big Billy had started growing longer in back as it abandoned the front and top.

"I *said* I was sorry," David offered.

"Well just watch it! We've had 'nuff trouble 'round here lately." Big Billy eyed the flooded riverbottoms across the nearby highway meaningfully.

"That's for sure," David mumbled, and reapplied himself to his roadwork.

Trouble! That *was* for sure, too; and most of it his fault. After all, he'd been the one who'd insisted on prowling around the woods when his pesky younger brother had thought he heard music outside two years ago this coming July 31st. And he'd been the one who had got (or been given, he'd never quite figured out which) the Second Sight, which had allowed him to see the source of that music, whence it had led him to a series of adventures that had kept his life out of kilter ever since. For that warm summer night David had learned that his everyday world was not the only one; that there were others that lay about the familiar terra-firma like wet tissue paper thrown against a globe, and *some* of them were inhabited. That night he had met the denizens of the closest: Tir-Nan-Og, one of the three principal realms of the Sidhe—the old gods of Ireland, maybe; had seen them as they embarked on one of the periodic processional Ridings that marked the quarters of their year. That was before he had gotten tangled up in their politics, before the last in a series of ever-more-perilous encounters had resulted in their king ordering the border 'twixt Earth and Faerie closed and commerce between the Worlds forbidden.

But there were other Worlds as well, lingering tantalizingly among the golden Straight Tracks that linked them. Galunlati, for instance, the Overworld of the Cherokee Indians, where he had journeyed in a vain attempt to thwart a war among the widespread tribes of Faerie. He had lost a Faery friend on that adventure—or been unwilling participant and first cause of his betrayal and subsequent capture, which amounted to the same thing—and his conscience had not truly left him alone since.

"Trouble for sure," David repeated aloud, "trouble with a capital *T.*" And then Big Billy decided to fetch another load of gravel, which was trouble of a different kind entirely.

Sprawling sleepily in the bathtub two hours later, with his buddy Darrell Buchanan's latest homemade acoustic blues tape slowly winding down on the Walkman, David was certain there was no part of him that was neither sunburned nor worn to a frazzle. Or if not *every* part precisely, then at least a considerable number of large and/or conspicuous ones. With a deft twist of toes, he adjusted the hot mix to a gasp shy of intolerable, and set himself to compiling an inventory of those ills for possible guilt-tripping applications. Sunburned shoulders, back, and arms to start with, and ditto cheekbones and nose, all because there hadn't been enough clear weather this spring for him to get his usual tan. And sore muscles in all the same parts (or at least the movable ones) not to mention hips and thighs in the bargain. Nor could he ignore shovel-born blisters on six fingers, a splinter in his right palm, and a numbed-and-blood-blistered toe where he'd dropped the hammer on it right before quitting.

And that didn't even count being pissed, which—he supposed—was also pain of a sort, though in this case not of the body but of the mind.

He flopped back against the porcelained rim to let the rising tide draw the stiffness from his body, eventually finding the gumption to corral the soap and actually tackle some of the grime that patterned his torso like a Jackson Pollock painting. And recapitulated his litany of lost opportunities.

He *could* have been gaming with Gary and Darrell and Aikin, for instance: exploring imaginary paper worlds with the half of the MacTyrie Gang that had no particular interest in studying for finals and would not have sacrificed a Saturday for them even if they had. But that, at least, he was just as glad he had missed. He'd seen enough of real alternate Worlds to last him a lifetime. The worst thing was knowing they were still there: a temptation barely out of reach, waiting and—he sometimes suspected—watching.

And speaking of watching, he was suddenly having a fine time watching the soap slide and spiral over his body. Unfortunately, the patterns began to remind him of the interlaced designs the Sidhe used, and there he went again, thinking about a chapter of his life that was over—except, he feared, it wasn't. That's what his best friend, Alec McLean, had told him time after time. ''You ain't seen the last of old Silverhand, I promise you.'' Or, ''Wonder what Oisin's doing now,'' or, ''Wonder if the war ever started.'' Yeah, Faerie might be closed off, but it damn sure wasn't forgotten.

Not when everything he encountered reminded him of it, including Alec, who wasn't even interested in such things.

Alec! He was another defunct entertainment possibility, though in this case not one entirely out of the picture yet. In fact, after supper he was going over to Casa McLean to brush up on his chemistry (his weakest subject, and Alec's second best), and to bounce a couple of ideas about his valedictory speech off him, to see if they found a better reception with him than they had with his in-absentia girlfriend, Liz Hughes, when he'd bounced them off *her* across the phone lines for forty-five minutes the night before.

And that brought him to that same Liz Hughes, who was the person he had *really* wanted to spend time with this weekend. But she had a bodacious final art project to complete, down at the private school she'd been attending in Gainesville for the last two years, and wouldn't be coming up this weekend anyway. He quickly banished thoughts of her though, because it didn't do to be naked and wet and soaping one's body while thinking about one's remarkably pretty lady, because it put him in mind of *her* plying the bar of Coast . . .

At least he still had Liz's token, indeed had never removed it since she'd surprised him with it last Christmas.

It lay on his chest now, right between his pecs: a coin-sized disc of cloisonnéd copper she'd made in jewelry class, that bore on one side a full-faced human head (rather like his own, he thought), and on the other a conventionalized heart. *Head* and *heart:* his and Liz's years-old conflict: the dichotomy that ever confounded him.

A swirl of heat into his armpits made him realize that the tub had finally filled to acceptable level, so he turned the water off with another twist of foot and set himself to soaking. A drip remained, though, a steady trickle that he found somehow soothing.

He was tired, so tired. He slid down lower, let the water float the soap from his body.

His eyes closed and he dreamed.

There was rain in that dream, and already he didn't like it because his dreams had been unpleasant lately—dark visions of war and death and conflict he suspected were slopping over from some unseen altercation in Faerie—never mind that he'd seen enough rain the last few weeks to last him a lifetime. But then the dream-self wrested free of even semi-conscious control, and there was nothing for a while but the hiss of sheeting water and vague, drifty images of running through a darkness full of cold prickles and slashing droplets all aligned at precise forty-five degree angles. He was lost on a stormy winter night, slogging along a road that *might* be the Sullivan Cove road, or might not, or maybe through woods where the long pine needles added their own prickles to the falling water. And there was something following him, something huge and cold and evil, with glowing yellow eyes. Something that hissed and made a rustly, squishy sound where it dragged itself across the sodden land.

Abruptly it was on him: a serpent that had no end he could see through the driving rain—a monstrous red thing with a triangular head the size of his car and ivory horns sweeping back from it and a kind of stony searchlight between that played back and forth and suddenly transfixed him so that he could only run in the slow motion pace of terrified dreamers, while the dreadful creature got closer. Its maw gaped; he tried to flee but could not; and then it had swallowed him, and he had climbed up into its forehead (which was, for some reason, hollow), and was gazing out its eyes. And then he was the serpent himself and gliding through the woods in search of . . .

What? Prey? Yeah, that's what he wanted: prey and vengeance. Vengeance, and . . .

Light ahead of him, and he slid into a clearing where the rain had drawn back to form a dry circle in the center of which a young man sat on horseback, facing away. No, not a *man,* the captive rational part corrected: one of the Sidhe, one of Lugh's black-cloaked guards. The figure twisted around in his saddle, and fear crossed the parts of his face visible below his helm, and he screamed—except that David couldn't hear it, only see the full lips pop open. Suddenly he knew the face. It was Fionchadd mac Ailill, his one true friend in Faerie, the one he had inadvertently helped betray, and he shivered reflexively because he knew Finny probably hated him now and would hate him more if David ate him. But suddenly he was no longer the monster but Fionchadd, and he was scared, not because he was about to be eaten, but because there were people coming at him with chains, with *iron* chains, and already he could feel their heat, and then that other became aware that David was watching him, and somehow turned around in his own head and said, very slowly and distinctly, "It is all your fault, you know."

David's heart skipped a beat and he jerked away, as if fleeing that accusation.

"No it's not!" he screamed. *"No it's not! No, no, no!"*

And back in the tub his real body flinched as well, and came desperately awake, the words still on his tongue.

"No! N—"

The word trailed off as he caught himself, and a chill shook him in spite of the steamy heat. Jesus, that had been real—so real. *Too* real, in fact, because some of it *was* real—or had been. He swallowed hard. Not a difficult dream to interpret really, he'd had it before several times in the last few months, or variations, anyway. Not always with the rain—that was a late addition, though he did tend to have it more often when it rained—but always with two elements. One was the serpent that his waking mind knew was called an *uktena:* a monster from Galunlati that he knew all too well because not only had he helped kill one, but because he had briefly *been* one, last year when the Sidhe had come seeking Fionchadd's betrayer. Anger had welled up in him, then; anger at his helplessness, and he had become the strongest thing he knew, the thing he now most feared, because he knew it reflected part of him, the darkest pit of his soul.

Yet still the memory infected his dreams—it, and the other recurring element: Fionchadd himself, now prisoner . . . where? He didn't know. He only knew that it was his fault. If only he'd—

With no more warning than a brief mechanical click the door popped open.

David sat up frantically, snatching a washcloth to obscure crucial portions of his anatomy, only to see with minor relief the freshly-clipped blond head of his seven-

year-old brother, Little Billy, staring him straight in the
eye, his expression an almost comical mixture of surprise,
concern, and curiosity.

"Sorry, Davy," he began. "Pa told me to find out what
the matter was."

David glared at him. "Shut the door, dammit!" Then,
when the little boy acquiesced—unfortunately with himself
on the inside, "What do you *mean* what's wrong? *Nothin's*
wrong 'cept I just had a whole afternoon blown to hell!"
He spoke deliberately loud, not caring if he were over-
heard.

Little Billy twisted in the frustrated consternation of one
whose good deed has gone awry and prodded David's
abandoned jeans with a small, bare foot. "No, Davy," he
said patiently. "I mean why was you yellin'?"

David rolled his eyes. "Was it *that* loud?"

Little Billy nodded solemnly. "Sho' was."

"Jesus!" David slumped further down into the water,
leaving only his head and knees exposed.

"Is something *wrong,* Davy? You been real jumpy
lately. And you been talkin' in your sleep a lot, I can hear
you even in my room."

"Christ," David groaned for variety. "What about?"

Little Billy shrugged, sat down on the toilet lid, and
dragged both arms inside his Batman T-shirt, which gave
him the appearance of an armless but well-endowed female dwarf. "Don't know, 'zactly. Mostly just stuff like
now. You know: 'no, no, no,' and 'it ain't my fault,' and
all. You woke me up doin' it last week. Two times!"

David didn't know whether to be irritated or grateful.
His brother's room was across the hall from his own, closer
than his parents' lair, which shared porch frontage with
the living room. He always slept with his door closed,
even when it was really hot, as did his folks. But the kid
didn't. It was thus irritating to be spied upon, but a relief
that it was his brother and not his parents doing the re-
conaissance.

"You're not mad at me, are you?" Little Billy inquired

hopefully, freeing his hands again. "Everybody's been real grouchy lately."

David started to reply that *yes*, he was angry, at having his bath interrupted and his sanity questioned by a seven-year-old, however precocious. But then he saw his brother's face, saw the real apprehension there.

He swallowed hard. "No, kid, I'm not mad, just tired. Tired and worried, and feelin' kinda bad about somethin' I did."

"Finnykid?" Little Billy asked, hopping down from his perch.

"Yeah," David acknowledged, as he levered himself out and wrapped a towel around his middle. "Finnykid."

"It wasn't your fault, y'know," Little Billy observed, and scooted out the door David obligingly opened for him.

The door closed abruptly and David found himself facing the steamed-up mirror on its back.

"Oh yes it *was*," he whispered to his strangely hollow-eyed reflection.

Prologue II: Behind the Lines

(north of Erenn—high summer)

The selkies had been swimming for three days and the nights between and not always through water—though what the curious red-purple stuff was they had passed through a half-day's hard journey back, neither had known. All that was certain was that it had offered less resistance than sea-water and had tasted and smelled like flowers: alarming, yet pleasantly strange. And this morning something far more perilous had happened: when seeking to escape a curious kraken, they had dived too deep and come fearfully close to an Edge! Indeed, Tagd, the larger one, the male, had accidentally slid a flipper through and still felt in the long slender bones the empty cold that lay below the World. The rumors were true, then: there were places to the north of Erenn where the sea bed had begun to unravel—either that, or had not yet taken form.

No such uncertainties had troubled them lately, though; and now a gradually rising bottom and the half-sounds of waves on a not-too-distant shore told them they were approaching land. Anticipation awoke in them, gave them direction, gave them drive. Tagd swam ahead, rising toward the surface since the waters were now too shallow for the ship-long basking serpents that were their chief threat. The female, Erioch, followed, swam faster, and breached beside him. Afternoon sunlight shimmered across sleek dark fur, even as it glittered on the endless water like diamonds strewn across a slab of rippled jade. Ahead, halfway to the horizon, was their goal: a shard of island, scarce more than a dark line above the sea, except for that which glistened there like a wet black finger accusing the cloudless heavens.

Another dive, through red coral now, though the sand it rose from was silver and black; another breach, and they made landfall.

Tagd dragged himself ashore, suddenly awkward, where before had been only swift, sure movement. He grunted, for the rock was hard and vitreous and bore many a scarce-smoothed edge that cut at his belly and flippers. A particularly sharp ridge gashed his tail, and he yipped, then stopped, feeling foolish, for he already endured far worse hurt than that. He glanced toward his right forelimb, saw what glittered there—at once the source of his pain and the key to his mission. It was a ring of silver completely encircling one of the slim bones, but overgrown by the skin and flesh that webbed it to its fellows, making it for the time a part of him. But that would not be much longer.

Erioch joined him, and he barked an order. A harsher bark was the reply. He closed his eyes and reached into his memory, found a shadow-shape there and called it forth.

There was a rush of pain, as if his whole sleek body had exploded and collapsed onto itself once more, and when he raised his lids again, he saw through the green eyes of a man. A woman stood beside him, slim and naked and well-muscled, with the same wide swimmer's shoulders and blue-black hair as he. A ring glistened on his black-nailed finger. Before him the tower taunted the sky.

He stared up at it appreciatively and a little in awe, for it was thing of rumor, a tale from the distant past made

manifest. It did not *look* like the stuff of legends; much
more it resembled a work of nature gone awry: a giant
tree trunk grown from that hard black glass which sometimes oozed from the bowels of the earth in the Mortal
World. Black it was, indeed; but in no wise uniformly, for
in places he could see through a little way, and here and
there complex patterns had been etched and hewn and
blasted into its sheen. Its height, he could not guess. As
tall as half a hundred folk as tall as he, it well could be.
And a fit birthplace for a warrior king.

Lugh Samildinach had been born here, so Finvarra's
druids told; he who was now Ard Rhi of the Daoine Sidhe
in Tir-Nan-Og, southwest across the sea beyond their own
Erenn—he who was now their foe. Balor of the Fomorians
had hidden his daughter Ethlinn in the distant top, fearing
a prophecy that declared that a son of hers would destroy
him. But in spite of all his efforts, a warrior of the Tuatha
de Danaan had found her, and the child he had begot had
grown to be lord of the youngest and strongest realm of
the Sidhe. Even now Finvarra's fleets fought his in the
south, and neither side was winning, though that was due
in large part to aid from the Powersmiths and Arawn of
Annwyn, who so far had kept Lugh from being overwhelmed by Finvarra's more numerous and far faster vessels.

"Truly, it is a wonder," Erioch breathed behind him.
"But we have no time now to stand staring."

Tagd scowled at her, but his expression softened as he
took in her naked beauty, their own smooth skins being
fair enough for Faery eyes, and there truly being no time
for the weaving of such frivolities as clothing from foam
and stray seaweed. And then he saw her eyes shift and
narrow as they caught some movement behind him. He
followed her gaze, called upon Power to see farther, and
saw as she did what broke the southern horizon: Ships at
full career coming their way—long, low *golden* ships with
blood red sails, each of which showed a golden sun-in-
splendor. And above them, but a little behind, more ves-

sels—but these rode the air a bow-shot above the waves, their oars slowly beating among the breezes.

"It appears we have come just in time," Tagd noted wryly.

A gull's cry answered him, and he turned to see a large white fellow gliding easily through the salty air toward them. It alighted on a knob of glistening rock, and before he had time to notice any more than a glittering around its throat, its shape shimmered and twisted and became a tall, pale-haired man, also nude.

"In time indeed," the stranger snapped, casually conjuring a short green kilt from a handful of kelp. "Know you that I am Engol, Watch-Warden of Ethlinn's Isle. If you have business here it would be wise to state it quickly."

"I am Tagd," the selkie informed him. "This is Erioch. If you are whom we seek, you will know how to receive our message."

A frown bent the Warden's dark, slanted brows. "You come from Finvarra?"

Tagd held up his hand. The ring caught a beam of sunlight and turned to fire.

Engol stepped forward and removed a similar ring from the chain that hung around his neck. He pressed it against the one Tagd raised to meet it. Light flared at the juncture for an instant, Engol's face froze for a fractioned moment more, and then he nodded.

"You are who you say," he acknowledged. "If you will follow, we may yet fulfill your errand in time." He indicated a shallow indentation in the glass of the tower, inserted his ring into a hollow there, and motioned Tagd to use his likewise. "By entering thusly, those within will know you bear a true message. Come, we must hasten."

For an instant the only sound was that of the slapping of waves on the glassy shore, and then a hidden something clicked, and a section of wall angled outward.

More men stood behind, and women, too, all of them tall and slim and dressed in serviceable tunics of green and gray. Their eyes were fierce and wary, and all clutched weapons hastily snatched from a series of trestle tables where they had evidently been rapidly donning armor, to judge by half-laced gauntlets and part-buckled vambraces that clad them, the shields and high-domed helms that lay about. The large, round room was lit by a shifting, gray-green light, and was empty save for the tables and attendant benches—probably some sort of seldom-used guardroom now awakened to use. The ceiling was domed, but not perfectly, for the circle of the walls was not exact, and a long ramp looped around the opposite side and disappeared through an oval opening between two carved obsidian ribs.

A few stared at their visitors' gleaming skin as Engol hurried them past, but most, when they saw their commander's haste, went back to their feverish vesting.

"How goes the war?" someone called, with the nervous tremor of one who had believed it would never touch him.

"You have only to look outside to know that," Tagd shouted back as he and Erioch sprinted after their host. "I think your spear will soon find living sheathing."

A murmur of alarm swelled the ranks, followed by a dull metallic clatter.

"But truly, how *does* the war go?" Engol asked in turn as he bounded onto the ramp. "Orders are not information."

Tagd shrugged as he joined him on the slope, though all kept moving. "Stalemate as of three days ago, which is the last we heard. You still guard Finvarra's prisoner; the Powersmiths hold theirs and add to their number daily, and among them Finvarra's daughters. Finvarra's main fleet encircles the Powersmiths' flagship in the Middle Seas as they have done all winter, but still cannot come at them, for Ilionin has raised a shield of Fire that burns the very water—though now that the Tracks are strong again, *that* could quickly change, if she grows restless with captivity and sends for reinforcements. Meanwhile Lugh and Arawn

awn harry Finvarra's back and the southern shores of Erenn as well, when the Tracks permit—hoping, I think, to
destroy Finvarra's ships faster than he can build them.
Lugh has the air ships, too, but few of them, and they are
frail, though even now some come this way.''

''I *knew* it,'' Engol spat. ''I told Finvarra it was a
mistake to hide the prisoner here, but he would not listen.
He had vessels enough to defend this place, he said. Lugh
would have to pass the entire coast of Erenn to come here,
if he even knew where the prisoner *was*. And this way the
war would not ravage his land. His lands, no; but what of
the *seas?* What of Manannan mac Lir, whose domain they
are? Does Finvarra invite a fourth foe?''

''I have heard no word of Manannan,'' Tagd replied.
''He keeps his silence, which in itself is strange.''

''But where will Finvarra move the prisoner, then?''

''We are to take him from here and swim north; no
more would it be good to tell you.''

''Ah, surely you are right, for siege will be joined, and
I could be captured. Still—''

''Can you not go faster?'' Erioch interrupted pointedly.
''This tower is passing high.''

''Aye,'' Engol chuckled. ''But there is more to this ramp
than seems apparent. One more turn and we are at our
goal.'' And so it was that they reached the top of Ethlinn's
Tower.

Once more the rings unlocked an unseen door, and once
more Tagd passed into a large round room.

And at last came face to face with the one who, through
no fault of his own, had set the greater realms of Faerie
in contention.

Slumped in a window alcove opposite, he did not look
like much: a slender, fair-skinned, gold-haired youth not
quite fully grown. Nothing special there—nor in his slanted
brows, clean-angled jaw, and full lips; *all* the Daoine Sidhe
had them. Not even his clothing was worth note, simply
a long robe the same colors as the room: black and gray
and white and silver. But his eyes were something else:

green and afire with anger and pain. He met Tagd's gaze
when the door opened, and started to rise. A heavy clank
drew the selkies' attention toward the noise.

Another thing was also true, then: Finvarra not only had
a prisoner, but that prisoner was shackled with Iron. He
shuddered at that, fearing even the presence of that ever-
hot metal, and wondered how the boy stood it. Wyvern
skin helped, of course, and the boy wore cuffs of that stuff
around his wrists and ankles, so that the heat was barely
tolerable. But still, it was not a fate one of his race would
have chosen.

The boy blinked back fury, his face contorted, and then
Tagd remembered another thing: this lad had already
known the Death of Iron, had suffered a spear-thrust (from
Ailill, his father, so it was said) that had pierced both his
body and his soul, sundering both, destroying one, and
wounding the other past hope of healing. Well, the boy
obviously had a new body now. But the wound in the soul
. . . ah, those *never* truly healed. And the Iron shackles
would sufficiently inflame it that it would take all the boy's
Power to remain sane. So that was why he had not escaped.

"Not much, is he?" Engol laughed harshly. "Such a
little thing to start a war."

"*Boredom* is what started the war," Erioch snapped
back. "A thousand years, nearly, since the last one, and
that because of a heifer!"

"A bull," Tagd corrected. "But you were the one who
would hasten."

"Aye," said Engol. And with that, he reached into a
compartment on the ramp side of the archway, withdrew
six hand-sized squares of silvery leather, and gave two
each to Tagd and Erioch, keeping a third set for himself.
"You may have to touch his bonds," he cautioned.

The prisoner did not resist when Engol jerked him to
his feet, did not react when the rings applied to the locks
made the chains fall from the shackles.

Nor did he protest when he was taken down the spiraling ramps and into the chaotic guardroom, nor when he at last faced open ocean.

Tagd scanned the horizon apprehensively. Lugh's fleet was closer now. He did not need to call on Power to see the suns glittering on the sails.

"Barely in time," Erioch observed irritably.

"What would you now?" Engol inquired.

"That you will see," Tagd replied, whereupon he stared at his left hand until a bit of webbing showed there, then gritted his teeth and tore the thinskin free. The prisoner saw, and fear enflamed his eyes, but it was too late. Engol held him while Tagd and Erioch stripped him, save for the Iron rings about his wrists. When he was naked, Tagd slit the skin at the base of the boy's neck with a fingernail and slapped the skin-patch across the bleeding wound. The boy shuddered, cried out weakly, but by then the *change* had come upon him. Tagd watched until it was finished, made sure the Iron bonds were still locked around the flesh above the flippers, now almost overgrown with skin. The prisoner-seal snarled at him when he grasped its shoulders, but he slapped it, then began his own *change*, even as Erioch did.

Engol bade them farewell from the shore, resumed his gull-shape, and flew south toward the fleet.

And two selkies and their prisoner started toward the sea.

They had not even reached the first line of breakers when something attracted their attention further out, beyond the most distant swells to the north.

Tagd halted for a moment, puzzled, and then his already round eyes rounded further with wonder.

For as he watched, a ship rose into view from beneath the very waves. Of some white material, it was, that might very well have been bone, and with sails of blue and silver, worked in an overall design of scales, over which three human legs in blue conjoined at the hips ran in an endless circle. Fear rose in Tagd, for this was not expected; this was not part of the plan. Was it some trick of

Lugh's? Did the Ard Rhi of Tir-Nan-Og command not only vessels of the water and of the skies, but of the deep seas as well?

But then Erioch barked a chuckle next to him, and he realized what had happened.

The vessel had fully risen now, and was gliding toward them, undisturbed by the breakers that flashed and fought around it. An instant later the carved wooden dragon at its prow tapped the shore.

A man stepped forward from where he had been hidden at the trailing rudder. He was as tall as anyone Tagd had ever seen, in Faerie or the Lands of Men, and more muscular than any warrior of the Sidhe he could recall. He wore a simple loose robe of blue and green brocaded velvet, open to the waist where a belt of golden shells bound it, and had hair sleek as wet black sealskin. Atypical for the Sidhe, a beard spread across his chest.

And apparently had no concern for his fine raiment, for he hopped across the low gunwale, landing chest-deep in the water, and strode toward the selkies.

"Do not bother to manshape for me," he called casually, for already Tagd was *changing* again. "I know you for what you are. Show me the sign, and I will show you one, and relieve you of your burden."

"Manannan mac Lir," Tagd managed to bark, ignoring both orders from surprise as he reclaimed his human form. "So you have entered the fray."

Manannan shook his head. "I owed Finvarra a favor, which he has now demanded. For the rest, I wait and see. Though," he added, gazing south, "it appears that someone else may have made my choice for me."

Tagd recovered himself, waded forward, and raised the ring. The Lord of Caer Ys met him, showed his own hand where an identical bauble glittered, twin to that so recently embedded in Tagd's flesh the pain had not yet left him. Silver touched silver, light flashed once more, and words poured into Tagd's brain without benefit of hearing: *Deliver your charge to this one, then be about your business.*

Tagd nodded stiffly and shuffled aside as the man stooped, lifted the prisoner (who was scarcely larger than a well-grown pup), and strode with him back to the vessel. He was still watching in stunned amazement as the ship slid away from the shore, turned gracefully, and slipped back beneath the waves.

"So Manannan now has the boy," Erioch observed in human shape from the spray-slapped shore behind him— just as the shouts of warriors reached them from the fleet to the south.

PART I

WINDS BETWEEN THE WORLDS

Chapter I: Ancestral Voices . . .

(Sullivan Cove, Georgia—Friday, June 13—oneish)

"Now who in the Sam Hill is *that?*" JoAnne Sullivan wondered aloud to nobody as tires whined and ground in the gravelly mud at the foot of the hill below her family's house, striving without much luck for traction on what in antediluvian times had passed for a driveway. She sighed and stuffed another dripping load of washing into the new Kenmore dryer in the kitchen's northeast corner before stalking toward the westward back door (the kitchen was in the downstroke of the old T-shaped farmhouse and flanked by porches on either side), snagging a tall glass of Dr Pepper as she went. Unconsciously she smoothed stray blonde hair out of her face and wiped her damp hands on the tail of the single surviving Clifton Precision Softball T-shirt she wore above cut-off Wranglers because it was too hot and sticky to wear any more and too messy in the kitchen to risk anything better.

"Turn that *down!*" she hollered left into the tacked-on den that made the base of the T, where a nearly-naked Little Billy was ensconced in front of the tube engrossed in "Chip 'n Dale's Rescue Rangers"—loud enough to drown out k. d. lang's latest on WZEL-FM, which *she'd* been listening to.

"But Maaaaa, *you* made me come in!"

"Hush up and mind me!" JoAnne snapped before she could catch herself. No sense being such a bitch over so little, especially when the protest was valid.

Not that it let him off the hook, of course: as soon as the sun had ventured out that morning the little varmint had been out there in it, muddying up the miniature Enotah County 'Possums gym shorts Davy had given him for his birthday and the burgundy T-shirt that matched 'em—which had been the genesis of the current round of washing. It had pissed her off mightily, too; and he had gotten sunburned in the bargain. By the time she'd hauled him back inside, his arms and cheeks were a fair match for the rest of his ensemble. She should have known better, though: he'd proven noisy at best and underfoot at worst, and his television was about to give her a headache she didn't need.

Wurrr-urr-urr-urrrrrrr.

Scowling, JoAnne sidestepped Tiberius, the yellow tomcat that tried to rub her legs, and eased onto the porch. Her brows practically collided, then, as she saw the heavy mass of clouds glowering above Bloody Bald out at the cove beyond Uncle Dale's place where Big Billy was supposed to be re-anchoring the old man's new trailer for the second time that spring. There were *always* clouds there now, and it gave her the willies. Magic, David said it was, though the border with *that* place was supposed to be closed off. But she didn't like it, not one little pea-pickin' bit!

*Wurr-urr-urr-urr-*uurrrrr.

The spinning persisted, grew louder, and she followed it toward the blood-red slash of the Sullivan Cove road and the spindly green shoots of the closest hunk of corn-field, mostly underwater now, as a result of last night's downpour. Or maybe it was the night before's—they were starting to run together.

A once-white Chevy S-10 pickup was slowly fighting its way up the drive, easing past her white Crown Vic, which was still in the ditch at the turnoff where it had slid that morning in utter disregard of the six loads of gravel her menfolk had unloaded the previous weekend, which had washed away three days later. Eventually the truck made it to the relative solidity of the side yard and squished to a halt, though the driver kept the motor idling. A stray beam of sunlight glanced off the bumpers and chrome light bar atop the cab, masking her frown with a squint. It was good to see the sun shining off *something* these days. Mighty good indeed.

The passenger door opened, dispensing a tiny, round-shouldered old lady in new Sears sneakers and a faded calico dress that had never heard of either color or fashion. JoAnne's heart sank: it was Minniebelle Coker, who lived in the next hollow up the main highway. At least eighty-five, Minniebelle was one of that vanishing school of mountain women who didn't believe in calling ahead and didn't think anything at all of dropping by unexpectedly to spend the day. Oh well, she *was* a good-hearted old soul, and anyway, it'd give JoAnne an excuse to sit down and cool off for a spell.

Minniebelle had paused at the door to retrieve something from the seat, then tottered across the soggy yard, leaving her grandson Marcus to clunk the door shut behind her. Marcus stuck his thin, ruddy face out his window and hollered, "Just got a call 'bout *another* goddam ruckus. Be back 'round three, if I can."

Minniebelle nodded, and JoAnne's heart sank further. That meant she had to put up with the old biddy for at least a couple of hours.

But still . . .

Taking one final swig from her Dr Pepper before abandoning it on the weathered gray porch rail, JoAnne navigated the creaking steps and walked barefoot through the

yard to meet Minniebelle halfway and relieve her of her
burden: a corrugated cardboard box in which nestled four
identical Ball jars.

"Thank-ee, gal," Minniebelle squeaked. "I reckon I'm
just plumb wore out and rotten. Ain't got strength for
nothin' these days."

"I ain't quite *that* far gone," JoAnne replied, trying to
retain some semblance of both humor and hospitality, "but
I'm pretty sure I'm a little bit mildewed."

"Ain't never seen such rain, 've you?"

JoAnne shook her head as she took Minniebelle's arm
and helped her up the steps. "Not in my lifetime."

"Nor mine neither," Minniebelle acknowledged beside
her. "This much just 'taint natural."

"Lots of unnatural things been goin' on, as a matter of
fact," Minniebelle opined with special emphasis half an
hour later. " 'Specially 'round *these* parts." She took a
swallow of ice tea and regarded her hostess sharply.

JoAnne eluded that gaze and stared out across the thick-
grown yard, thinking she probably ought to get David at
it come Monday morning. They were sitting on the front
porch now, eating the morning's biscuits globbed with the
fresh batch of strawberry jelly which had been the contents
of the mysterious jars. Minniebelle was a famous canner,
and this was only the first of many loads she'd drop by
over the summer, as things came into season.

Unfortunately, though, she was also a famous gossip
and busybody, and the last thing in the world JoAnne
needed was for somebody to start asking questions about
"unnatural" things. 'Specially when there really *had* been
strange things goin' on that she knew about, and probably
a right smart more she didn't.

"Mighty strange things," Minniebelle offered again.

"Like what?" JoAnne asked innocently, having decided
it was best to find out exactly what her guest knew—'cause
what Minniebelle knew was bound to be the maximum anybody did.

"Like . . . oh, like all that sickness you folks had two summers ago: first pore ole Dale and his stroke, and then the littlest 'un just turns off for a while. You ever find out what'uz wrong with 'em?''

JoAnne cleared her throat uncomfortably: what was she going to say? They'd been sick and healed, that was true, but she didn't believe half of either the cause or the reason herself, and didn't want to believe even that part: that there was a whole other world overlaying this one, a world where magic happened and once in a while crept out to torment her family.

All these things flashed through JoAnne's mind in an instant, but her reply was the well-rehearsed line she'd used on the non-local parts of the family—and on Minniebelle herself at least twice before.

"Miracles happen. They just happen, and I'm glad they do."

"Seems to me like you been usin' up more'n your fair share, though," Minniebelle shot back. "Both of 'em sick one day and healed the next. *I* ain't never seen nothin' like it."

"I hadn't either," JoAnne replied truthfully, thinking of the year she'd spent wondering how the healing had been accomplished before she'd followed another old lady up the mountain and found out the truth of the matter.

But Minniebelle was not to be daunted. "And *then*," she continued, forging ahead, ". . . JoAnne, I hate to say it, but your oldest boy's just gone plumb off of the kazip. Why, I've heard all kinds of things 'bout him. Just acts strange and all, and then last summer when everybody thought him and that Hughes gal had run off that time, and them Gypsy-folks got their wagons burnt—why, law! My boy Marcus *seen* that part, 'cause he'uz ridin' with the sheriff that night, and he seen that fire. Oh, he told what they told him, too: said it was fire runnin' fast on spilled gasoline, but he told me what he really seen: said there'uz a strange boy there just waved his hand and made that fire. Said he rode off and wasn't ever seen again. Said there'uz some mighty fine horses there, too . . . just a little *too* fine, if you catch my meanin'. Wouldn't you say *that* was strange?''

JoAnne finished off her second biscuit and checked her watch, wishing Minniebelle would just go on home. She even considered offering her a ride—except, of course, that her car was stuck beyond redemption. As for the pickup, which would have made it, Big Billy had taken it over to Dale's.

''Well?''

''I ain't got nothin' to say,'' JoAnne replied shortly. ''It's our business and Davy's and his buddies. Everybody come out all right.''

''Yeah, I reckon so, far as *you* folks're concerned. But Marcus got in a lot of trouble over it 'cause they was too many holes in his report. But that ain't the last of it, neither . . . there'uz that stuff the next day: all them lights up on the mountain: *I* seen that! Was out Sunday mornin' huntin' for 'sang, and walked up the ridge, and seen them clouds come a-rollin' in toward that mountain over yonder''—she pointed left, to where the shoulder of the proper Appalachians crowded in. Lookout Rock, JoAnne knew, was what she was talking about.

''But they weren't no ordinary clouds, no si*ree,*'' Minniebelle confided. ''They'uz like them clouds in that movie thing—*Close Encounters,* or whatever ye call it: that'un 'bout them spaceships, and that crazy man made a model of out of the mashed taters. Only I watched real close, an' I seen shapes in there. Couldn't make 'em out, but they looked kinda like boats, or somethin': long, skinny boats with great wide sails. And then them clouds come back and they all vanished.''

''So you think we've been havin' spacemen visit us up here in Sullivan Cove?'' JoAnne managed a serious laugh in spite of her discomfort, for Minniebelle had certainly seen true—just interpreted it wrong.

''I've seen stuff 'bout it in the *Enquirer:* Folks loses time, or forgets where they were, and all; and they find out them saucer folks has carried 'em off. Shoot, I hear they even carried off Elvis!''

JoAnne rolled her eyes. That clinched it: Minniebelle was about to slip right on off, and she didn't know whether to be grateful for the change of topic or worried about the poor old woman's mind.

''An' another thing ain't natural,'' Minniebelle went on blissfully, before JoAnne could reach any sort of conclusion. ''All this rain! Why, law, girl, I've seen rain, but nothin' like this. Straight down all day. Clear sky one minute, and clouds the next—and . . . why, land, the dreams I been havin'!''

JoAnne's eyes narrowed abruptly. ''What *kinda* dreams?''

''Bad dreams, gal: dreams 'bout hatred and killin', and . . . and *monsters!*''

''I been havin' nightmares too, and so has Davy. Can't hardly sleep for 'em.''

''*I* dreamed I got mad at Marcus and stuck a knife in 'im! Woke up in the night and I had one in my hand, and was walkin' out the back door toward his trailer!''

''Jesus, Minniebelle, you be careful!''

''*Jesus,*'' Minniebelle observed pointedly, ''ain't got *nothin'* to do with it.''

''Minniebelle!''

''So where's your young'un now?''

''I got *two,*'' JoAnne snorted with unexpected impatience.

''I got ears to *hear* the littl'un; it's the big'un I was wonderin' 'bout.''

''He's over at the lake with his buddies and their gals, I reckon—'cept his gal ain't up here yet. Some kinda pregraduation cook-out, or somethin'. He's graduatin' tonight: first honor.''

''Smart boy, I always said. Smart and polite and good lookin'—*real* good lookin'—'cept he needs a haircut. But weird.''

''I'd thank you not to talk 'bout Davy like that!''

"But he *is!* Everybody knows it. Why, them things he goes on about—"

"Goin' on 'bout things don't make you weird," JoAnne snapped, feeling her day's suppressed irritations start to escape their bonds. "Davy knows things, is all. He *likes* to know things. There's two things that makes folks think you're weird, Minniebelle," she added, her voice rising with every word, "knowin' too much—and not knowin' enough! Up here folks say Davy's strange 'cause he's smart and interested in things most folks ain't. But down there in Athens where he's gonna go to school it's you and me that'd be strange 'cause we're so ignorant! Do I make myself clear?"

"Books don't make you smart, neither, gal," Minniebelle gave her back promptly, though her usual feistiness was edged with something harder and her blue eyes looked cold as steel.

"They sure don't!" a male voice rumbled unexpectedly, as Big Billy sauntered out of the house, stuffing the tail of a clean white T-shirt into his jeans, though he seemed to have already sweated through it. JoAnne jumped a little, having neither heard him come in the back door nor tromp down the hall.

"Maybe me and Minniebelle was havin' a private conversation," she flared. "Ever think about that?" (What *was* gettin' into her today? She wasn't this bad when she was on the rag, yet she was picking fights everywhere. This had to stop and quickly, before she went *too* far.)

"Looks mighty public to me," Big Billy drawled. He sat down on the swing and scratched his belly absently. Davy had finally got him to running, and he looked as good as he had in years. He seemed to have dropped another couple of pounds, too, JoAnne noted, trying desperately to shift her train of thought and thus defuse the potentially explosive tension. It was hard, though; good looks didn't help her husband's tongue or his temper, which were no great shakes at the best of times.

"Minniebelle brought us some strawberry jelly," she

managed finally, reaching down to pick up the tomcat that had arrived along with her spouse.

"Strawberries, huh?" Big Billy grunted, casting a distrustful blue eye toward Minniebelle, whom he was a little afraid of. "Surprised you got any. Everything *we've* got's under water." He swept his hand in an arc before him indicating the flooded bottoms. "Might as well hire Chinese and raise rice."

"I got me a greenhouse," Minniebelle beamed. "Don't rain in there 'less *I* want it to."

"Good jelly too," JoAnne observed, relieved at the slackening of the previous moment's hostility.

"Have to try some," Big Billy replied, and fell silent.

"Least it's not rainin'," JoAnne added warily, checking her watch. "Uh, Minniebelle, I hate to do this, but I really need to start gettin' ready for graduation." She winked at Big Billy over the old lady's head. "Bill'll run you home, won't you, Bill?"

"I reckon," Big Billy mumbled sourly, starting to rise. "If you don't mind ridin' in a muddy pickup. 'Course I gotta go get it first. Left it over at Dale's."

"Can't keep nothin' clean round here," JoAnne offered.

Minniebelle stood up so abruptly JoAnne started, sloshing tea into her lap. *"Well I never!"* the old lady shrilled, like a cat whose tail had been rocked on. "Why don't you just come out and *say* it, 'stead of pussyfootin' around?"

JoAnne gasped incredulously. What in the *world* had brought this on? Minniebelle was a pretty straight shooter, but she wasn't usually rude—and JoAnne thought she had a thicker hide than to get huffy over honest talk.

"Say *what?*" she finally choked.

"That I ain't wanted here! You can *keep* the damned jelly," she added. "But don't 'spect nothin' *else* this summer!" Suddenly she was shaking, her wrinkled face red with rage.

The last bonds on JoAnne's control unraveled. "I don't want *nothin'!*" she shouted back before she could stop.

Big Billy's eyebrows nearly intercepted his receding hairline.

"You ain't gonna *get* it, neither!" Minniebelle raged on, heading for the front steps.

"Well, I . . ." JoAnne broke off as she saw the gasp of realization that suddenly rounded the old woman's lips, the sudden horrified brightening of her eyes before they filled with tears.

"Why . . . I . . . I don't know what made me say that," Minniebelle sobbed. "I didn't mean it, none of it. I just got real mad of a sudden, and wanted to . . . to *hurt* somebody."

"Yeah," JoAnne whispered shakily, taking her in her arms. "I felt it too."

Big Billy looked puzzled but went back inside to begin the trek back to Dale's. "Foolishness," he muttered, as he slammed the door behind him.

The tomcat scratched JoAnne for no obvious reason.

Chapter II:
. . . Prophesying War
(a tower—no place—no time)

Silver—and gray, and crumbling stone, and the persistent clink of the Iron chains that bound him: these filled Fionchadd mac Ailill's days.

How long had he stared at the ill-made walls of his prison? How many risings of sun and moon had passed him by? Except that he was not certain there *was* a sun or moon in this strange shattered place, at least not as there was in Ethlinn's obsidian tower from which he had lately been spirited—though of his time there he remembered little because he had spent all his Power keeping the pain at bay. Here there was only a sporadic brightening in the silver-white haze of the close-looming sky—a brightening that drew closer every day, as if some celestial body inscribed a slow progression that might sometime bring it in line with the single slit of window that lit the round tower chamber that was his world.

Or might never.

As to the room itself, it had curving stone walls and a floor of concentric circles of precisely cut gray flags inset with spirals of silver that here and there lapped up the walls and in four places reached the domed ceiling and spread out once more, though cracks and flakes and fissures disturbed the complex pattern.

For the rest, he had a silver-framed bed with torn sheets of rough gray silk, and a coverlet of ragged gray fur, and a table and chair of gray wood gilt with silver. The simple breeches and sleeveless tunic he wore were also of that non-color, and made of plain coarse wool; and his pierced and gathered shoes were of nondescript gray leather. He had chains, too: Iron-alloyed bonds lined with wyvern skin that bound his wrists and ankles to the wall and trailed across the floor behind him when he paced out the narrow limits of his freedom. But even that metal was dull: gave off no reflections, so that Fionchadd could not see the green of his own eyes, or the gold of his hair, or the pink of his lips and his tongue. His skin was pale—too pale to offer much contrast, and he had thought more than once of slicing open his veins so that the gush of red would relieve the monotony that drugged his sight. Not suicide that cut, for such was an impossibility with his kind. Oh, he might sever the ties between body and soul for a space of seasons, but the two would rejoin in time, and there was nothing he could do to forestall that reunion. And his captors would still have his body, and when the two reunited, the cycle would start all over with his situation not one whit better.

So Fionchadd had only to sit and wait and gaze out his window at a vista of white-silver water across which four bands of silver light slowly spun with the tower itself as their hub, until they merged with the like-colored sky of this strange, tiny land no one had heard of. Straight Tracks, he thought: roads between Times and Worlds. But who had ever seen them in silver?

He had asked once, queried the friendliest of the Erennese guards; but the man had told him little. Finvarra alone knew of this place, he had discovered, but almost nothing more except that it was not truly a part of Faerie. He still hoped by careful questioning of his captors to learn the full, true tale in time. It was something to do, after all, a puzzle to fill the spaces between more troublesome concerns, the principal one of which was winning his freedom.

But escape eluded him, because of that same pain that dulled his mind and would not let him draw on the Power that should have let him choose any number of shapes and so win free. There were two kinds of pain, too; one he had learned to live with, and one that was troubling and new.

The first, the wound in his soul, had never healed. It ached always, a gnawing between his thoughts, around his movements; so much a part of him he could no longer remember what it was like before. It, he had mastered; it, in a sense, he could numb—as he could ignore the slap and hiss of waves outside and the tangy smell of salt water, and center on other sounds and odors. But that did not mean it was not present.

The other agony was born of the Iron rings that bound him, for the fires of the World's first making yet burned in that metal and never cooled. It was tolerable—barely, if he was careful; but of it, too, he could not be free.

And a final thing he could not elude was fear. For himself, of course, but more importantly for his mother, the Fireshaper Morwyn, whose fate he did not know except that she had offered herself up in exchange for his freedom when Finvarra had demanded she surrender herself for judgment because of her role in the deaths of his half-mad sister and her twin, his own equally insane sire.

Evidently that had not happened, however, for he had not been released, and he had heard vague rumors of the ship that would have delivered her being intercepted by her mother's Powersmith kin. There were tales, too, of a massive battle waged between the Powersmiths and Finvarra's folk, of Finvarra's daughters taken hostage and Finvarra fleeing in the shape of an albatross, then turning his full wrath on Lugh and attacking both north and south,

while a third force tried to intercept the Powersmiths en route home. This last had supposedly succeeded, but the Powersmiths had raised a shield of magical
fire around their fleet which not even Finvarra could shat-
ter.

All this he had slowly found out the previous autumn.
Winter had come then, and in previous years both the
Tracks and seas of Faerie would have been impassable.
That was before the Powersmiths had learnt how to build
ships that could sail in any weather and promptly built a
fleet of them for Finvarra—an action they doubtlessly regretted now, since he'd heard something about an impass:
the Powersmith fleet besieged that same navy. As for Lugh
and Arawn, who did not have the new, stronger, vessels,
he supposed they had used the interim to muster forces
and augment their fleets so that they could come to their
ally's aid, now that the Tracks were once more growing
stronger with the approach of Midsummer.

As for himself, he knew things Finvarra wanted also to
know, and his un-loving uncle had spent most of the winter trying to discover those things.

The torture was new. Before, the bonds were only to
prevent his escape by distracting him enough to dampen
his Power. But lately things had changed. At least—so
far—he had resisted.

They were coming now, he could feel the dull tread of
heavy feet on the invisible stair that wound up from somewhere below. Closer and closer, and a door opened in the
wall and two figures entered; squat, muscular manshapes
not quite shoulder high on him, cleanshaven all over to
better display skin that gleamed like waxy, dark-green
leather where it was not covered by loincloths of short
white fur and arm-and-leg bands and torques of polished
silver. *Djinn*, Fionchadd knew, who could work with
Iron—unlike his guardsmen, who were men of the Sidhe.

No words passed between them as they approached. He
tried, as he had tried a hundred times before, to summon

Power to blast them, but it would not come; the pain had caused its flame to burn too low.

Without dispatch, one of the djinn seized his left arm, spun him around to draw both wrists together, while his companion grasped Fionchadd's legs, subduing their pointless thrashings with the skill of one long practiced, and with speed not even his Powersmith kin could have equaled.

The rest he knew from grim experience: chains shortened until his limbs were drawn to the corners of the bed; his tunic rucked up to his armpits, his breeches to his feet, then hair-fine needles of Iron deftly applied so that they wrought neither wounds nor bruises, but only tiny holes—and delicate, almost crystalline pain.

"Tell ussss," one demanded, in a sort of hissing whisper. "Tell ussss of the place you came from. Tell us of the land beyond the fiery waterssss."

"Finvarra would know thissss," the other took up. "Tell ussss, and no more will we harm you."

But Fionchadd would not tell and was glad he had given away the torque that contained one of the seeing stones that *would* have told, had Finvarra got hold of it, and gladder yet he had destroyed its twin before his capture. Oh, he would not have known the Words that called the images showing all the ways of that other World Fionchadd had traversed in hopes of finding a way to safe-haven for his mother, but he had no doubt the Ard Rhi of Erenn would have eventually discovered them. Finvarra's druids were mighty, and his own Power also, that of the Tuatha de Danaan—far mightier than Fionchadd had expected, for had Finvarra not somehow found a realm that was not of Faerie, nor the Mortal World, yet in some way of both, where the Tracks ran not gold but silver? Such a thing Fionchadd had never heard of, and with such things, what other arts might the Lord of Erenn command?

"Tell ussss!" the hissing persisted.

No! He had friends there in that other place beyond the

World Walls—three at least, even if one of them—Alec
McLean—had inadvertently betrayed him. As for the other
mortals, David Sullivan and Calvin McIntosh, they bore
no taint at all. Them he would not abandon.

"The sssecret," the other one hissed, as pain entered
Fionchadd's abdomen and ran in cold fire down the nerves
of his legs. A needle turned, and the fire reversed itself
and fled along his ribs, making it hard to breathe. A slight
pressure, and he lost control of his water.

"The sssecret," the first one echoed. "Tell us of Galunlati."

Galunlati? Fionchadd wondered. *I have not told them
that word—or have I?* He tried to think of the last time
they had come to him and could not. Maybe he had said
something then. Maybe. But they would get no more out
of him, no more at all.

"The sssecret"—and pain.

"The sssecret"—and pain.

·And then *more* pain, and Fionchadd fled into a dark
place inside himself where he had hidden once before when
the death of Iron had come upon him. And there he stayed,
while agony ripped his slender body and left no outward
sign.

Help, he thought. *Help me, help me!*

For he knew someday the pain would find him even
there, and then, despite himself, he would reveal all he
knew.

(another tower—Tir-Nan-Og— high summer)

The wind had shifted around to the north, and with it
came rain and the rumor of war.

At guard atop the northmost tower of Lugh's northmost
citadel, Froech felt the former as a stinging upon his face

and knew the latter by some subtle resonance in his bones. Power, it was—Power used profligately to raise the storms that had harried Lugh's realm for days, drowning the outposts and coastal forts along the wild northern shore with tidal waves that crested far inland and smashed the low-lying woods that stretched south between here and Lugh's principal hold, shattering trees a hundred spears tall to splinters with blasts of unholy lightning. Such storms frightened him—he who had seen the Quarters change four thousand times. And such storms as these, Froech very much feared, could even reach outside Faery.

At their heart was wild Power, Power that had been born elsewhere, wrapped around the very stuff of nature, and directed. But now, he knew, the wielders of that Power had come as well. They faced not the storms alone, but the stormmakers in the bargain. The first attack in any Faerie war was always with the weather.

So it had been when first his kindred had been swept by the Tracks to this clump of Worlds and had found themselves in Erenn. The Firbolg had been there before them, who were of olden times their kin; and before their hosts ever joined in war Badb and Macha and the Morrigu went to Tara and brought mists and clouds and darkness over the whole place, following that with showers of fire and blood. Three days it had lasted, before the druids of the Firbolg broke it. He knew; he had been there. And so it had ever been.

Grimly he scanned the horizon, fair angular face set, dark brows glowering from under his helm, black hair twitching wildly where it flowed unrestrained across his back. He clutched his wine-red cloak around him and shivered, wishing he could draw warmth from the sun-in-splendor emblazoned on it. There was cold in that rain, a cold that should not be present this far south in Faerie. A moment more he would watch, then make his report.

Steps sounded on the dampening flags behind him. He glanced sideways and saw Andro, his flame-haired blood-friend, striding toward him, hand hovering, as their hands ever did these days, near his swordhilt. Andro's eyebrows lowered, as he too turned his gaze north and sniffed the air which now smelled strongly of lightning.

"So Finvarra's minions have landed, have they? Well, it had to happen. Beat us into weariness with storms and then attack. Break the spirit, and the body follows it down."

"But why here in the north?" Froech wondered. "When Lugh's principal strongholds lie south and east? Surely if they were whelmed the north would quickly follow."

"I have wondered about that too," Andro replied. "And only now have I contrived a possible answer."

"I wait—but hurry, for this we must pass on."

"It is the forests themselves Finvarra seeks to destroy," Andro said heavily. "Only think, brother: Erenn has little wood, and not even Finvarra's druids can make it grow faster than it will. He has built many ships and lost many ships, and even before this war we traded him timber from our groves."

"And now he has lost more ships and can build none to replace them . . ."

Andro's face brightened. "But Lugh can. Yet what of the rest of the war? What of the message that came this morning? Is it as I have heard? Has the war truly shifted our way?"

"This sea war, maybe," Froech replied thoughtfully. "But I think it has all been a diversion. Finvarra never attacked with all his fleet; he kept some in reserve, and with them he has come against the forests, for without wood Lugh cannot build ships any more than can he."

"Ah! An evening of the scales, then . . ."

"Aye, but would *we* were not in the balance."

"All for a pair of half-mad twins."

"All for the Laws of Dana."

"A life for a life."

"And ten thousand deaths thereby."

Andro nodded sadly. From a pouch he drew a prickly shape: a caltrap, it was called: four thorns of a certain kind joined at their centers by druidry. He laid it in his palm. Another nod, and Froech clamped his hand atop it, and as one they squeezed them together. Pain flowed into them, and with it blood. But with that blood flowed Power, doubling and redoubling as it mixed and mingled.

And so it was that Froech and Andro both gazed north and saw the land stretch long before them, thick with the corpses of trees. But they saw too the clouds that overlay those trees like a blanket of doom, and beyond those trees—still leagues and leagues away—the white lace of waves on a distant, storm-tossed shore.

Those waves were not empty though, nor was that shore, for ships lay there at anchor: black ships with black sails emblazoned with scarlet eagles. And all along that coast came the glitters of spears reflecting ever-increasing lightning, and war drums that echoed the thunder, as Finvarra of Erenn at last brought battle to Tir-Nan-Og.

"Dana help us all," Froech sighed, as Andro put on raven's form and flew south with a message dark as the weather.

Help me! another thought tickled his mind—but was gone before Froech knew it was not his own.

(Sullivan Cove, Georgia—Friday, August 13—mid-afternoon)

"David!" Alec McLean cried. "Christ, man, you gonna sleep all day?"

David dragged his eyelids open and levered himself up on his elbows, still seriously muddle-headed. He stared first at his best friend's concerned expression; then, automatically, at his own near-naked body in search of incipient sunburn. For the time of year he was as pale as he'd ever been: the glaze of gold on arms and legs, chest and shoulders was mostly last summer's leftovers—and the residue of the previous weekend's forced labor.

"And what're you doing way out *here?*" Alec demanded. "I like to never have found you."

"Huh?" David finally grunted, sitting full up and shaking his wild-haired head, as his fingers adjusted the waistband of the skimpy red Speedo he wore in place of his accustomed cut-offs. It had been a birthday present from Liz—as much *birthday* suit as *bathing* suit, she'd giggled when he'd opened it back on January 16. Today's pre-graduation cookout was its official unveiling. Too bad she'd not been here to witness it. Too *damn* bad.

"Sleep," Alec supplied patiently, "as in 'sleep your life away.' "

"Huh?" David mumbled again. And then the dream slammed into him and he shivered as if someone had flicked ice water across his chest. He blinked, saw the waters of B.A. Cove ten feet beyond his rock begin to chop slightly as the afternoon wind picked up. "Feels like rain," he managed. " 'Course it *always* feels like rain these days."

Alec grimaced, squatted on the next slab down, and commenced toweling his still-damp hair. He smelled of sand and lake water. A pair of blue gym shorts were plastered to his slender body. "I think that was an evasion, David. Is something wrong?"

"Damned straight, if it rains tonight!"

"No, I mean worse than that."

Quick blue eyes darted left, seeking across an acre of broomsedge to where the rest of the MacTyrie Gang— Runnerman Buchanan, M.H. (for Mighty Hunter) Aikin Daniels, and G-Man Gary Hudson—were clustered beside Apocalypse Now, Darrell's VW van, busy assembling a mid-afternoon barbecue, while their respective ladies: Sheila Groves, Janie Spenser, and a very pregnant Tracy Jensen—and Darrell's older sister, Myra, who had invited herself along to sketch—looked on with vast amusement.

This party was the official opening of summer: the first sunny day after school let out; tonight's larger bash at Gary's would be a one-timer and a sort of prequel to his wedding the following weekend. *If* David survived graduation. He inventoried the scantily-clad bodies once more and sighed. The most important one was still missing.

"Liz isn't here." It was part statement, part accusation.

Alec snapped the towel against David's shoulder. "She'll be here, man; don't worry. She can't help it if they gotta make up all those snow days they missed last winter, but no way she'd miss your graduation—*Mr. Valedictorian!*"

David shrugged. "No big deal, that. Not in a class of fifty."

"Nobody else even came close."

"Barbara Justus did; so did you."

"Except for English."

"Self-sabotage, that," David chuckled, thinking of Alec's English-teacher father's consternation at his son's apparent inability to deal with the arcana of his chosen profession. Give Alec a program to construct or a formula to memorize or an experiment to run, he was fine. Give him a sentence to diagram or a verb to conjugate or a poem to explicate, and he went to pieces. His spoken and written language was fine, it was the *theory* that was somehow beyond his comprehension.

A comb replaced the towel in Alec's hand; in an instant his short brown locks were neat as normal. "As I was saying: something wrong?"

David reached over and mussed him up again, noting absently that his sorry attempt at a mustache was missing—victim, no doubt, of a pre-commencement parental order. "Why do you ask?"

"Shoot, man," Alec snorted, nonplussed by the attack, "when I found you here every muscle on you was so tight I thought you were gonna explode, and your face was scrunched up like . . ."

"Like what?"

"Oh never mind the effing *image*. It's the *fact* I'm concerned about." A pause; then, "More dreams?"

David nodded reluctantly. " 'Fraid so."

"Fourth time this week I make it."

"Fifth: had one last night—woke me up and I couldn't get back to sleep. That's what put me out now."

"Faery stuff again?"

Once more David nodded. "I thought it was over," he said at last.

"Lugh warned you, though," Alec noted. "He said that war didn't keep borders. He said we'd feel it . . . what were his words? 'When the skies turn dark and rains fall heavy and you dream of death and murder, remember that perhaps they are reflections of darker things in Faerie'?"

"Something to that effect." David studied his feet, staring absently at the golden hair dusting his legs and toes.

"Bad one this time?"

David nodded mutely, swallowed. "There were . . . *two,*" he said hesitantly, "one was in some kind of grubby enclosed place like a prison, and a feeling of fear and pain and of someone wanting help, and that's all I can remember." He closed his eyes, shook his head again. "It was real confusing, just feelings mostly. But the second was more vivid. I . . . I was standin' on a tower or something, looking out over a forest dark under thunderclouds, and then there was this terrible feeling of dread, of something awful begun. And then somebody turned into a raven, and I felt something . . . I don't know . . . something tickle my soul. Something kinda like that other dream." He shuddered suddenly. "I think you're right, Alec; I think it's like Lugh predicted. I think there's war in Faerie. The other dreams were just snatches: towers and warriors and a sense of unease. This was much more concrete."

"But how?"

Another shrug. "Who knows? Maybe things are so bad even the World Walls can't contain it all. Maybe their emotions are so keyed up over there they're startin' to seep through.''

Alec shuddered in turn, and David knew he was thinking of their earlier encounters with that Otherworld that overlay their own. He'd never come totally to terms with the multitudinous contradictions implicit in that. But then, he'd never come totally to terms with most of Faerie. Alec was a rationalist at heart, and Faerie either defied logic, or forced a redefinition.

Alec took a deep breath. ''There's another explanation, you know. Something a lot more reasonable.''

David cocked an eyebrow inquiringly.

''Guilt, David: plain old-fashioned guilt. God knows I've felt it myself. Still do.''

David shook his head. ''I've considered that a lot, but I think there's more to it than that. If it was only me havin' 'em, I might believe it. But ma's had 'em, Little Billy's had 'em, Uncle Dale's had 'em. Shoot, even poor old Minniebelle Coker's had 'em, and I think they're gettin' worse.''

Alec frowned. ''A pattern there: all members of your family—'cept for Minniebelle.''

''I think it's more the *place*, Alec. There was a fight at the church across from my house last Sunday that you could hear clear across the hollow.''

''And you really do think it's slop-over from Tir-Nan-Og?''

David slapped his hands on his legs. ''What else *could* it be?''

''Search me. But just think a minute, oh Mad One. Tir-Nan-Og overlaps here, that's true—but it overlaps this whole part of the country, so there ought to be contention all over too.''

''Are you blind, or what?'' David snapped. ''News has been *full* of stuff about domestic violence and hospitals runnin' over and that kinda thing. Crime rate's *way* up in Atlanta and Chattanooga and Knoxville.''

"Coincidence. Full moon or planetary alignment or something. All the blessed rain, maybe. Besides, *I* haven't felt anything."

"Yeah, but haven't you noticed how wired everyone is at school lately? Who knows who else is havin' dreams and not sayin' anything because they're just too strange?"

"Just end-of-the-year apprehension."

"You think!"

"More than you, apparently."

David fell silent, staring once more at the group at the van, knowing he needed to rejoin them, but feeling no desire to be social. "There's one way to find out for sure, you know," he said, meeting Alec's gray-eyed gaze meaningfully. "You could use the ulunsuti."

Alec looked away. "Uh-uh, no way, man!"

David took him by the shoulder. "Not even once, bro? Not even for me?"

Alec shook his head. "Not even for you."

"But Uki gave it to you to use. He didn't give it to me, or to Calvin, he gave it to you and he told you to study it."

"I didn't deserve it, though. He gave it to me out of some misguided sense of honor."

David glared at him. "Are you *sure* about that? He's a . . . a demi-god, after all. I think he knew what he was doin'."

"Maybe—but he didn't ask me."

"But still—"

"Look, David," Alec flared suddenly. "I've got the damned thing, and I do what I have to do to keep it from going crazy. But no way am I gonna spend my time fooling around with a magical jewel out of the forehead of a goddam monster!"

"Where's your scientific curiosity?"

"In my other pants!"

David regarded him seriously. "You realize what just happened, don't you? We got contentious—more than we should have, and faster. No warnin', just slam-bam, thank-you-ma'am.''

"So you really think it's something to do with the dreams?''

"No, I think the dreams are something to do with it.''

Alec took a deep breath. "These dreams, Davy—has there been any sign of—?'' He broke off, his eyes misting.

"Of Eva?'' David finished, remembering the Faery woman who had used Alec to betray Fionchadd the previous fall and whose last-minute change of heart had saved them both when the uktena David had become had overwhelmed him. "No.''

A sigh. "Never hurts to ask.''

David laid a hand on his shoulder. "Just hurts, period, right, man?''

Alec nodded sadly. "Jesus, David. I loved her . . . I thought; and then she . . . But then she said she really did love me there at the end. I wonder if she still does.''

"Do *you*? That's the important thing, the part you can control.''

"I *shouldn't,* that's for certain . . . but— Oh Christ, man, I don't *know!* If I saw her again I don't know if I'd kiss her or kill her.''

"You need a woman, guy; a *real* woman. A year's long enough to do without.''

"Almost a year,'' Alec corrected. "And don't forget that a year ago we were both celibate—and had been forever.''

David grinned and stood up, suddenly finding it necessary to distract himself from what he was thinking and the effect it was having on him, which would be all-too-evident in the Speedo—not that he cared around Alec, but the others . . . A year since the first time . . . Lord! And almost two weeks since the last . . .

Alec eyed him wryly, missing nothing. "I think a cold dip's called for.''

"Yeah, and then a cold brew.''

"And a loose shirt with a very long tail."

David grabbed a handful of pine straw from the detritus around him and poured it over Alec's head. It stuck in the damp spikes, making him look like one of the wild men he'd seen in a book on medieval art.

Alec reached down to grab a retaliatory handful, but by the time he rose once more, David was already dashing into the shallow water.

"Lo! The dead has risen," somebody called from beside the van.

"If they only knew!" Alec chuckled, as he followed David in.

They swam for perhaps five minutes in unseasonably cool water that was red from washed-in clay; and then David emerged and toweled down, finally wrapping the gold-and-purple terrycloth around his waist Egyptian style. By the time he rejoined the group, however, his "affliction" was threatening to return. He deliberately walked barefoot across the roughest turf. The distraction helped, but not enough. An oversized white shirt made him feel considerably safer.

"What's up?" Gary asked wickedly, handing him a beer and a burger.

"Funny you should ask," David giggled, staring meaningfully past Gary's brawny figure to the obviously bulging tummy of his girlfriend. "You in particular, I mean."

Tracy raised a dark brow delicately into even darker hair, wordlessly daring David to go further. "It'll be a gorgeous kid, anyway," he managed lamely.

Gary laid a hand on his lady's tummy. "I can already feel the little guy doing push-ups."

"Long as he doesn't do side-straddle-hops when we're at the altar," Tracy laughed, planting a wet one on her sweetie's cheek. "Always assuming it *is* a guy," she added pointedly.

"There but for the grace of God," Alec began, before David elbowed him in the ribs.

"Huh?" asked lanky blond Darrell Buchanan, a dollar short and a day late as usual. Then, "Oh, you mean—"

Sheila Groves, the shapely blonde girl Darrell hung out with—mostly, David suspected, because she looked like him—tugged Darrell's track-team ponytail sharply. "Don't say another word, Runnerman. You're absolutely certain to be sorry."

"He's already sorry," M.H. Daniels chuckled before his own lady, the considerably taller Janie Spenser, shushed him by shoving a hotdog in his mouth.

"So am I," David agreed, stifling a guffaw, "sorry you didn't do that sooner. I—"

He stopped in mid-sentence as a drop of rain needled his shoulder, and glared up into a rapidly darkening sky.

Fifteen minutes later the sudden shower had abated, having briefly forced all nine of them to take shelter inside the van and to drag the grill under the overhanging awning. The others had gone back to the lake for one final dip, and David, who was still moody about Liz's absence and bothered by his dream, found himself alone with Myra. He'd never been around Darrell's older sis much, since she'd been away at college most of the time he'd known the big D (who'd arrived from Atlanta in time to join the tenth grade and the MacTyrie gang at the same time). Nor had he noticed how pretty she was, even now when she was utterly without makeup. She was slim and blonde, to start with (her hair bound atop her head like a furry fountain), had great cheekbones, and her eyes were marvelous. Her brows were too pale though, and ditto her lashes. Darrell's, by contrast, were darker, but where the family looks made Myra pretty, they merely made Darrell foolish. Myra picked up a pad and began sketching. "Something wrong?" she asked to break the silence.

David shrugged noncommittally. "Not really," he lied, wishing people would stop asking that question.

The hand paused in mid-stroke. "You miss your lady, right?"

David focused on her rapidly moving fingers. "Yeah, partly." It was true too, in spades. But he had other things on his mind as well.

"Well, think of it this way; she's not here now, but there'll be no more separations. Darrell's told me how she's been going to school in Gainesville the last two years, and how you've been about to go crazy in the meantime. But you're together now; and I for one am glad to see it."

"That helps a lot," David said sullenly.

"What I'm saying, guy, is that in the context of the rest of your life, a couple of hours now won't matter."

"Easy for *you* to say."

"Harder than you think. I'm here with a bunch of neat folks, and with some great landscape to draw, but what am I doing? Thinking about my boyfriend, Scott, down in south Georgia digging up shark teeth."

David froze. Shark teeth reminded him of the uktena scale he had stuffed in his back pack, which he had first thought a shark's tooth. It was one of several mementoes he had of last summer's adventure in Galunlati. But worse, it was a reminder of what that scale could do—like turn him into a monster. A chill actually made his teeth chatter.

Myra put down the pad. "Something *is* wrong, isn't it; and not just missing your lady? Yeah, I know, I've noticed it: all this rain, all the wind, it's like a war going on in the sky. And it's not just a physical war; it's like a war in your head, a roaring in your soul. It's like the tension you feel before a thunderstorm, only it never ends, just gets tighter and tighter. I've sensed it ever since I got up here. And Darrell says it's been going on for days."

David nodded, wondering suddenly what Myra knew, how much Darrell had told her of the strange things that had happened to him. Runnerman knew most of it now; Lugh had forgotten (or neglected) to renew the Ban of Silence he had imposed on those who knew of Faerie, so they had been free to inform their friends, trusting to the impossibility of it all to enforce discretion. But what had Darrell told Myra?

"I've felt something similar once," Myra continued darkly. "At a Renaissance fair down in Athens. The weather was freaky there too."

"I heard about that," David replied. "Did a lot of damage and all."

"Real freaky," Myra repeated; then, more lightly: "Hey, how 'bout holding that pose for a while!"

"Sure," David said, looking a little puzzled. He froze where he was: leaning against the van with one of the awning poles in his hand. Myra applied herself to her drawing. A moment later she was finished, and handed him the pad for perusal.

Goosebumps prickled over him. It was him, all right, but Myra had changed his shirt to a coat of ring mail, his bandanna to a cap of iron, and the pole to a wildly barbed spear. But what gave him pause was the background she had sketched in: a desolate, wind-swept shore covered with shattered trees. The sun was unnaturally huge and fiery and directly above his head, its entire many-rayed disc shadowed by the outstretched wings of an eagle. David had seen them both before: for the sun was twin to that which was emblazoned on the surcotes of Lugh's warriors, and the eagle was the sign of the royal house of Erenn: that of Finvarra.

"Nice," David said, "but where'd you get this symbol?"

Myra would not meet his eyes. "I . . . I don't know, it . . . it just came to me."

Thunder sounded then, and the rains returned. His friends pounded up from the beach.

"Can I have this?" David asked.

Myra nodded. "I'd like to draw you again, sometime, too. You've got a real nice body."

David blushed and looked away.

Gary was the first one to the van, having beaten his

running rival, Darrell. "Christ, is this rain *never* gonna stop?"

"When the sun beats the eagle," Myra said, and fell silent.

David, crouched in the back, could only stare at her and wonder.

Chapter III: Carolina Reverie

(Sylva, North Carolina—Friday, June 13—sunset)

The sun was still a hand's breadth above the western mountains when Calvin McIntosh pushed through the screen door and padded onto the cabin's porch. He scratched his bottom through a convenient hole in his jeans, settled himself into the unpainted rocker that in the last year or so he had come to think of as his own, and gazed out at the vista beyond the peeled pine railing: mountains upon mountains as far as his very sharp eyes could see—maybe all the way west to Tennessee or south to Georgia. Closer in were the beeches and oaks and ashes that crowded around the cabin, their leafy summits level with the porch's cantilever floor because of the steepness of the slope. But they rapidly lost their definition as he stared further into the haze of the Smokies. And lingering near the sun were clouds, also in long, low layers, so that Calvin could not be sure where land ended and sky began.

So be it, then. Maybe it was not wise to think of the two as separate. Everything was ultimately one; that was

one of the things he had learned here at the haven he shared
with Sandy.

One of many things.

Sandy Fairfax was somewhere in her middle twenties
and taught physics in the local high school; he had only
left his teens a month before and did nothing at all that
would make sense on an employment form except wander
around and learn, but somehow it had never mattered to
either of them. He asked questions about things he didn't
understand, and she answered; she wondered about things
she didn't comprehend, and he speculated. She gave him
science and economics and business and philosophy and
ethics (and food to eat—what he didn't hunt—and a *fine*
motorcycle to ride a roof and a bed to share); and he gave
her woodscraft and herblore and metaphysics and magic
(and the sweat of his brow often enough, like today when
he'd re-roofed the smokehouse). For though Calvin Fargo
McIntosh had grown up in Atlanta, he was three-quarters
Cherokee Indian, and trying very hard to become a wizard.

This evening, however, the only magic he had in mind
was that of contentment, of being in a place he loved,
surrounded by fantastic scenery, and feeling good about
his long day's labor. He sighed happily, propped his strong
bare feet on the railing, and took a sip from the cup of
coffee he had brought with him from the supper table.
Sandy was in there now, cleaning up, since he'd cooked
(venison burgers and wild mushrooms). She'd join him
shortly and they'd watch the sun set and the night arrive
and talk about—who knew what.

Maybe magic tonight, because they hadn't in a while,
and after all, he *did* know more about the arcane lore of
his people than anyone living, probably—at least from
firsthand experience; and by slow degrees had been initi-
ating her into its mysteries as well. It had not been easy,
of course; but who *could* believe there were Worlds beyond this one, that anybody could actually travel to if they
had the art? Asking someone to believe that was asking a

lot, especially to a scientist like Sandy. Eventually, he'd had to actually show her. *Not* by taking her to Galunlati; he had neither the power nor the permission to do that yet. But by performing the ritual and going there himself. That she *could* believe: him in the middle of his Power Wheel one minute, and gone in a puff of flame the next. It had hurt him fearfully—the transition always did. But it had been worth it, because it had lowered the last barrier between them. From then on there had been endless questions, and eventually Sandy had found herself trying to contrive a unified-field theory of physics/metaphysics to embrace the cosmology of all the overlapping Worlds.

There was so much she didn't know, too; and so many questions he could not answer, because he only knew a little about one World besides their own. She really needed to talk to his friends down in Georgia: Dave and Alec, and all. They'd spoken to the folk of one of the *other* Worlds and knew what was up. Yeah, maybe this summer he'd take her over there and they'd hash out some stuff. Maybe even next weekend—he had to go anyway, to be in Dave's buddy's wedding.

He fished in the pocket of the sleeveless denim jacket that hung open over his chest, and pulled out the packet of photos he'd picked up that day from the Eckerds down in Sylva. He'd shot them the previous August, but never got around to developing them until now. A lot of 'em hadn't come out, but enough had to provide a reasonable record of those friends he'd just been thinking of.

The first was one of Mad Davy Sullivan standing alone in a high mountain pasture, with a line of dark forest to his right, and behind him a picture-postcard of sprawling lakes. A little shorter than Calvin, and built more like a gymnast than a runner, Dave was nevertheless wearing running togs: white gym shorts and a burgundy de-sleeved sweatshirt which depicted his school name and mascot: the Enotah County 'Possums. He was also barefoot, and was pointing to his tootsies with one hand and shrugging theatrically with the other.

Calvin couldn't help but grin. He'd made that the last day he'd been there, when Dave had been unable to find his shoes anywhere and had decided to undertake his morning run without them. Not wishing to put his friend at a disadvantage, Calvin had joined him and done likewise. Unfortunately, it had been a mistake to try to out-macho that particular white boy. The stone bruises had nearly killed him, and it had taken nearly a week for the blisters to heal.

The next photo was one of Dave's home, a white frame farmhouse crouching atop a steep hill on the knees of a forested mountain, with a strip of bottom land on one side, and a series of hilly pastures on the other. Dating from around the turn of the century, the house had obviously been added onto several times, and sported three distinct porches, though only two were visible in this view.

The following shot was of Dave and his Candyapple Red '66 Mustang, the one he called the Mustang-of-Death. It seemed to have had a near brush with its namesake, too, because it was missing the right front fender, and the passenger door was blue. He wondered if Dave had ever got it back like he'd wanted it after the accident—he'd never actually seen it intact.

He skipped quickly by a series that showed the Enotah County landscape. It was not that different from the territory around here, though the Carolina mountains might be a touch higher than their Georgia counterparts, and there seemed to be a few more artificial lakes filling the valleys over there.

And then he found a picture of a gaggle of teenaged boys standing in front of a neat Cape Cod bungalow. They were the MacTyrie Gang, Dave's gaming and run-around buddies: tall, lanky Darrell "Runnerman" Buchanan, who was handsome in a foolish sort of way, and who, as a member of his high school track team, wore his hair in a scraggly pony tail Calvin was certain Dave wanted very badly to emulate. And dark-haired "G-Man" Gary Hudson, who also ran track, but was into serious body building (he had doffed his shirt and struck a pose for the photo). He was the one getting married—make that *having* to get married.

Between them was slender Alec McLean, dressed very hi-tech in his black parachute pants and T-shirt, and with his spiky haircut and earring. That hipness was an illusion, though, because Alec was the most conservative— and, after Dave, the brightest, especially in science—of the lot. Finally there was the one he didn't really know, because he'd been gone most of the time Calvin had spent over there: Aikin Daniels, just a solid, nice-looking middle-sized guy in silver-framed glasses, cammy fatigues, and a black T-shirt that depicted a howling wolf. Dave had said he was the sportsman of their crew, and something of a loner, though the gaming campaigns he orchestrated were noted for their imagination. He was also, apparently, the last one to learn about the Worlds.

Only two pictures to go, now. The first was of Dave's girlfriend, Liz Hughes, and showed a pretty, pointy-faced red-haired girl holding a camera of her own. She was very slender (exactly the way Calvin liked 'em), and had green eyes that radiated a challenging sparkle. In the photo she was wearing white cutoffs and a green Abolish Continental Drift T-shirt.

The last shot showed the ruins of a mid-nineteenth century cabin nestled in a mountain hollow. The place had been knocked off its foundations, and was skewed every other way as well, with not a window pane intact. The front porch had been smashed to kindling, and large sections of the tin roof were missing. A crumpled burgundy Volvo 240 lay stuffed into one corner.

That was Dave's uncle's house: the one that had practically been destroyed when the Sidhe had ridden from their World to demand that Dave surrender Alec, whom they believed to have betrayed them. Calvin had been instrumental in setting things right afterward, and that had been the thing that convinced him to follow the way of the shaman and try to learn the secrets of his people's magic, to which end he had returned more than once to Galunlati to study. As for Dale Sullivan's house—he'd heard the old guy had given up on fixing it and had moved a house trailer onto the lot behind the ruins.

"You miss them, don't you?" came a soft voice behind him, and before Calvin could turn, a woman settled herself on the bench built into the railing to his right. She was as tall as he was, and slender, with hair that would have been brown had the sun not been at it for years, and had it not been so long—nearly to her waist in back. In another time she would have been called a hippie, at least by looks and lifestyle. But she knew more about lasers than living off the land, more about halogen gasses than hallucinogenic mushrooms, more about quantum theory and cosmic string than canning and macrame. At the moment she was wearing a dashiki a friend had brought her from Malawi, and sipping delicately at a glass of Chablis. He frowned minutely at that, for he never touched the stuff by principle, never mind he was still not quite of legal age.

The frown became a wry smile as he shuffled the photos back into their mailer and returned them to his pocket. "Yeah, I miss 'em a lot."

"You could call them, you know; I don't mind."

Calvin shifted restlessly. "I know you don't, and I've tried, as a matter of fact—'bout half a dozen times in the last two weeks, tryin' to find out what's up with this blessed wedding. But all I get are those damned recordings." He adapted a nasally computerized tone: " 'We're sorry, but your call cannot be completed as dialed, please check to see that you have the correct number,' or 'We're sorry, but all circuits are out in that area, please try again.' Oh, I got through once, but Dave couldn't hear me, even though I could hear him. Something really weird's goin' on with the phones over there—apparently they're havin' some really wild weather, or something."

Sandy's brow wrinkled thoughtfully for a moment. "There's been stuff on TV about that, something to do with alternating high and low pressure systems that seem to pop up and vanish without any warning, but just in that one place, possibly due to sun spots. A huge amount of rain more widely spread; lots of wind and lightning. I'm not surprised the phones aren't working half the time. Maybe you really should go over.''

"Maybe I will.''

" 'Course you've been saying that for months . . .''

"I know, but—but I need to work with Uki, and when I'm not doing that, I just like to hang out and do nothing. Learnin' magic takes it out of a guy.''

"Hitchhiking to Mexico was nothing?''

"I had to find out some things, get a feeling of being in a place with some real history. I hate this idea of all time bein' *now*. Everything that *is* came from somewhere else, or some *thing* else. There's nothing original in the world. But it's when people won't see that that trouble starts. People aren't apart *from* biology and history, they're a part *of* biology and history.''

"Very sage—for a mere beardless boy.''

Calvin stroked his smooth chin. "Do you disagree?''

"I don't think so, though I'd need to meditate on it some more.''

"Well, seein' other Worlds, other planes of reality, kinda makes you doubt your own. You sorta develop a need to anchor yourself as strongly as you can.''

Sandy curled her feet under her and took another sip of wine. "So how does that jive with prophecy, then?''

"What d' you mean?''

"Well, doesn't your friend have a prophetic stone, or something? How does that work?''

"Oh, the *ulunsuti*. It's the crystal from the head of a monster that lives in Galunlati, called the uktena. I've told you about helpin' to kill one, right?''

"Yeah.''

"Right, well, basically you concentrate on the crystal and on what you want to know, and it just kinda shows it to you—including the future, if that's what you're askin' about. To do anything major, you have to prime it with blood."

"But does it show you *the* future, or simply *a* future?" Calvin shrugged. "Can't say."

"Arrgghhh!" Sandy grumbled. "Just when this was starting to get interesting. But seriously, I really would like to know more; any chance you could borrow it? Or maybe take me over to see it?"

Calvin frowned. "Well, it belongs to Alec—was given to him quite specifically. He's got enough sense of the rightness of things not to let it out of his hands. It's really a big responsibility, and he takes it like one. But if you'd like to go over sometime . . . Hey, how 'bout tomorrow? I really do need to check up on the blessed wedding plans anyway."

She shook her head. "Gotta work on those damned end-of-the-year evaluations all day. But sometime, seriously. I think if I understood how the ulunsuti deals with time I could come closer to sorting all this out."

"Well," Calvin said, as he polished off his coffee, "what *I* have to figure out is how many shingles I have to split in the morning to roof the garage."

"Thought you were going down to Georgia."

Calvin shook his head. "Who can say?"

"I'll leave it to you," Sandy sighed. "I've gotta go warm up the old calculator."

She left him alone, then; and Calvin once more stared out into the evening. To the west the sky had darkened perceptibly and the sky was awash with clouds like hovering buzzards. He thought he heard distant thunder.

Chapter IV:
Commencement

(Enotah, Georgia—Friday, June 13—evening)

". . . and now the valedictorian of this year's senior class: David Kevin Sullivan." And with that monotone introduction echoing tinnily around Enotah County High's Burns Memorial Auditorium, Dr. Anthony Taylor returned to his seat between the county school superintendent and the local probate judge.

David took a deep breath and stood, hearing his cheap gown rustle and feeling the burgundy nylon briefly snag on a ragged corner of the metal folding chair where he had been waiting nervously next to Barbara Ann Justus, who was second honor and head cheerleader, and Nat Berrong, the superintendent's son, who had done the invocation. His footsteps sounded impossibly loud as they slapped across the well-oiled boards. Damned Sunday shoes! He'd wanted to wear his Reeboks, but his ma wouldn't hear of it, just like he'd wanted to wear jeans and no tie, and been denied for the same non-reason. The ponytail, however, was still intact and neatly secured with a burgundy-and-silver velvet ribbon. Another deep breath as he stepped up behind the podium and fished out his index cards. A third, as he gazed out across the expectant multitude and began.

"Friends, family, faculty . . ." he commenced, then had to pause to clear his throat. Someone on the front row giggled, and he felt his cheeks grow warm. "Friends, family, faculty," he repeated. "I guess you all just heard Principal Taylor say who I am, and what I am; and I guess you all know why I'm here. I reckon, too, that you're all expectin' the same kind of speech you hear year after year: about the challenges of the future, and steppin' out into a brave new world, and all that stuff. But I'll tell you something right now: I was gonna *make* a speech like that. I *rehearsed* a speech like that all last week, even memorized it, 'cause that's the speech they gave me to say, and I may be about to get myself into a heap of trouble by sayin' something else now, but I'm going to anyway, 'cause if I used the one they gave me it'd just be one more piece of high school, one more example of doing what other people tell you to do, and not thinkin' on your own, which is what life's supposed to be about."

He paused nervously, eyes darting everywhere, feeling Dr. Taylor's glare burning into him exactly as they had when he'd been summoned to the office in the eighth grade for pulling the fire alarm. "One thing, though," he went on, "you don't have to worry about me tellin' you off, or cussin' you out, or anything, I'm not. I've got a speech I've worked up myself, and that's the key word: *myself.* I've got a fair store of facts floating around in my head right now, but I figure today's the first day of the rest of my life, so the first thing I gotta do is start putting 'em together *myself . . .*"

He went on, repeating the words he'd composed over the preceding week, the one he'd committed to memory along with the other he'd actually recited at rehearsal, careful to maintain his mountain drawl so folks wouldn't think he was too uppity. Somewhere around a third of the way along he sensed the whole place relaxing as the audience decided he wasn't going to say anything too incendiary in spite of his by-now-universal nickname: Mad Davy Sullivan. His basic text was simple: school was grist for the mill, you learned facts, but the things you *really* learned were things about getting along with other people: making friends, sucking up to teachers, when to tell the truth and when to lie . . . It was all amazingly savvy, he thought—and would have been, if he'd come up with all of it himself. But the truth was, it was mostly a synthesis of things he'd heard Uncle Dale say, or David-the-Elder say, or even Liz. Surprisingly, a little of it also came from his father; they'd had a long talk or two over Christmas. By the time he'd got to the middle, he'd gone onto automatic and was scanning the crowd, picking out faces he'd already found before: his folks—Big Billy in suit and tie for the third time David had ever seen him so, Little Billy likewise but with the tie askew, Uncle Dale in white shirt, clean khakis, the stubby ponytail of his own that had scandalized David's ma when he'd shown up in it that evening. She was there too, of course, looking absolutely smashing, as she could do when she wanted to, though the padded shoulders of her black-and-purple dress were maybe a little extreme.

A further scan yielded more familiar faces. Alec's folks: Dr. McLean and his wife, Geraldine; the one beaming, the other nursing secret grudges that his son's English grades had kept him out of either top spot. Gary's dad was there too, the former race car driver who now ran the BMW dealership in MacTyrie that somehow found enough retired rich expatriate Atlantans to stay afloat, but who found himself spinning wrenches as often as pitching sales. And there was Darrell's family: Myra the artist, and his mom, who taught business at MacTyrie J.C. and nursed on the side, while his lanky dad managed the athletic program and coached tennis.

And, wonder of wonders, there was Aikin's forest-ranger father and his mother the archaeologist, together for only the third time David had ever seen them so (their respective careers demanded they live apart, though they were madly in love with each other). There were others too: friends who had graduated previous years, younger folks watching older brothers and sisters pass out of their lives, eager for their own places in the sun.

But one face was missing. David studied the rows and aisles again, having now come to the third of the four points he had planned. No, *there* she was, way in the back, making her way as unobtrusively as she could down the aisle to squeeze in by his ma: his lady, Liz Hughes. Lord, she looked good—red hair cut so that it resembled feathers, short on top but past her shoulders on back and sides; medium-blue dress accented with lace and patterned with flowers.

He grinned in spite of himself, and continued, "Now I don't want you to think that I've *got* all the answers, or even *think* I've got all the answers or maybe even *suspect* that I've got all the answers. But I've got a heap of questions that ought to keep me busy for a while, and I hope the rest of my classmates will have, too; 'cause I've seen too many of us go out and get old in two years. I . . ." He paused, blinking, staring at Mike Wheeler in the fourth row, who had just shot a rubber band at him. He ignored Mike, his nemesis of the last twelve years, and looked back at Liz. She was gazing at him, too; but then he saw her start, squint up at the ceiling as if searching for something among the steel I-beams. The lights dimmed abruptly, browning out as the power station at the edge of town shunted in different lines. Suddenly he realized it was raining—raining hard. Probably it had been for a while, but the new auditorium was so well insulated, he hadn't really noticed.

But he *did* notice when the lights went out entirely and lightning flashed outside, strobing the room stark white. Normality returned before he could say anything stupid, though; and he heaved a sigh of relief, grateful he was nearly done. Behind him he could hear Dr. Taylor fidgeting nervously.

"And so in conclusion," he went on quickly, "I'll say something that's been said many, many times before, but only 'cause it's true, and only 'cause I've decided it really is what I ought to say: Today *is* the end; but it's the beginnin' too, and no one knows what the future holds. Thank you, ladies and gentlemen; and apologies to you, Dr. Taylor, and to our class sponsors, for springin' this on you, but I guess I've got a nickname to live up to, and I wouldn't want to let anybody down. Thank you again."

And with that he returned to his seat.

"Good job," Barbara whispered beside him, but he scarcely noticed. The school superintendent was addressing them now, and then would come the *alma mater* and the conferring of diplomas. In the meanwhile, he sought out Liz. She was still there, but something was definitely wrong: her face had gone blank, as if she were a thousand miles away. He saw her blink, shake her head, saw his ma speaking to her, almost certain the words were "Are you okay?" The worst thing was he couldn't go to her. She was sensitive, he knew: able to take herself out of herself sometimes; able to get impressions, feelings—even images—from inanimate things. *Scrying,* it was called, searching for something with part of that thing as a focus. Then he realized, to his horror, that she still had his ring: the ring Oisin had given him years ago, that was still a part of Faerie, though it no longer held any magic.

But it could still be a focus, couldn't it? And war was probably raging in Faerie and leaking though into this World as weather, and maybe as dreams and emotions, too. That was what was causing the rain, he was positive now—and he bet Liz had somehow picked up on it, because her face was white as bone. He knew too that if he tried, he could probably key into it as well: simply let his mind go blank and see the war, like he had earlier that day at the lake. But he didn't want to. What he wanted to do was to tend to his lady.

Barbara elbowed him back to reality. "Wake up, Davy," she whispered. "It's almost time."

The power flickered twice more during the superintendent's address and once again during the F.F.A. band's spirited electric rendition of the school song, which was set to the tune of the "Battle of New Orleans" and began, "In 1925, a 'Possum took a trip . . ." And then, right after Dr. Taylor had asked them all to rise and the first row had made their way into the wings, the room blacked out entirely and stayed that way. There were shouts for a moment, and one scream, and a series of uneasy whispers, then silence as, for no clear reason, five hundred people listened to the pounding of rain on the flat tar roof and watched a mad laser show of lightning cavort across the parking lot like some enormous carnival ride gone wild.

David closed his eyes, tried to tune out the sound—and gradually heard the rumble of thunder change to cries of rage and madness and the bellowing of beasts as he abruptly found himself witness to a battle raging in Faerie. Finvarra's forces had conjured a tornado to flatten Lugh's host, who had sheltered in a holly grove, and Lugh's druids were fighting back with a twister of their own, to which they had added balls of ever-burning fire. But the worst thing, the ever-present thing, was the water: water falling so hard it was like endless sheeting needles of cold steel, stabbing both earth and flesh with more fury than he could imagine. He was in someone else's body, he realized: a woman's this time, and she had fallen, was drowning, but just as that dawned on him he came back to himself.

Somehow he was standing. Blinking. The lights were on, though fitfully, and he could hear the whine of the auxiliary generators coming on line beneath the floor.

"Evelyn Anita Adams," Dr. Taylor intoned shakily, and David saw a short, chubby girl slump across the stage. "Angus Darrell Buchanan," the litany continued, as the audience slowly relaxed. "Aikin Carlisle Daniels . . . Gary Madison Hudson . . . Alexander Marion McLean . . . Annabella Thurmond . . . Christina McKenzie Walls . . . Ronald Ezekial Zukowski."

And at last (which pissed David off a little), the three

honor students who remained on the stage. "Barbara Ann Justus . . . Nathanial Samson Berrong . . . David Kevin Sullivan," and he was walking across the stage again, shaking Dr. Taylor's hand mechanically, taking the scroll bound in burgundy-and-silver ribbon, pausing at the end of the stage to flip his silver tassel to the other side of his mortarboard before returning to his seat.

Music started immediately, the F.F.A. band doing the march from *Star Wars,* of all things. As one his classmates rose and processed out. But David barely remembered it. All he could think of was seeing Liz, telling her what was up, seeing if she was okay.

Somehow it was over.

All but the worry and the rain.

David was not prepared for the postpartum chaos that greeted him after the ceremony. One moment he was walking down the aisle trying to feel more like the Luke Skywalker the music suggested and less like the smirking shorter-than-average high school kid wearing goofy-looking regalia he was certain was the image he projected; the next, he found himself literally in over his head with bodies. Shoulders, necks, faces swelled up around him, almost stifling him as he tried to force his way to the less-crowded fringes of the hall outside the auditorium. Once he saw his mother's blonde hair, Uncle Dale's weathered, angular visage, but then Alec had grabbed him by the shoulders and was steering him onward while Gary thrust his muscular torso through the crowd, fiancée in tow.

A hand reached out to him, another voice called con-gratulations. An elderly great-aunt stopped him to kiss him and shake his hand and tell him how good he looked, how proud she was of him.

But where was Liz? He had to find her, find her fast, discover what was going on with her, see if it was anything like what had happened to him.

Suddenly he was alone, his friends whisked away by the same extended-family clangor that he knew he should also be seeking. He stopped, stood on tip-toes, scanning the crowd, aware of the smell of oiled boards and the gleam of trophy cases to either side of the semicircular entrance lobby. A flash of white proved to be Uncle Dale's hair, and he started that way, found his folks just as the mob eddied away, with Little Billy running on ahead, grinning from ear to ear.

And *there* Liz was, matching his brother's grin, but with trouble in her eyes. He tried to grin back, took his mortarboard in one hand and bowed low in a Cavalier bow. The grin widened.

" 'Bout time," he teased when she had come near enough to hear him above the din.

"Sorry I was late," she panted. "It took me *forever* to get over the mountain. Had to stop three times 'cause I couldn't see, and the car nearly drowned out twice. Jesus, David, is it ever gonna stop raining?"

He did not reply immediately, simply gazed fondly at her. A lot had changed in the nine months they'd been an official couple. They'd passed the stage where all they did was make out, the one where all they did was talk. They had reached the level of intuition where they could dispense with casual conversation and cut to the matter at hand.

Liz drew her eyes away uncharacteristically, swallowed, then looked at him again, managing to restore the grin.

He raised an eyebrow.

She giggled. "Sorry . . . I . . . I know we need to talk, but . . . gee, I can't help being caught up in the moment."

He blushed furiously, started to unzip the gown.

She stopped him, fished in her purse for a camera. "No Davy, not yet. I want to remember this: you in your regalia, and probably not for the last time."

"Christ!" David grunted, rolling his eyes. But he dutifully allowed himself to be positioned before a relatively blank wall. His ma and pa had crowded around, but Little Billy was off looking at trophies.

"I thought I was done with pictures this afternoon," he

growled, thinking of the half-hour session at home, with him in every variation of kith and kin united by him in the foolish nylon gown. Synthetic renditions of Renaissance clothing juxtaposed with hi-tech haircuts and a late-nineteenth-century farmhouse thrown in for background was a little too mixed a metaphor for him, though he was probably the only person he knew who would have noticed the incongruity.

Three flash cubes later he was finally allowed to shrug out of the cap and gown, which he delivered to Little Billy who promptly donned the mortarboard. The diploma he surrendered to his pa with a mumbled comment about him having helped finance it, but his ma promptly snatched it from her husband's startled hands and stashed it in her purse along with the three honor scrolls he handed her next: one for being Star Student, one for being a National Merit Scholar, and a third for winning the Strickland prize for best English student.

The crowd was thinning now, folks wandering down the steps and out onto the porch where they peered up at the streaming skies and wondered what was the best way to get to their vehicles. Not a few men were dispatched with umbrellas to fetch rides as close as possible for their not-so-foresightful kin.

Aikin rushed up, his gray-green eyes bright with merriment behind their thick lenses. "Hey, Mad Guy, you coming to G-Man's party?"

"Wouldn't miss it," David replied with forced enthusiasm, then glanced quizzically at Liz. "Uh . . . but we may be a little late."

"Be there or be square," Aikin chided, bouncing away to search for his own lady.

David's parents were backing away. "You going to that party then?" JoAnne asked.

"I told you before I was, and yeah, I'll be careful, and"—he glanced at his pa—"I won't have anything to drink."

Big Billy shrugged. "You're a man now, gotta make

your own decisions—ain't that what you just said? 'Sides, I thought Miss Lizzy was drivin'."

"She is," David acknowledged, recalling the skirmish he'd had with his ego earlier that day when he'd been torn between doing the macho thing and taking his Mustang, and the rational thing, which was to let Liz drive. Good sense had won out—to a point, since it was a fact that the M-of-D was a real handful in the kind of rain they'd been having lately. Liz's little Ford EXP, by contrast, did nicely in the wet, as long as you didn't go too fast, which she wouldn't do. Still, it felt a little weird being chauffeured to his own graduation bash.

"Catch you tomorrow, then," Big Billy called with surprising cheerfulness, then ushered his clan away.

Uncle Dale lingered for a moment and stuck out his hand. "Congratulations, boy," he said. "I'll give you my speech later, right now's your hour. You go and have fun with your friends—but be careful. Seems to me there's a lot more going on behind the scenes than meets the eye." He wagged his ragged brows skyward and winked knowingly.

David nodded back and took off his tie, stuffing it in his pocket. His final act at Enotah County High was to seek out good old locker #301 and remove the duffle bag he'd stashed there. While Liz watched in some amusement, he exchanged his tight new shoes for his comfy sneakers.

"So," he said when he had finished and the two of them were padding down the now-almost-deserted hall toward the entrance, "what happened back there?"

Liz's hand tightened in his, and her breath caught. "I . . . I don't know, Davy. I've been real edgy ever since I came through the gap. I know you've been talking about a lot of bad vibes going on and all the rain and all, but I didn't know it was this bad. But then at the ceremony I was looking at you, and it started raining, and suddenly I saw someone else—Lugh, I think, standing in front of a host addressing the troops, or some such. Lord, it was weird."

"Want to talk about it? We don't have to go to the party."

She shook her head decisively. "Sure I want to talk about it, but *after* the party. This is still our prime reality, David. We've *got* to get our priorities straight. Tonight . . . tonight, let's try very hard to be the people we were before we *knew* so much."

David couldn't help but grin. "I'd as soon keep some things like they are!"

A mischievous smile. "Good point."

"Though I kinda wish we could do it for the first time all over again."

She bent close, whispered in his ear, "You can still do it for the first time as a high-school graduate!"

"And talk this Faery thing out afterwards?"

"Sounds good. I—"

Alec appeared out of the shadows to their left and jingled the keys of his dad's newest Volvo. "See you in MacTyrie?"

"Not if I see you first!"

Chapter V: By Diverse Waters

(MacTyrie, Georgia—Friday, June 13—evening)

"Actually, if you *want* to talk about it, we can," Liz offered five minutes later, as she maneuvered Morgan, her black Ford EXP, along the water-glazed highway between Enotah and MacTyrie. For a miracle, the downpour had abated as soon as they'd reached the city limits, and there was no longer so much as a drizzle, though the highway was like a sheet of black mirror reflecting Liz's halogen headlights and those of the occasional oncoming car. She could not see the white-painted margins, though; and only the amber reflectors made the center line visible. Her face looked hard and intent, not at all like an eighteen-year-old who would graduate in another week.

Slumped beside her David grunted noncommittally and shrugged with equal indecision, finally venting his frustration by rolling down the window (though the AC was on), and letting the cool night breeze flagellate his neck with his now-unbound hair. *Head and heart,* he thought, fingering Liz's medallion through his open shirt. *Heart*

and head. Patience and priorities. Calm and . . . bullshit.
He vented another, louder grunt.

They were passing the first marina now, cruising above
it on a long, deep fill. The dark bulks of houseboats riding
high in rain-fed water obscured the white slabs of dock
and squares of cinderblock baitshops. Beyond them lay a
gray-silver arm of Langford Lake, placid and sated as a
sleeping satyr, and beyond *it* were the softly rounded
masses of the Appalachians. David's gaze wandered that
way, then skyward, to see the clouds flying in ragged tat-
ters, and—barely above the serrated horizon—the fitful
light of a single star.

"I guess you *don't* want to, then," Liz supplied when
he made no articulate answer.

"I . . ." He exhaled explosively. "Oh fiddle, Liz . . .
Of *course* I wanta talk! I'm going crazy trying to figure
out what's goin' on. I mean I really thought we were done
with this when Lugh closed the friggin' border! I honestly
hoped I'd finally get a chance to be just a normal kid. And
then all this happens . . . I . . . oh shit, just forget it!" A
fist into the seat cushion vented his feeling of impotence.

"Davy . . ."

"*Forget* it, Liz; we already decided to let it slide tonight, at least as far as the party. I mean it *is* kind of a
one-shot deal. Besides, do you really *want* to get into anything heavy when we've got the incipient married man to
contend with?" This last sounded a little forced, but it did
bring his thoughts around to other things, like Gary's impending wedding, at which the MacTyrie Gang were to be
groomsmen.

Liz chuckled, perhaps sensing that David's mood had
lightened a fraction. "Don't forget the incipient *bride!*
God, if I hear any more about wedding dresses I'll go
crazy!"

"Or tuxes!" David managed to laugh in turn. "She's
changed the color scheme three times. One *more* and me
and the boys're gonna make it blue denim!"

"Either that or a rope and ladder?"

A grin, not forced. "Good point. Maybe we'll arrange an elopement."

Liz peered at him slyly from the corner of her eye. "You guys giving him a bachelor party?"

David kept both his face and voice neutral, though his eyes sparkled mischievously in spite of his mood. "Why, Liz, what makes you think we'd do something like that?"

"Any excuse for a party, of course: any reason to get loud and obnoxious and crude."

An eyebrow lifted. "And when have you seen me either way?"

She paused. "Never, actually—but I have my spies!"

"Ah, but how good are their sources?" David laughed again—and disgraced himself by trying to sing "Secret Agent Man" *a cappella*.

The road was almost dry here, and Liz urged the little car onward at a faster clip, though she ignored David's pleas for her to race when Aikin's old Chevy Nova passed them. Their theoretical top speeds were about the same, he suspected.

By the time they had started up the small mountain that was gateway to MacTyrie, the clouds were nearly gone; and when they crested the gap at its summit, the moon was actually shining. David fiddled with the PAUSE and VOLUME on the stereo, which was playing Saint-Saëns's "Organ Symphony," arranging it so that the massive organ chord that heralded the final movement thundered in just as MacTyrie swung into view: a sparkle of lights embracing a curve of lake on the one hand and itself encompassed by an arc of mountains on the other. The ensuing strings complemented the twisting road on the downhill side nicely.

An instant later they sped across the bridge, and two miles further on they were in town, passing Alec's street and navigating the small business district, including Hudson BMW, before making a sharp uphill left just past the far city limit sign. They trundled along a narrow gravel road for a ways, winding first between pine woods, then among the steep roofs, exposed beams, and bogus plaster siding of Starshine Acres condominiums. An abrupt right put them across the saddle of a second small mountain, and the first left thereafter brought them, after a quarter mile, around behind Gary's house. They were maybe a mile and half from Alec's house. There were no dwellings further on.

Hudson Hall—as David called Gary's place—was not particularly remarkable to look at. Built before mountain architecture had succumbed to glass and angles, it was simply a sprawling ranch perched on the peak of a mountain so that one side peered down on MacTyrie, and the other, where Liz parked among a score of other cars, looked across the swimming pool and bath house toward another arm of lake. These last were what gave the place its special character, and it really was a palatial spread— one even Gary's dad could not have afforded had the Baptist minister who had built it not been defrocked and forced to leave the county under circumstances so scandalous they'd required him to liquidate his estate at fire-sale prices.

A bank of sliding glass doors fronted the patio, and those in the middle, which let into the family room, were wide open. David could see scads of classmates there already, as well as a steady stream of folks crossing the patio. Most were still in their dress clothes from graduation, though a fair number had changed to grubs or trendier garb. One—the foolish Darrell—was apparently wearing his graduation gown, boxer shorts, and nothing else to the consternation of a glowering Sheila Groves, who had switched to white jeans and a black The Cure sweatshirt.

Gary met them at the door, beer clandestinely in hand, mortarboard cocked jauntily above his Tom Cruise grin, muscular physique displayed to advantage by a black tank top. A beaming Tracy Jensen was tucked under his other arm, an oversized man's dress shirt masking her swelling belly.

"Welcome to my camp," he intoned. "I guess you all know why you're here."

"My name's not Tommy, though," David gave him back, quaffing a quick, secret swig before raising a hand in salute to Gary's dad, who was passing through with another bag of Ruffles, which he deposited on the (officially dry) bar before turning to glower at his only son.

Tall and thin, clad in a BMW racing jacket and matching cap (leftovers of his glory days with Bryan Webb Racing), Harold Hudson had once been remarkably tolerant when it came to adolescent alcohol consumption—until one of David's classmates had bought it big in an accident and word of the subsequent parental liability suit trickled down. Official policy for the party (and there were notices to that effect all over, though David knew there'd be exceptions) was therefore "don't let me see it, and don't do it on the property."

Harold's glower turned to a smile when he saw David, though, and he pointed speculatively at a bottle of Coke, there being too much din to holler.

David's raised finger put him on hold. He gave Liz a quick kiss and headed for Gary's bedroom, where he changed into the cut-offs and jersey he'd brought along in his duffel bag. The jersey, a graduation gift from Alec, was bright red and sported a gigantic V on the front and the number one on back, with a star emblazoned on the chest. The cumulation of David's latest batch of academic honors.

"Real modest, Sullivan," Rob Marshall intoned as he emerged.

"If you got it, flaunt it," David replied smugly, eyeing Alec who was wearing a similar shirt with the number 3 on the back and its own symbolic esoterica scattered here and there.

And then someone put Indigo Girls's latest on the stereo and cranked up the volume. Liz, now in white shorts and David's old Governor's Honors jersey, grabbed his hand, and for the next forty-five minutes David lost himself in music (with occasional forays out to grab a Coke or a handful of nuts or chips). For a while, at least, he forgot about his disturbing theories.

An hour later the rain was still holding off, though the clouds were gathering again, massing above the flanking mountains like ominous guards hovering around a prisoner. Tired from a second bout of frenzied dancing, David and Liz had wandered out by the pool to cool off. His jersey was soaked through; she had pushed her sleeves to her shoulders. They flopped down on the redwood bench farthest from the house. A low brick wall behind them held out the forest and the night. Through the glass doors they could see multitudes of their friends still gyrating crazily—to Fine Young Cannibals, for the nonce. But more and more couples (mostly) had staked out parts of the great outdoors. The diving board had been an early casualty; others were leaning against, or reclining on, various cars. Their end, however, was fairly unpopulated. At least David could hear the cries of katydids above the buzz of voices and the thump of music. Liz took his hand.

"Had enough?"

He frowned. "Have you?"

"I asked first."

"I'm still enjoying it, but . . . I wouldn't mind if you wanted to leave now." He glanced at the sky. "Might be wise, in fact, if those are any indication."

"Lord, I'm sick of rain," Liz sighed.

"And we've still got things to discuss—that really do need discussing."

Her eyes twinkled merrily. "And other things to catch up on, too!"

"Oh?"

She nuzzled his neck, nipped the ear Myra had pierced that very afternoon (his folks still hadn't noticed the tiny stud). He responded in turn, drawing her close and letting his hands wander across her back and hips. Her arms went around his neck, and for a while they forgot everything.

And then, "So *this* is where you got off to!"

David pried himself free and looked up, to see Gary and Tracy trotting forward, Gary down to skimpy black swim trunks, though Tracy was still fully dressed. Gary was maneuvering with difficulty. Darrell (apparently now dateless) was trailing along behind, with Alec and Aikin a few yards behind *him*, evidently to make sure the abandoned and obviously shitfaced Mr. Buchanan didn't fall in the pool and off himself.

"Yep, here we are," David acknowledged archly. "You *need* something?"

Gary patted Tracy's tummy happily. "Not a care in the world, m'lad: got my diploma, got my acceptance at MacTyrie J.C., got me a pretty lady, and gonna be a dad-eeee!!!!"

"All of which we knew," Alec observed dryly.

"And I'm *drunk!*" he shrilled. "It's my party, and I don't have to go home!"

"But I do," Tracy noted with resignation.

"You can take my car," Gary offered, inclining his head toward his red Plymouth Laser—the new bulbous model that had replaced the old one, which he had totaled. His dad wisely kept him out of Bimmers, except for special occasions when he'd lend him a 735 or (like the prom) a new 850i.

"Yeah, but the night's still young, eh Sullivan?"

David nodded and glanced at Liz. "Uh, yeah. But look, G-man, I think we'd better be travelin'. It's a great party, and all, but—well, we partied all afternoon, and I kinda need to spend some time with my lady."

"Nod-nod, wink-wink!" Darrell chortled loudly, poking Alec in the ribs.

"Yeah, and I've sorta got a headache," Liz added. "Squinting through the rain all the way from Gainesville'll do it to you."

Gary's face broke into an evil grin. He flopped an arm awkwardly across David's shoulders. "Uh-oh, Sullivan, a *headache!* Looks bad for the home team."

"Yeah," Alec chuckled, more tipsy than was his wont, but he'd probably be staying over.

"Better watch it!" Darrell guffawed, eyeing his running buddy. "You may wind up like G-man yet!"

David blushed to his ears, remembering the few weeks of real fear he'd experienced after the first time he and Liz had done it. Neither of them had exactly been prepared, and . . . well, the image of himself as a freshman at the University of Georgia with a small blond papoose stuffed in his backpack had haunted him for days, though he had to admit that it did have a certain charm. Since then they'd been more careful.

"Not likely," David mumbled.

"You got something 'gainst my baby?" Gary slurred.

"Not a thing, lad," David replied, standing. "Long as it's yours."

"*He,*" Tracy inserted. "Dr. Nesheim called right before graduation."

"Another G-man? Oh, Lord!"

"Hey, congratulations!" Liz cried.

"He's got the *ceeeegars* ordered already," Darrell added, slapping Gary on the back.

Gary glared at him.

" 'Course none of us smoke," Alec noted.

"Who's next? is what I want to know," Tracy giggled, eyeing David and Liz speculatively.

"Who knows?" David mumbled, as Liz rose beside him. "But seriously, folks, we need to be movin' on. Got deeds to do and promises to keep."

"Etcetera, etcetera, etcetera. Okay, then, party poopers."

"Right. See y'all later."

"Thanks for coming," Gary called. Without warning he turned and dived into the pool. The first shriek that followed was Tracy being splashed by the tsunami that marked his passage. The second was Aikin and Alec heaving Darrell in beside him. The last sounds David heard before Liz turned the key and rolled up the window was

"Smoke On The Water" thundering out the back door, and the last thing he saw was Alec and Aikin improbably involved in a tickle duel with each other while a soaking Darrell wrung out his sopping graduation gown above them.

The clouds followed his example with a vengeance.

By the time David and Liz had reached Sullivan Cove the downpour had abated somewhat, but the branch that followed the road was still running high, red and frothy with runoff from both the fields and the hills above them. She'd had to set the wipers on full most of the way, and had spent a lot of time scrunched up close behind the steering wheel squinting through the windshield at the near-horizontal sheets. Twice, in spite of low speeds, they had aquaplaned. They'd passed two cars off the road, too, but wreckers and the Georgia State Patrol were already in attendance. The lights were out in the Ignorance Creek community, though, and also in Fairplay and East Damascus (there was no West)—legacy, probably, of blown transformers.

Liz eased the car along the muddy road, trying to stay in the high spots where a trace of gravel yet remained. Fortunately the road was not as worn as many, mostly because only the Sullivans or their visitors used it, except for the paperboy on weekends, and the small congregation of the Sullivan Cove Church of God on Sunday morning.

They passed David's house on the left, the ruins of Uncle Dale's cabin a half mile further on. David strained his eyes in the darkness, trying to make out the trailer the old man had slipped in behind it. It was too bad, though, that his favorite uncle had been reduced to that in his old age. Oh, he'd heard the excuses: too much trouble to fix the house, and he planned to leave it to David anyway, so he'd rather let David build the kind of place he wanted than stick him with something he might not like. But that didn't make him feel any better when it was his fault the place was trashed to start with. It also reminded him of the inevitability of Uncle Dale's death, and that thought chilled him.

A short way further on forest closed briefly in, and then they reached the turnaround at B.A. Beach. The rain had stopped again, but they did not get out to make their way across the field of soggy broom sedge and through the line of trees to their usual lakefront makeout site. Instead, Liz turned the car around so it was pointed back the way they had come. David reached into the glovebox and pushed the button that popped the hatch, and they climbed into the long carpeted platform behind the seats. Too short to stretch out in, really, the upholstered cylindrical cushion Liz stored there made a good support for their heads. Feet propped on the high trunk sill, they looked out on the night. David shivered when he thought about the image they must project: rather like a snake's head agape, with them reclining in its jaws.

They did not look at each other, simply twined their fingers and relaxed into each other's company.

"So what do you think's going on?" Liz asked at last.

"Oh, Lord," David began, "I don't know where to start."

"How 'bout with the rain? This much can't be natural."

David shrugged. "Well, it has to be something to do with the war in Faerie. Remember Ailill? Ailill *Windmaster* they called him, 'cause he was born in a storm and therefore had a natural affinity for 'em. He liked to make 'em, too, according to Nuada. Would sense 'em forming in Tir-Nan-Og, help 'em along, and then send 'em through the World Walls to bother us."

"Right—but he's out of the picture now."

"Yeah," David agreed. "But remember last fall when the Sidhe were out to get Alec and we were all holed up at Uncle Dale's? They couldn't actually attack the house, so they juiced up the weather and brought storms down on us—worse than these, actually. These have just been goin' on longer."

"So you think this is Sidhe doing?"

"I *know* it is! It's the war in Faerie. Lugh said it would happen and it has: it's come to Tir-Nan-Og, and the results are resonating even here. And remember what Calvin told us about what Uki said? That the storm at Dale's was felt even in Galunlati? It's the same thing here: storms in Faerie leaking through the World Walls to clobber us."

Liz shuddered and drew closer to David, resting her head against his shoulder and stroking his bare thigh absently. "Must be a hell of a war. It's been going on for days."

"Days here, sure; maybe no time there at all. You never can tell how time runs on the other side."

He felt her nod. "Good point. But, gee, Davy, how much longer *can* it go on? If it rains like this all summer, nothing'll get done: everything'll mildew, and gardens won't grow, and the tourists all stay away by droves."

"No loss that!"

"You don't make your money off 'em. A lot of folks do. Think about them!"

"Okay," David conceded. "But you know what really bothers me?"

"I give."

"That it's all our doing, really. Alec's fault if you look at it one way, or ours if you get to the *real* bottom."

"Don't say that, David; we've been over it before."

"But it still bothers me—I guess it's got to be practically an obsession. If you and I hadn't got things going he'd have never gotten jealous of you. If he'd never gotten jealous, he'd have never been vulnerable to manipulation by that Faery woman who betrayed him."

"Would you rather we'd never gotten together?"

"No, of course not. But I wish we'd been more aware of the effect we were havin' on him. I mean, shoot, Liz, he's my best friend, has been forever, and then suddenly he's odd man out. That *has* to be a bitch to deal with."

"He has to grow up."

"Well he did a lot last summer, let me tell you. It may have ruined him, too."

"How so?"

"Well, with women, for one thing. He's hardly dated at all since then."

"He didn't date *before* then, either," Liz pointed out.

"The pickings are rather slim, if *you* notice."

"That didn't stop Gary and Darrell and Aikin."

"They're not as picky."

"Okay, I'll grant you that. But even so—"

David interrupted. "I mean being shafted's one thing; practically everyone goes through it. But Alec wasn't just shafted; he was tied up and roasted over a long, hot flame, then sauced with guilt and left to stay warm in the oven. I mean, most folks' exes don't deliver their friends to enemies who threaten to kill them, and use the weather for weapons."

"Well, I can't argue with that."

"Know what's weird, though? I think he's still in love with her. In spite of all she did, Alec's still in love with Eva."

"You sure about that?"

"Well, he's more or less said as much—and she *was* his first."

Liz pinched his side. "That's *lust*, David, not love!"

"Yeah, but even so, she did admit there at the last that she loved him—at least that's what he told me."

"Unfortunately, I wasn't there when she died," Liz replied slowly. "And anyway, I was kinda concerned with other things—like whether *you* were dead or alive."

"I still think it's possible, though—"

"Okay," Liz said decisively, and David knew she was seeking to divert the conversation. "So we've established that it's the war in Faerie causing the shitty weather. *And* we've established that it's all our fault for ignoring Alec—which in a way it really is, though I think the Sidhe would've found something else to fuss over even if Fionchadd hadn't been captured. What about the newest stuff?"

"My dreams, or yours?"

"You've had 'em too?"

David nodded. "For the last week. I didn't tell you on the phone 'cause walls have ears, and I didn't want to upset the folks any more than I had to. I've told Uncle Dale, Ma, the Gang—but I didn't know who might be listening on your end, I mean the phone down at your dad's isn't exactly private. So," he added, "you wanta go first?"

Liz took a deep breath. "Well, it's basically like I said. I was just sitting there with your mom and dad, looking up at you on stage and thinking how handsome you were. But then the weather started acting up and I started getting real edgy, like I've been since I got back up here, and then I started, like, picking up vibes all around—not *trying* mind you, not scrying, just picking up feelings like a lot of nervousness, a lot of anger, a lot of hostility. It was like a pot about to blow. Fortunately, there was a lot of happiness and excitement too, and that kinda damped it down. But it was strong, Davy, *really* strong. I don't usually feel things like that unless I try really hard, but these just came. But anyway, I started fidgeting with the ring, the one Oisin gave you, that's not supposed to be magic anymore. And the next thing I knew I wasn't looking at you. I was looking at Lugh standing up on some kind of platform talking to the troops. I . . . I must have got in touch with Oisin, or somebody, because I was sort of vaguely aware of him. But . . . I don't know. It was just really scary, coming on me unasked like that."

David whistled. "Fortunately, mine haven't been that bad. Nightmares mostly, the last week or so. Just a feeling of dread—of being hurt, maybe. Images of soldiers mustering, of storms above forests, of ships plunging on wild seas. Until today."

"Okay . . ."

"Today's was much clearer. I sort of drowsed off at the cove, and then suddenly I was in someone's head—Froech's, I think. I was keepin' watch on top of some kind of tower, seein' the clouds come in across sweeps of forests—the biggest forest you ever saw. And . . . I had a friend there, I think, and we talked some, but I can't remember what they said—maybe they were speaking Sidheish, or something. But I think the gist of it is that Finvarra really has landed. There was something else, too: a message sent by raven, and . . . and there at the last . . . I . . . I think it was a cry for help.''

"From Froech?''

David shook his head. "I don't think so. I don't know where it came from. I don't even know if he was aware of it. But when I woke up that was what was ringing in my mind: somebody in trouble. Somebody needing help.''

"But who? You've got lots of friends in Faerie.''

David shrugged. "Who knows?''

"Fionchadd, maybe?''

"That I doubt. He's supposed to be captive in Erenn. I don't think thoughts reach that far.''

"But you don't know.''

"No, of *course* I don't!'' David snapped.

"Christ,'' Liz whispered. "You know what you just did, don't you?''

"What?''

"You got bitchy for no reason.''

"I . . . You're right—I did the same thing to Alec earlier.''

"Don't worry about it. I've been fighting it all evening. That's why I wanted to dance so much at the party: so I could burn out nervous energy and wouldn't have to guard my tongue all the time.''

"I hate to say it,'' David told her, "but I think that's more slopover from Faerie.''

"But the border's supposed to be closed!''

"Yeah, but according to what Finno told me, Lugh can't really physically seal it without great cost to himself. He has to actually *nail* himself to his throne with a dagger, and he can't do that—not and be commander. What I think he did was simply forbid commerce and maybe juice up

the glamour a little. As far as the barriers are concerned—
the natural ones, if they *are* natural, I think they're the
same. I think the Sidhe still cross into our World on their
Ridings when the residue of iron forces them off the Tracks.
I just think they take extra precautions not to be seen. But
what worries me is that we're coming up on another of
their high days—Midsummer's—and the Walls Between the
Worlds are usually thin then. And if the weather's this bad
now and the war's still going on then . . . God knows
what'll happen.''

"You got any ideas?''

"Other than wishing I could stop the war? No. But even
if I did, I couldn't do anything. I couldn't get there if I
wanted to, not by any direct route. And anyway, I think
they have to let you in.''

"It's a moot point anyway.''

"But, God, Liz, I feel so bad about Finno. He was my
friend. He liked me, I liked him. Even Alec liked him—
and now he's a prisoner, maybe even dead beyond return.''

"No word on that?''

"Nothing. I've tried to get Alec to use the ulunsuti and
check things out there, but he won't. Maybe I'll try again,
though. Maybe together we can convince him, 'cause I
really do think things have kicked up a level, somehow.''

"Right. Well, now we've assessed the troubles of two
Worlds, how have you been doing otherwise?''

"Missin' you, of course.''

"Me too.''

"Lookin' forward to never missing you again. 'Bout
time, too.''

"What about Mr. McLean? He decided what he's gonna
do?''

"Goin' to Georgia, of course. Couldn't stand to go to
MacTyrie Junior. His dad's all for it, too.''

"Still shadowing you?''

"Well, we *are* gonna room together—at least officially.''

She looked at him askance. "What's *that* supposed to mean?"

"Uh, well, Darrell's sister Myra says she'd feel better if there was somebody stayin' at her studio some. So I thought you and me . . ."

"David!"

"It was *just* a *thought.*"

"Indeed!"

"Know something?"

"What?"

"I'm tired of talkin'."

"Then don't."

They didn't, and for a long time the only sounds were of quickening breathing and of hands against cotton and denim, and eventually against bare flesh. The cold prickle of rain on their feet finally brought them back to the world. Lightning flashed once, and then it was pouring. Liz glanced at her watch. "Jeeze," she groaned. "I've *got* to get on home."

"Too bad," David panted. "But there's always tomorrow."

"Tomorrow I have to go back to Gainesville and study. I have finals Wednesday and Thursday. And Friday you get to come see *me* graduate."

"I still can't believe you guys built up so many snow days. I mean, you're further south than *we* are."

"I'll believe anything about the weather anymore, David. Anything at all!"

It was raining harder than ever when Liz finally got them back to David's house. So hard, in fact, that she almost hit the becalmed Crown Vic before she saw it. David insisted on getting off at the bottom of the hill, pointing out that she'd only mess up her car by trying to navigate the white water of their drive. A quick final kiss, and he was in the darkness and sprinting up the sodden slope, instantly soaked to the skin and practically blind.

The back porch light was on, though; and with that as guide he made it to sanctuary.

His pa was long since in bed, but his ma was still up, reading Andrea Parnell's latest in the kitchen, which she preferred to the den. David granted her a quick, grumbly greeting and dashed into his room to dry off and change, emerging a short while later in gym shorts and—atypically—a short blue bathrobe. JoAnne looked up and smiled as he poured himself a cup of coffee from the pot on the stove, then smoothed it out with a generous portion of cream and sugar.

"Have a good time?"

"All but the weather."

"Might as well not even talk about that!"

David rolled his eyes. "Tell me about it."

She looked up at him, face serious. "Maybe *you* should tell *me.*"

"Well," he began, "I don't think it's natural."

She put the book down. "Figured it wasn't."

"I—" A frantic pounding on the back door interrupted him. David glanced up, startled, meeting his ma's expression of alarm.

"Now who on earth could *that* be?"

David grimaced and padded over. He flipped on the porch light and almost cried out as he wrenched the door open.

"Liz! What . . . ?"

"The highway's washed out," Liz replied dully, as David hustled her in. She was absolutely soaked. Her hair looked like streams of blood and her clothes were molded to her body like a clammy second skin.

"Well don't just *stand* there, come in!" Joanne ordered. "Get her some coffee, David, and some towels." She ushered Liz to a seat by the dining table, then closed the door, pausing to gaze out into the night. "Figured that old culvert'd go sometime," she observed when she returned. "Bill always said they didn't put it in right. How bad was it?"

"Pretty bad," Liz replied breathlessly. "It's washed out on either side. Road's completely cut. I guess I'll have to call my mom and have her meet me on the other side."

"The Devil you will!" JoAnne snorted. "You ain't calling your mama out in a night like this! You'll stay here; we'll call her and tell her what's happened and she can get you in the mornin'. Sides, it's probably what your life's worth to try to cross the creek on foot now. Best to wait it out. Where's your car?"

"I parked it just inside the church road. Was afraid somebody'd hit it otherwise."

"You walked all that way?"

"It's not that all that far." She paused, managed a smile. "Besides, it was more like running."

"Evidently," David noted, fishing an assortment of towels out of the dryer, all of which he handed to Liz before busying himself concocting a fresh pot of coffee.

Liz took the towels gratefully and began dabbing her sodden clothes. JoAnne looked on for a moment, then rose decisively. "Come on, gal, that won't do no good. I'll stick them clothes in the dryer and you can wear one of my robes and nighties in the meantime. You can stay in David's room."

"And I'll stay . . . ?" David wondered from the stove.

"Upstairs," JoAnne told him pointedly.

"I was *gonna* suggest the couch."

"The foldout one in the den?" Liz inserted. "I can stay there if you like. I don't want to put David out of his room."

"You're stayin' in David's room," JoAnne said firmly. "And that's that."

"But *I* could—" David began.

His ma eyed him sharply. "You *really* wanta do that?"

"Good point," David conceded. "The monster'll be up early tomorrow to watch cartoons."

"Yeah," JoAnne said, though he had an idea she knew his true motivation. The hall floor didn't squeak anything like as much as the attic stairs did, and JoAnne Sullivan had sharp ears.

Liz followed David's mother toward the bathroom. He saw her duck inside and emerge a short while later dressed in the pink housecoat his ma had handed in. The collar of a white nightgown peeked out from under it. She sat down beside him and sipped at her coffee, saying nothing. Her eyes, when David saw them, looked awful.

"Long day."

She nodded. "And too much goin' on."

The silence persisted, but David caught the buzz of the living room phone being dialed and of his mother's voice speaking low.

"I just called your ma," JoAnne reported, rejoining them a short while later. She winked at Liz. "I figured if I talked to her she'd know nothin' fishy was up twixt you and David."

David blushed.

Half an hour later they all went to bed. David hesitated at the door to his old room to kiss Liz good night.

"You know," he whispered. "This is the first time you've ever stayed over here—and in my room yet!"

"So?"

"I just hope it's not the last!"

And with that he padded upstairs, pausing as Liz closed the door to blow her one final kiss.

Chapter VI: A Summoning

(Sylva, North Carolina—Friday, June 13—past midnight)

Calvin was not certain if he was awake or asleep when the rattlesnake spoke to him. He was in bed, that much was clear: it was past midnight. Sandy was curled on her side next to him, one bare leg outside the covers; he was lying on his back, still lolling in the afterglow of a hard day's work and a long evening's loving. (It was true what they said about older women, he decided, grinning.) But there'd been a certain lack of passion this time, as if both their minds were somewhere else. And then they had talked for a long time in the darkness, with Sandy trying to explain some of her theory of magic and multiple Worlds as they related to physics. He'd understood parts of it, but when she'd started going on about Straight Tracks and trying to liken them to cosmic strings, he had suddenly felt her theories creeping past the boundaries of his intellect. One moment he comprehended; the next she was speaking gibberish. Eventually she'd fallen silent, but he'd remained awake, staring at the ceiling.

That was when he became aware of the snake.

At first he thought it a shadow, an image of a window spreader cast on the handmade rag rug. He considered getting up to investigate, but something stopped him. The light was strange and murky, not at all like the welcoming moonlight that should have been present.

Maybe he slept.

Maybe he *still* slept when he became aware of the slow dry hiss of scales on wood beside his head and turned to find himself face to face with a monstrous diamondback coiling around the bedpost a bare six inches from his nose. Chills raced over him. But then—to his surprise, yet somehow not—the snake opened its mouth and spoke.

"Come," it said. "Hasten, for Uki calls you."

Before he could reply, the snake was gone. Or maybe had never been. Maybe it was only another shadow cast by a tree on the headboard.

But Calvin did not believe that.

Moving as quietly as only years of pride in that art could make him, he slid from the bed. The sheets made the barest whisper as he left them; his feet scarce thumped on the bleached pine floor. He moved toward the open door that led into the other room, pausing to snag a pair of jeans from the chair, gritting his teeth as the zipper buzzed slightly across the arm. Another pause by the door to retrieve the sports page of the *Asheville Citizen* and a certain white doeskin bag he had left there (the medicine pouch that lay on his chest he *never* removed), and he entered the kitchen-great room, whence he passed through the open front door and stepped onto the porch. Moonlight draped the pale wood with white and blue, and Calvin waited until he had crept down the long, steep steps on the northern side to dress.

Fog enfolded him, then, creeping up from the surrounding trees, and he knew that magic was afoot in the world. What had Uki told him when first he had left Galunlati? "Our Worlds touch but seldom now, and that only in mists and the dreams of madmen." Did that mean he was mad?

Did it matter? One thing only was clear: He had been

summoned. And a summons from Uki could not be ignored.

He wandered through the fog for a short while, aware
only of the forest reaching out to circle him, though he
could not see the trunks around him, only the ragged summits of pines looming above the white tendrils, dark
against a moonlit sky.

Eventually he came to the place he had sought without
conscious volition: the small, round clearing that housed
his Power Wheel. He and Sandy had camped there sometimes—when they grew tired of even the rudimentary com-
forts of the cabin. It had also been the site of their first
loving, last June under the summer stars. It was therefore
a Place of Power (to use Dave's term), because someone
had given it Power by loving it, and he himself had an
emotional investment there. When the time had come for
him to construct a Power Wheel, it had been the natural
choice. Sandy understood, she had even deeded it to him,
as if she knew by instinct that the fact that it was a gift
made its Power even greater.

Hardly daring to breathe, he made his silent way to the
center and knelt by the pile of ancient ashes that remained
from his last visit. The fog had drawn back, he noticed,
but yet waited at the limits of the ring; the moonlight was
bright enough, nearly, to show the patterns of colored sand
he had sprinkled upon the loam. Taking a deep breath, he
reached into the doeskin bag and fished out two objects.
One was a common disposable cigarette lighter, the other
a triangular sliver of some glassy material roughly the size
of his palm. It was milkily white, shading to clear at its
edges, but two of its points bore a shimmering ruddiness,
as if they had been dipped in blood. It was a scale of the
great uktena, and tonight it would be the key to another
World.

The ritual was deceptively simple, though he knew that
long hours collecting and preparing ingredients and not a
little pain went into the empowering of the scales—rituals
that Uki had only recently imparted to him as well. An-

other breath, and he took the scrap of newspaper, crumpled it into a ball, placed it in the center of the clearing, and set it alight. Had he had time to do things properly, he would have used leaves for tinder and added sticks and branches and certain herbs, and made the fire with flint or pyrite, for natural things had more Power in such a working. But he was in a hurry, and the fire was what ultimately mattered, not the nature of its making. A third deep breath. Did he really want to do this? Was he ready to endure the agony once more?

Did he really have any choice?

When he judged the flame to be brightest, he thrust the scale into it. The fire immediately flashed out to embrace the world with light like a magnesium flare. And at that precise moment, Calvin cried out, his voice not loud, but very very clear, *"Hyuntikwala Usunhi!"*

Light engulfed him, and he could see nothing but white, and then the light ceased to concern him, and all he felt was the horrible pain of the crossing. It was as if he were being flayed alive, as if his body were being consumed a cell at a time by gleeful lightning. He tried to scream and could not, tried to pass out and was denied.

Abruptly the pain swept away, and Calvin blinked and opened his eyes into daylight so bright he first thought he had been struck blind. The scream he'd held suspended escaped as a gasp.

Eventually his vision began to clear, though the pain came creeping back disguised as heat. He blinked, wiped his brow, wishing he'd brought along the beaded headband that usually bound his long black hair from his eyes. Another blink, and his eyes had adjusted to the unexpected glare.

Before him a waterfall thundered into a mighty gorge. On either side and behind him were the outer fringes of an endless wood—maples here, mostly, and maybe a few beeches. He surveyed them absently—and frowned, for the leaves, which had been greening with springtime when last he'd been here, were now crisped and sere.

And a little ways off to the left a figure was turning around. It was a man—or manlike: well over six feet tall, with the features of Calvin's people. His skin was not red-brown, though, but almost pure white, and seemed to contain some inner fire. He had long black hair in braids past his waist and was wearing (as he always did) a white deer-skin loincloth beaded with patterns of snakes and lightning—the same symbols that decorated the gold bands coiled about his muscular arms and legs.

"Siyu, Edahi," he said. "I see you have received my summons, though truly I had hoped to see you sooner."

"Siyu, adawehiru," Calvin replied. "Sorry, Uki, I've been . . . busy."

"You will be busier," Uki told him promptly, his face gone quickly grim. "For there is much you must hear, much we must discover, and then much we must decide."

Calvin nodded and puffed his cheeks thoughtfully. He glanced up at the glowering sky, thinking, inanely, that blue heat was hotter than red.

"It's—*warm,"* he said carefully, by way of breaking the silence.

"That is the reason I have called you," Uki replied, pointing toward the heart of the heavens.

The sun was wrong: was much closer than it should have been. But worse, it seemed to be slowly pulsing, gradually shifting size.

"Someone is shaking Nunda Igehi," Uki said, and led the way into the woods.

Chapter VII: Dark Night of the Soul

(Tir-Nan-Og—high summer)

War, Froech thought, surveying the mounted host that flanked him beneath fringes of dripping boughs as far as he could see to either side, was a great deal more trouble than it was worth. It was one thing if you were mortal: you charged, you fought, you either lived or died, and that was the end of it. But war among *immortals*—ah, that called for other rules entirely. There was still fighting, of course; but with the Sidhe even the weapons were different. In Faerie, battle began with trials of Power, because that was the way it had always been and the way the Laws compelled it. But Power was slow to horde and fast to disperse, so those initial forays usually progressed quickly to spears and arrows, then to axes and clubs and swords, and finally to knives, and—more frequently than he liked— to one's own hands around a foeman's throat.

But what was the point? One killed—or was killed; one died, and then one day or ten days later (if the wounds were minor) or longer if there was greater hurt—one rejoined soul and body and fought again, and the whole vain cycle was repeated. Oh, aye, it hurt to die; he had already done that once—by a wyvern's disemboweling claw. But the pain was like anything else: it came, and it vanished, and eventually the memory faded.

Unless one of two things happened. The first was not likely: that was the Death of Iron, which clove body from soul and wounded both alike past hope of easy rejoining. Iron did not exist in Faerie, though, and no one of that World could wield it.

The other bane was if there was no body for the soul to rejoin, though even that problem could be overcome. Generally a man would join his spirit to a babe in the womb and so grow up that way. More rarely a man or woman of great Power would by slow degrees reform a body from the very stuff of Faerie. That could take years, centuries even; but what were a score of either to the immortal Daoine Sidhe of Tir-Nan-Og who were his comrades—or the kindred folk of Erenn, who were his foes?

Yet on such things victory hung. Men fought, men were killed, that was the way of battle. Yet the real conflict sometimes came after in a mad scramble to recover the fallen. Women most often did this, for they were not so strong as men and so more likely to be wounded in war, and also they were the source of wombs in which the dead could be reborn. As soon as a skirmish ended, they were on the field, carrying away the wounded, searching the grasses for slivers of severed flesh to be reattached and thus hasten some warrior's healing; at times battling the women of the foe for possession of the slain.

The trick, then, was to destroy the bodies of the enemy dead with fire or sorcery; or to rend bodies into such small bits that full healing would take a thousand years. The only victor, Froech knew, was the one who could kill the most of his adversaries and keep them dead the longest.

But at least it was not as easy for the Erennese as it had once been, for they had lost the Cauldron of Rebirth in a conflict with the folk of Annwyn. Affairs should be more equal now.

Except that, somehow, war had been brought to Tir-Nan-Og.

The wind shifted: warm air from the south, whipping his long black hair into his face because he had been too vain to bind it and had thought the intricate cheek guards and equally ornate nasal of his high-domed helm proof enough against random breezes. That breeze brought odors, too: stagnant water (from the fen on whose fringe they met); and well-oiled metal; and the musk of horses that never changed between the Worlds, though they wore horns or feathers or scales. New, however, was the cinnamon-sweet smell of the Watchers who crouched before them in their countless head-high ranks, domed shells ablaze with the pearlescent interlaced spirals lacquered upon them, their heavy, clubbed tails inscribing strange patterns in the mud as they surveyed Finvarra's host.

They were an innovation in this campaign. Always before Lugh had used them to ward certain of his borders from unwelcome visitors, but using them in war . . . it remained to be seen if they would work. It had taken almost a month to assemble enough to be useful, and longer than that to imprint their tiny minds with a rage to order. But *if* it succeeded . . . there would be few enemy dead indeed, for the beasts ate only freshly killed meat. And what man, Sidhe or otherwise, would rejoin his soul to what churned in the guts of a beast?

Who indeed? The very thought made him shiver.

A lur horn sounded abruptly, and backs stiffened all down the line. Froech glanced left, to his friend Andro, who grinned at him from beneath the fringe of beard that was atypical of Faery men, and patted the salamander on his shield, and then further down to Andro's lady, Fuilte-gerne, who rode beside him, beautiful face grim as the crows stamped on her helm in the mark of the Morrigu's house. The warrior to his right he did not know, but he spoke to him anyway.

"It would seem we are at last to it, brother. What think you, will we carry the day?"

"The day, I think; the war I doubt," the soldier said. "For all we fight on our own land, Finvarra's hosts are greater and his sorceries far stronger."

"Yet ours hold. His druids have tried and failed, and now must pause to recover their strength."

"As do our own, an even match."

"Not so even," Froech laughed. "For they shall take away few dead."

"Let us hope not. And let us hope the Watchers know friend from foe."

"Lugh says they will."

"But they are not truly his to command. Even he mistrusts them."

And then the horns sounded once more: two blasts, then one, sliding silver into the air, but quickly loudening to fill the world. Froech frowned, looked forward, across the brass-scrolled plates that armored his jet-black stallion to the looming bulks of the Watchers. Another set of notes in a certain rhythm ordered the battle: four short calls, which carried with them coded orders.

Arrows, it would be, as he had guessed: arrows to arch across the Watchers as soon as the foe came into range. And come they would, too, for already the Watchers were ambling forward, and would continue if unchecked until they forced the enemy either to fight or fall back before them. The former was most likely, for Finvarra's men held the less-certain ground: fen in front, and less than a league behind them, ragged cliffs. They had to advance or be lost.

Already the Watchers had covered a half-score paces, but Froech held his ground, bow at ready, eyes half closed as he sought to raise a glamour to confuse whoever of Finvarra's levies might choose him as his target. He wondered what Finvarra's troops were thinking, there across the oozing slime in the black-and-scarlet livery that was as out of the place here as his own deep red and gold would have been in the misty glens of Erenn.

And then horns again, from across the way, and Fin-

varra's men moved forward, their white horses stepping as
one. Arrows flew from that line, but Lugh's troops had
expected them and raised blazing shields to consume them
with arcane fire. The second volley was the same, and
then it was their turn to shoot, and shoot they did: launch-
ing shafts that split as they flew, and turned one to fire,
and one to ice, and quenched the shields Finvarra's men
raised against them or set their sable cloaks ablaze.

And still he sat unmoving, while the Watchers drew
nearer the foe. Already there were dead there, and the
odor of blood strong in the air; and that smell roused the
beasts' tiny minds and drove them on with ever-increasing
fury.

Arrows flew again, and spears this time: silver-edged
as only Goibniu could make them. But those spears did
little harm, for they could barely reach the Sidhe, and slid
off the armored heads and shells of the Watchers. One,
though, had found its mark and pierced a Watcher in the
soft spot between head and shell, and even as the blood
gushed out, its fellows were upon it, disrupting the line
for nigh ten paces about. And it was into this opening
Finvarra's forces flew: breaching the ranks and thrusting
into Lugh's host with weapons flailing.

Lugh's men forced them out again in a rout that left
corpses strewn across the mud: corpses which the women
quickly claimed and hauled away to fuel the bonfires, lest
the smell of their blood too much excite the beasts.

The Watchers were halfway across the fen now, and the
going was slow, for Lugh had not reckoned on the effect
their great weight would have on that shifting, oozing surface. But another note had sounded, and the troops were
moving as well, pacing their horses slowly.

And then Finvarra's men were charging, shields raised,
spears braced, diving toward that line of moving flesh—

—And meeting it: bringing hooves down on armored
heads, breaking off stubby horns, blinding red eyes, diving
between or leaping over to break their ranks and so come
to Lugh's host at last.

Few made it, and those that remained behind found their mounts also mired in the muck or pierced by arrows.

But no few of the Watchers died as well, and Froech saw the one directly before him stumble to a halt with a matched pair of spears in its eyes and begin clawing frantically. Its fellows moved on, but Finvarra's forces were already diving toward the gap, and Froech kicked his own mount forward to meet them, as Andro did likewise at his side.

It was hand to hand then, horses dancing about, maneuvered by mind or heel alone, fen-gasses rising between to choke the air as swords clanged hard against shields and men grunted and sweated and swore. The sun beat down but it was not an ally of Lugh's, no matter it was his sign, and Froech felt the heat begin to rise in him. He could have banished it, but Power demanded concentration, and he had no time for such, not when he had to keep alive, had to keep his shield up and his sword moving in post and parry. His adversary was larger than he—huge for a man of Faerie—and his charger likewise, and Froech felt himself pressed back—yet not toward the line, not toward his friends, but toward the body of the Watchers. His horse stumbled as it trod the dead monster's tail, and it was all he could do to keep his balance and meet the blow that smashed down at him. Another blow, another backward pace, and the horse was having trouble avoiding the Watcher's corpse. A sword flashed out again, and he met it—barely. But a second stroke bit through his shield and into his collar bone, and he had no choice but to cast aside his protection lest it too much encumber him. Even as he did that, even as he spun his sword in a maze-dance before him, his foe had discarded his own shield and reached toward him, grabbed a lock of unbound hair and jerked. Froech had only a moment to realize what was happening before a sword ripped toward his throat. The blow missed his neck, but found the arm he raised to protect himself, and then he was falling while all the world went red.

Pain flooded through him when he hit the ground, and

his vision cleared. He had just time to see that clouds were forming in the north with unnatural haste and to hear the grim chanting of the druids once more commencing their craft, before cold bronze wrenched his soul from his body.

David awoke into darkness. He sat up, glanced around, momentarily disoriented. As his eyes adjusted to the gloom, he could make out the steep angles of the attic ceiling, the narrow bed where he lay uncovered because the tiny room was summer-hot in spite of the open window that blew rain-cooled air across him. That air smelled of dust here, too, not of sweat and fear and battle. But it seemed as if the sounds of warfare still came to him, until he realized it was rain on the roof.

"Jesus," he whispered, then noticed he was shivering, though not with cold. That had been the worst one yet: so very real . . . and somebody he had known as well. The whole thing was starting to get to him. It was one thing when you had to deal with rain as a matter of course, as one of the inconveniences of life, and ditto for contention. Then you merely had to watch your step and try a little harder. But when it was your fault, and you couldn't do anything about it—that was a thousand times worse. It was like that awful sick moment last year when he'd lost control of his car and knew he was about to crash. Everything had gone into slow motion and he'd known absolutely that he was gonna hit, but not how hard or with how much damage. Except that this time the irresistable force was coming at *him* and he was powerless to avoid it.

Restless, he climbed out of bed, tugged on his gym shorts and threw the robe around his shoulders more from a desire for psychological comfort than any physical need. Barefoot, he padded downstairs, wincing as his tread brought more than one set of creaks from the boards of the narrow stairwell. So much for his ma's precautions.

Right at the bottom and down the hall; hesitating, but not stopping, by the door of his sanctum, and again to glance in on Little Billy who slept peacefully in his own room. Once in the kitchen he closed the hall door behind him but didn't latch it, thought of switching on the light, but decided against it. A glance over his shoulder, and he made it to the counter beside the stove, where he knelt and rummaged quietly through the detritus there until he found a bottle of Big Billy's Jim Beam. That was what he needed, something to deaden his memory, to banish the horrible images.

He snagged a squatty glass from the dish drainer and opened the freezer compartment at the top of the fridge. Four ice cubes, and the whiskey went over. It took more than he'd intended—Pa would know some was missing— but his was the greater need now. If Big Billy gave him any grief, he'd simply level with him. They'd argue, of course, but he'd get the better eventually.

Thus fortified, he crept out the back door (open, except for the hooked screen, to let in the night breezes that cooled the house in lieu of air-conditioning), and sat down on the edge of the porch. A long swallow almost made him choke, but he caught it in time and let the cold fluid set fire to his throat, feeling its warmth flood through him. The rain had slackened to a persistent drizzle, and he stared for a while at the patterns it made in the ever-growing puddle at the base of the steps. The steady drips diving off the roof scant inches beyond his feet were a sort of frame: bright silver pillars against a background of gloom-shot gray. Tiberius the tomcat came up to him and curled against his side. He could feel the prickle of water on his toes as drops smashed themselves on the steps and showered them with liquid shrapnel.

To the right, at the limit of vision, he could almost see Bloody Bald. Lightning flared there, a shimmer in the darkness like a flame seen through layers of gauze. War went on there, he knew, war in Faerie. He wondered what had become of his friends among the Sidhe. Lugh, he supposed, was leading the charge. Nuada and Morrigu were Lugh's lieutenants, so they probably had major roles as well. Oisin, the old human seer, was doubtlessly advising. And the others he knew less well: Froech and Regan, Cormac and Forgoll—how did they fare? It was all pointless, too: a thousand lives altered, the very land changed, all because of him.

Footsteps sounded soft on the bare boards behind him. He did not turn, because he knew them, though he had never heard them just that way. Silently Liz folded herself down beside him, gently displacing the cat. She rested her head on his shoulder. He took a drink, felt the burning in his throat, his head growing muddled—which was precisely what he had intended.

"Something's wrong." Not a question.

He nodded and took another swallow. "Another dream, Liz. It was Froech this time." He shuddered violently, until she slipped an arm around him and drew him close. "More vivid than ever, and . . . oh, God, Liz; what am I gonna *do?*"

"Do you always have to do something? This time there isn't anything you *can* do."

"I . . . I felt him die . . . I was there, in his head—and I felt him die."

She gasped softly, then paused. "You can't worry about that, David, he'll be reborn, they all will. The Sidhe *can't* die."

"No, but they can feel pain, just like us. They claim they're used to it; but how can you get used to havin' your throat slashed or your head cut off? And if you did, what would it do to you? I *liked* Froech. He was sort of like me: wild and impetuous, even if he was a thousand years old. But will he like me now? I caused this mess, in the last analysis, so will *any* of the Sidhe like me? I mean crap, girl, any way I try to reason it out I come to the bottom and find me being nosy on a summer night. Am I supposed to assume the Sidhe won't make the same conclusions?"

"It wasn't just you, though," Liz said. "The Morrigu had a hand in it too, remember? She's the one who saw you assume the Second Sight position, the one who sensed the Power of the Sidhe in you from some ancestor of yours she'd dallied with, the one who woke the Sight in you. You only had the desire and the potential. No, if it's anyone's fault, it's hers.''

''I hope she's happy, then. Morrigu, they call her: *great queen.* But queen of what? Of the dead? She oughta be in her element now!''

''I thought you said her thing was combat. Lawful combat—enforcing the rules, and all.''

''Yeah, but even if I blame it on her, that doesn't change the situation.''

''Which is?''

''Shoot fire, just look around you! Weather gone wild, contention in the air, war in another World causing the equivalent in this! You think I like havin' to live with that, knowin' it's all my fault?''

''But it's *not* your fault!''

''Yes it *is!* The only question is: what am I gonna do?''

''I . . . I don't know.''

''And it's gonna get worse, too. As Midsummer's Day approaches, it'll just get worse. Mark my words.''

''Maybe you should leave town for a while.''

''Yeah, sure—and let all hell break loose while I'm gone? What about that? Good God, girl, I could come home and find my folks with their throats cut. Pa's got that much violence in him, so has Ma.''

''So then . . .''

''I think it's time I started acting instead of just bitchin'.''

''Okay, then; I'll turn it around: what *are* you gonna do?''

''Well, for one thing, I'm gonna go see Alec and make him use the ulunsuti so I can maybe find out what's goin' on in Faerie. I'm gonna talk to Uncle Dale, probably; and I'm gonna try to get hold of Calvin.''

''Okay, then,'' Liz said. ''See, things are better already; you've got a battle plan.''

''Yeah,'' David sighed. ''But how do you stop a war?''

"One man at a time, and one side. You remove the cause."

"If we can even *find* the cause. Sometimes I get the feeling the Sidhe are doin' this just for giggles."

"Maybe so."

"Guess I'd better get in now, though. Folks'll be out here next."

Liz nodded, and they stood. For a long moment they remained there on the porch, close together. David enfolded her in his arms and bent his head into her neck, stifling a sob.

When they parted at the base of the stairs, he saw that her eyes, too, were shiny.

Back in the attic a short while later, he lay down naked atop the covers, then shivered and climbed underneath, hugging his pillow close like the teddy bear he had abandoned years ago. Never in his life had he felt so alone.

Chapter VIII: Universal Secrets

(Galunlati—summer)

Though Calvin had spent a considerable amount of time in Galunlati during the previous nine months, he had visited the place Uki led him to only for very special functions—certain prayers and meditations, rituals such as that which empowered the uktena scales to teleport, the passing on of particular bits of lore. To reach it, they walked for perhaps half an hour northwest from Uki's home in the caverns above the gorge Hyuntikwalayi. During that journey, by some unspoken agreement, they did not converse, and Calvin found himself becoming keenly aware of his environment. The trees grew closer together here than any other place he had seen, and eventually he noticed that the oaks and scattered dogwoods were gradually being replaced by cedars and laurel—plants of vigilance. More than once he felt the hair rise up on the back of his neck. The light slowly shifted in color as well until it bore a distinct greenish tinge that in no wise lessened the almost-blinding glare. Nor had the heat abated, though they walked in a semblance of shade. If anything, it had become even *more* stifling in the windless spaces of the

woods. He could see very little ahead, for the tall shaman's wide, white shoulders filled most of the trail.

Abruptly Uki stepped aside and ushered Calvin into a
circular clearing perhaps thirty yards across, completely
covered with hard white sand: his Power Wheel. The light
was nearly unbearable, but by squinting Calvin was able
to reacquaint himself with its particulars.

The perimeter was faced with a high wall of dark laurel
beyond which cedars glowered. But what caught Calvin's
attention every time he came here was that each of the
cardinal points was marked by a lightning-struck tree,
which were very strong medicine indeed. That to the north
was blue, the east red, the west black, and the one to the
south, from which direction they had entered, white. He
had been unable to copy them when he'd made his own
amateurish duplicate, and had been forced to substitute
wood from a single tree painted appropriately.

A final quick survey showed him something he *had* cop-
ied, though: The sand was not actually pure white, but
quartered by yard-wide strips of darker gravel leading from
each tree to the center and girding the clearing as well, so
that the configuration was that of a circle divided by a
cross. A magic sign: sigil of the Four Councils Sent From
Above, and also of the World. And well he *should* know
that, he thought wryly, for in those days before he truly
appreciated its significance, he had gotten that same symbol tattooed on his bottom.

He knew better now, of course. Someday he would have
it removed.

- Uki seated himself at the point where the southern arm
joined the others and motioned for Calvin to face him on
its northern twin.

"Now," the shaman said, when Calvin had positioned
himself, *"now* we may talk freely. I imagine you have
many questions."

"Uh, yeah," Calvin replied uneasily, finding it difficult
to sit still on the hot sand. "What's goin' on with the
sun?"

"You have gazed upon it," Uki replied. "Look again and tell me how it seems to you."

Calvin lifted an eyebrow dubiously, then dared a tentative skyward glance. Was Uki crazy? You didn't gaze straight at the sun and keep your sight, at least not for more than the instant he had risked before.

"It will not harm you here! Now *look!*"

Calvin swallowed, took a deep breath, and stared straight at the solar disc, startled to realize that he really *could* gaze full on it without discomfort. In fact, he had never seen it so clearly; it was almost like peering through a telescope. It blazed at the zenith, red and furious, and Calvin was certain he could actually make out the sunspots that pockmarked its surface, the solar prominences that rose and fell upon it. He held his breath, caught up in wonder. But something really was wrong—the great star was pulsing, quivering a little, flinging off mass with wild abandon, and if he tried very hard, he thought he could feel the heat increase with each flare.

"It's . . . moving," he whispered finally. "And it's awful bright."

"Shaking," Uki affirmed, nodding.

"And let me guess: this isn't normal; leastwise it sure wouldn't be back home."

Uki nodded again. "Yes, there is a wrongness—a great wrongness, and it troubles all of us here. I have met with the Chiefs of the three other Quarters, and none of us have found answers."

"No ideas? *That's* hard to believe."

"None to speak of," Uki replied calmly. "But perhaps I should relate the whole tale. To begin, the last time you were here nothing was wrong; Galunlati was as it should be. The seasons came and went in their proper times, and Nunda Igeyi was neither too bright nor too dim. The rain came when I called, and the winds answered my need, and all was well. But six hands of days ago, Nunda Igeyi began to grow hot. The increase was slight at first, but quickly became greater, so that many of the plants began to wilt, and it sometimes took all my effort to bring the rain while at other times I had to strain to keep it away, for it seemed to come from nowhere, and with great violence. Finally we saw changes in Nunda Igeyi itself, and then we recalled with fear how when this Land was made Nunda Igeyi was too close and had to be moved nine times before Galunlati grew cool enough for anything to live.''

''Right,'' Calvin said. ''But we've talked about this, about my lady's idea that the sun's probably the same for all the Worlds, or at least how the suns of all the Worlds hereabout are probably interrelated, kinda like shadows of each other, and how in our World the earth moves, not the sun. So it was probably *Galunlati* that was moved then. I know over on our side small differences in the tilt of a planet can make a major difference in its weather.''

The discussion that followed was one of the strangest Calvin had ever had. He had explained something of conventional cosmology to Uki before, and the shaman more or less understood it, though he had trouble with the terminology, which did not translate too well. The gist of it was that Calvin's World was the primary World, or at least the most complete one, and its sun was therefore the primary sun—but that there were others, visible in adjoining Worlds like Galunlati or Faerie—suns which probably occupied the same part of space/time occasionally, but not always, rather like a multiple star with the secondaries in other Worlds—except that they occasionally all collapsed back together and occupied the same space but in different dimensions. Sol's gravity was strongest, though, and its solar system was complete with fully realized planets.

But Sandy had theorized more, had decided that gravity might not be confined to one's own universe, but might pass through what Dave called the World Walls and influence other Worlds as well. Thus, while Earth was round, the Worlds that clustered about it did not have to be, as long as Earth remained to anchor them. It was rather like bits of wet paper dropped upon a globe: they held their own shape and substance, but depended on the globe to hold them and give them strength. Certainly Galunlati was not complete, at least not in the sense Earth was—this Uki had told him. There were places where one could literally walk to the edge and find nothing beyond, though Uki thought the Land as a whole was slowly growing, which also seemed logical to Calvin, if Galunlati was still drawing mass to itself, as all incomplete Worlds probably did.

The part that was hardest to get across, though, was the theory Sandy had come up with to explain Straight Tracks. Basically, her thinking was that a large mass like the sun produced gravity "waves" which inevitably encountered the gravity produced by other heavenly bodies as well— and by extension, heavenly bodies in other Worlds. Those interfaces made the waves focus into strips like the "lines" where soap bubbles joined together, and these were the Tracks—essentially accretions of concentrated gravity. Where a bunch of Tracks intersected, mass began to accumulate and eventually formed Worlds—but they still needed the gravity of a large body—like the Earth—to keep them together, otherwise they might start to decay.

"So Galunlati actually depends on your Land for survival? I do not like this," Uki mused thoughtfully when their discussion had finally wound down. "Yet I think such a thing could be. It would explain much about the differences between the Lands as I perceive them."

"But not the problem with the sun, I gather."

The lines in Uki's brow grew even deeper. "Unless something is *changing* the amount of this . . . *gravity* Nunda Igeyi produces, and that change is tugging Galunlati back and forth. We are smaller than your Land, after all, while Nunda Igeyi is doubtless the same as your own."

"But what about the pull of our World?" Calvin inserted. "Seems like it would attract Galunlati more than the sun—*either* sun."

"Hmmm, yes, an interesting notion: Galunlati caught between the pull of two Lands. The problem is how to stop it, for if what you say is true, Galunlati may soon cease to exist. It may burn up—that is what we feared. But if I understand this gravity right, Galunlati could be torn apart as well.''

"Jesus," Calvin whispered slowly.

"What we must do," Uki said, "is to find out what is causing Nunda Igeyi to shake and how to stop it. First, though, there is something I must show you."

Calvin watched silently as Uki removed a pouch from his beaded belt and drew out an earthen jar from which he shook a transparent crystal about the size of his closed fist. A single line of red ran through it from one side to the other, like the septum of a papaya. Calvin recognized it immediately as an ulunsuti. He'd worked with this one once or twice before, usually to help Uki check on the weather in the more distant parts of Wahala, the Quarter that was effectively his kingdom. It had other uses as well, but Calvin had mostly heard of them, not been witness. This should be interesting.

Uki placed the ulunsuti between them on the sand, the wide end exactly centering the Power Wheel. Though Calvin knew what was supposed to happen next, he swallowed nervously.

"Fear is to be overcome, not denied," Uki told him. "Were you not fearful, you would not truly be a man."

Calvin nodded and stretched out his arm. Uki took it gently, and Calvin tried to watch without flinching as the shaman drew blood from his palm with an obsidian knife, before handing the blade to him to reciprocate on Uki. Eyes locked with each other's, they lowered their bloody hands to the talisman.

Light flared there, but it was cool light, though Calvin could feel warmth flowing out of the crystal, linking them in some uncanny way.

"Now go into trance," Uki whispered. "When you are ready, gaze at the ulunsuti and follow where I lead."

"Right," Calvin replied softly, and closed his eyes, focusing only on his breathing, letting each breath go longer and deeper, inhaling through his mouth and exhaling more slowly through his nose. He felt himself start to go under, felt his eyes sliding back in his head, and with great effort opened them again.

The blazing crystal filled the world, but very quickly his vision narrowed to the line of red at its center. And then he was falling into it, further and further, only distantly aware of the touch of Uki's mind.

Suddenly he was somewhere else. It was dark at first, but then the darkness was lit by countless hazy spheres—one of which swam nearer, and he saw that it was itself made up of a seeming infinity of glowing, shifting strands. He stared at it and became aware that it was twinned—no *triplicated*—no, that there was a whole *series* of spheres and half-spheres and fragmentary spheres, some of them superimposed upon each other, others overlapping, others standing alone at a little distance, each made of filaments of a different color but connected to those of all the others as well. And then he looked beyond the spheres and saw straight lines of light flowing out from the spheres to make a vast webwork like a three dimensional fiber-optic spiderweb a-glimmer in the black. At places those lines crossed, and made brighter spots, and sometimes they merged with those spun from several spheres and made very bright spots indeed. One of those intrigued him, and he willed himself closer, saw that it was also a sphere of white, but that threads of red flowed into it from one of the other spheres, so that the white sphere had a splotch of red on one side, and then he saw lines of gold coming in from another of the overlapping spheres, and saw that they joined into several splotches. He understood—he thought.

And with that realization, he was back in the Power Wheel.

"God Almighty," he gasped.

"You have seen what few men have," Uki told him. "You have seen the pattern of the Lands."

"And the white's ours, right? And the red's, maybe Galunlati, so the gold must be . . ."

"What you call Faerie. But now enter the ulunsuti once more, for I would show you another marvel."

Calvin swallowed and slipped back into trance. This time Uki took him close to what he supposed was the sun of Galunlati, though he could sense the greater strength of the nearby earthly sun as well. But now Uki brought him near one of the strands of red that reached from that sun *to* Galunlati, and Calvin saw that it did not run straight, but kept bowing and shifting out of true, rather like the wavelengths in a string. They swept toward the sun again, and then were inside it, and Calvin could see a thousand tiny filaments reaching from a golden sphere there to shake the red. Uki brought him nearer yet, then carried him along a golden strand back to the sphere that was the earth, until suddenly they could go no further.

Again Calvin returned to himself. He stared at Uki curiously, too stunned to speak.

"I have shown you as much as I can," Uki said. "Something disturbs Nunda Igeyi—the red threads you saw; yet the disturbance does not come from our Land or from your Land. It comes from that place that lies on the *other* side of your Land from this. What I would have you do is find out what is causing it."

"How?" Calvin wondered. "Why can't you find out here?"

"Because though the ulunsuti can show us the pattern of the Lands, it can only *look* into those, like yours, that lie beside it, which Faerie does not. I therefore ask that you use the ulunsuti I gave to your friend Alec McLean to spy into the Lands that I cannot reach and see if the source of this disturbance can be found there."

"Hold—" Calvin cried, looking down and shaking his head. "This is too much, I've gotta think."

"Think then," Uki told him, "but do not think long, for the fate of three Lands may depend on your finding out what is shaking Nunda Igeyi."

"Yeah, I know," Calvin groaned. "It's just—just a lot to have to swallow all at once. But I'll see what I can do.

And now I think of it, I bet this has something to do with the weather in my World as well.''

"I have no doubt," Uki said. "For weather depends on very little things indeed: dust, the weight of the air, the direction of the wind . . ."

"And magic?" Calvin smiled.

"If you wish," Uki replied. "And now I think it is time you were gone. If you learn aught, return here; I will be waiting with eagerness." He fished in another pouch and produced an uktena scale identical to that Calvin had burned to arrive there.

Calvin took it and pulled out his cigarette lighter, but Uki shook his head. "The old way would be better."

"Whatever," Calvin grunted apprehensively, and stood.

At a sign from Uki, Calvin squared his shoulders and closed his eyes, and at a word, he raised the scale above his head, clutching a point with either hand.

Uki clapped his hands a certain way, and Calvin had only time to feel the air go still and thin and cold when a bolt of lightning stabbed down from the heavens to engulf the scale—and spread to enfold him as well, consuming him with the familiar agony.

Before he could even gasp, he was standing once more in the center of his Power Wheel. It looked exactly the same as before, except that the sky was lighter. By the length of the long tree shadows and the filigree of red on their topmost branches, he guessed it was almost dawn.

Sandy met him halfway to the cabin: a tall figure in denim and plaid taking shape from a remnant of mist.

"You look like death," she said. "I was just coming to look for you."

"I *feel* like death too," he sighed. "And you couldn't have found me until just now."

Her eyes narrowed. "Coffee's on."

He wrapped an arm around her waist. "Good. And then I'd best be goin'."

"Going where?"

"Down to Georgia—to try to save the world."

A low chuckle. "Damn, and I've still got papers to grade!"

"I'll be back, love, never fear. And then we've gotta do a lot of talkin'. I may just have found the key to your questions. Trouble is, the room beyond's full of a whole lot bigger puzzles."

She stopped in place and regarded him seriously. "You weren't lying, were you? About having to save the world?"

"No," he whispered sadly. "But I wish to hell I was."

Chapter IX: Company

(Sullivan Cove, Georgia— Saturday, June 14—morning)

David would have liked to have stayed in bed much later the morning after his dream than he was allowed, but as it was, the sun was shining fitfully through the grimy window in the eastern wall when he was awakened by the sound of something smashing downstairs. Glass, it sounded like, and there were words close on its heels, heated words accented with profanity. Which meant that, sunshine or no, it was still business as usual at Sullivan Manor—though given the temperaments of his folks, it was hard to tell if this was an ordinary disagreement or a magically induced one. Having no desire to make his debut in the middle of an altercation, he vented a mournful groan and dragged the covers back over his head.

A door slammed and he winced, then heard footsteps coming up the stairs. He tensed, suddenly alarmed, since he'd gone back to bed bare-assed. Not that it mattered, really, at least not as far as Liz was concerned, though the notion of her catching him naked in bed in his own house with his folks downstairs was suddenly a lot more alarming than the both of them that way by the lake or up on Lookout, or in his long-lost magical boat under the stars. He

sat up quickly, checked the cover—and breathed a vast
sigh of relief when the head that emerged at the top of the
stairwell proved to be that of his younger brother.

The little boy (not so little now actually; he was seven
and had finished first grade with straight A's, of which he
was vastly proud)—pranced over to the bed and plopped
down atop David's left leg.

"So what's up kid?" David asked him, twisting round
to ruffle his hair.

"Pa sent me to get you up."

David yawned. "Figured that much. What else is goin'
on? What's the ruckus about?"

"Ma burned the toast and the coffee was too weak,
'cordin' to Pa. He throwed the butter dish on the floor."

"*Threw* the dish," David corrected. "God, I hope Liz
didn't see that."

Little Billy rolled his eyes. "She did, though. Me and
her just about laughed at 'im!"

"*She* and *I*," David corrected again.

His brother frowned, "Aw, Davy, how come you're always changin' me? *You* say stuff like that."

"Yeah—when I'm bein' careless, and around here who
cares? But *you* gotta know better. You'll grow up and be
seriously brilliant someday, and we can't have you talkin'
like a mountain hick."

"*You* don't talk like a hick."

"No, but I have to watch it when I'm away from here,
or I'll backslide. But anyway, so what's Liz doin'?"

"Foolin' with breakfast, I reckon."

"You're a big help."

"Davy!"

David made a sudden dive for his brother and managed
to snag an arm before Little Billy could escape. It took
more effort than he expected to reel him in (the little
booger was surprisingly strong), but eventually David got
him in range of his other hand and began tickling him
unmercifully. Little Billy giggled and twitched and wiggled and tried to retaliate (dangerous, since David was

himself far more susceptible than he liked to admit), and eventually their gyrations brought them closer to the edge than David could compensate for, and the whole kinetic mixture of boys and bedding flopped noisily to the floor. An on-the-fly check that neither was hurt and they were at it again—until heavy footsteps sounded downstairs and Big Billy's voice rumbled up the stairwell like distant thunder.

"You boys quit actin' crazy and get down here. I gotta headache!"

They froze instantly, faces locked in resigned glee, David with his right leg and a hunk of blanket wrapped around Little Billy's lower body, and his left arm prisoning both his brother's while he assailed an unprotected side; and Little Billy with his right hand snaked free and stuffed into David's especially vulnerable armpit.

A quick set of smirks followed an exchange of knowing looks from almost-matching sets of blue eyes, and David released his prisoner, flinging a substantial hunk of bedclothes over him as he scrambled back to the bed and dived for the gym shorts he'd left on the bedpost. His brother was ahead of him, though; and finally realizing David's atypical state of undress, snatched them from David's startled fingers and ran for the stairs, grabbing the bathrobe as an afterthought.

"Why you little—!" David shouted, then flopped back on the bed and shut his eyes against the violence that had suddenly erupted in him, that had made him, for the tiniest instant, want to chase down his brother and literally break his neck.

"David! Breakfast!" His ma's voice this time.

"Just a sec!" he hollered back, trying very hard to regain control. A glance down at his naked body and the humor of the situation finally dawned on him. He exhaled the breath he'd been holding as a giggle.

The upshot of Little Billy's thievery was that David was forced to make his entrance downstairs in much the same

garb as a Roman senator, but with rather less dignified
effect.

Liz, whom he could see from the foot of the stairs, was
on the phone in the living room. She lifted a brow in
amused surprise as he rolled his eyes in her direction
and darted into his room to don a pair of cut-offs and a
T-shirt. He looked very sheepish when he entered the
kitchen.

Big Billy was nowhere in sight, though the Saturday
Atlanta Journal and Constitution seemed to have been
hastily abandoned; and his mother was sweeping up the
detritus of a broken plate and muttering to herself. The
smell of charcoaled bread permeated the room.

"I just don't know what's got into him," JoAnne com-
plained as David poured himself a cup of coffee. "He's
crankier'n an old she-bear."

"We *all* are, Ma," David said, taking a sip of the controversial beverage, which really was pretty weak. "It's
like I told you: all the hostility in Faerie's sloppin' over.
We'll just have to be extra careful."

She rose and eyed him wistfully. "That's easy for you
to say; you can think things like that and keep 'em in your
mind; me and your pa's a lot more set in our ways."

"You gotta be the one to do it then, and just cut him
some slack."

"What do you think I *been* doin'?" she snapped, then
caught herself. "And damned if I didn't just do it again.
Don't know what's gonna happen if this keeps up."

"Something's gotta give," David said flatly. And with
that remark, he fell silent.

—Which allowed him to key into Liz's conversation.

". . . Yeah, right, Mom; but it's like I told you, I don't
have to have clean clothes. I'm just stranded, not ship-
wrecked. I've got plenty of stuff back in Gainesville and
I need to study more than I need to look good. We're
talking chemistry here, not home economics."

A voice chattered back rapidly, and Liz grimaced ex-
pressively then: "Yeah, I *know* I could come around—*if* I

didn't mind going through Clayton or Hiawassee, but it'd take longer to do that than it would to get back to Gainesville. I mean this is the only road north for miles. I—''

She was cut off by more angry-sounding chatter, but finally managed to break in again. *''No,* Mom, the car's *fine;* it's not stuck or anything, and I already called the patrol, and things are okay over the mountain—shoot, you can tell that by looking out the window!''

Curious about that last remark, David stood and wandered to the eastward back door, pausing in transit to retrieve a sliver of plate his ma had missed. The sun was still shining fitfully, illuminating the porch's gray boards and the long slope of side yard above the scrap of cornfield that separated the Manor environs from the main highway and the larger field on the other side—the one where he had first seen the lights of the Sidhe two summers before. But what caught his attention now was the road: an almost-stationary line of cars that snaked down off the mountain to the right, and an only slightly faster moving one that appeared from beyond a hump of mountain to the left. David guessed the road was still out and the G.S.P. was re-routing traffic—turning it back, really, as there was no effective way to detour them. As he watched, a mammoth earth-moving machine hove into view from the southern side.

Shrugging, David turned back into the room and snagged a slice of toast. Just as he sat down he caught the last snatch of Liz's conversation. ''. . . Sure, Mom, I'll be careful. I'm gonna stay here a little longer and see if traffic clears a little, and then head out. I'll call you soon as finals are over.''

She hung up the receiver and returned to the kitchen, where she plopped down beside him and helped herself to the remains of a cold cup of coffee. ''Lord, Davy, mothers are such a *pill,*'' she announced, for the moment apparently forgetting the puttering JoAnne.

''Yeah,'' Little Billy agreed, transiting through with the

funnies in tow on his way to a rendezvous with the morning's cartoons. "Big, ugly, *nasty* pills!"

"William Thomas!" JoAnne snapped.

"Watch it, kid," David chuckled. "You've gotta live here a while longer yet." He looked back at Liz. "So what's up?"

"Well, I called the patrol and they said things were fine over the mountain, just the culvert out here which has blocked the whole highway, so there'd be some traffic but no problem. No rock slides, or anything. Unfortunately, they won't have the road fixed until this afternoon sometime, and probably only one lane then, and I've gotta get back as soon as I can so I can study. So I'm gonna hang around here till after lunch and then go straight to Gainesville. That's what I was calling Mom about. I left some laundry over there last time I was up, and she was making a big deal about it, and I just about went wild trying to convince her that everything was okay, that I could get to school fine, and that your mom washed my muddy clothes and loaned me some clean ones."

David started at that. He'd never considered that Liz and his ma were close enough to a size to swap clothes, though now he looked, he realized those were his ma's jeans Liz was wearing, along with one of her blouses. Come to it, though, his ma *was* in pretty good shape for a woman in her early forties, and she'd worried off a bit of weight in the last year as well. Even without makeup she was still pretty good-looking, though the crow's feet at the corners of her eyes were getting more prominent by the month, and her hair a little duller. She was also beginning to acquire a trace of looseness in her cheeks and neck.

A lingering glance at Liz confirmed it: they really were almost the same. For the first time in his life it occurred to him that Liz was really not a girl, but a woman. He wondered, though, if she—or anyone—would ever really think of him as a man. At five-foot-seven, with white-blonde hair and still only once-a-week stubble, he really did wonder.

Liz appropriated the last of the bacon. "You still going over to Alec's?"

"Do bears perform necessary bodily functions in the woods?"

"You know more bears than I do. Do they?"

David grinned back, catching the reference to the bears he had met in Galunlati. "Yeah, well . . . But seriously, I don't see any way around it. Knowin' bad news is better than not knowin' anything sometimes. So I guess I'll head on over as soon as I can. I don't think I really dare call."

"May be a while, then," Liz said. "But hey, the sun's back out anyway."

David looked up. "It *is*, isn't it?"

Liz swallowed her last mouthful of toast and polished off her coffee. "Think I better go move my car, too. I didn't look real closely at where I parked last night, just tried to get it out of the main drag."

"Mind if I come along?"

" 'Fraid I'll get lost?"

Something about the flip tone of her reply rubbed David the wrong way. He started to tell her to can the sarcasm, then frowned. *Was* she being sarcastic? Or just conversational? He frowned further and bit his tongue. Jesus, it was getting to him, making him irritable and fractious and jumpy. None too soon for her to leave. Maybe he ought to go with her.

"Sorry," he began, "for what I *nearly* said just then."

She studied him seriously. "Yeah . . . I think I know what you mean. Lord, I hope the whole summer's not like this."

"Me too," David said, and opened the back door. By the time they reached the bottom of the hill she had almost caught him.

As he and Liz neared the turn-off that led from the Sullivan Cove road to the Sullivan Cove Church of God roughly an eighth-mile from his house, he caught sight of an image so absurd it made him laugh out loud.

The little white church was set back a fair bit from the road, perched on a low hill that had been partially denuded of trees except for a smattering of oaks and walnuts. There was a small graveyard before it and to their right, by the gate of which Liz's car sat. But what caught David's eye was further up by the church proper. It was mid-morning of the first day of their annual all day revival, and though the main highway was blocked, that didn't mean that the congregation meant to be cut off from the sweet love of Jesus. Apparently no members lived on the Sullivan Cove side of the main highway, either, because there wasn't a single car in the parking lot. But there was a steady file of suited men and well-dressed women picking their way down the low mountain behind the church. The sight of them—tottering old folks, loud teens, taciturn adults, and fractious children—all parading through the woods, occasionally slipping and sliding as they made the last slope above the churchyard, was more than he could stand. His laughter rang loud through the valley.

Liz looked sternly at him. "Don't do that Davy. It's not nice! One of those old folks could fall and get hurt!"

"But I can't *help* it!" David chuckled, eyes wet. "They must have parked across the mountain up in Coker Hollow and be comin' across that way. It's not but a quarter mile or so as the crow flies."

"If you want to go with an old crow . . ." Liz finished.

"Well they can't get through this way, the road's blocked. I've gotta admire their dedication."

"Yeah," Liz said as she unlocked her door, "and I need to be admiring the way back to your house." She paused. "Think I'll take a look at the damage first, though."

David sighed. "Want a passenger? Maybe I'll get some idea when I'll be able to get over to Alec's."

"Let me know what happens with that, okay?"

"Of course! But shoot, girl, you're not even gone yet. You did say you were stayin' through the afternoon, didn't you? I mean, jeeze, why don't you just spend the night and let 'em get the road really fixed and the traffic straight-ened out? You can study up here, I'll be quiet, I promise.''

"Yeah, but my books are down there! I did that delib-erately so I wouldn't be tempted!''

"You devil!''

"You should talk,'' she said mischievously. "You're the one doing the tempting now.''

He grabbed her suddenly and planted a sloppy wet one on her mouth.

"Jesus, David! Not here in front of these folks!''

"Give 'em something to preach about!'' David laughed. "Show 'em some sin just waitin' to happen!''

" 'Get thee behind me, Satan!' '' Liz giggled in turn, as she slid out of David's grip and climbed in, reaching over to unlock the passenger door.

"If I'm Satan,'' David continued from inside, "then that makes you . . . ?''

"Missus Satan?''

"We're not married that I notice,'' he protested, wish-ing he hadn't mentioned that word, which Liz had a time or two. Not that it was a *bad* idea, but not yet . . . not quite yet. The image of the papoose returned, but coupled with it was Liz in bathrobe and curlers holding a copy of *Soap Opera Digest* in one hand and a coffee pot in the other, while he balanced tiny replicas of a sprawling brick ranch and a station wagon in either hand. He'd seen too many cartoons, he knew. Far too many.

"Uh . . . no,'' he managed. "Lilith, maybe?''

"Thought she was Adam's first bride.''

He shrugged, feeling chagrined at his ignorance of his own mythology. Now if she'd asked him about Cuchulain . . .

"Maybe,'' Liz said, backing the car into the muddy road and turning east.

"Well,'' Big Billy announced to the world at large, "that sure is a fine mess.''

David, who, with Liz, had joined him on the gravelly

shoulder of the main highway, nodded—a gesture precisely mimicked by Little Billy. "That's a fact," he replied.

He stared at the scene before him: steep, raw bank on the left crested by a file of trees where the terminus of a series of steep ridges had been sliced away to make way for the highway, the far slope pitching steeply down to the Coker Hollow road—next up the highway from Sullivan Cove. The creek flowed out of there, too, and the highway had forded it until last night. To the right was the narrow end of his pa's bottomland, bounded to the east by the rest of the creek, and beyond by Enotah National Forest, all beneath a heavy loom of clouds that now and then to let through shafts of fitful sunlight. And straight ahead was the highway, mostly invisible beneath the gleaming bulks of slow-moving vehicles.

The road was cut all right: a ten-foot slice taken out straight across, with the thick, hard strata of pavement visible above a base of clay and granite gravel. The vast corrugated cylinder of the displaced culvert lay crumpled and abandoned at the absolute apex of their field. As for the creek that had caused the present havoc, it was back to normal, no more than the usual foot or so deep, and David wondered once more at the amount it had taken to wash something like that out of the ground. On either side of the break the blue-and-gray bulks of the Georgia State Patrol's Crown Victorias (and one pursuit Mustang) blocked traffic, blue-suited patrolmen equipped with bull-horns and whistles maneuvering traffic in each direction while a dump truck emptied its second load of gravel, preparatory to inserting a fresh culvert. Liz was probably right: they'd doubtless have at least one lane open by that afternoon. He'd have to be careful, though, next time he came barreling over the hill up ahead.

"Gosh!" Little Billy gasped. "Did that li'l creek do all *that?*"

"Sho' did," Big Billy replied. "I tried to tell 'em when they put that there thing in that it 'uz too little, but they wouldn't listen. I been here a long time, seen how much it can rain."

"Yeah," David said, finding himself for once in agreement with his pa.

"Good thing it didn't happen 'fore commencement, though," Big Billy added philosophically. "Otherwise you'd've been givin' your speech to the cows and gettin' your diploma by mail."

"Maybe so," David chuckled, struck by the image of himself addressing his impassioned paean for independence to the unflappable Madame Bovary, while her new calf, Voltaire, looked on. "Or maybe they could have worked up some kinda satellite link, or something. Video cameras here feedin' into the high school. Diplomas comin' in by fax machine."

"We don't have a facts machine," Little Billy observed.

"No, but we have a *fact* machine," David told him. "One 'bout three feet tall and blond-headed!"

"That's a fact," Big Billy put in, and David started, surprised at his pa's joke. Odd, he thought, how the weather made everybody else irritable and left Big Billy alone. Or maybe they'd just all sunk to his level of grumpiness and he felt less outclassed now.

"Gonna be a bitch come Monday, though," Big Billy went on. "They don't have that thing fixed by then we'll have to go to Helen to pick up groceries."

"I'll go if you like," David volunteered quickly. "If I can't get to MacTyrie I won't have anything else to do." And besides, he added to himself, it'd keep him out of the house and out from underfoot. The first day of summer vacation stuck on Sullivan Cove with his rascal brother, his moody ma, and his sweat-of-the-brow-raised pa, was not a notion he relished.

"Maybe so," Big Billy grunted. "Reckon we oughta get on home. Reckon I might even apologize to the old lady."

"Might be a good idea," David acknowledged, exchanging expressions of relief with Liz, who took his hand and started back to the car she had parked at the end of the road.

They had almost reached it when he became aware of a subtle variance in the steady drone of traffic that had been turning around behind him: something beyond the idle of engines and the crunch of tires and the occasional squeal of an overstressed power steering pump. He frowned, then recognized it as the sound of a motorcycle—a big one, thumping expertly through the maze. He stopped in place, searching, and found it: a Bimmer R 80 G/S, shiny and black, headlight on, as was the law in Georgia. Not new, but still impressive. He stared at it appreciatively, and turned to go, sparing the merest glance toward the rider: a muscular fellow in black helmet, black leather jacket, jeans, and Frye boots. But as Liz tugged his hand gently onward, he heard the cycle's engine gunned, and turned again—just as it ground to a halt behind him. Already wired (he was always that way now) David tensed, ready to assault the cyclist with some scathing remark.

And caught himself just in time. There was something familiar about that grin, about the blaze of perfect white teeth and full lips above a square-cut chin. And then he figured it out: that skin was ruddier than it ought to be, and the cheekbones a tad wider.

He squinted through the visor, then caught the glint of a beaded necklace above the jacket collar and the gold stooping falcon pins that decorated either lapel.

"Calvin!" he cried, dropping Liz's hand and rushing forward. "Hey, folks, it's Calvin!"

They stopped in place, turned and began to approach: Liz calmly, Big Billy at his usual saunter, Little Billy at a full-tilt run.

"Long time no see, keemo-sabe," was all Calvin could get out before Little Billy was tugging on his leg. "Hey, Thunder-kitten," the Indian added, removing his helmet. He reached over to rub the small boy's hair. It was a reference to Little Billy's favorite TV show of the previous summer.

"Awww, that's old stuff," Little Billy piped. "It's ninja turtles now!"

"Oh yeah," Calvin said quickly. "Those are the guys with the Italian names, right? Hope they don't have one named Caravaggio."

"Huh?" wondered the Brothers Sullivan as one.

"He liked little boys," Calvin mouthed to David over Little Billy's head.

"Oh," David mouthed back, then; "Hey squirt, why don't you take off and let me and Mr. Fargo catch up and all, we'll be along, don't worry—that is," he said, "if you're up for lunch at the old home place."

"Always!" Calvin cried.

David aimed a kick at his brother's backside. "Now scat, kid."

"Awwww, Davy!"

"I said *scat!*"

Calvin raised an eyebrow, and then neither of them could hold back any longer. A quick high-five ensued, followed by a hearty, brotherly hug made awkward by the fact that Calvin was still astride the cycle. "So how's it goin', man?" he asked, shaking out his mane of black hair—longer now than when David had last seen it. There was an ear stud too: another falcon.

"Let me guess, you need a bed, a bath . . ."

"All of the above," Calvin chuckled. "But more to the point I need to talk to you."

"Any particular reason?"

"Good things and bad things."

"Give me the good first."

"No, he has to give me a *hug* first," Liz inserted, joining them.

"Glad to oblige." Calvin grinned. "And I'll give you a better one once we get to Dave's house."

"You said something about good and bad things . . ."

David supplied. He loved Calvin like a brother, but he didn't quite trust him around Liz yet, even though he supposedly had a girlfriend, the never-seen Sandy.

"Oh, yeah, right," Calvin laughed, releasing Liz. "Good things first, I guess: I need some ideas about a wedding present for G-Man."

"You came over here to ask me *that?*"

"I came over here 'cause I got some *real* disturbing news last night—or this morning, or sometime. Stuff that I need to bust tail on."

"Sounds serious."

"It is," Calvin affirmed. "But not so serious I can't spare sometime for lunch," he added, eyes twinkling. "We can rap till then."

"Well that settles one thing," Liz said. "I'm certainly gonna hang around a while longer now!"

"I hope so," Calvin replied, once more grinning at her.

"Your bike?" David asked, to change the subject.

Calvin shook his head sadly. "Sandy's. But let's not stand here blockin' traffic. Hop on and I'll give you a ride."

David hesitated, glanced at Liz.

She shrugged. "Go ahead. I think I know the way on my own. And I know how much you like wheels."

"I think you can make it part way up the drive now," David said. "Just park where you can."

"I've *got* a brain, David! *And* eyes!"

David rolled *his* eyes at Calvin and climbed on behind him, while Liz returned to her car and began turning around.

"So," David wondered as Calvin trundled off, "where'd you come from all of a sudden?" He paused, wrinkled his nose, then chuckled. "No, let me guess: from Our Lady of the Smokies?"

Calvin's stubby nose wrinkled as he sniffed. "Damn! Thought she scrubbed all that off me 'fore I left. God knows she like to have scrubbed nearly everything *else* off—what she didn't wear off other ways!"

David giggled and wondered when he'd get to meet Calvin's squeeze. Thus far all he'd seen was a fuzzy wallet photo of a pretty, though rather hippie-looking lady.

And then he had no more time to wonder, for Calvin was wheelstanding down the Sullivan Cove road.

"Well," David announced a few minutes later, when he, Calvin, and Liz were ensconced in his bedroom, "welcome to Georgia!"

He was reclining on his elbow on one of the flanking twin beds while Liz sat on the floor beside him and Calvin eased his feet out of the boots and white socks. The Indian wiggled his toes blissfully. "New shoes," he offered by way of explanation. "Birthday present from . . ."

"I bet I know," David laughed. "But what about this trouble?"

"Well," Calvin began, "I guess you know I've been kinda out of touch lately, 'specially since Christmas, but the fact is, it's not really my fault. I've been spendin' time in Galunlati. You remember Uki said I could visit, so I've been goin' every chance I get." He fished in his pocket and brought out an uktena scale. "I burn one of these to get there, and he gives me a new one every time I come back. It hurts like hell to transit, though; and I don't much like to do it unless I have to, or can stay a long time. In the meanwhile, I've been livin' with the woman I told you about."

"Sandy," Liz supplied.

"Yeah," Calvin went on. "I've told her about all this stuff we're involved in, the Worlds, and all. And she, being a physics teacher, has been tryin' to figure it all out rationally. But anyway, I've been kinda keepin' tabs on what's goin' on over here too, I . . ."

"You've heard about the shitty weather then?" David interrupted.

Calvin nodded grimly. "That's why I'm here, partly."

And with that he told them about his most recent visit to Galunlati.

"Whew," David said when he had finished. "So what's the worst-case scenario?"

Calvin shrugged. "Well, Uki seems to be afraid Galunlati'll be destroyed, and that would affect things here. But I think maybe the worst thing is that the sun itself could get unbalanced someway."

"Like go nova, maybe? You've *gotta* be kidding?"

"No, but it's apparently tied up with the Tracks somehow. Sandy thinks they're some kind of inter-dimensional manifestation of gravity. But apparently something's been drawin' on the power of the Tracks, and that's been causin' all *kinds* of trouble over there. I needn't tell you how precarious the specs are that keep this place habitable."

"Good point."

"Yeah. I mean in Galunlati, which was apparently *made* in some way, they moved the world nine times before they got it right—course the folks there thought it was the sun was moved, but you get my drift. It's no big deal here—yet; Faerie and Galunlati are both fragment worlds and more or less depend on ours to keep together. But they're also more susceptible to disturbances at a cosmic level. It's like gravity: it doesn't take as much to perturb the orbit of a small object as it does a big 'un."

"And Galunlati's a small object, relative to us, right?" David wondered, trying very hard to grasp the complex concepts.

"Right. But still if anything happened to it—or Faerie . . ."

"It might upset the balance here."

Calvin nodded emphatically. "Right!"

David shook his head. "Where'd you learn all this, anyway?"

"Books, Uki, Sandy, common sense, you name it." He paused. "I don't reckon you have any ideas?"

David shifted position. "As a matter of fact I do."

He briefed Calvin then, about his dreams, the war, his theories about it.

"God!" Calvin said, standing up and pacing the space between the beds. "Yeah, it all makes sense now. And it really is critical that we find out what's goin' on over there."

"I'd thought about tryin' to stop it, if I can," David said slowly. "Had the idea anyway, though I'm damned if I've got any notion how. I mean, how do you stop a war, man?"

"Like I told you, David," Liz inserted. "One man at a time, and one side."

"Easy to say, hard to do."

"But at least we agree on the first step."

"Right," Calvin said. "Soon as lunch's over we bop over to see Mr. McLean."

"There's one minor problem with that," David noted.

"Oh?"

"Road's out twixt here and there."

"Is that all?" Calvin laughed. "No problem, long as I got the bike." His gaze fell on Liz. "Only holds two, though."

Liz grimaced resignedly. "I guess I'll just have to trust you guys then, and it's probably just as well. At least maybe I can get some studying done this way."

David's eyes narrowed. "I thought you left your books in Gainesville."

"I did," Liz replied. "But not my notebooks."

"You're not leavin', then?" David inquired hopefully.

"Not yet, foolish boy! Do you think I'd run off with something like this going on? But I really do need to study, and somebody probably ought to tell your folks what's going on. Uncle Dale too."

"You got it."

"What I've *got,*" David said, "is a case of the hungries! Let's go see if ma's got lunch ready, then boogie. I'll give old Alec a call and tell him I'm comin' over, just not why, or with whom."

Calvin looked briefly worried. "He *is* okay, isn't he?"

"More or less. Still pining for Eva some. I think he's

Chapter X:
Eavesdropping

*Lord, get me outta this with my head on frontwards and
my skin intact,* David was praying with surprising fervor
for an adolescent agnostic as Calvin laid the Bimmer far
over to negotiate the last sharp turn on the MacTyrie
mountain at what David knew with absolute certainty was
preposterously more than legal speed. He tightened his
grip on the Indian's leather jacket and closed his eyes, as
his body tilted in sync with his friend's. *Use the Force,
Luke,* he thought, as gravel brushed his left cuff. He had,
he decided ruefully, a certain amount more sympathy for
Alec, whom he had terrorized with his own brand of mo-
torized mayhem since he was a highly-illegal fourteen.

The bike straightened abruptly, and he heaved a sigh of
relief and opened his eyes once more, certain he'd heard
Calvin chuckle. At least they were almost to their destination.

And at least it was not—for the moment—raining,
though David suspected that he might arrive pretty damp

anyway, either from perspiration, or maybe from peeing in his pants from sheer terror.

A wayward June bug found its way around Calvin's head and thwacked David smartly on the upper lip; its mate smeared itself across his face plate. He flinched, swore softly, and blinked back tears. When he could see again, they were on a straight, and Calvin was really winding the cycle out.

Moses, save me. David gritted his teeth and hung on.

Over the MacTyrie bridge (eyes closed again), around a final series of blessedly more gradual curves, and Mac-Tyrie loomed before them. Just inside the city limits they turned left onto Alec's street, then right into his drive. Calvin cut the engine and walked the cycle the last few yards out of courtesy to Dr. McLean's usual afternoon nap. David climbed off shakily and checked his watch as casually as he could. At least his britches were still dry.

The watch read 2:35 P.M., which meant they had made the journey in eighteen minutes and thirty-six seconds—a new record. And they could probably have made it even faster had not the main road been out. Instead of turning down the Sullivan Cove road and then onto the main drag—and into the trickling traffic—Calvin had turned left at the bottom of the driveway, then cut through the church environs. From there it had been a short jog overland, following the trail into Coker Hollow, where they'd jumped the creek and cut into the main highway above the break. Traffic had been heavy at first, but Calvin had proven expert at weaving in and out of it, using the shoulder when necessary, but with absolutely no regard for David's nerves, which were as shot as they'd ever been.

As if sensing David's distress Calvin turned and grinned at him. "You okay, man? You look a little pale even for a paleface. Or is that maybe a touch of green?" The grin widened wickedly.

David exhaled in relief. "Jesus, Man . . . I think you left my stomach somewhere back in Enotah . . . and my right kneecap 'bout three miles up the road."

"Oh, come on, I didn't take that curve *that* tight."

"I don't know about that . . . I started to scream and sucked up three hundred feet of ants and two dead possums!"

"My ass!"

"Yeah, and that's another thing. I think mine's up 'round my shoulder blades. Did you *have* to jump the creek like that?"

"It was faster than going 'round."

David aimed a kick at Calvin's denimed backside and followed him up the sidewalk between the dogwoods and banks of ivy that comprised most of the yard.

A camo-clad Alec opened the front door before they could knock, and David shivered at the blast of air-conditioning. Alec's mom was from Wyoming and had never truly adjusted to either the heat or humidity of Georgia summers—of which the present one had been a particularly virulent example in both regards.

Calvin had not removed his helmet yet, and Alec was staring at him in confusion.

David raised an eyebrow. "One mysterious visitor comin' up."

Calvin flipped up the tinted plastic, and Alec's face broke into a grin that stretched from ear to ear. He reached out to shake hands and found himself drawn into a hearty hug.

"Hey, man, how's it *goin'?*" Alec managed to croak as he tried to slap Calvin's back.

"Not too bad," Calvin replied in his most innocuous tone as he set Alec back down. "How's your own bad—" He stopped himself a hiss short of "self," and David guessed he was fearful of resurrecting the negative memories he knew that term evoked for Alec. "How're *you* making it?" he finished lamely.

"Dandy, just dandy," Alec answered, still beaming, "—'cept for the blessed rain," he added with a peculiar half-snarl.

A vigorous nod. "Yeah, *tell* me about it."

"If you'll tell me 'bout what *you've* been up to," Alec shot back.

"You got two hours?" David groaned.

"I got all day!" Alec cried airily. "I'll just go snag us a couple of D.P.s, then we can head upstairs."

"D.P.s?" Calvin wondered, when Alec had darted off.

"Doctor Peppers," David replied. "It's sort of his and my totem beverage."

"Ah," said Calvin. "I know all about totems."

David started. *"Do* you? You've never told me yours."

"I have too," Calvin assured him. "Just not with my voice."

David was still staring at him when Alec thrust an ice-cold can into his hand.

"So," Alec wondered five minutes later, "what's up? What's all this hush-hush stuff?"

David took a long swallow from his D.P. and exchanged troubled glances with Calvin. "Well, gee, man: it's like this . . . you know what's been goin' on with the weather and all, and what I think about it, right? Well, Calvin's got an idea about it, too: a real disturbin' one, and some evidence to back it up. But we can't prove anything without your help."

Alec frowned uncertainly. "I'm not sure I want to hear any more."

"Yeah, but you really ought to anyway. See—"

"Let me tell him," Calvin interrupted. "Look, McLean, it's like this . . ."

He went on then, recounting the details of his most recent visit to Galunlati.

"Whew!" Alec whistled when he had finished. "You really think it's that bad? That the war in Faerie could have a negative effect on the friggin' *sun?* I mean, look folks, fooling around with the weather's one thing, but the sun's ninety-zillion miles from here and Sagan only knows how many times bigger than the whole friggin' planet! You're telling me that the actions of a couple of Faery dudes are gonna mess up the *sun?*''

"I said it *might,*" Calvin replied a little irritably, "It sure seems to be havin' that effect in Galunlati. It's smaller than this world, don't forget, and not as massive. It'd therefore be more susceptible to anything that messed with the gravity over there, just like it's easier to fool with the moon than the sun."

Alec frowned again. "Maybe so. Let me think about it a while, okay? I never can keep the physics straight on that."

"Uh, yeah . . . but, well, uh—there's something *else* we need for you to do," David said carefully. "And we don't have a while for this one."

A thick black eyebrow lifted. "Like what?"

David took a deep breath. "We need to find out what's goin' on in Faerie. Maybe if we know what's happenin' there **we** can do something to forestall further disaster, both here *and* there. Use the ulunsuti," he added, as calmly and sincerely as he could. "Use it to spy on Faerie. Maybe that way we can at least be forewarned. We might even use it to get word to them about what all their foolin' around's doin' to us."

"No," Alec stated flatly, not meeting David's eyes. "No deal."

"But *why?*"

"I . . . I just don't like to use it, David. It *scares* me, man!"

"But why? I mean I *know* you've been doing minimal upkeep on it . . . I read up on it some in *Myths of the Cherokee,* and it agrees with what Uki told us: you're supposed to feed it blood once a week, and once a month heavy-duty blood or it'll go wild. Since it hasn't gone wild, I presume you've been feedin' it blood. Not," he added with a touch of sarcasm, "that you've bothered to let me know."

Alec's mouth worked, but he still did not look up at his friend.

David clamped a hand on his thigh and squeezed hard. "You have been, haven't you?"

Alec nodded sheepishly.

"Hey, man, don't worry 'bout it. It's what you're supposed to do. It's part of the responsibility of havin' the damned thing."

Alec turned at him, face grim. "But don't you *understand,* David? How many times do I have to tell you? *It's not rational*—and I'm a rational person." He gestured around the room. "All this stuff: the computer, the TV, the CD player, the VCR: all of it makes sense. You line electrons up a certain way and push a button and off they march. You turn current on and off, and letters appear or math gets done or lines get drawn. But you take a piece of God-knows-*what*-kind of transparent material out of the head of a monster snake from another world and feed it blood and it shows you the future—that I can't accept. It freaks me out. It just doesn't *fit!*"

"And therefore it scares you," Calvin finished for him.

"Yeah, something like that," Alec conceded. "I guess . . . I guess I figure that if I accept that, then everything else will be suspect, and my whole reality system'll fold up like a house of cards."

"You could think of it as opening up like a flower instead," Calvin suggested. " 'Stead of shuttin' it out, maybe you should be tryin' to work out a . . . a unified field theory of magic, or something."

"Give me a *break!*"

"No, think about it, McLean," Calvin went on reasonably. "We know a fair bit about the cosmology of Faerie, or you guys do, anyway. Why not try to put it all together and work out more? That way we might learn something really useful, and you wouldn't have any reason to be scared of it."

"You forget one thing."

"Oh?"

"Yeah . . . like that people have been trying to work out a unified field theory of our known reality for years and haven't got anywhere. How's an eighteen-year-old supposed to throw Faerie into the mix and get an answer any sooner?''

"Good point, but—"

"But we're getting *beside* the point," Calvin broke in. "I mean look, McLean, it's your property, you can do what you want with it. But if you don't want to try it, at least let me do it. I've been trainin' with Uki some, I know the technique."

A shadow of strain crossed Alec's features. "No," he said again. "Then . . . oh crap, guys, okay . . . but just once, and that's it. Deal?"

Calvin shook his head. "I can't agree to that. But just once *today* unless something really serious is going on, how 'bout that?"

"And we each get a vote," David added. "Two out of three does it, and we all try to be sensible about it. Do what's right, not what we want to do. Head over heart, and all that."

Alec sighed. "Reckon I don't really have any choice then, do I?"

"You've always got a choice," Calvin told him. "But sometimes you don't know what you're really choosin'."

Alec did not reply, but pulled out the top drawer of his night stand and withdrew an earthenware pot plugged with a thick bark stopper. He tipped it on its side and shook out a white deerskin bag which bounced once on the bedspread. Alec loosened the drawstring and emptied the ulunsuti into his left hand where it glistened tantalizingly. David gasped involuntarily as a stray beam of sunlight lanced through the window and struck it, projecting a rainbow onto the R.E.M. poster on the wall behind them— a rainbow whose red stripe was preternaturally bright.

"What now?" David asked.

Alec shrugged. "I've never used it prophetically. The first time I used it at all, I was just staring at it and wondering about something. I was kinda tired and dreamy and all, so I wasn't making any real effort, but then suddenly it took control and gave me the answer I wanted. And then later when you were hurt, we used it to call you back.''

"Right," Calvin inserted. "You use it to focus mental energy."

"Whatever." Alec glanced at Calvin. "Guess you'd better tell us what to do and we'll try to follow. You're the shaman here."

David giggled suddenly, and both his friends looked at him. "What's funny?" Alec asked, scowling.

"Oh, just that up until now it's always been me playin' boy-sorcerer, and now it's you-all! I don't have a bit of magic to my name, 'cept Second Sight that can't see anything, but here you both are playin' with Cherokee mumbo-jumbo.''

Calvin cleared his throat. "Okay, guys, we've got a job to do.''

"We're waitin'," David told him, grinning attentively.

Calvin frowned thoughtfully. "Well, this may be a major working, and since we don't have the kind of power Morwyn had when she used it to spy out the future, we'd probably better all try to do this together—" He looked at Alec. "Sorta like we did when we called David back. Also," he added with a sigh, "I suppose we oughta do what we can to enhance our power."

David cocked an eyebrow. "What'cha got in mind?"

"Two things right off: We'll have to do this sittin' on the floor hand-in-hand with the thing between us, but if you just do that, it kinda cramps the energy flow—so one thing we can do is to drop our britches and sit with our bare knees touchin'.'' He flopped down on Alec's bed, and began tugging off his boots, while Alec and David did likewise on the floor and windowseat respectively.

"And the other thing?" Alec wondered when Calvin had stripped down to falcon T-shirt and black briefs, and he and David had rejoined him in a sort of lopsided triangle on the faux-Persian throw rug beside Alec's bed.

"You won't like it."

"I *already* don't like it."

Calvin snagged a boot and reached into the top, to draw out a potent-looking hunting knife. "Blood," he said. "We prime it with blood. *Our* blood."

Alec rolled his eyes.

David sighed. "Might work. Won't hurt—much—to try. One of us, or all?"

"All," Calvin replied. "That would be strongest."

David nodded. Alec closed his eyes and swallowed.

Calvin bit his lip, held out his left hand and made a quick stab along the length of his index finger, allowing bright red to show, then handed the weapon to David. David followed suit, more quickly than he'd expected, for the blade was unexpectedly sharp and he cut further and deeper than he intended before he knew it.

Alec went last, and hesitated longest, but finally he too drew the blade along his finger.

Calvin took the ulunsuti and placed it on the center of the intricate design. Then, at a nod from him, they all reached forward and smeared their life-essence across the crystal. It remained there for a moment, veiling the glitter, then slowly faded as the ulunsuti absorbed it. But where before the talisman had shone softly, now it blazed with an arcane light, and the red line in the center was bright as fire.

"It does that when you feed it," Alec admitted.

He started to wipe his still-bleeding hand on a convenient dirty sock, but Calvin restrained him. "Leave it till we're finished. It'll aid the power flow. Now," he added, "we all join hands and touch knees and try to concentrate on the red line in the crystal—and keep one part of our minds open to the question: just wonder real hard about what's going on in Tir-Nan-Og."

"Shouldn't we maybe have a more specific goal?" David wondered. "I mean, we don't want the ulunsuti to get confused. Maybe we should try for a person—Lugh, or somebody. He should be fairly close by, so to speak, and we know him and know what he looks like—and he might be less alarmed than some if he detected us spying on him.''

''Good idea,'' Alec agreed. ''Anything to take the heat off a tad.''

''Okay then,'' Calvin said. ''Grab hold and let's to it.''

David took a deep breath and took his buddies' hands: Alec's firm but a little soft, Calvin's much harder and rougher, though with a certain gentleness of touch that surprised him. Another breath and he let his eyes go out of focus, trying to see only the ulunsuti's red septum. He resisted the temptation to close his eyes; tried, rather, to call Lugh's face to mind: long black hair, narrow, angular chin, flowing mustache, blue eyes . . .

Nothing happened for a moment, but then the red slowly expanded. David felt his eyes drawn toward it, and his other senses seemed clearer as well. He was aware of Calvin's hand and knee to the left, of Alec's to his right, but now he thought he could detect a gentle flow of warmth spreading from Calvin's flesh into his own, up his arm and across and into Alec, while a parallel flow entered his knees and flowed through his groin and back down his other leg.

But an instant later he forgot that, for his thoughts had turned to Lugh, and this time the image formed rapidly. One moment he saw only a line of red, and then it had been replaced by a vista he had seen before: Lugh's primary palace—the one at the heart of his kingdom.

In plan, it was shaped like a star; with six lesser, towered points, and six greater. Each tower was white and two hundred feet tall, and each bore a banner on top: a golden sun-in-splendor upon a field of crimson.

David did not know whose body he shared, only that it was gazing north. He saw the terraced grounds of the keep, the narrow band of open country that surrounded them—

But where forests had once ringed the castle, marching a hundred leagues in a thousand shades of green edging slowly to blue and then the not-color of the horizon, now was only devastation.

It was destroyed, all of it: the stuff of a thousand navies a million times larger than Finvarra's. Trees a hundred—a *thousand*—feet tall, all straight and true and so ancient many must have started growing when Tir-Nan-Og first gained mass enough to hold their roots; those same trees lay on the ground, broken, rotting, torn to pieces by the fury of Finvarra's storms which had laid open even the land itself. It reminded David of two things almost simultaneously: the ravaging of the Amazon rain forests he'd been seeing nightly on the news, and the devastation in Siberia following the explosion of the Tunguska object: trees blown flat, radiating from a common center.

But it was not man's greed nor nature's caprice that had wrought this, but a war that embodied them both. Storms: wind and rain, all driven mad by magic. And followed by Finvarra's hordes, which now marched toward Lugh's citadel.

From the northmost tower a figure looked down on Finvarra's troops spread across the land like black ants, their lines stretching far into the shattered forest to merge with the scattered smokes of the trees that had been set aflame lest even their hulks be used to build new vessels.

A woman rode forward from Finvarra's host: a tall Faery lady astride a huge black horse, both liveried in the black and scarlet of Finvarra's house. She took off her golden helm and looked toward the tower, raised her voice to the folk who stood above.

"Lugh Samildinach," she called. "High King of the Sidhe in Tir-Nan-Og! Know that I am Macha, Mistress of War of the Sidhe in Erenn, second only to High King Finvarra who may not touch your soil until you relinquish your claim!"

"I know who you are," Lugh shouted back, not bothering to remove his black helm. "Why have you come here? Why have you blackened my land?"

Macha laughed, the sounds clear even in the weighty air. "Ships must have wood, Ard Rhi; and wood you had a plenty, far more than Finvarra. And now wood you have no more. The seas are heavy with the wrack of your fleets, and they may not be rebuilt. You have no longer any way to attack Finvarra. I have come to ask your surrender.''

"And what of the boy?'' Lugh inquired casually.

"Fionchadd? He has been hidden where no one can find him. Not even I know where he now resides.''

Lugh's eyes bored into her, even from that distance. "Do you not? No, I suppose you speak the truth. It would be exactly like him. True form for the Spider King.''

Macha ignored his remark. "Ard Rhi, I await your reply.''

Lugh sighed with theatrical nonchalance. "If it is an answer you must have, I fear I must give you one you will not like.''

"And what is that?'' Macha asked. "Do not forget that we can kill the boy past hope of return.''

"I have not forgotten,'' Lugh said. "But do not *you* forget that this is my land and that there are certain things I can do that Finvarra cannot, certain weapons I have at my disposal.''

"Finvarra knows too well of your weapons,'' Macha snorted. "And he knows that both Arawn and the Lord of the Powersmiths have forbidden you to use the Horn of Annwyn.''

"Ah,'' Lugh chuckled, "but does he know of *all* my weapons?''

"I doubt not that he does. He certainly knows of the flying ships.''

"All?''

"He knows that you have none that can best him.''

"Ah,'' Lugh cried, his voice growing steadily stronger. "But I do not *need* to best Finvarra; at the moment, I only need to best *you!''*

"A boast, but in vain!''

"Is it?''

And with that he whipped off his cloak and stood revealed in scale armor as golden as the sun. He stepped to the top of the northmost merlon and spread his arms, and only then did Macha notice the bundle he bore—a long, dark object wrapped in scarlet velvet.

A Word, and the golden binding-ties fell away, and Macha gasped in dismay. The tales were false, then; the Spear of Lugh had not been lost in the Second Battle of Mag Tuired.

And from his lofty perch, Lugh grinned and raised his arms, and the spear in them, and with that movement the clouds broke and sunlight streamed through and struck the spear, and at another Word, light poured forth from it.

Macha cringed, expecting to face flaming doom, but the flames did not touch her: They struck behind, to find purchase in the shattered woods. An instant only those broken forests steamed, and then burst into flame that quickly merged with the tentative fires already set there. And in that instant Macha knew her folly. Lugh had tricked her, lured her far inland, far from her sources of supply, with a whole forest at her back. And as the flames rose higher, Macha heard the screams of her forces trapped there, and those of her men who had suddenly found themselves cut off from any hope of returning home. And then she felt the fury of the sun burn down upon her and knew fear such as she had never known.

"You were speaking of surrender," Lugh said mildly. "Any time you please, I will hear yours."

"I am ready," Macha gritted, as the man beside her became a raven. "I already send word to my master."

"Is it peace, then?" Lugh demanded.

"Aye, for a time," Macha conceded.

"Time is all that matters," Lugh told her. "Go back to your master now. Tell him that what you have seen is but a shadow. Say to him that Midsummer's Day approaches and my Power waxes day by day as it draws nigh. Tell him that if I do not have Fionchadd safely in my keeping by midnight on Midsummer's Eve, with dawnlight I will lay waste his fleet; and if that does not suffice, at noon, when my power is at its greatest, I will set the Power of the Sun against Erenn itself."

Macha nodded, her beautiful face pale as sorrow. "I will relay that word," she whispered.

"See that you do," Lugh replied, lowering the spear. And then the image faded.

"Jeeze," Calvin gasped. "Talk about good timing!"

"Yeah," David exhaled his own relief. "We look in just as the war's concluded."

"If it *is,*" said Alec, standing and reaching for his jeans. "I don't think that's gonna be sufficient."

"Why not?" David asked. "Lugh may need ships, but Finvarra needs men, and Tir-Nan-Og's stronger than Erenn, at least that's what Nuada once told me. What choice does Finvarra have?"

"He evidently still has Fionchadd, for one thing," Alec observed. "He can still blackmail Lugh. 'Course that's apparently what he's already *been* doin'."

"And there's a far worse thing," Calvin added darkly.

"Oh?"

"Yeah. What he just did probably further stressed out the sun."

"Oh, Christ, you're right!" David groaned. "I forgot about that. I guess I figured that Lugh's gonna take the battle to Finvarra now, so we'll be all right. But I forgot about what Uki said. We already know that usin' Power puts stress on the sun. And I'll bet you dollars to donuts that that deal with the spear just then was even worse. And think about this, guys: we're all assumin' Finvarra'll surrender, 'cause that's what we'd do. But suppose he doesn't? Shoot, he's immortal. His whole kingdom can go and he'll still be reborn. All of 'em will be, probably, though it might take 'em a spell." He paused, giggled at his inadvertent joke. "But what may not make it is a World. Erenn might survive, our World too, but what about Galunlati? It's weaker than either, more tenuous."

"What're you saying?" Alec asked slowly.

"What I'm sayin'," Calvin replied, "is that if Lugh uses that spear on Midsummer's Day, it could very well destroy Galunlati. And if it goes . . . I don't wanta think about what might happen here.''

"Like, you got a worst-case scenario in mind?'' Alec wondered.

"Maybe,'' Calvin said. "I think—''

He got no further because a heavy knock suddenly shook the door.

As one, they started, neither of them having heard any-one open the front door, much less come up the stairs.

Alec had already opened his mouth to speak when a voice reached them from the landing outside. "Hey, come on, guys; it's me, Gary!''

"Christ,'' David cried. And then suddenly realizing he was still in his skivvies, he grabbed for his pants.

Alec grabbed for the ulunsuti.

Calvin simply sat and waited.

And Gary turned the knob and walked in.

"I thought you locked it,'' Calvin said to Alec.

"I thought *you* did,'' came Alec's startled reply.

"Glad you didn't though,'' Gary chortled. "Is this a seance or a circle-jerk?''

Chapter XI: Dark Days Ahead

"What does it *look* like we're doin'?" David replied archly, hoping to distract Gary so that Alec could finish secreting the ulunsuti.

Gary was too quick for him, though, and stared first at Alec, then straight at David. "I don't *know*, Sullivan. What *does* it look like?"

Alec grimaced sourly, and David heard the soft thunk of the crystal striking the bottom of the protective jar the paranoid Mr. McLean had tried to conceal behind his back. He could tell Alec was about to say something really snotty and had just started to warn him when Calvin interrupted from where he'd been hidden between David and the door.

"G-man!" he bellowed happily, leaping to his feet. "Hey, guy—it's good to see you!"

Gary's eyes pirouetted back-and-forth in brief confusion, to be replaced an instant later by a twinkle of joyful recognition. "Tonto, my man! What're *you* doin' back there!" Then, as another sort of realization dawned on him, "Hey, that *your* bike outside? The G/S 80?"

"Sorta." Calvin grinned, and David, who had finally found a chance to slip on his jeans, hoped he'd take the hint and direct the conversation that way—or any way except toward what they'd been discussing. It occurred to him that the bike was probably what had brought Gary inside in the first place.

"Oh wow!" Gary continued enthusiastically. "Those things won the Paris-to-Dakar half a dozen times! Sharp, man, *really* sharp!"

"Yeah, right," Calvin affirmed, trying to sound modest, but beaming like a fool. "And thanks." His eyes slid toward the blue-and-white BMW patch on Gary's coverall, and David realized, for the first time, that though it was Saturday afternoon, Gary was wearing Hudson Motors livery and had black grime under his nails. Not for the first time he considered the incongruity: a bright Atlanta-born boy who shared the MacTyrie gang's love of gaming and general weirdness, but at the same time didn't hesitate to get his hands dirty under the hood of a car. It all worked, actually, G-man had been planning to study automotive electronics at Georgia Tech before news of Tracy's pregnancy had made him reassess his future. He was *still* going—but had decided to attend MacTyrie Junior for a year before making the leap.

"It's what *I* do, too," Gary said, in confirmation. "I—" He broke off suddenly and blinked at Calvin, who still had not put on his pants. "But hey, man, mama didn't raise but one fool and it ain't me. You guys're hidin' something, ain't you? Or do you *always* sit around in your drawers?"

David tried to look guileless, while Alec simply tried not to look at all, though he had managed to ease the ulunsuti back into the night stand.

"I repeat," Gary went on, "you're obviously up to something, and I doubt this was a circle jerk—which leaves me with my other suggestion. So why don't you guys just level with me, or do I have to invoke the M-gang oath? There's no Ban of Lugh cookin' now, remember?"

David nodded reluctantly. "Yeah, well—you're right, we were kinda foolin' around with some stuff."

"What *kinda* stuff?" Then, "Damn! You were playing with that magic rock Alec's got, weren't you? The one he won't ever let me look at."

Alec's expression clouded, but David rolled his eyes and nodded again, while Calvin looked on, scowling.

"Well, jeeze, boys," Gary went on. "Don't let *me* stop you. I mean just cause we're best friends and all . . . !"

"Cut it, G-man!"

"Cut *what*, Sullivan? What *I* want cut is about ten feet of crap."

"He's right," Calvin interrupted quickly, once more exchanging glances with David. "He's got a right to know." He faced Gary. "You guessed it, man. We were messin' with the ulunsuti, tryin' to get it to prophesy. Alec's not had much experience with it, and I have, so we thought we'd try out its prophetic function. Thought we'd start on something easy, so we checked out next week's weather."

David breathed a mental sigh of relief. That had been a close one. Calvin hadn't lied, but he hadn't told anything like all the truth either.

"And did it work?" Gary wondered suspiciously.

Calvin smiled cryptically. "We'll have to wait to find out, won't we?"

Gary shrugged and flopped down on the window seat, and David had to consciously repress a sigh. That meant G-man was prepared to stay for a while.

Gary turned his gaze toward Alec, looking very bright-eyed and prim. "So, McLean, how 'bout cluein' me in on the procedure, then. Show *me* the future, and all?"

Alec stiffened. His lips were already shaping a *no*, but David shook his head at him, hoping Gary wouldn't notice—and that Alec would take the hint.

He succeeded on both counts, but it made little difference because Gary suddenly stood up (narrowly missing the low ceiling in the dormer). "The weather!" he cried.

"Shit! Hey, could you, like, show me the weather for the *wedding?* That way I'll know how to plan!" His grin widened, and David knew he was on a roll now. "Oh, Christ, folks! Hey, could you show me the *whole thing?* Kind of a sneak preview? It'd be a real trip to spy on your own wedding!" He turned and grinned at David. "That way we can be sure ole Darrell don't forget the ring."

David could not help grinning back, but by then Gary had grabbed Alec by both shoulders and was shaking him energetically—something like a cross between an overly-friendly beagle and Hulk Hogan. "So how 'bout it, Mach-One? Come on, get that ole' rock out and show yer buddy what's up. You can do that much, can't you? I mean, think of it as a wedding present or something."

Alec looked mightily uncomfortable, but David and Calvin caught his eye over Gary's shoulder and signed consent. "Up to you," David mouthed, where Gary couldn't see.

"Oh, crap, G-man," Alec groaned at last, as he extracted himself from his brawny friend's clutches. "I reckon I owe you that much—but I can't guarantee anything." He turned and began fumbling in the drawer.

A disturbing thought struck David, then; and he glanced down at his hands—and was relieved to see that the blood-stains were gone. Evidently the ulunsuti had absorbed every drop. He wondered what would happen if it contacted a really deep wound. Nothing, probably, since Alec had cut himself badly on a windshield wiper blade back in the fall and used the crystal immediately thereafter. But, he suspected, it was a thing better not tested too carelessly.

Alec produced the ulunsuti and simply stood hesitantly for a moment, looking doubtfully at Calvin.

The Indian caught the signal and sank to the floor.

Gary hesitated in turn, hands on the zipper of his coverall. "But don't I have to strip or something?"

Calvin shook his head. "Not for this. We were doin' something a little harder earlier, and that meant usin' more skin-to-skin contact to enhance the power. This won't be any big deal.''

Gary frowned uncertainly. ''But you said you were checkin' on the weather . . .''

''We were,'' Calvin replied quickly, ''but on a more theoretic level, kinda. We were sorta trying to find out what was causin' these everlastin' downpours.''

Gary's eyebrows lifted in curiosity. ''And did you?''

Calvin nodded vigorously. ''The sun—which means we can't do much about it.''

''What the hell?'' Gary grunted, and took a place between David and Calvin.

The ritual was familiar enough this time, requiring only a pinprick of blood as primer. Once more they sat in a circle, hands joined, knees touching, staring at the ulunsuti.

''Just think about the wedding,'' Calvin whispered. ''Let's all concentrate on that.''

David took a deep breath, and did.

Gary had never experienced the ulunsuti's power before, though he had encountered something similar when Liz had scryed in his presence the previous summer—the night David had been kidnapped by Morwyn. Still, he hardly knew what to expect, so there was an instant of blind panic at the beginning as he felt something gently take hold of his mind. He fought it briefly, then heard a voice inside his head telling him to relax, to think only of his object of desire. A long, shuddering breath, and he forced himself to zero-in on the line of red—and on his wedding. He had pictured it a hundred times already; was as romantically obsessed with it as Tracy, though he doubted she knew that. And somehow the image in his head slewed and shifted, as dream became concrete reality.

He gazed, as from a great height, upon a low, grassy hill, and his heart leaped when he recognized it, for it really was the place he and Tracy would become man and wife. It was also a piece of abandoned pasture his dad owned a ways out of town, and God knew he *ought* to recognize it 'cause he'd been having to mow the blessed place (or try, at any rate, given the rain) for weeks in preparation. His labor looked to have done some good, too; because there was only a short, soft stubble of grass there now—that, and cars and people. The lower slopes and the dirt road that looped around it were packed with vehicles of every description, but he thought he saw David's battered Mustang, Alec's Volvo, and Darrell's VW van, his dad's old 2002. And beyond . . . beyond were mountains and a gleam of lakes beneath a sky of absolute blue and a sun of purest gold/white.

He was among the crowd now, and that was strange, until he realized that he'd always envisioned the wedding as an onlooker, probably because that was the way he had experienced every one he'd previously attended. He strained to make out faces, saw his dad, his mom—standing apart, but still beaming, Darrell's sister Myra, David's uncle Dale. And he saw that his last source of concern (beyond the weather) had been taken care of, for the hill was dominated by a tall archway made of furring strips but covered with the roses he'd been secretly raising in Dr. McLean's greenhouse ever since Tracy had accepted his proposal.

Now they ran rampant over the whole structure. That was the place, the open-air chapel where he and Tracy would become one being.

Closer now, and he could hear music—the closing bars of "Jesu, Joy of Man's desiring," (Tracy's choice), segueing into the Rolling Stones "Angie," all rendered on synthesizer by Darrell's sister's friend, LaWanda, who'd come up from Athens special because she was the only person they knew who could play classical straight and still do rock gently enough to please the old folks without stripping it of the energy that fired the young.

The scene shifted for a moment, blurring; red filled the image, and Gary blinked. When it finally clarified, he seemed to have jumped ahead to the actual ceremony. He saw himself, immaculate in white tux, Tracy beside him in the long dress her mother had made from her own wedding gown, its train barely enough to tickle the green Astro Turf they'd used for a walkway because she didn't want grass stains.

And there was the minister: Reverend John K. Seckinger from MacTyrie Methodist, who hadn't balked much at the mixture of mainline Christianity and subtle paganism in either the ceremony or the vows.

And to the right, also in white, but each with ties and cummerbunds in their totem color, his buddies from the Gang: Darrell, his best man; and David and Alec and Aikin—and the at-large member, Calvin. Three of the five, he observed absently, were wearing ponytails. All were grinning like idiots.

The bridesmaids he could not see as clearly, except for Liz's red hair, but he knew them. Two were Tracy's sisters, another was a friend who had graduated the year before, and the final one was the Angie the song was for. (There was a song for each bridesmaid and groomsman, though he'd balked at Darrell's suggestion of "Welcome to the Jungle" and substituted "Bad Company." Alec's more thoughtful choice had been R.E.M.'s "The One I Love.")

The processional began ("Also Sprach Zarathustra"), and the minister beckoned them forward. They processed past beaming friends, and then the music stopped, and it was as if the sun suddenly shone brighter. "Beloved friends," Rev. Seckinger began. "Today—"

Emotion welled up in Gary, making him choke. He blinked, eyes misting. That was enough; he didn't want to see anymore. Some things just shouldn't be foreseen.

He coughed, blinked again—and returned to reality—just as his beeper sounded.

"*Shit!*" he muttered. "Guess Dad's wonderin' why I'm not there yet. Reckon I—" He paused, staring at his friends, who were still entranced. "Ooops—sorry!"

But the spell was broken. One by one his buddies emerged from the trance, but he was too elated by what he had just seen, too filled with anticipated joy—and too pissed off about the beeper—to notice the expressions of abject shock and fear that passed among his companions as, without waiting permission, he picked up Alec's phone and dialed Hudson Motors.

Calvin was the first to recover, but David was the first to assess the situation and risk speaking, though he shot warning glances at his friends. "Jesus, G-man," he managed. "Don't tell me you're workin' *today*."

Gary put his hand over the receiver and nodded obliviously. "Need the cash. Dr. Nesheim tore hell out of his 635 and Dad promised it to him by next week if he'd deliver the baby free."

David grimaced in resignation, knowing of Mr. Hudson's barter system that got him a heap of gratis services—everything from child delivery to house painting to having his taxes done.

Gary spoke to his father for a moment, more than a little irritation heating his voice, then slammed the receiver down and turned apologetically. "Sorry guys, gotta go," he said.

"Our loss, too," Calvin replied, standing. "Catch you later . . . I hope."

Gary shrugged. "Can't say. Looks like it's gonna be an allnighter. I just hope Trace appreciates what I'm doin' for the bairn."

"I'm sure she will," David mumbled absently as he joined his friends afoot.

Another shrug. "Hope so." And Gary was out the door.

Alec closed it behind him and let out a long breath. His face was white, and only with difficulty could he slump down on the bed. There were tears in his eyes. "Christ, guys, did *you* see what *I* saw?"

David frowned and shook his head as if to clear it, more frightened by something he had seen there at the end than he was willing to let on. "I . . . I'm not sure," he stammered. "I . . . saw everything very bright and clear—and

then right after the vows, everything . . . changed, and
then I saw so *much* stuff all at once I still haven't sorted
it all out yet.''

Calvin looked at him sharply. ''What *kinda* stuff?''

David started to reply, but Alec interrupted. ''Death.''
He buried his face in his hands.

David eased down beside him and slid an arm around
his shoulders, noticing that Alec was trembling almost uncontrollably. ''Maybe you ought to lay it out straight, man.
Maybe we *all* should.''

Alec took a deep, sobbing breath. ''Well, at . . . at first
it was all just regular stuff: the wedding—viewed from
outside, I guess; 'least I could see myself, and then the
ceremony, and then there was this noise from somewhere
else—I guess that was Gary's beeper, and it kinda jerked
him away, only I stayed, and then things got really jum-
bled, and I only caught images; but then things clarified,
and I saw—they were walking out from under the arch . . .
and . . .'' His voice broke, and David had to hand him a
sip of Dr Pepper before he could continue. ''Oh, God,
guys, you mean you really didn't see it?''

''I'm not sure,'' David hedged. ''Not exactly, I don't
think.''

Alec swallowed awkwardly. ''Well . . . it was . . . it
was nothing at first—just the wedding and then real happy
and all, and then blammo: lightning right out of a clear
blue sky hits Tracy and . . . and *kills* her.''

''*Jesus!*'' David gasped, exchanging troubled glances
with Calvin that did absolutely nothing to reassure him.

''Or *somebody,*'' Calvin remarked. ''Are you *sure* she
was dead?''

''Her face was smoking and her eyes were gone. That
dead enough?''

Calvin nodded grimly.

Alec's eyes were wild. ''Don't tell me you guys didn't
see that!''

''I didn't,'' Calvin replied, then paused, frowning. ''No,
actually maybe I did. I . . . I saw them leavin', lookin'

happy, and then things got confused like you said, and I only caught flashes, like superimposed images. In one there was a kind of skull face, and in one we were runnin' toward them and it felt real urgent, like we were tryin' to stop something, or whatever, and people were screamin', and—"

"I saw them get in the car," David inserted suddenly. "Or at least, in one version I did."

"But I saw her *dead!*"

"Which means . . . ?" Calvin began.

"Which means we each saw something different," David replied at last. "We saw futures piled on each other, maybe. Alternate realities." He closed his eyes, tried to work it out logically but failed. It was all too much. *Way* too much.

Alec made a dive for the phone. "We've gotta call G-man and tell him not to go through with the wedding!"

David grabbed him in transit. "Not yet. I don't think it's that simple."

Alec stared at him blankly, blinking back more tears. "Sure it is."

"No, think a minute," David said quickly. "Even if we tried to stop it or delay it or move it, we'd have a hard time gettin' anyone to go along, even G-man. I mean, I saw a *lot* of futures: some where Trace survived, and a couple where she didn't. And one—" He paused, shaking his head as the awful images crowded close again, getting clearer the more he tried to remember them. "In one I think I saw her dead somewhere else the same day; so one way or another something's evidently gonna get her. Movin' the location won't be enough, I don't think. And I saw us tryin' to stop things, and us not tryin' to stop things, and us not there. *And* I saw 'em well and happy."

"So what are you saying?"

"That I'll bet you dollars to donuts that lightning you saw had something to do with the war in Faerie sloppin' over, which means Lugh's truce won't last. Shit, man, think about it: lightning doesn't just strike out of a clear sky. Not when it's noon on Midsummer's Day and the King of the Fairies just happens to have a weather-related ultimatum expire around the same time.''

"And . . . ?" Alec prompted, having recovered his equilibrium somewhat.

"I think we've got to try to stop the war."

"You have *got* to be kidding! We're just kids, *human* kids, and you're talking about major-league magicians here. Why not try to stop the wedding instead? That'd be a whole lot easier."

"I wouldn't bet on it, McLean," Calvin interrupted. "Besides, I don't think we *can*. I saw futures where we weren't there, but only a couple where Tracy didn't die."

"Which means we've now got *two* reasons to try to stop the war in Faerie."

"Oh no!" Alec cried helplessly. "You've really gone off the deep end this time. There's no way we can do that, not with us cut off from Faerie!"

"And how *do* we stop a war anyway?" Calvin asked curiously.

"Simple enough," David replied, though he didn't really believe it. "We remove the proximate cause."

"You mean . . . ?" From Alec.

David reached over and ruffled his best friend's hair, and realized suddenly that sometime in the last thirty seconds or so he had made an irrevocable decision. "Yeah, Fool-of-a-Scotsman, we simply find out where Finno is and spring him."

"Whew!" Alec finally managed, but squared his shoulders. "That's a pretty big order, man."

"Yeah," David agreed. "But it sounds like the crystal showed each of us different futures. There has to be a reason for that. We didn't all see the same thing, which leads me to think that time really can go several different ways at that point."

"Which still leads us back to what to do."

Alec reached for the phone again. "Well, like I said, the *first* thing we've gotta do is call G-man."

Once more David intercepted him. "I don't think so. It'd only freak him out, and that's not necessary—yet. The wedding's not till Saturday, right? We've still got time to get a lot done between now and then if we get on the stick."

Alec was not so certain. "I don't know, guys."

"Okay, then," David sighed, "we hedge our bets. We try to find out what we can, and if we hit a snag by . . . by Wednesday, we've still got plenty of time to work on Gary."

"Why Wednesday?"

"'Cause Tracy left this mornin' to shop and stuff down in Atlanta and won't be back till then."

"But *David* . . . *!*"

"I'm sorry, Alec, but I really think that's the thing to do."

"But didn't you *see* her? Didn't you see Tracy dead?"

David nodded grimly. "Yeah, but I also saw her alive—*all* of us alive."

He did not tell his best friend that in one version he had also glimpsed all of them strewn across the meadow like the fallen rocks of Stonehenge.

PART II

CLOUDING UP

Chapter XII: Battle Plans

(Sullivan Cove, Georgia — Saturday, June 14 — late afternoon)

Liz could tell by the way David was moving when Calvin let him off the cycle that something was wrong. There was a tension in his step that was not typical, a hunching of shoulders against more than the sprinkle that had just begun. Standing on the Sullivans' back porch, she was unable to hear the boys' parting conversation, but evidently it was a matter of some urgency because Calvin nodded emphatically and his words rang loud but unintelligibly in the clammy air. David reached up to undo his helmet and stuffed it in one of the cycle's matching saddle bags, not pausing to fluff up his hair. Calvin promptly wheeled the bike around and splattered off down the drive. When David turned toward Liz she was shocked at how haggard he looked.

She met him in the yard, drew him toward the open barn door. He followed, not protesting, let her seat him on a bale of sour-smelling hay.

''Something's wrong.''

David shrugged helplessly and buried his elbows in his thighs and his chin in his hands. ''Maybe . . . yeah. Oh, hell, I don't know. We . . . we got Alec to use the ulunsuti to check on Faerie. It was what we expected: there's war— only they apparently just concluded some kind of truce. I'll give you the details later.''

She laid an arm on his shoulder. '' 'Cause there's bad stuff that won't wait, right?''

He nodded. ''Am I really that easy to read?''

''Sometimes.'' She waited for him to reply.

Eventually he did. ''The *bad* news is that the truce may not last for more than a week or so—until Midsummer's Day, max. Lugh's given Finvarra an ultimatum, and if he follows through on it, it's gonna be like Calvin's worst nightmares. You think what we've had lately's bad; wait 'til this hits! Lugh's gonna be usin' the whole power of the friggin' *sun* to blast Erenn.''

''But that's still not what's getting you. Not really.''

David shook his head and told her about Gary's intrusion, about what they had seen—or thought they'd seen— afterwards. Liz could feel her chest tightening, her muscles growing tense.

''And you really think there's no choice but to try to stop the war?'' she asked when he had fallen silent. ''You won't even *consider* trying to postpone the wedding?''

Another shrug. ''We talked about that, and we're still keepin' it open as an option, but we all saw multiple futures, and in most of 'em something bad happened. In a couple we evidently *tried* to stop it and couldn't. I think Gary'd go along, if we told him. But Tracy's the problem. If we started going on about how she should put off the wedding 'cause she's gonna be struck by a bolt of Faery lightning, there's no way she'd believe us. Even if Gary told her, I doubt she'd believe. I mean look at the trouble I had convincin' you and Alec when I first found out about Faerie.''

''You could *show* her.''

David grimaced in frustration. "Maybe—'cept she's out of town as of this mornin' and won't be back until it's practically too late. But the bottom line's that *we've* gotta stop the war. One way or another it all comes down to that. Soon as Calvin gets back we're gonna try to find out how."

"Where's he gone?"

"To pick up Alec. You and me are supposed to brief Uncle Dale, while Alec tries to get hold of the gang—or Aikin at least; he's more level-headed than Darrell—and tell them what's up. Somebody needs to know—just in case."

"And then what?"

"Calvin and Alec'll meet us over at Uncle Dale's, and then we gotta do some *serious* plotting."

Dale Sullivan took a long swallow of coffee and 'shine from an intricate golden chalice of dubious origin (that kept whatever was in it exactly the same temperature until it was emptied, yet never froze or scalded his lips or hands—as he'd discovered to his surprise), then set it down on the formica end-table beside him. He leaned back in his rocker (survivor of his wrecked cabin), and peered intently at the four young people who looked back at him with equal intensity, waiting for him to speak. His gaze lingered longest on David, and David found himself squirming.

"I thought we 'uz done with this stuff," the old man said at last. Not mad, David was relieved to note, though he'd detected a slight note of irritation. No, his tone was more one of resignation, of things hoped for but not expected.

David cleared his throat. "We *all* hoped it was over, but none of us believed it. Lugh even warned us, remember? Shoot, he's been warnin' us ever since Morwyn killed Ailill. I can still remember what he told her."

"What?" Calvin wondered suddenly.

"Oh, Lugh told Morwyn that she might have precipi-

tated war by killin' Ailill, and she said that she was a
Powersmith and that the war would sweep by her. But then
Lugh said—let's see, I think I can get the exact words:
'You will come to know this, Fireshaper: that when war
ravages Faerie, perhaps even breaks through to consume
the Lands of Men, that every one who dies, man or Faery,
will die cursing your name.' I think we've 'bout come to
that.''

"Yeah, if we'd only listened then, we might be free of
this,'' Alec noted sourly.

"No use frettin' over *ifs*, though,'' Dale replied. "Time
now to start thinkin' 'bout *thens.* ''

"Which we've already said,'' David grumbled in frustration. "What we *need* is ideas. Like, how do you end a
war when you can't even enter the bloody theater of battle?''

"Are you absolutely *positive* about that?'' Calvin inquired. "I mean, are you *really* sure you can't work the
Tracks?''

David shrugged. "As sure as I can be of *anything* to do
with this. I can't *work* 'em, that's for sure. I can't even
see 'em unless they're activated, and that's not very likely
these days.''

"You ever try?''

"As a matter of fact, yes. Once last winter. I— Oh,
never mind.''

Yet David cast his mind back to a cold day in January—
his birthday, in fact, the 16th, when he'd gone up the
mountain to try that very thing. It had been the dark part
of the year, the time he hated most. Clouds for weeks,
and cold for even longer. He'd found himself wishing for
summer, wishing so bad he could do like Oisin had once
done, and give him a day of sunshine from some far future
June. He'd sought out the place where he knew the Track
lay, sat for hours staring at a strip of ground where nothing
grew but moss, and even that was hidden under the snow.
Nothing had happened, *nothing*. Magic had utterly abandoned him.

He shook his head abruptly. "I told you about it, Liz, Alec. Don't you remember?"

"Okay, then," Dale inserted, clearing his throat. "So you can't get to Faerie. But answer me this: If you *could* get there, what would you do? I doubt Mr. Lugh'd take too kindly to you folks walkin' up to him and sayin', 'Hold on here just a minute.' "

David chuckled in spite of himself, having entertained exactly that notion. "Well," he began slowly, "since the war's bein' fought over Finno to start with, I guess the simplest thing would be to spring him from wherever he's being held and proceed from there. I thought of that, actually, but it just seems too preposterous now I've had time to think a little more."

Alec stared at him incredulously. "Still on that, huh? Well, *that* oughta be simple enough," he added sarcastically. "All we've gotta do is search God knows how many Worlds that we can't get to anyway!"

A scowl from Dale silenced him. "Are you *sure* just rescuin' that boy'd end the war?"

"No," David replied. "But that's what started it. Hostages and counter-hostages. Morwyn was gonna give herself up in exchange for Finno, but obviously that's not happened."

The old man looked thoughtful for a moment. "That may be true, now I think on it. I've read some of your books, and seems to me I recall that they went to war over a cow one time."

"And over an insult to a King they deposed," David added, thinking of Bres.

"Cows *more* than once, if the books're right," Calvin chimed in. "I've been readin' up on 'em lately, too."

"I've been afraid to," David admitted. "It's too strange seein' one reflect the other and still tryin' to keep up with the inconsistencies."

"That's a fact," Dale agreed. "But that don't solve our problem. Given that freein' Mr. Finny'd end the war—which it might do or might not—appears to me that brings up two more things: findin' him and freein' him. And once you've got him free, what're you gonna do with him?''

David frowned. ''Return him to the Powersmiths if we can. Finvarra won't dare mess with them; all he can do is bluster.''

''We'd have to be careful, though,'' Liz noted. '' 'Cause if Finvarra ever figures out it was humans—never mind *which* humans—that sprung Finno, he might cause trouble in our World.''

''*Real* careful,'' Alec said shakily. ''He's no fool.''

''But the borders are sealed,'' Liz pointed out.

''Not exactly,'' David countered. ''Lugh put a ban on commerce between the Worlds. He didn't actually physically seal the borders 'cause he has to join himself to the land to do that. But you're right about one thing: if there *is* a way to Faerie, it's through the Tracks, and I don't know how to work 'em. Oh, I can find 'em, sometimes— the Sight's good for that—but I can't just walk onto one, activate it, and wind up where I want to go. Shoot, even the Sidhe don't really know what they are; they just know how to get around on 'em.''

''But are *all* of them closed?'' Calvin asked pointedly. ''Lugh may have closed the border between here and Tir-Nan-Og. But what about the border with Erenn? Finvarra's his own man, isn't he? What's to stop him from comin' here on his own?''

''Well, the Worlds don't overlap right,'' David said. ''Tir-Nan-Og overlaps *now,* but I think Erenn overlaps the early eighteenth century, and Annwyn the thirteenth, or something. And that doesn't even take into account the fact that *this* World was in a different place in our space each of those times. If I even *try* to think about *that,* I get a headache. And then—''

''All of which presupposes we can even find Finny,'' Calvin interrupted. ''He may not be accessible at all, 'specially if we can't use the Tracks. I was kinda countin' on 'em.''

"Yeah, but we'll simply have to use the other resources at our disposal, I guess," David sighed. "Whatever magical whatsis we've got: the ulunsuti, for instance, and whatever you can do, Fargo. Probably oughta check with Uki and see what he suggests, too."

"Well, then," Liz said, taking his hand. "That's not so bad. And remember that you and me and Alec all know a lot about Faerie, you especially—and that I can scry."

"I keep forgetting about that," Alec admitted. "You never used to be able to."

"No, I've *always* been able to, a little. But I've gotten much better at it lately."

David's face brightened. "So that means you could use it to find Finno?"

"Maybe," Liz replied uncertainly. "But I'd need something that belonged to him—a part of him would be even better, like blood, for instance. The last time I tried to find somebody who was lost in the Worlds I was using a bit of Ailill's blood." She looked at David. "You got anything of his?"

David frowned, taking inventory of what he had left from Faerie: a suit of chain mail, a few bits of clothing Morwyn had given him, an odd bit of jewelry, but nothing from Fionchadd.

"This do?" Uncle Dale asked suddenly, pointing to the golden coffee-chalice.

David glanced at it uncertainly. "I'm not sure. Finno gave it to you, but it was gold from this World, and Morwyn actually made it, not him—though I'm still a little puzzled that it works, since Lugh said magic stuff would lose its power."

"Which argues for more than a verbal closing," Alec pointed out.

"Spells, maybe? Or a stronger glamour?" David suggested. "*I* don't know."

"I've got it!" Calvin exclaimed suddenly. "I really do have something that belonged to him."

David looked puzzled. "Huh?"

"The torque!" Alec cried, slapping the arm of the green velvet sofa he sat on. "The torque that he used to record the trip through Galunlati. He gave it to you when you parted."

"I don't suppose you've got it with you, do you?" Liz wondered hopefully.

Calvin shook his head. "Negatory. I didn't exactly know I was comin' over here till I found myself on the way. And I sure didn't think I'd find myself plottin' jail breaks from Faerie."

"So where is it, then?"

"Back at my lady's house in Sylva."

"Hold on a minute, guys," Alec interjected, "we're forgetting something."

"Oh yeah, like what?"

"Well, we're sitting around talking about scrying, but we've got the ulunsuti here now—it's in my pack, Calvin made me bring it. So why not look for Finno now? I mean, it worked before when we were looking for Lugh."

David's face brightened. "Yeah, Fargo, any reason not to give it a go?"

Calvin's brow wrinkled thoughtfully. "We could, I suppose, but—"

"No buts," David interrupted. "We've gotta do it—I mean presuming you're still willing," he added to Liz.

"Same ritual as before?" Alec wondered.

Liz shook her head. "I'd rather go solo first, if you don't mind. I . . . I'm kinda insecure about this kinda thing. It's . . . well, ideally you've gotta open your mind to other people, and that really does kinda freak me out."

"Whatever you say," David told her, patting her hand. "It's your call."

Liz nodded, and seated herself in the middle of the floor. Alec handed her the ulunsuti jar and she removed the crystal reverently and held it in her hand. A moment's pause, a series of deep breaths and she began staring at it, her eyes growing ever wider and more unfocused until David could see only the thinnest ring of green around her enormous black pupils. Her breathing became shallower and shallower.

For perhaps two minutes she remained that way, and then suddenly she blinked and looked up at them. Her face was grim, but she said nothing until she had put away the ulunsuti and returned the jar to Alec.

"So?" This from David.

"I . . . couldn't find him. It was all so chaotic, so confused. I kept trying to picture his face, kept calling on him, but I kept getting other images, other faces—other *emotions!* God, the emotions! It was . . . I think it was the war, 'cause they were certainly Faery faces, and most of 'em in armor. Oh, there may be a truce, kinda, but there's still so much . . . I don't know . . . *karma* over there and leaking through from there to here that I can't focus on anything. I'm sorry, folks."

"How 'bout if we all tried together?" Alec ventured. "Like we did over at my house, or when we found David's spirit last year."

"No," Liz told them flatly. "I *can't,* not now. It took all I had to find my way in and back, and at that I nearly lost myself—couldn't tell what was me and what was somebody else. I can't look for Finno and hang on to you folks too, at least not this way, I . . . I'm not that strong. I guess I really do need the torque."

"I could use the ritual of finding," Calvin suggested. "That worked before."

"It might," Liz admitted. "But frankly I'm . . . I'm just not up to it, not this soon. That was scary, *real* scary."

David took her hand. "That's okay, girl. We understand." He glanced at Calvin then. "Any ideas now?"

"Well, for one thing," the Indian replied, "the problem may not all be Liz's. The ulunsuti can only look one World away, and we're not sure Finny *is* one World away; he could be in one of the Worlds that touch Faerie but not here. The ulunsuti can show us what's in Worlds that touch ours, and the near future but that's about it, and even then its limits depend on the strength of the user. Like, it's harder to see something far off than nearby—and how likely is it that old Finvarra'd conveniently hide him in our backyard, much less Lugh's?''

''Well, then,'' Uncle Dale inserted unexpectedly. ''Seems to me you've got a choice 'twixt a maybe thing and a sure thing. I'd go for the sure thing if I had the time—which you do. I'd get hold of this torque and see if you can't find Mr. Finny with it.''

''How soon *can* you get it, Fargo?'' David asked.

''Couple of hours at least,'' Calvin replied, frowning. ''It'd be faster if we all went over to Sandy's, if we can pull it off. I mean, we *are* on a short schedule, folks.''

David and Alec exchanged weary glances, and Liz too looked troubled. ''I've got school,'' she groaned. ''Got a big final coming up. And I've managed to get my car stuck again,'' she said sheepishly.

''Oh Lord,'' David sighed, glancing toward the yard, where the black EXP was enmired to its bumpers. ''I forgot about that.''

''That doesn't mean I won't do it, though,'' Liz said. ''I can go over there, do the scrying, and still get back in time to get to Gainesville late—*if* I can get somebody to get the car out. Ma'll be POd about it, but—well, she'll just have to deal with it.''

Uncle Dale grinned. ''Yeah, I 'spect there'll be a lot of pissed-off parents 'fore this is over with. But just you leave 'em to me.''

''Lord, yes,'' David groaned. ''I can just imagine me havin' to clear this with Ma and Pa. They'll let me go, but they won't like it. What about you, Alec?''

''Do you *really* need me?''

''Fool-of-a-Scotsman! Of *course* we need you; you're Lord of the Ulunsuti. Don't forget that. You're actually master of the most power, and don't forget that, either!''

''Yeah,'' Calvin said. ''I can work it, but not without your permission. Rest of the stuff I know's mostly good on the other side.''

"Crap," Alec sighed in turn. "Well, I reckon I don't have any choice, do I?"

David flopped an arm on his shoulder. "I reckon not. But the folks'll be used to us runnin' off by now. We'll just tell 'em we're goin' over to see Calvin's place. No big deal. Besides, come fall we'll be on our own anyway."

"Good point," Alec admitted uncertainly.

David rose to his feet. "Okay, boys and girls, let's to it. We'll go to my house and get some stuff—Alec, I'll lend you some gear if we need it. Then it's off to Sylva to scry for Finno, and then . . ."

"I'll have to report to Uki," Calvin reminded them. "I could do it here, but it'd probably make more sense to find out what we can beforehand. The more I have to report, the better. Besides, I need to tell my lady." He glanced at Dale speculatively. "Mind if I call and tell her to expect company for dinner?"

"Be my guest," Dale replied, nodding toward the phone.

"And then I'll go on to school from there," Liz added. "If I can get my car unstuck," she added pointedly.

David frowned. "Hmmm. That's a problem. We don't really have time for that now. So . . ."

"I'll take care of yore car, Miss Lizzy," Uncle Dale assured her. "You young'uns go on. Take David's car, and I'll get Liz's out and drive it over later, if you want. Or you can run her on down to school and you and me can take her car back later. Just give me a call."

"Or Liz could take somebody and I could take somebody on the bike," Calvin suggested.

"No way!" came twin horrified shrieks from Alec and David.

"Enough of this," Liz sighed. "Let's just get going."

Chapter XIII: Just Visiting

(near Sylva, North Carolina—
Saturday, June 14—
early evening)

Gravel spat and sputtered and threatened David's head-lights as he saw Calvin's bike fishtail around the steep curve ahead of him to disappear beyond an outthrust mass of laurel. He gritted his teeth and swore silently—and wished there was a gear lower than first.

In spite of their best efforts, it was after seven o'clock and he still hadn't got the Mustang-of-Death the last quarter mile up the pig trail that was purported to be Sandy's drive, though it looked to be more moss and weeds than gravel. The problem was neither steepness—though there was enough of that to make a Range Rover think twice—nor curves, nor even the loose roadbed. It was simply a capricious washboardedness that reacted with the car's wheelbase at exactly the wrong frequency and made it bounce and jump sideways every time he tried to go above about five miles an hour—which he felt he had been doing for at least a day.

"Damn," David muttered, aloud this time, as a final set of ruts sent the tail-end half sideways and set twigs scampering along the sides. Liz in the passenger bucket echoed his sentiment, and Alec in the cramped backseat added, "In spades."

"Just hang in there, Mach-One," David sighed. "We're almost there—I think."

"Yeah," Alec countered, "but *I* think my butt's somewhere down around Franklin."

"How 'bout your nerves?"

"Nerves? *What* nerves? Oh, you mean those things that oozed out of me after you passed that semi on the blind curve? The things that went skulking off into the bushes with their tails between their legs? They—"

"It wasn't blind."

"*I* couldn't see."

"Of course not! You had your eyes closed!"

"That's okay," Liz chuckled. "So did I."

"That makes three of us," David giggled, and Alec cuffed him.

"Yeah," David laughed, "but you could always've ridden with Calvin." He glanced in the rearview mirror and saw Alec's slightly green face assume a shocking pallor.

"Once was enough," Alec replied quickly. " 'Course I could *also* have driven *your* car . . ."

David shot him a glare that would have melted lead, but a sudden steepening of the trail brought him back to the task at hand. The way had narrowed among a stand of birches that rose pale on either side, and just as he was certain the car wasn't going to be able to pull the precipitous grade, the road finally leveled off and opened up, and they were there.

Straight ahead a gravel oval about the size of his folks' side yard had been scooped into the loose schist of the mountain that towered above it to the left, and to the right was what he had first thought a pile of fallen timber, but which proved to be a shingled carport angling off the corner of a long, rustic building. Calvin's borrowed bike peeked out from under one side. A formidable-looking red-and-black Ford Bronco poked out the other. David doubted the winch on the front bumper was ornamental.

"Well, folks," David announced, "we're here."

Calvin met them at the back door and handed David a frosted mug full of some frothy dark liquid. David took it, sniffed it tentatively, and took a sip—and almost gagged at the bitter taste.

"What's the matter, Dave? Can't abide your native fire-water?"

"Tastes like burned horse piss!" David sputtered back. "What *is* it, anyway?"

"Guinness Stout, of course. Ireland's national brew."

David made a face. "Somebody squeeze it out of a peat bog?"

"Let me try," Alec volunteered, reaching for the mug—just as Calvin handed him its twin. He raised a questioning eyebrow at Liz. "I didn't know if you partook or not."

Liz cast a glance back down the alarming slope and nodded vigorously. "I do now!"

"You still abstain?" David asked Calvin, steeling himself and risking another taste.

The Indian nodded.

A musical voice interrupted, floating toward them from somewhere inside. "You forgetting about the glass of hard cider we had on my birthday?"

Calvin blushed and eased the door open, motioning for his friends to enter. The wrought-iron latch, David noted, was homemade—probably a local antique.

David let Liz in front of him and followed her into a vestibule maybe eight feet square, sided with knotty boards nailed at a forty-five degree angle. Rough hunks of skinned tree-trunk marked the corners, each of which offered a branch to a point straight above their heads in an organic semblance of a gothic vault. The arching spaces between were augmented with racks of deer antlers, including a very impressive eight-pointer. Doors opened off on either side, each hung with a woven tapestry depicting mountain

sunsets. That to the left was closed, the one to the right
ajar enough to expose a toilet and an antique footed bathtub, and the one straight ahead opened against a wall.
Warm light came through from beyond, probably candles.
There was still no sign of the woman with the wonderful
voice.

David shrugged and went on ahead, entering a large
space that obviously doubled as kitchen, living room, and
dining room. The beamed ceiling (also peeled pine) rose
to the full height of the sloping roof, and an open door
beyond let in a breeze off the porch and a fabulous view
of mountains.

Immediately to their right was a huge stone fireplace,
and in front of it a woman was standing.

In spite of the sunburned gold of her hair, David at first
thought she too was a Native American. Maybe it was the
shape of her face, or the arch of her nose, or the way she
carried herself—or simply the way she looked at him as if
she saw more than was there. Behind him he heard Alec's
sharp intake of breath and realized that she also looked
more than a little like his lost love, Eva—except that this
woman was wearing gray-green cords, a souvenir shirt
from The Who's latest tour, and a brief, heavy-fibered vest
that looked handwoven.

Suddenly the woman smiled and the ice was broken.
"Well, looks like you folks made it up Coon Hound's
Despair! Come in, grab a chair; I'm Sandy."

David shook her hand, then flopped down gratefully on
an overstuffed love seat beside the low green sofa facing
the fireplace. Liz joined him. Without waiting permission
he tugged off his shoes and socks and flexed his toes and
ankles gratefully, running them through the thick fur of
the sheepskin that lay on the bleached pine floor. He
glanced at Alec. "So sit down, man."

"Yeah, have a seat," Calvin echoed, returning from
whatever nameless errand had detained him out back.
"Liz, what *do* you want to drink?"

"Water's fine."

"It really is, too," Calvin assured them, trotting into the kitchen corner to run a frosted glassful which he handed to Liz before turning his gaze to David. *"You,* however, don't get anything until you've finished what I gave you to start with."

"You don't like it?" Sandy asked, sounding a little disappointed. "It was my idea."

David tried to smile. "A valiant effort, but . . ."

"I'll finish it," Alec volunteered, having already polished off his own. David handed him the mug and raised an eyebrow in Calvin's direction. "Got more of that branch water, sir?"

"I've got some bourbon to go with it," Sandy offered, then caught herself. "Lord, what a loon I am, offering liquor to folks your age like it was goin' out of style. If the school board ever found out, they'd run me out of town on a rail."

"Without their scalps, though," Calvin appended over his shoulder, grinning wickedly as he filled a mug for David from the tap.

"I won't tell."

Calvin handed David his water and cast an amusedly appraising glance at Alec, who was still leaning against the fireplace. "So have a *seat* McLean! You waitin' for a written invitation?"

"Thanks," Alec replied, "but I'll stand a while longer, if you don't mind. Have *you* ever ridden over that road in the backseat of a Mustang?"

"I bet he hasn't," Sandy laughed. "But I have. I've got a recliner with a built in massager if you like. It's in the bedroom."

Alec managed a weak smile. "Later." He glanced at David. "I guess Calvin's told you we've got serious business."

"Which we can talk about after supper," Sandy said, rising. "Plotting the salvation of Western Civilization always goes better on a full stomach."

"Venison," Calvin noted simply.

Alec poked David in the ribs as Calvin led them to the table. "Wonder if it'll beat the old family recipe?"

"Time will tell."

Time did. The venison was excellent: back strap cut into thin discs, dipped in milk, then dredged in flour, lightly garlic-salted and peppered, and then quick-fried. Eaten while still hot and crunchy, it was tender enough to be cut with a fork. David decided he'd need to fool with the family recipe some, even if it was for stew. There was also wild rice and tossed salad and homemade brownies with black walnuts for dessert.

Eventually Calvin pushed back from the table. In a series of efficient moves, he whisked away the dishes and cutlery and loaded them into the sink. Five minutes later they were sitting on the front porch, watching the first ruddiness of evening creep into Carolina.

"So what's this problem you folks have?" Sandy asked at last.

Calvin told her his part first, but when they came to the section where they had spied on Tir-Nan-Og, David took over; and then each took a turn describing the wedding, since neither had seen it exactly the same.

Sandy had little to say throughout, though she nodded occasionally and jotted down a few notes now and then. Finally she looked at David. "Well, I think you're right about one thing: Obviously you should try the simplest solution first. Find out where this Fionchadd fellow is and go from there. And also, much as I hate to admit it, I think you're probably right in deciding to take matters into your own hands before you tell your friend about the threat. I really can't fault your logic or your motives. But I'm like Liz: I really think you've an obligation to warn both your friends if this scheme of yours goes awry."

"Oh, we're definitely goin' to," David assured her, "for whatever good it'll do. But thanks for the vote of confidence." He glanced at Liz, then at Calvin. "Well, boys and girls, I think we've probably wasted enough time. Liz has to get back to school, and I need—well, I just need to *know* something. So let's get the show on the road. You got the torque, Fargo?''

Calvin did not reply, but slipped into the house and returned an instant later with a ring of thick gold just big enough to slip around someone's neck. It was patterned with spirals and granulated gold-work, and cloisonné lizards were worked around its circumference. One end was knobbed by a strange transparent jewel, the other was missing. Calvin handed it to Liz. ''This do?''

Liz took it uncertainly. ''I think so. I know I've got vibes off David's ring a time or two. Once in particular.''

''I've still got the ulunsuti,'' Alec volunteered, nodding toward his red nylon backpack. ''If you still want to try what we were talking about over at Uncle Dale's.''

''You mean use the ulunsuti to focus, and I use the ritual of finding?''

''While Liz tries to scry using the torque,'' David finished.

''Merge the magic of two worlds?'' Liz asked doubtfully.

Calvin nodded. ''Worth a try—if you're up for it.''

''Yeah,'' David said. ''What do you think, Liz? Wanta try to use 'em both?''

Liz shrugged uneasily. ''I don't reckon it'd hurt to make the effort. Worst that can happen is that I'd fail again.''

Calvin took a deep breath. ''Just remember one thing, folks, Fionchadd may not *be* one World away, in which case we may not be able to find him. I mean we *do* have to consider that.''

David frowned. ''Yeah, but I think he's reached me once, in a dream, which argues that he's nearby.''

''Good point,'' Calvin conceded. ''Only one way to find out for sure.''

Sandy still had not spoken, but was watching with real interest, a cup of Irish coffee in her hand.

David stood decisively. ''Okay, gang: let's do it.'' He

paused, looking at Liz, whose face was tense with antic-ipation. "Hey, you okay?"

She nodded. "I . . . I'm scared, a little. And I really don't want to do this, but I think it's the necessary thing, really the only thing. But I can't help wondering what we'll do if we can't find him. I mean, if he's further away, we may not be able to get there from our World at all, and if we have to try to figure out the Tracks—well, I'm *real* dubious about that."

Calvin took her arm. "You don't *have* to. I can give it a go."

She shook her head. "Sorry guys, but I think it really does have to be me."

They retreated inside and, at Calvin's urging, changed into shorts, then cleared a space in the middle of Sandy's living room—a place conveniently demarcated by a cir-cular rug in the shape of a Power Wheel, though Sandy said she had got the idea out of a Susan Cooper novel. Calvin stared at it a moment, then nodded and scooted it a couple of feet to the left so that it was precisely under the apex of the roof. He took the ulunsuti jar from Alec and placed it in the center, then motioned Liz to seat her-self behind it, facing east. He squatted down on the east-ern arm and pointed David to the north. "Your Power comes from there," he explained. "The Sidhe come from the north, at least relative to Georgia, and your Galunlati connections in the form of Yanu are from there as well. Alec, my man, you get the south."

" 'Cause I'm from Atlanta?"

"Right."

"Which leaves the west for me," Sandy sighed. "Be-cause that way lies the Land of the Dead, and I'm closer to that than you guys, right?"

"You folks must've been talkin' a lot," David told Cal-vin.

Calvin rolled his eyes. "White woman ask many ques-tions."

"This is creepy," Liz said hugging herself, obviously

trying to remain calm. "Combining two different magical traditions, and all. And I hate to say it, but I feel kinda silly."

"So did I when Oisin told us all to strip naked in Uncle Dale's barn," Calvin chuckled. "You get over it."

"Tell me about it," Alec muttered, glancing nervously at Calvin. "Do we need to prime the pump?"

"Prime it?" Sandy wondered.

"With blood," Calvin replied. "It gives you surer results."

Alec grimaced sourly, even as he began baring his arm. "I feel like a bloody pin-cushion."

"Bad pun, McLean."

"Meant to be."

Calvin shrugged. "Let's try it without, first. If the torque's as strong as I think it is, it should be enough. How 'bout it, Liz?"

She shrugged in turn. "All this ritual's new to me. My granny just taught me to trust my feelings; she just showed me how to breathe and let go of myself and see what my brain was really thinking when I wasn't watching. But since then I've decided that desire and belief are prime triggers. Now—let's get started."

She took a deep breath and unstoppered the jar, then emptied the ulunsuti from its bag and placed it back on the center of the rug before her. Next, she placed the torque atop it so that it curved around the crystal, took one gilded end in each hand, and closed her eyes.

David simply stared at the talisman. He was aware of Sandy to his right, of Calvin to his left, conscious of the pressure of their knees against his own. But he centered on the ulunsuti. It was easier here than at Alec's or Uncle Dale's, perhaps because of the environment. The ceiling between the rafters was dark now, though the beams themselves were limned with candle fire.

But the brighter flame was the ulunsuti. It caught the last furtive beams of sunlight and sucked them in, caught the uneven flicker of the candles and claimed them for its own, to grow brighter and brighter as he watched. He was aware of Liz, too, somehow; of her reaching out to him as the mystery of that linkage became more natural. That was strange, too, he realized distantly. A year ago they'd never have considered such a thing: a mingling of minds. But he'd touched her mind now, and her body as well, and for an instant he wondered if what Eva had told Alec was true: that exchange of bodily fluids conferred or amplified Power. If that was true, he and Liz certainly had a link with each other.

But then there was no more time for speculation, because he felt himself drawn into the crystal.

Liz took another breath, feeling a prickle of Power that was not her own. She closed her eyes against the sudden glare of the ulunsuti and tried to envision Fionchadd's face. Distantly she heard drumming, and knew Sandy had begun a soft tapping on the small tom-tom she had brought. That helped a lot, helped bring her out of herself, helped her center. Calvin had also begun to chant, very softly, keeping time to Sandy's rhythm. She did not try to make out the words, though she knew they were familiar.

"Sge! Ha-nagwa hatunganiga Nunya ulunsuti, gahusti tsuts-kadi nigesunna. Ha-nagwa dungihyali. Agiyahusa aginalii, ha-ga tsun-nu iyunta datsiwak-tuhi. Tla-ke aya akwatseliga. Edahi digwadaita."

More deep breaths, letting the sounds soothe her, open her memory to Fionchadd. She tried to imagine his face above the torque, though she had never seen him wear it. Smooth beardless skin, narrow chin, high cheekbones that complemented the slant of his green eyes and elegant black brows. A mouth that was wide and pretty and a little mocking, quick to joy, to lust, to the merest touch of evil but with a softening that had come into it lately. Long blond hair curling past his shoulders.

Fionchadd? she called, and was aware that she was floating—or that part of her was. *Fionchadd?*

She drifted further, aware that this had never happened

before. It was as if the torque were tugging her toward it, making her one with the metal. She could sense every grain, every twist and spiral. Could feel the strange alloys of which it was made, the sparks of the jewels that tapped the hidden powers of the universe.

Fionchadd? The crystal swallowed her, sent her spiraling. The chant rang loud in her ears, and she followed it, let it take her, became one with it, took its words into herself and repeated them over and over, centering on her goal.

Unreality whirled and shifted. She was aware of the torque again, dragging her onward.

Abruptly she was in a room. Fionchadd was there, chained to a bed, his rumpled gray clothing stained with blood. He looked groggy. Chains bound his hands and feet, his neck. A strip of thin leather hung across his naked chest. A dagger lay atop it. An *iron* dagger it must be, for the Faery boy was writhing. She wanted to go to him, to rip away the bonds, but something stopped her.

"Where is this Galunlati?" someone was saying. "Lugh threatensss us and Finvarra would come on him from behind through this ssstrange place. Lugh is no friend of yoursss. You mussst tell usss, if you would sssave your fosssster-father's people."

"My foster-father has deserted me," Fionchadd spat, and looked away.

"He will have you back if you will tell him. He will exalt you among the Daoine Ssssidhe."

"I do not wish—"

"Very well."

A scaly hand lifted the dagger, another removed the hide. The dagger was restored but rested on bare flesh now; the point coming nigh to his navel, the hilt to the base of his throat. He writhed, screamed, hid within himself, but Liz trailed him there.

Fionchadd! she called, with no voice.

Liz? he had time to call, and then the pain truly found him.

And through him discovered Liz.

She screamed, though she could not, and jerked free. Her mind whirled, she was vaguely aware of herself moving, of Fionchadd's form fading away. *David,* she shouted and he was there, anchoring her. *We have to find out where he is,* he said, and she steeled herself and saw: A tall tower made of stone with a silvery glint, but with a look of age and decay about it, the whole surrounded by water—a lake maybe, or was it some sea? for the silvery surface was alive with waves and silver Tracks swept across its surface. There was precious little land between the tower base and the shore. Nor did there appear to be any door. Beyond was nothing: the edge of the World itself, maybe, and she was aware of reality twisting further.

Liz! again, and with it another wash of pain, and she could stand it no longer.

There was an instant of agony and she was out of herself entirely—lost. For a panicked moment she floated helplessly, powerless to return to herself. Then she sensed something, followed it eagerly—and glimpsed wars and armies, entire forests lying shattered. *Tir-Nan-Og,* a part of her realized, even as she felt herself whirled away again. Eventually the spinning stopped and she heard chanting. Lost, fearful, she moved toward it, saw seas that were alive with light and tenuous clouds of Tracks, all laced with a *nothing* that was darker than black.

And then a fleet—a floating island of black ships that lay off a Faerie coast. Somehow she was above them, looking down—so far down she could see the edges of the World, the Tracks as they rode the seas of Faerie, something of the non-stuff between. And she saw *more* fleets—at least three. One in black that bore the scarlet eagle of Finvarra, and another sailing from the south that showed the golden sun that was Lugh. And the third bore an emblem she could not clearly make out, save that the sails were gold and the emblem crimson, and that it moved slowly from the east. *Powersmiths*, something told her.

She looked closer, suddenly was there, seeing everything as clearly as if she were standing on deck.

"How many days until we meet?" someone was saying. A man's voice, one of a score of gold-clad seamen who lolled against the rail as the oars plied the shimmering waves of their own volition.

"No one is certain," another answered. "The seas are fickle; so are the Tracks. Had I to guess, I would say at least two."

"And then we put an end to Finvarra for certain, take him captive and make him relinquish our own."

"Aye—if Lugh joins us in time."

"He will. He has never failed us. Besides, it is *his* southern harbor Finvarra plans to attack."

"Aye, but he makes a capricious ally."

"Not with fear of us as a motivation."

"True, but we fear him too, or at least the captain does. It would not be good if he used that spear again."

"One reason we are to join him, so I have heard. The King wants an end to this war."

"And well he should."

A pause, then. "Did you hear something?"

Another. "No, but I felt the ether stir. I do not think we are alone."

Liz felt eyes come at her. A mind brushed hers, knew her alienness.

"Human!" it breathed. "But how?"

She tried to turn and flee but could not. "One of Finvarra's spies?" that mind cried.

No! she tried to scream, and back in the room her lips moved in that sound. "Help."

Calvin started. He'd been following Liz, but then had lost her. Or she had lost him. He had caught a glimpse of land and ships, then she had vanished—until the word had come ghosting into his mind: *help!* And the only help he knew was the magic of his people. He closed his eyes, shut out the ulunsuti, concentrated on the formula he had been slowly chanting, and tried to think of Liz.

"*Sge! Ha-nagwa hatunganiga Nunya ulunsuti, gahusti tsuts-kadi nigesunna . . .*"

And somewhere upon the Faery ocean, Liz heard. She followed that voice, let it rip her free from the mental walls that held her.

And then she remembered her task: Fionchadd.

She had seen Fionchadd, did not want to see him again . . . yet she had one thing left to do: she had to *find* him, pierce the World Walls there about, and see where in her own World they lay. She steeled herself, drew on the strength she felt flowing into her from her friends.

The tower was the key. Slowly she rebuilt the memory.

Cold, then: cold and dark and falling. A resistance against her mind: present, then gone. World Walls, a part of her knew, and then she had a sensation of flying, of fleeing that place. She touched fog and felt colder yet— impossible for one who had no body. An image clarified: the tower! But with it came another wash of unbearable pain, and she had no choice except to flee—but at least she could choose her route: across the sea to the edge— *through* it. And then silver enveloped her in a fine mesh, and then, so suddenly the familiarity made her cry out, she saw something she recognized.

A city spread before her, night-lit. She knew those buildings: the silver cylinder of Peachtree Plaza, the Regency Hyatt House's famous blue dome, the red marble slab of the Georgia Pacific Building, the elegant new IBM Tower. And to the left almost at the limits of vision was the low, humped mass of Stone Mountain.

Atlanta!

The shattered stone tower returned for one final instant, and with it a fading *help,* but before she could reply it was gone, replaced once more by the shimmering facade of IBM's *nouveau-art deco* showpiece.

"I think he's in Atlanta," Liz said aloud, and fainted.

* * *

David felt his heart catch when he heard those words, but then his concern was for his lady. He leapt forward, broke the circle, even as Sandy ceased drumming and Calvin stopped the chant David had also unconsciously taken up. Calvin was on his feet in a moment, splashing cold water on Liz's face. She stared blankly for an instant, then blinked. ·

"Atlanta," she repeated, looking up at David. "How much of that did you catch?"

"Enough," he managed, as Sandy rose shakily and staggered for the kitchen.

"Enough for sure," Calvin agreed, joining David to help Liz back to the sofa. *"Damn!* Two kinds of magic workin' together, and five minds!"

"Yeah, and goin' every which way," David added. "Jesus, I don't *ever* want to do that again."

"Atlanta," Alec mused, as if he had not heard them. "Oh, come on; you're not serious!"

"He's in Atlanta," Liz repeated. "Well, not Atlanta, really. I think it's another World—a bubble off Tir-Nan-Og or one of the other Faerie realms, or something, and accessible only from there—and maybe from here, since we were able to look through to it. Maybe it's like Powersmithland, sort of, which is accessible only through Annwyn—so folks in Faerie thought—but also touches Galunlati. But it overlaps Atlanta, I'll bet you anything."

"Is it always that . . . traumatic?" Sandy wondered, returning with a pot of hot cider she'd put on before they began. She looked pale, but otherwise seemed none the worse for her first encounter with magic.

Calvin fixed her with a searching glance and an inquiring eyebrow, but she shook her head and mouthed, "I'm okay."

Liz spared her a wry grin, and helped herself to a long swallow of cider. "No," she said, "that's the worst it's ever been."

And then she repeated what she had seen and felt and heard as best she could.

"That stuff about the ships is real interestin'," David noted, his thoughts linking up almost more quickly than he could blurt them out. " 'Cause it looks like three fleets are convergin', one of Finvarra's, one of Lugh's, and one of the Powersmiths'. I bet I know where, too," he added. "Lugh's got a major port down around Savannah, I've seen it on one of those projection discs of his, and they mentioned something about defendin' Lugh's southern harbor, so I bet that's where they're goin'. We already know Finvarra's been causin' a lot of grief in the north of Tir-Nan-Og, and we know Lugh's given him an ultimatum. But that doesn't mean old Finvarra won't try to fight. Shoot, that whole mess in the north might even be a feint to draw attention away from that fleet."

"But what does this actually mean in terms of your plan?" Sandy asked.

David took a deep breath. "It means that *if* we can spring Finno, we've got a goal to try to get him to. The Powersmiths are his people, and looks like a bunch of 'em are gonna be fairly close to the coast. If we can get him to them, we can hand him over. Slam-bam, thank-you-ma'am, end of war."

"Except that we've still got a couple of problems," Alec said slowly. "Like, now that we've found Finno, how're we gonna spring him? And once we've freed him, how're we gonna *get* him to the Powersmiths? I mean, we can't go through Tir-Nan-Og, the border's closed—which I suppose means Faerie itself's closed as far as this century's concerned. And there's no way we can get to Erenn and try to get through there. So that leaves three choices: we take him via our World, via the Tracks—or via Galunlati."

"But we've already *been* through that," David sighed in exasperation. "I don't know how to *work* the Tracks, and I think it's too dangerous to try to learn now. And I *don't* think it would be too cool to bring him into our World, for fear Finvarra'd come after him."

"Which leaves Galunlati," Calvin snapped bitterly. "Somebody *else's* World." His face darkened, hardened, his voice became suddenly cold. "It's always that way with you folks, isn't it? You're always willin' to risk someone else's property, someone else's resources. What makes you think Uki'd be any more eager to have us go marchin' through there than anybody else? He doesn't want undue attention either, don't forget."

"You got any better ideas?" David retorted, feeling unexpected anger, even though he knew the words were true.

"No, I *don't* have any other ideas," Calving spat. "But we're merry well *not* goin' through Galunlati!"

"Suppose it's okay, though?" Sandy interrupted reasonably, laying a hand on his arm. "It's possible, after all, and I'm sure if you think about what you said you'll realize that you've kinda overreacted."

"My ass!" Calvin grumbled.

"Yeah, but you've gotta go there to report to Uki anyway," Alec retorted. "There's no harm in bouncing the rest off him. All he can say is no. Maybe he'll even have some ideas we haven't thought of."

"Maybe," Calvin conceded with a grunt. Finally the Indian stood, poured himself a cup of cider—frowned long and hard at it, and added a mere drop of bourbon. David raised an eyebrow.

"Okay, so I overreacted, and I'm sorry," Calvin muttered. "I understand where you're coming from. But there's more to it than that."

"Yeah, well, I shoulda thought it out better too," David admitted, crossing to hook an arm around Calvin's shoulders. "But hey, guy, we've gotta get goin'."

"Goin'? Goin' *where?"* He paused. "Hey, no *way,* man; you're not goin' with me! Uh-uh!"

"Why not?" David shot back. "We've been before and Uki knows us. Besides, you need someone who can explain the situation in Faerie."

"But how'll you get there?"

"Same way as you," David replied, fingering the pouch in his pocket. "I'll burn my scale."

"It's not treated. They have to be treated to do that."

David raised an eyebrow. "Do they? Oisin gave me mine. Maybe it *was* treated. And anyway, there's only one way to find out."

"Either that, or he could go and bring you back one," Sandy said, sparing a wry glance at her sweetie.

Calvin's nose twitched sideways in a sour grimace. "Oh hell," he grumbled, "I don't guess there's any real choice, is there? I mean, what you said really does make sense. 'Sides, I'd hate to have to make two trips. And actually," he added slyly, looking at Alec, "I *do* happen to have a couple of spares. They're some I used to practice the technique on that makes it possible for 'em to transit worlds."

"Then you could fix mine for sure," David said.

Calvin shook his head. "Takes too long and I don't have all the ingredients, so I guess you'd better use mine. I mean it's a risk, and all; I won't lie about that. But I think it's safe. As best I can tell if it doesn't work, it simply doesn't work."

"Doesn't strand you in Limbo, or anything?" Alec inquired doubtfully.

David looked at him. "You don't have to go if you don't want to. We won't hold it against you."

Alec rolled his eyes. "Yeah, I know I don't—and I don't really want to—but, well, I guess I owe it to Uki. I mean if I can help him out, I suppose I should."

"Even if it involves doin' more magic?" David asked.

"Even if it does."

"It hurts," Calvin warned. "Hurts a lot *more* to go back. That's why I don't go often."

"I can stand pain," David told him flatly, while Alec slowly nodded.

"Just think about poor Finno," Liz reminded them. "Think about iron burning you forever."

"Are you going too, Liz?" Sandy wondered.

Liz shook her head. "I don't have a scale. Do you?"

"No," she sighed wistfully, gazing speculatively at Calvin. "At least not yet. I want to go when I've got time to talk, and that isn't now."

"And time's a-wastin'," David said, and that ended it.

Ten minutes later, David watched as Calvin built a tiny fire in the circle of the stones at the center of his Power Wheel and, when it was burning well, took the three scales, placed them on a piece of corrugated cardboard, arranging them so that the points touched in a rough pyramid. He then set it carefully atop the flames.

"Best we hang on to each other," he whispered. "In case things *don't* come off."

David nodded and grabbed Calvin around the waist with one arm, drawing Alec in with the other as the Indian maneuvered them so that they stood almost atop the flame, the smoke already clogging their nostrils. And then the cardboard caught, and an instant later burned through. One flame touched a scale, and the world exploded into light.

"Hyuntikwala Usunhi."

David screamed as his body was torn apart, flung into another place and reassembled. Calvin had warned him, of course, but he was not prepared. The last time he'd followed a rabbit. It had taken a long time, but there'd been no pain. He thought for a moment he might crawl back from Galunlati—maybe crawl on broken glass and shot-up tin cans. Anything to avoid doing that again.

He blinked, felt the residue of pain leave him, but was not ready for the heat that already burned against his skin: the too-hot sun of Galunlati.

Chapter XIV: Shuttle Diplomacy
(Galunlati—summer)

David wiped his brow and looked around, already perspiring from the double-dose of Galunlati sun that came partly from the sky and partly reflected up at him from the blazing white sand of Uki's Power Wheel. He had not been there before, though he had heard Calvin mention the place, and usually such things roused his curiosity. But this time he would have given a lot to be lying in a dark forest pool somewhere, cooling his heels in mountain water. That was the problem: there was no wind to cool them, not even enough to twitch the foliage on the sentinel cedars—scarcely surprising, given that Uki was a lord of the weather and that even a breeze would have disturbed the patterns wrought in the scorching sand. But now that lack of breeze only made it hotter. David risked a glance skyward, saw the sun unnaturally bright, unnaturally red. He looked away quickly, but even that brief glimpse had given him afterimages and made his head hurt. He could not tell if the surrounding trees were browning, or if that were only an optical illusion born of over-stressed eyes.

Calvin saw his actions and nodded mutely, and David

thought he looked worried—as worried as he'd ever seen him.

"Whew," David laughed nervously. "I see what you mean about travellin' that way. I wouldn't want to do it any more than I had to."

"Tell me about it," Alec agreed, and David noticed his friend was very pale.

"I *did* tell you," Calvin shot back. "Maybe you'll listen next time."

"We *needed* to come," David retorted, flashing Calvin a warning glance. "You know that."

Calvin nodded sourly, and David wondered what had brought on his sudden bout of moodiness.

"Hot," Alec ventured.

"Hotter'n when I left," Calvin muttered grimly, but David thought he was trying to get a grip on himself. "And that was only a day ago, more or less. Even allowin' for the time differential, that's bad." He paused. "Something else's wrong too: we called on Uki, and the scales usually take you to whoever you call on, unless you're thinkin' real strongly about a different location—but we wound up here."

"So you think . . . ?"

"I think it's another function of Lugh's latest . . . indiscretion."

"Makes sense, I guess," David sighed. "But jeeze, could it have made so much difference so soon? I mean, crap, man; we're still dealin' with a friggin' *star* here, and a hell of a lot of distance."

"And forces we don't understand," Calvin finished. "And those forces focusin' through *others* we don't understand. But we ain't gonna get any answers here. Come on boys, let's travel, it's about a half hour hike."

And with that he led the way into the woods.

"You know," Alec mused as they shouldered through the encroaching laurel and followed Calvin onto a path, "it's too bad we couldn't convene some kind of grand council—take folks from our world and Galunlati and

Faerie and set them together and talk cosmology, try to figure all this out. Our physics and their magic, and . . ."

"You sound like Sandy." Calvin chuckled in spite of
himself. "And actually, I'd like to see that too. Find out
about the Sidhe and all, how they got here, and all that.
And then set Uki down and get the history of Galunlati,
and see how that jives. All I know about it so far is that
it's essentially a made place."

"Made?" Alec wondered aloud. "By whom?"

"I'll tell you later," Calvin said. "It's too complex to
go into now."

"But *Cal*vin!"

"Shh," Calvin whispered. "I need to think."

They walked in silence for the next several minutes, and
David was grateful for any chance to relax—to take in
mental energy instead of spending it. Oh, it was still hot
there in the woods, but at least it was pretty as well, and
for the moment he didn't have to be responsible. Thus, he
was a little disappointed when Calvin's abrupt "Ho, we're
nearly there," brought them to a halt.

"What . . . ?" Alec began.

"Shhh!"—from Calvin.

Alec frowned but David laid an arm on his shoulder and
cupped his hands around his ears, motioning toward the
trail before them.

Calvin suddenly trotted on ahead and was soon gone
from view. They followed as quickly as they could, given
the terrain, and David saw Alec's nod of acknowledgment
as he became aware of what David had noted. First it was
a sound—more a vibration, actually—that crept through
the moss beneath their feet. Like distant thunder it seemed,
but David knew it for its true self: Hyuntikwalayi—Where-
it-made-a-noise-as-of-thunder, the vast waterfall that in his
World overlapped Tallulah falls. But the closer they came,
the more he became aware of a second sound: a sort of
low-pitched chanting.

The way brightened ahead, and David caught sight of
Calvin once more. An instant later they stepped into a

wide, rocky clearing. Straight ahead, maybe a hundred
yards off, a stream cut the open place from north to south,
its upper reaches lost in a mass of mountains. A trail ran
beside it, David knew from past experience, though it
eventually bent off to the northwest before going north
again—ultimately to Atagahi, the magical lake of healing.

To the right, though, the view was far more evocative,
for that way the stream plunged abruptly over cliffs into a
spectacular deep gorge. A wisp of mist arose from beyond, and the sound was louder, almost deafening. Rocks
rose to a gentle peak right beside the point where the river
dived over, and at that point a figure stood, arms outstretched, gazing at the sky.

It was Uki, though David had forgotten how tall the
Chief of Wahala was, how disturbingly white his skin
shone—though his bones and features were those of Calvin's people. As it was, he resembled a near-naked version
of the statue of Christ overlooking Rio de Janeiro. David
could not make out the words of his invocation, so merged
were they with the thunder of waters.

Calvin signed them to a halt, and they paused until the
chanting ended. Eventually Uki's shoulders sagged, and
he turned. It was a moment before he saw them, but then
he looked up and quickened his pace in their direction.
An instant later he had reached them, was extending his
hands in the style he had learned from David the last time
he was there. David had to crane his neck to look into his
face, and when he did, he started at the change. Worry
had etched lines where no lines had been, had deepened
those few creases already present, hollowed the cheeks
beneath the high cheekbones. If an ageless being could be
said to have aged, Uki had done so.

"*Siyu, adawehiyu,*" Calvin replied formally, bowing:
Greetings, very great magician.

"*Siyu, adawehi,*" Uki replied in kind, nodding to each
of them. But then his stern face broke into a wide, welcoming grin. "*Siyu! Edahi, Sikwa Unega, Tsulehisan-
unhi!*" he cried to Calvin, David, and Alec in turn,

greeting them with their names in the archaic Cherokee he spoke: He-Goes-About, White-'Possum, and The-Resurrected-One respectively. Then, more seriously, "You have returned, Edahi, but I fear you bring no good message."

Calvin shook his head. " 'Fraid not—but I've learned a lot. More'n you want to hear, probably."

"If it is much you have learned, then it will take long to tell, and that is a thing best done where it is cooler," Uki said. "So come if you will, and visit with me a while."

Calvin and David grinned, though Alec was trepidatious, but they all followed Uki toward a narrow path that snaked down the inside of the gorge and led under the waterfall to a large, dry cavern.

David looked about apprehensively, expecting to find the place crawling with the snakes and giant tortoises it had held before, but there was no sign of them—though the sandy floor bore the twisted marks of their passage.

"Where're the girls?" Calvin wondered aloud, in reference to Uki's two disturbing half-sisters, the Snake Women.

"Gone to the north and south to learn how the land fares, gone to seek council with the mighty."

"The mighty?"

"With the Red Man of the East and the Black Man of the West and the Blue Man of the North; with Awahili the eagle, and Awi Usdi the Little Deer and Yanu Tsunega the White Bear of Atagahi; and even with Tsistu, Chief of Rabbit kind."

"I was wonderin' about that," Calvin mused thoughtfully. "I wondered if there wasn't something you folks could do here."

"In truth, there is little," Uki told him, "though we make the effort. Mostly we try to maintain watch on Nunda Igeyi to see that it grows no brighter, and call the clouds often to shade the land. But without Kanati, little can we do. I have tried to bring the cooling rain, but can no longer find it. I fear Kanati has deserted us.''

"Kanati?" Alec wondered.

"One of the gods," David supplied. "I think he's Uki's father."

"He is," Uki said. "But he is gone from here now and returns only when he pleases. But come, I am a bad host. We will eat and drink and then you will tell me what has transpired."

They followed the shaman into an adjoining cavern, and David spent almost a whole minute simply inhaling the cool, moist air. Uki disappeared, to return with a white deerskin and a series of pottery vessels. These proved to contain whole chilled mushrooms, honey, blueberries, and some kind of celerylike greens with a tongue-soothing dipping sauce. There was also ice-cold water, which they pulled from a large earthenware pot with gourd dippers.

"Now," Uki said, when they had refreshed themselves, "what news do you have for me?"

Calvin sighed wearily and told Uki as much as he could about affairs in Faerie, with David supplying the details about the intricacies of Faerie politics.

Uki said little while they spoke, though he did interject a question from time to time. When David got to the part about Lugh using the spear to draw on the energy of the sun, though, Uki hunched forward attentively. "Yes," he muttered. "This makes sense, for not a day past Nunda Igeyi suddenly grew very hot indeed. And it matches a thing I have been thinking."

He went on to explain how he believed that when Lugh drew on the power of Faerie's sun, he also drew on the power of the suns in other Worlds as well. Earth's sun was too strong for even a very powerful being to affect it, but the same was not true of Galunlati's weaker one.

"However," Uki continued, "I think there are more important things you must tell. Did I not hear you say you thought you had found a way to stop this war?"

David nodded and told him of their sketchy plan to rescue Fionchadd.

"So once you have found Dagantu, once you have freed him, what then?" Uki asked at last, giving Fionchadd his Cherokee name, which meant Lizard—because he moved like one, not because of the year he had spent in that shape. "Will not those who have imprisoned him follow you? What is to keep them from entering your Land?"

"Fear, mostly," David replied. "They don't dare draw too much attention to themselves, since our World doesn't believe in magic and I'm afraid there'd be more magic afoot than the Sidhe like—and that's not even countin' the problem they have with iron."

"It also depends on where Finny's bein' held," Calvin added carefully. "We thought he was captive in some part of Faerie subject to Finvarra—like Erenn. That'd make the most sense, but when Liz looked for him, she found him . . . she's not sure, but geographically it . . . seemed to be near Atlanta, which is a large city in our world many days walk from us—though we probably won't be walkin'."

"We really can't tell until we know more," Alec interrupted. "As it is, we're unbelievably lucky Finno's even on this side of the Atlantic. Otherwise, we'd really be calling in favors we don't have with you trying to get to places from which we could maybe reach Faerie, or asking for teleportation magic, or I don't know what all."

"Fortunate indeed you are," Uki said, "and I think your plan is wise. But one thing yet concerns me: You say you fear pursuit into your world if your foe finds you have stolen your friend. That is reasonable enough. But what troubles me is that you have also spoken of a need to get him to the land of his mother's folk—"

"*Grand*mother's folk, actually," David corrected. "His mother's mother was a Powersmith, her father was brother to Annwyn's queen."

"I am set straight," Uki laughed, nonplussed. "But

whatever the relationship, there is a thing you are not tell-ing me, is there not? A favor you wish to ask?''

Calvin nodded sheepishly. ''Saw right through us, didn't you? But yeah, we are kinda in a bind. See, Finvarra shouldn't know about Galunlati yet, unless he's got more spies at Lugh's court than we know of, but he does know something's up—knows there's another World that borders ours, just not where it is or how to get there. But I doubt he knows that the land of the Powersmiths can be reached from here. Lugh has nothing to lose by our freein' Finny, so if Finny is being held close to Tir-Nan-Og and we wind up there when we try to teleport, we may be okay any-way—we'll simply turn Finny over to him and have done.''

''But if you do not?''

''That's what I'm gettin' to. If we can't get Finny to Faerie, and can get him to our World, we run the risk of havin' Finvarra follow him into our World. So what I was hopin' is that we could kinda keep the *option* open of bringin' Finny back into Galunlati, at least briefly, if we really have to. Once here, we can either send word to Powersmithland, or else—if you'll let us—go through Gal-unlati until we're fairly close to where that naval battle's gonna be, and then switch back there.''

Uki nodded grimly and frowned, but he looked relaxed. ''I do not like this,'' he said finally. ''I do not like the idea of becoming ensnared in the workings of other Lands, and I fear to see this war spread through all the Lands. Yet if it is not stopped, if Lugh uses this weapon on Mid-summer's Day, we may all be doomed. Surely he knows this.''

''I'm not so sure,'' David interrupted. ''I think Tir-Nan-Og—all of Faerie—is more secure than Galunlati. I don't think even Lugh would be so suicidal as to know-ingly risk his own World.''

''There are many variables,'' Uki said. ''Too many, yet you have given me much to report to the Council. Still, time is critical, and Edahi has said more than once that it is easier to get forgiveness than permission. Therefore, you have my permission to proceed—but cautiously, and only if there is no other choice, for I do not want attention drawn to Galunlati. Should you succeed in freeing Dagantu, you may enter Galunlati if need be. I would urge that you do so only if necessary. Since there is a battle a-borning to the south, I would also suggest you make the transfer there—you will have less territory to travel through.''

''There aren't any uktenas down there, are there?'' Alec asked nervously.

''No,'' Uki chuckled. ''But I would beware of bears and rabbits.''

David frowned thoughtfully. ''Uh, speakin' of critters, there's something I keep meanin' to ask you. I . . . I keep wonderin' about you and snakes and the uktena. I mean the uktena was your enemy, right? You had us kill it. And you're supposed to be standin' guard over the Snake Women—your sisters; and you don't like havin' snakes around. Yet you wear them as ornaments, and everything I've read since I left here indicates that snakes are important in weather magic. I can't reconcile the two.''

''It *is* a hard thing to understand, is it not?'' Uki replied, smiling. ''But remember the heart of our magic derives in part from similarities and in part from things that are part of more than one world at once. Snakes move like water, therefore they may help bring the water. They are neither fish, though they have scales; nor beast, though they go upon the land; nor bird, though they lay eggs. In this they have power, and that power may be used to bring rain, which is water between earth and sky, which may be solid or liquid or even air.''

''I see,'' David said. ''Sort of . . . But there's another thing that puzzles me.'' He paused, swallowed. ''If lookin' at an uktena causes death to the seer's family, why didn't our folks die when I turned into one last fall?''

''Because you were not truly in your Land, for one thing,'' Uki told him. ''There was so much magic afoot that your power could not get through. But more importantly," he added, "you were not yourself truly evil."

David had just started to inquire further when Calvin shushed him.

"No time for that now, White 'Possum, we've got other things to talk about." He eyed Uki speculatively. "We still need one favor."

Uki raised an eyebrow. "Oh?"

Calvin looked embarrassed, an expression David had seldom seen him wear. It made him look younger, and David decided he tended to think of Calvin as being older than he probably was—and then realized he didn't really know his friend's true age.

"Uh, yeah," Calvin mumbled awkwardly. "I told you we may be able to spring Finno by goin' to wherever he is and simply unchaining him. Trouble is, we don't really know how to get there, since the only way that might work is closed. So we were sort of wonderin' if you could lend us a few uktena scales to burn, so we could maybe try to get there that way."

Uki frowned. "Those scales are rare and precious and not to be used capriciously. It takes much medicine to prepare them. This you know."

"Right," Calvin affirmed. "And I'm afraid our plan may require a fair number, just in case. But we can always bring 'em back if we don't use 'em. And I'd be glad to help you make more."

"How many?" Uki asked gravely.

Calvin's brow wrinkled in thought as he counted on his fingers. "Let's see, at least two to get there, if he's only one World away and if only two of us go, which is probably the minimum we could get by with: somebody who knows Faerie and somebody who knows Cherokee magic—me and Dave, I guess. And then three to get us back to our World with Finny—or twice that number if he's *more* than one World away. And then three more to get here, if we have to use that option—assumin' we can't jump straight here, which I doubt we can, given that we can't *see* two Worlds away with just an ulunsuti. The last is a contingency,'' he added hopefully.

"And more yet to get you to the Powersmiths and more yet to get you home again when this is over,'' Uki groaned wearily, though his eyes twinkled. He sighed dramatically and strode off to his chamber once more to return with yet another pouch. He emptied it onto the floor in a cascade of ruddy, vitreous color. "These are all that remain of our winter's labor,'' he said, "for only certain scales may be used. I will try to make more, should you need them, but these are all I have now. And remember, it will take three for you to return to your own Land from here this time.'' He sorted through the pile and wound up with thirty scales. "Six hands I have but I cannot give you all. Will four hands and two be enough?''

"More than enough, I hope,'' Calvin said after an instant's calculation. "If not—well, we'll just have to wing it.'' David watched as Uki swept all but eight of the scales back into the pouch, which he then handed to Calvin, before distributing three of the remainder among the boys.

The shaman disappeared again, to return a moment later with a medium sized leather pouch which bulged in odd places. This too he handed to Calvin. "Should you attempt what I suspect you will, Edahi, you may find the contents to be very useful. Go now,'' he added, "and take the scales with my blessing and the blessing of Galunlati. I will do what I can here, but I fear the battle will be mostly yours, and truth to tell, what you have told me sounds too simple, for surely Finvarra will have posted guards. Remember what I have said: use the scales sparingly, for they are rare and cost much to empower—as well you know. Avoid my Land if you can, but if you cannot, make the crossing in the south. Now come, I will call down the lightning.''

David cringed at that, yet knew it was no worse than the flames they had come through to reach this land.

Uki rose and led the way to the shelf behind the falls. Once more he bade them hold their scales aloft; once more he had them close their eyes and think on home. A word from him, a certain chant and a pattern of claps—and lightning flashed down from the sky and pierced the falls and sent them first into agony and then back into Carolina.

CHAPTER XV: Into the Breach

(Sylva, North Carolina—Sunday, June 15—early morning)

The first things David heard when he found himself once more in Calvin's Power Wheel were Alec's muttered "Damn" and Calvin's relieved "Whew!" A yip of surprise a bare second later might have come from either of the women, but David was too startled by the cessation of pain, the resumption of noise after the abrupt transition, to identify its origin, and by then whoever it was had regained her composure.

It was now full dark, and in the moment it took his eyes to adjust from glare to gloom, he wondered how long they'd been gone, how time in Galunlati translated into time in his World. A check of his watch did no good: it had stopped, which did not surprise him. Someone cleared her throat and he spun around and saw Liz and Sandy still sitting on the de-barked logs that surrounded the Wheel. They'd obviously left at least once, though, because they were both nursing steaming mugs, and Liz had acquired a large green serape which she had draped around her shoulders. It was not cold, but there was a decided nip in the air which made David shiver from the contrast with the oppressive heat they had left behind.

"Lord!" Sandy exclaimed, rising and stretching luxuriously. "I don't know if I could *ever* get used to seeing that; never mind what it does to theories about the conservation of matter, and all." While she spoke, she was unscrewing the large thermos she held, while Liz fumbled in the wicker basket beside her. "Liz said you were all coffee drinkers," she continued, stifling a yawn as she took one of the mugs Liz produced, and filled it. "Unusual for young folks, I'd say—but then, you're unusually civilized young folks."

David took the mug gratefully and sniffed it, noting the strong aroma. Fortunately he liked it strong. There was a hint of cocoa, too: mocha. "Like the mugs?" Sandy inquired absently. "Got 'em at a Renaissance fair down near Athens."

David examined his. The smiling face of a wizard looked back at him. It reminded him of Oisin. He smiled back and wondered if Sandy was talking about inconsequentialities for their sake or hers.

"Nice," he said, glancing at his watch again. "Uh, what time is it, by the way?"

"Four in the morning," Sandy replied promptly, yawning once more. "You've been gone about six hours. Want some breakfast?" she added hopefully.

"*Love* some," came Alec's quick response, and David too realized he was hungry again, in spite of what he'd eaten in Galunlati.

"But we need to get goin'! We don't have time to—" Calvin began to protest, until a scowl from Sandy froze him in mid-sentence.

"Haven't we already decided that saving the world goes better on a full stomach?"

The silence that followed was more proof than David needed that Calvin too was running close to empty.

* * *

Half an hour later, full of bacon, sausage, omelets, and waffles—and about a gallon of juice and coffee—David and his friends stumbled from the table to the circle of seats in front of the fireplace. The sky outside was barely pinkening.

"Well, that was good," Calvin said, "but I reckon we'd better be gettin' down to business."

"Sounds good to me," David yawned, taking a place at Liz's feet. Alec joined him; Sandy slipped in at Calvin's side.

"So what'd you find out?" Liz finally blurted.

A sigh, and Calvin began sketching in the details of their meeting with Uki; and David found himself nearly nodding off in spite of the urgency of their situation. He hadn't slept well the night before—nor the night before that. Add the painful transition to and from Galunlati, a fair bit of exercise there, plus a lot of mental gymnastics, and he wasn't surprised that it was all starting to catch up with him.

"So granting that Uki's given us permission to use Galunlati and given us some scales to burn, where does that leave us?" Liz wondered when Calvin had finished.

"It leaves us with two immediate problems," Alec replied pragmatically, rising to poke up the small fire they had built more for company than comfort. "How do we get to where Finno is, and how do we rescue him?"

"Three problems, actually," David corrected sleepily. "Where *is* there? All we know's that it's near Atlanta—we think. And probably in another World, since Hot-lanta oughta overlap Tir-Nan-Og."

"Got any notions about that?"—from Liz.

"One, maybe," David said, rubbing his eyes. "I think Finvarra found some secret way to this place he's stashed Finno—and it's not very big, so if you didn't know to go there, you'd probably miss it."

"So he may not even know about the possible border with our World?" Alec wondered.

"Which means?"

"Which means we gotta go there," David replied heavily. "Fortunately old Fargo here's got an idea about that."

"Right," Calvin agreed. "And the sooner we get at it the better."

"Like when?" Liz asked, stroking David's hair absently.

"Tomorrow?" Alec ventured.

Calvin looked at David with a mischievous twinkle in his eye. "Actually, I was thinking more like now."

"Now!" David cried pitifully. "You have *got* to be kiddin'! I can barely hold my eyes open—and you're not much better!"

"Would you rather wait and risk Tracy's life?" Calvin shot back. "It may be almost a week until Midsummer's, but we've gotta leave time for things to go wrong!"

"No!" Sandy said firmly. "Time or no time, you guys are dead on your feet. You're gonna rest some before we even consider any more of this. Come on, I've got plenty of crash space—plenty of floor, anyway."

They bedded down—all of them, including Sandy—in a semicircle of sleeping bags before the fireplace. Calvin drew the loose-woven drapes, which had the effect of dimming and softening the light without actually plunging them into darkness. The fading fire was their only illumination. Sandy had put an Alan Stivell harp tape on to help them relax, and its delicate melodies wove through the gloom, mingling with the hush of breathing as they all tried to sleep. But there was a lot of shifting and thumping and twisting, too, as bodies strove to find rest brains were slow to provide.

"So you mean to start out from *here?*" Alec asked, finally breaking the uneasy silence.

"Quiet!" Liz mumbled.

"But I'd sleep better knowing what was gonna happen when I get up!"

"Alec!"

"Oh, why the hell not?" Calvin agreed. "I more or less feel the same way."

"So . . . ?" Alec prompted.

"So Finny's prison may be in or near Atlanta, but the scales can transport in space as well as between Worlds, so there's no reason *not* to start from here. I mean, it'd save a shitload of time. All you've gotta do is know someone of Power where you're goin'—or have someone with a lot of mojo to send you, like we did."

"Which still presupposes two things," Alec yawned: "That Finno's Power's the right kind, and that he can help us if he wants to—and that the scales will even work where he is to get you back. I mean you might find yourselves stranded, if the Powers of one World don't transfer to another, which they don't always do."

"Fascinating," Sandy muttered under her breath. "We have *got* to talk about this some time. But not now," she added pointedly.

"There may be another problem, though," David said slowly. "Somethin' even Uki seems to have forgotten."

Calvin propped up on an elbow and stared at him, scowling. "What's that?"

"You need to have been where you're goin'."

The lines in the Indian's forehead deepened. "Crap," he groaned, falling back against his pillow. "You're right! How could I have been so *stupid?*"

"Yeah," Liz said, glancing sideways at David. "But if it *is* Faerie, you *have* been there. Maybe if you held on to Calvin when you burned the scale, that'd do the job."

"What about trying to send word to Lugh and have him help us?" Alec suggested. "Wouldn't that be the simplest thing? What about just using the scales to get *there* and tell him, instead of us trying to spring Finno on our own? Obviously Lugh's better equipped than we are."

"Maybe we *should* try that," David agreed uncertainly. "We might be overlookin' the obvious by assumin' we can't get to Tir-Nan-Og."

"Worth a try," Liz affirmed.

"Except for one thing," Calvin reminded them. "We've got a really limited number of scales. If we try and succeed, we're fine—maybe. But if we try and fail, we don't have enough to get us back to our World at the end. And since we need to keep our options open, we need to conserve those scales. It takes a long time to get the stuff together to set 'em up, and we can't afford to spend 'em like they were Marta tokens, or something."

"So you think . . . ?"

"I think we need to stick to our original plan first. Try to save Finno ourselves, and then if that doesn't work, use the remainin' scales to try to get into Tir-Nan-Og and hope we can get somebody there to listen to us."

"Yeah, I guess you're right," David yawned, turning over. "I was just hopin' we could get out of havin' to go through that pain more than we have to."

"I know the feelin'—literally," Calvin sighed. "But sometimes it just can't be helped."

"Okay," Alec said. "So now we've gotta decide how we're actually gonna do the deed."

"No!" Sandy growled from her place beside Calvin, "Now we've *gotta* get some shut-eye!"

Not even Alec dared to argue with her tone.

"Me and Calvin'll go, I guess," David announced from his place at the dining table late that afternoon when they were all up and alert and eating again. "Him for the magic, and me as native guide, or something," he continued. "Not that I know much about Faery magic, 'cept by instinct. Any ideas, Fargo?"

"Well," Calvin replied, sopping up the remnants of a bowl of venison stew with a biscuit, "now that we know where we're goin', I think we can just use the ulunsuti to check in there—if Alec and Liz work it right. It's Alec's, so he needs to keep by it, and she's the only one who can scry. So if we go and something happens, they'll at least know what, and be able to take alternative action."

"And we can leave them a couple of scales to use to try to get to Lugh, if they have to," David added.

"Good idea."

"So how're you gonna do it, though, once you're there?" Alec wondered.

David shrugged helplessly. "Unfortunately, I haven't got around to that yet—there's so much to think of all of a sudden. Argghhhh!"

Calvin grinned. "I've been thinkin' about it, though. Since I'm not certain exactly where we'll land—whether in land or water, I think we probably oughta have a contingency." He looked at David. "You still got your other scale?"

"The ones Uki just gave us? I thought you had 'em."

Calvin shook his head. "No, the one Oisin gave you— the one you used to shapeshift."

David reached for the pouch in his pocket, then drew it back quickly, suddenly alarmed. "Uh-uh, no way, man! Not me! Never again! I can read it in your eyes! You want me to skinchange!"

"Uh, not exactly," Calvin replied reasonably. "I think *we* ought to skinchange—or be prepared to if we have to. I think we ought to go through in swimmin' togs, just in case we land in that water we saw. But since we don't know how far we'll have to swim—"

"I'm a good swimmer," David informed him. *"Real* good."

"Yeah, so am I, but that doesn't mean I can swim as far as we may have to. But we could if we became fish, or otters, or whatever."

"No fucking way!"

"But *why?* You've done it before, man."

David swung on him. *"Because,* Fargo, it scared me to death last time! I almost lost myself in the uktena, I did terrible things, and nearly did worse ones! Shoot, man; you were there: you and Liz had to call me back, and that was under pretty controlled conditions! You think if I shift in some other World it's gonna be possible to do that?"

"David—"

"Besides, *you* can't shapeshift!"

"Can't I?"

"You've never done it!"

"No," Calvin shot back. "But I know how it's done, and I've got a spare untreated uktena scale, which is all you need!"

"So you're willin' to try something that major in a World you've never been in with someone who might go wacko on you?"

"That's about the size of it, isn't it?"

David rolled his eyes. "Oh crap, Fargo, I must be get-tin' old. A year ago I'd have said sure, but now I'm really freaked by the whole idea. But . . ." He threw up his hands in resignation. "Oh, why the hell not? I mean my luck's held so far."

"Yeah," Calvin said, grinning. "And besides, we may not even have to do any of this stuff. I'm hopin' we can land in the tower itself, grab Finno, and zap outta there in a blaze of uktena scale sparkles."

"What about the guards?"

"Good point," Calvin acknowledged. "So we just look through, and wait until they're not there. Now come on," he added, draining the last of his cider and rising from the table. "Let's collect some gear and get goin'. I think I've got some spare togs that'll fit you."

"But what about the chains?" Liz reminded them, ris-ing as well.

"I'll take care of that," Sandy assured them. "I've got some bolt cutters somewhere 'round here that'll make mince-meat out of 'em."

David and Calvin changed in the bedroom. Calvin lent David a pair of gym shorts which fit him nicely and a Maggie Valley T-shirt that was far too big. A pair of old sneakers completed the ensemble. "For walkin' on the rocks, man; or in case there're barnacles. Those things'll trash your feet in a second, y'know. If we don't need 'em, we can kick 'em off. Too bad we don't have any life vests," he added with a teasing grin—"just in case *you* need one."

David ignored the jibe and for the next hour and a half helped his friends rummage through the house in search of odd bits that might be useful—rappeling line and tackle, a couple of hunting knives—and a pair of small mixed-nuts cans with plastic lids which caused David to raise an eyebrow in curiosity.

"Survival kits," Sandy informed him, clunking them onto the kitchen counter. "In case you have to stay a while. Hope you won't need 'em, but it's better to be safe than sorry." She proceeded to waterproof them by wrapping them in double plastic bags and tucked the whole mess into a pair of blue denim fannypacks, one of which she handed to David. "You may have to adjust that one, it's mine, but better not to go without."

David shot a sly glance at Calvin. "I thought you could survive with just your teeth?"

The Indian grinned, displaying a fine set of choppers. "I just prefer not to."

David scanned the room, hoping, he supposed, to find one more cause for delay, one more important thing they'd forgotten.

Calvin headed for the door, and paused, then turned and dragged David bodily out. "No way we can really be prepared, man," he confided. "Sometimes you just gotta grab yourself by the balls and jump."

Ten minutes later they rejoined their friends at the Power Wheel. Sandy had rebuilt the fire and it blazed merrily, giving psychological solace where no physical comfort was needed.

"So let me be sure I've got this straight," Sandy said. "You guys are gonna go to wherever this friend of yours is, cut off his chains, and try to bring him back by burning the scales—that's simple enough."

"Except doing it, of course," Liz noted.

''While we keep watch through the ulunsuti?'' This from Alec.

''You got it,'' David replied. He turned to Liz. ''You up to it?''

She sighed and laid her head against his shoulder. ''Sure. It's just that I'm still a little tired—more mentally than anything else, and tired of worrying about you. I know you've gotta do this, but part of me doesn't want you to. Part of me's scared, David, scared you won't come back.''

He nuzzled her hair. ''Hey, girl; don't worry. Well, no, *do* worry—but no more than you have to. I've done stuff like this before and come through okay.''

''Yeah, but you've always been prepared before, and I've always been where I could help you—almost always,'' she amended.

''*See?*'' he chuckled, knowing she was thinking of the time Morwyn had captured him and sent him to raid Lugh's dungeons. ''I did okay then. Luck got me through.''

''And Lugh's connivance.''

''Liz—!''

''Enough, David,'' she whispered. ''Just be careful.'' And with that she kissed him on the lips and released him.

David glanced around, suddenly embarrassed, and realized he'd completely forgotten his companions.

Alec was looking amused, and Calvin and Sandy were simply gazing at each other. Strange, that was, with her so much older—or was it? Alec's ma was older than his dad by almost that same difference. He shrugged. None of his business, anyway.

Calvin and Sandy's fingers trailed apart, and they all reassembled by the fire.

''I think,'' Calvin said, ''that we ought to all focus on our target, and then when we have, David and I go. That sound good?''

''Whatever you say,'' Alec replied.

''Okay, then, folks; let's do it.''

The ritual did not take long to set up: they sat on woven

mats just to the south of the fire, which was in the center, using the same arrangement as before except that this time they each slit a finger with Calvin's knife, placed them on the ulunsuti, and left them for a moment.

"I don't think I need the torque now," Liz told them. "I've sort of got the feel of this thing, though I'm damned if I know how to explain it. But I *do* think it'd help if we were all involved."

And then there was no more time for speculation, because the instant David looked at the ulunsuti, he was sucked into it. *Liz?* he cried in panic, and was suddenly with her; Calvin was there too. But where were Alec and Sandy? They were supposed to be anchoring them. Maybe they were, but then Calvin took control, was showing them the Worlds as Uki had shown them to him in Galunlati: *all* the Worlds—the Lands of Men a bright flame, Galunlati and Faerie—and others plastered over it, overlapping into infinity, all captives of the webwork of the Tracks. This was different, he realized, for here there were no World Walls, just layers. He thought of something, tried to call upon the Sight, and saw the patterns of threads clarify. He gazed at his own World, but saw Faerie overlying it; focused on one part and saw Tir-Nan-Og—and discovered that the beams of light that were the Tracks had a different glitter there where they touched his World. He brushed one, felt it push back, but knew somehow he could get through. World Walls? It hadn't been like that with Calvin and Alec.

Suddenly Liz reasserted herself, and he now saw only the pattern of the Tracks that lay about the Earth. She seemed to be sorting colors, and finally found one: A few silver threads among the gold. There were four of them, leading back to what David vaguely recognized as Scotland. No, wait, there was a fifth that led to Ireland, and . . . a sixth that snaked from Erenn under the golden glitter of Tir-Nan-Og and lay between it and our World, not quite touching.

Liz followed it, and he went with her, with Calvin.

Abruptly he saw it—saw Fionchadd's face as it must be
when colored by Liz's memory and attitudes—a little more
mockery there, a little more threat, but then, she didn't
know him as well as David did. The face solidified,
changed, became Fionchadd's real face, and David became aware of Fionchadd's presence as well. Pain washed
him for an instant, and David flinched, but Liz held firm.
And this time his vision cleared, to show him once again
the sea-girt tower. Then they were drifting toward it, slipping inside: And there was Fionchadd, chained to a bed,
but conscious. David's breath caught with relief. The room
was otherwise empty.

A touch of his shoulder was Calvin drawing him back
to reality. He blinked, nodded, and joined the Indian before the flame. Calvin reached into his pouch and pulled
out two scales, one of which he gave to David. (He'd left
the rest with Sandy, just in case, except for the three they'd
need to return.) David took it and did quick inventory of
his gear: clothes, shoes, fannypack, bolt-cutters, Liz's token for good luck, the separate uktena scale he would use
to shapeshift if he had to, now slung around his neck on
a rawhide cord and clasped by coils of twisted silver. Calvin also wore one that way, along with his own pack, and
the thonged pouch containing the teleportation scales.

"One thing," he whispered to Calvin. "If we have to
shift, our gear won't change with us. If that happens, keep
the scales that get us back 'round your neck, or grab 'em
in your teeth—unless you've got claws that can hold."

"Right," Calvin replied. "I'll keep that in mind.
Now—you ready?"

David swallowed nervously, nodded once more, grabbed
Calvin by the wrist—and cast the scale into the fire, calling
out as he did to Fionchadd. Beside him, distantly, he heard
Calvin do likewise.

Flame filled the world then, and light, heat beyond heat
reached out to embrace David and he was in it—but . . .
but something was wrong! The agony continued longer
than it should—longer and longer. Somehow he felt Cal-

vin's other hand grasp him, heard the Indian's unformed scream—and then it was as if they were being stretched tighter and tighter until their very atoms slid apart—until they could stretch no further, and snapped them back on themselves, shattering utterly.

The world vanished, spun; color, temperature, time itself vanished. And then David felt something solid thump against his back.

He opened his eyes—and saw Liz looking down at him. Other heads swam into view and he gasped. His head hurt abominably, and it was a moment before he realized what had happened, where he was.

"Didn't work," he grunted—and fainted.

It was Calvin that David first saw when he reawakened a short while later. "I guess I'm just like one of those expensive French wines," he managed to mumble. "I don't travel real well."

"I guess you don't," Calvin chuckled. "Remind me not to go on any extended trips with you."

"I'm scared of heights too," David added, then, more seriously: "What happened?"

"We didn't make it," Calvin replied simply. "We got close, I think, but something kept us out."

"Sealed borders, maybe?"

A shrug. "I think it was just that it's too far away. The magic could take us there, but not put us back together."

"Which leaves us back to where we were a day ago," David said wretchedly. "Except we've one less option, and two fewer scales—*and* we've got a lot less time to think up a solution that's gonna be a whole lot tougher."

"Real optimist, ain't you?" Calvin chided him. "I've already thought of one possibility."

David raised a weary eyelid. "Let's hear it."

Calvin took a deep breath. "Okay. Well, Uki and me have spent some time talkin' about the Worlds and all, teleportation, and stuff. He's shown me part of how to make the scales do the job, but we've talked about the ulunsuti, too.''

''Oh yeah?'' Alec interrupted, suddenly interested, and apparently forgetting that he was not supposed to like magic.

''Yeah,'' Calvin went on. ''We know it's really powerful. It can spy on other places and times, though how it does that I can't figure out, 'less it sorta acts as a some kinda reality focus—but anyway, it's partly made of the same stuff as the uktena scales, only a lot more powerful, accordin' to Uki. So one day I asked him what would happen if someone tried the ritual that makes the scales teleport on the crystal itself. I wondered if that might not make something *really* powerful.'' He paused then, for effect.

''Well, *did* it?'' David asked eagerly.

''I don't know,'' Calvin replied. ''Uki said he'd never tried it nor heard of it being tried. He said there were never enough ulunsutis around to risk.''

''So you want to experiment on *mine* now?'' Alec cried protectively.

''If we have to and you're willin','' Calvin replied.

''No way.''

''He told me something else, too, Alec: He told me why he gave you that crystal.''

''And why's that?''

''He's got one of his own, of course; and he used it to look into our futures while we were there the first time. He evidently didn't see a lot of this current crisis, or I think he'd have acted sooner. But he saw you and Liz usin' an ulunsuti to watch me and David pass out of the world. I . . . I thought it was what we just did, and he'd seen it wrong somehow; but it must not've been. He couldn't see clearly, he told me, but he said there was a gate. Until now I thought he just meant the fire you throw the scale into, but now I think he meant a real gate. I think the ulunsuti can open a *way* to another World.''

''Ah-ha!'' David exclaimed. ''So that was what he was

talkin' about when he said that about you attempting what he suspected you would.''

''Yeah,'' Calvin grunted noncommittally.

''So we do it, then?''

''No,'' Calvin replied. ''Not yet. First we need to get closer to where we think Finny is, just in case the gate only opens in space. And we need the blood of some large animal to prime it.''

''Uki told you this?''

''Basically, yes.''

''What this means, folks,'' Alec said, ''is that we've got miles to go before we sleep.''

''What *kind* of large animal?'' Liz wondered suddenly.

''Leave that to me,'' Calvin told her with a smile. ''Come on, gang, we gotta travel.''

''*Tonight?*'' David groaned, unable to suppress a yawn.

''Would you rather regret it a week from tonight?''

''No,'' David sighed, standing and stretching until he thought his back would snap apart. ''I guess you're right.''

''I *know* I am,'' Calvin told him, as he led the way out of the Power Wheel.

Interlude: A Call

(Sullivan Cove, Georgia—Sunday, June 15—11:30 P.M.)

The phone rang loudly in the dark, and it took Dale Sullivan half-a-dozen tries to lay hands on it.

Half awake, he brought the receiver to his ear. "Hello?" he yawned, scratching his side absently.

"Uh, sorry to call so late, but is this Dale Sullivan?" A woman's voice, musical, but a little nervous.

"Uh, yeah, shore is. What can I do for you?"

"Uh, well, you don't know me, but my name's Sandy— Sandy Fairfax. I'm a friend of Calvin MacIntosh's."

"Right," Dale said, still fumbling for the light. "I know him. He's not here now."

"No," Sandy said. "I know he's not. That's why I called you. I think there're some things you ought to know."

Chapter XVI: A Night in the Woods

(Jackson County, Georgia—
Sunday, June 15—very late)

Five hours after leaving Calvin's Power Wheel, whatever apprehensions David might have had regarding the salvation of either his friends or his World had been sublimated by a much more immediate concern: staying awake. In spite of having slept through the morning and most of the afternoon, fatigue had caught up with all of them them again in the last little while and was making its presence known in no uncertain terms—either that, or their biorhythms were screwed up something awful, or maybe it was the simple fact that having your body taken apart and reassembled took as much out of you as a hard day's work, and having your consciousness out flying around had much the same effect.

Unfortunately, it was the middle of night and he was driving to Atlanta.

He'd been fine when they'd decided to press on that evening, hoping to get as close as they could to the real-world analog of Fionchadd's prison under cover of darkness, since none of them were certain what they might have to do or where, except that whatever it came down to would best be accomplished without any unwelcome scrutiny. And he'd still been okay while they'd packed and plotted and putzed around the house far longer than he liked. But now he was beginning to regret not having pushed harder for Sandy to drive, as she'd volunteered to do before Calvin reminded her that she had a post-planning session at her school the next day that she absolutely could not afford to miss. Her peculiar living arrangement had raised some eyebrows over the previous year, and though she was a good and highly-regarded teacher, there were elements in her local school system that disapproved of her lifestyle and would avail themselves of any opportunity to ostracize her, so she had to be careful not to rock the boat too much.

So it was that David found himself piloting the Mustang-of-Death down the long, empty stretches of I-85 between Commerce and Jefferson at just shy of midnight, with Liz and Alec cutting heavy Z's in the right side shot guns, and Calvin only fitfully awake behind him. The trunk was packed with an assortment of gear assembled for a variety of contingencies, but immediate reality had narrowed to the rush of white line across the dark pavement and the harsh whip of wind through all four lowered windows— the car, a '66, had no A.C., and they were in rather close quarters. The noise also helped him stay awake, aided by the lively beat of the B-52s' latest album being tracked on the University of Georgia station they'd been listening to ever since they'd come in range fifteen minutes before. Alec had still been functional then, and it had been his suggestion. He was asleep now, and David was considering several alternatives. He'd have put in a tape, but the humidity had got to his cassette player sometime lately, and after it had eaten the new Midnight Oil, he'd called it quits.

And what he *really* wanted to call quits to was driving. His eyes were about to go: they were burning like crazy and he'd been blinking them far too often, and not because of the Sight. Worse, he had more than once caught himself on the ragged edge of veering off the road. Fortunately there was coffee that Sandy had sent along, but that only made him want to pee again—and they'd made two pit-stops already, to his chagrin. To take his mind off his bladder, he put himself to wondering about it all once more, about Calvin and Sandy—about how in the world they were going to rescue Finno. And with that came not awe, but dread: dread of the pain of the transfer, fear of shapeshifting, of losing himself. The horror of failing and knowing that though his World would probably survive, others might very well not. It was too much, he realized, too much for a guy to have to put up with when he was only five months past eighteen.

He tried to exile the notion, to concentrate on the situation at hand: white lines and a reflective-silver-on-green sign that hove suddenly out of the darkness bearing the legend JEFFERSON: 5 MILES. He started: hadn't the last one said eight? Where had the last three minutes gone? He blinked, shifted position, stuck his head out the window to try to wind-whip himself back to full alert. And cranked the radio louder. A glance in the rearview mirror showed Calvin finally sacked out. So what was the deal . . . ? "We'll go to Atlanta," they'd said, and this was the quickest way. Only which way now? There were several routes to Atlanta, so if they stayed on the interstate, they'd hit the perimeter in about forty-five minutes. The IBM Tower was smack in the middle of town, but what was the best way to get there?

The left side tires crunched gravel and David jerked reflexively, aware he'd faded out while actually making a conscious effort not to. He wrenched the wheel to the right and swore softly. One or the other shook Calvin from his stupor. "Damn, Sullivan, you tryin' to get us *killed?*"

"It'd solve some problems," David retorted wearily.

"Want me to drive?"

"You're no better off than I am, Fargo. But you can talk

to me if you want to, help me stay awake. We've only got another hour or so.''

"Only takes a second to splatter us across four lanes," Calvin yawned back. "But I've been thinkin'. I hate the idea of any more delays, but it's not gonna do any good for us to try this when we're dead on our feet. Besides, there's something else we need anyway, so I was just thinkin' . . . let's see, we're nearly in Jefferson, so why don't you turn off there?''

"Ask and it shall be given," David chuckled wanly, pointing to the exit sign that had obligingly appeared on the horizon. "US 129, to Jefferson, Athens, and Gainesville. Which way now, mon?''

"Left," Calvin instructed. "I know a place near here where we can chill out for a while.''

"You got it," David sighed, and shifted to third as he braked and changed lanes to head up the gentle exit ramp. "Left, you said?" he asked at the top, pausing to vent a yawn of his own.

"Yeah." Calvin yawned back offhandedly.

"Where are we?" Alec muttered from the right side of the back seat where he'd been curled into a cramped and rather angular ball, his long legs a problem in spite of Liz having moved her seat all the way forward.

"Close to our goal," David told him. "Closer, anyway.''

"Wake me up when we're there," he slurred back softly, and closed his eyes once more.

"Just go south," Calvin told David. "It's only 'bout fifteen more miles.''

The distance passed quickly and fairly painlessly. David had finally begun to acquire his second wind, and, now that there were some curves in the road, was finding more to occupy both his hands and his reflexes.

They trundled through tiny, rustic Jefferson and even tinier Arcade, which was hardly even a town; still heading south, traveling through rolling hills that were about an even mix of farms and forest. As they crested a low hill roughly ten miles out of town, Calvin leaned up and spoke into David's ear. "Okay now, slow down, it's up here somewhere, just let me find it—off on the right." David eased off the gas, but still had to brake hard to catch the road that suddenly darted out from behind a stand of pines. The tires squealed in protest. Liz squealed in irritation at having been so inelegantly awakened.

"Where are we?" she mumbled grumpily.

"Just what I was about to ask," Alec chimed in from the back seat. "For that matter, *when* are we?"

"Nearly midnight, and south of Jefferson," David replied. "And closer to bed."

"Not bed, precisely," Calvin corrected. "Let's just say closer to *sleep.*"

"Where to now, Fargo?" David wondered, as they puttered down a narrow paved road between ranks of scruffy pines. A small church and graveyard slipped by on the left, a house on the right, one light burning. Somewhere a dog yipped.

"Couple of miles on, dirt road, lefthand side."

David shrugged and followed Calvin's directions into what was now purely forest, and at last turned onto what looked suspiciously like a well-maintained logging road— until it became progressively more overgrown.

"Here," Calvin said at last.

David took in their surroundings: a small clearing almost overgrown with bushes and long grass, surrounded by more of the tall, stringy pines. He could see sky through their sparse branches, though—and bright stars. The only sound was the hiss of air through needles and the distant cry of an owl.

"You know the owners?"

"Know their son, met him at Boy Scout Camp once. Don't think they'll mind if we camp out here for the night, long as we don't hurt anything—'specially if we don't leave any sign we were here, which means we can't risk a fire. The north may be soggy to the core, but not this part of the country."

"Didn't know you were a Scout," David observed, as he shut off the car and climbed out.

"Wasn't," Calving replied, as he followed suit. "Grandfather took me down to their big set-up at Rainey Mountain a couple of years ago to do a demo. Met this guy there. Visited him again last year while I was roamin' around."

"What kinda demo?" This from Alec.

"Medicinal herbs."

"Oh, right, I'd forgotten about that."

"So where do we sleep?" Alec wondered.

"We've *got* bags," David noted with a touch of sarcasm. "And the ground looks pretty soft over there where the moss is. We can sack out there. Or you can crash in the car if you want to."

"No thanks," Alec protested, stretching again. "I'll take the ground. I've had enough of the M-of-D lately."

"And I'll take wherever you are," Liz whispered, seizing David's hand.

"It'll be the ground then," he said, digging a pair of nylon bags from the trunk. "How 'bout you, Fargo?"

"I'm gonna wander around for a bit," Calvin replied absently. "Be back when I get back."

"Take it easy," David called.

"You got it. Just remember: save me some food. And *no* fire!"

"Right."

David watched, but was never certain when Calvin passed from view among the trees.

"Lord, I'm tired," Alec groaned, as he unrolled his bag and stretched out on a flat, mossy spot.

"You got it," Liz agreed, following his example.

David slipped his bed roll between his friends, then returned to the car for the cooler Sandy had lent them. "There's a little coffee left, and some hot cocoa. Got some cokes, too."

"Cocoa," Liz decided instantly, "to soothe our nerves."

"What's to eat?" Alec inquired.

"Venison sandwiches and tater chips," David replied. "We should've stopped at that last Golden Pantry."

"And called out for pizza?"

"I wish," David sighed, applying himself to a sandwich—homemade bread, as it turned out.

They ate in silence, too burned out for conversation. David wondered again where Calvin was, but knew he could take care of himself. The wild was his turf, after all, and Calvin had essentially been on his own for several years.

Eventually they all snuggled into their bags. David lay back in his, arms folded above his head. The night had warmed up some, and in spite of the pesky mosquitoes, he took off his shirt. He was not surprised when he found Liz's head in the hollow of his arm, her fingers gently stroking his bare chest. He took her hand, held it against his heart. "I'm scared," he whispered to her.

"You're a hero," she whispered back, and then weariness claimed them.

David woke once an indeterminate time later, strangely disoriented. He gently disengaged Liz's hand and looked up. Fog had drifted in from somewhere, dense, white, low-lying stuff that made even the nighted trees go strange where they reared above it. Moonlight caught one of those pines and sprinkled stars among its needles, indistinguishable from those in the sky. A spiderweb glittered between twin dead oaks to the right, wrought in diamonds and silver. He glanced around, searching for Calvin. He didn't seem to be in evidence, but that didn't necessarily mean anything. He could be asleep in the car. Or, if the fog had trapped him somewhere, he was probably woods-wise enough to stay put and wait for morning to burn the stuff away.

And it really did have a calming effect, he realized. He closed his eyes again, slid down in the bag against the chill, and kissed Liz's hand once more.

She mumbled something, and he mumbled back, and then her soft breaths were lost in the murmur of the woods.

Somewhat later, David was startled awake once more by Calvin poking him on the top of the head with a bare toe. He started to protest, but the silhouette raised a finger to its lips and silenced him, motioning him to follow. David nodded, and as quietly as he could slid out of the bag. The fog had lifted a bit, but Calvin's body was still indistinct in the half-light. Must still be a few hours till dawn. David picked up his shoes but did not put them on until he could lean against the hood of the car. His feet made almost no noise among the pine needles.

Thirty or so yards further on, he caught up with Calvin. The Indian was almost naked—clad only in a loincloth that appeared to have been hastily improvised out of one of Sandy's handwoven scarves belted with a length of twine from which depended a matched pair of pouches. Golden uktenas David had not seen before glistened balefully on his muscular arms, though the moon had stolen all their color, and he wore his beaded headband. His hair looked strange, though: slick with moisture—too wet for the fog to account for. When he turned, David saw that his cheeks and chest were painted with designs that might have been hawks or eagles. David felt something thrust into his hands, looked down and saw the coffee thermos. It was cool and wet, as if it too had been dipped in water.

The silence was uncanny, as if the lurking fog swallowed all sound. The fog . . . there was something familiar about it. David caught Calvin gently by the arm, gestured around him, mouthed the word *you* and sketched a question mark in the air.

Calvin nodded almost imperceptibly.

When David had followed Calvin a hundred yards further on, he saw why Calvin had raised this mist. A tiny snow-white deer stood in the trail, its dainty form so bright it reflected the moonlight like a mirror, its delicate antlers extravagantly branched and shining like new-cast silver.

David held his breath, knowing instantly this was no creature of this World. Faerie then? But no, Cherokee myth spoke of such a beast: Awi Usdi, the Little Deer: Lord of Deer-kind in Galunlati. Was this him, and if so, why had Calvin summoned him?

Calvin took a deep breath and settled himself into a low crouch. Very softly he began to chant in the liquid syllables that David knew were his native tongue, then slowly reached into the grasses at his side and pulled out something David recognized: the many-wooded bow Uki had given him their first time in Galunlati. He had one like it; wished he'd remembered to bring it along. Calvin crept forward, once more softly chanting. Abruptly there was movement to the right: a flash of half-seen gray-brown shape amidst the leaves, the white flag of tail that gave its name to the local species of deer.

"Usinuliyu Selagwutsi Gigagei getsunneliga tsudandagihi ayeli-yu, usinuliyu . . ."

—And a sudden tension in the air as Calvin pulled back the string . . .

"Yu!"

The arrow flew.

The whitetail did not cry out, did not move, simply collapsed where it stood. That was strange too, for usually it took arrows a while to kill, but by the time David remembered that, Calvin was beside the creature and wrenching the shaft free of the hollow behind the shoulder blade. The deer's eyes found David's for a moment: clear and moist—then dulled abruptly, and by then Calvin had looked back at him. For the first time he spoke. "Quick! The thermos."

David nodded mutely and provided what he'd been asked. Calvin took it, and with one quick movement of his knife, drew the blade across the deer's throat, holding its head while a sporadic stream of blood dribbled into the container. When it slopped out onto his hands, he stood and backed away.

"Shouldn't we . . . ?" David began, but Calvin shook

his head and pointed behind him. The white deer was back, and with it a thickening of the fog. Indeed, the fog seemed to congregate around them, as if drawn there from all quarters of the wood. Something about it sent chills up David's spine. Calvin waited an instant longer, then took a deep breath and whispered one more chant. The fog melted away then, as if the trees absorbed it; and of neither animal was there any sign.

Calvin turned, grinning, but David could see sweat sheening his body and relief on his starlit features.

"Whew," the Indian whispered. "I wasn't *at all* sure that'd work; that's the first time I ever tried it on my own."

"Tried what?" David asked. "Or rather, which?"

"To raise a fog, to start with," Calvin replied. "Uki taught me that. It functions as a gate between here and Galunlati but you can only use it at certain times and for certain reasons. The ritual Oisin used to send us through the first time's too complicated. Mine's easier—but before you ask: no, we can't use it to get to wherever Finny is. Uki wasn't even sure it'd work here, but I had to try. That's why I left: I had to go purify myself: go to water, perform the ritual as a man of the Ani-Yunwiya."

"And let me guess," David appended. "You summoned the king deer and got him to intercede."

"I *had* to, Dave. I could've killed a deer tonight anyway, probably, 'cause there're certainly plenty around. But it'd have been out of season, even if I'd thanked it and covered the blood; so I had to get Awi Usdi to intercede, to explain my errand—though he already knew about it—and to take the body away. To leave it'd raise too many questions. Besides, I owe it to my friend whose land this is. Awi Usdi has promised me he will bring another deer here, one from beyond these lands, one with many points. No one will know."

David's gaze wandered back to the thermos in his hand. "But why'd you even bother to bring me along? Surely you could have done this alone. Not that I minded, or anything," he added hastily.

"We are friends, brothers almost, and I thought you would like to witness," Calvin replied simply. "And also, I needed someone to carry the thermos, 'cause I was afraid the taint of civilization would weird out the magic. Anyway," he added, "we need warm blood to accomplish our mission, and that oughta keep it that way for a couple of hours. I couldn't tell you earlier, 'cause I was afraid even that would queer the ritual. But once the fog came, once I spoke to Awi Usdi, I needed a second. Thanks, man, for being there."

"My pleasure," David said, thinking of just how wonderful it had been: a new mystery. Suddenly he realized just how much he missed magic. That it was Cherokee, more his regional heritage than any rites of the Sidhe, made it all the better. He wondered suddenly if Calvin would help him learn it.

They had reached the car now, and Calvin ducked around to the driver's side and stripped off the loincloth, then began wiping away his warpaint with a sock. Naked in the moonlight, David saw him briefly as he really was: a boy, true; but a Man of Power as well, that power reflected in the proud, keen lines of his body.

Calvin wasted no time. Jeans and falcon T-shirt returned, ditto his Frye boots, minus one sock. David checked his watch, startled to see that it was nearly four o'clock. "Best we ride again, I guess," he whispered wearily. "I'll go wake the others."

"Right," Calvin agreed. "We still need to get to Atlanta as early as we can and find some place where we can work what I've got in mind. A patch of woods would be best. Fortunately, the place is full of 'em."

"Right," David echoed uncertainly, and left to awaken Liz with a kiss.

"What time is it?" she asked sleepily, as David applied himself to the much more recalcitrant Alec. "I thought we were gonna sleep till dawn."

"Can't," David told her. "Somebody's liable to catch

us and ask questions. Calvin's got what he came for. We need to move, need to be in Atlanta in about an hour. That'll still give us a little time before sunup.''

Liz nodded and helped herself to the last of the cocoa in the remaining thermos, while Calvin came up to help rouse Alec—which was not a thing easily accomplished. David risked a glance at the sky. It was clear, but already lightening in the east. They'd have to hurry. But, he realized, he felt good. The sleep might have done part of it, little though there had been, but he suspected magic had something to do with it as well.

"I've been thinking," Liz said a moment later. "Since we're this close, maybe I ought to scry again. I got a sense of Atlanta last time, but maybe it was just trying to give me a familiar landmark, or something. One thing, though: I . . . I'm not sure, but I think the second time it didn't look quite the same. It was like . . . like the place had shifted, or something.''

David eyed her warily. "If you really need to . . ."

Liz shook her head. "I'm not wild about doing it again, that's for sure; it gives me a headache. But we really don't want to go awry.''

"Good point," Alec acknowledged from where he was combing his wayward hair with the aid of David's outside mirror.

By the time Alec and David had rolled up their sleeping bags and put away the night's detritus, Liz was ready.

"I won't ask you about that little errand of yours and Calvin's," she whispered to David when he caught her momentarily alone. "But I hope an explanation'll come along some time.''

"Soon enough," David replied, and then Alec and Calvin returned and it was time to begin.

They did not bother with the torque this time, nor did they prime the ulunsuti with blood. "We'll do that if we have to," Liz informed them, "but it's like—I don't know. Scrying like I used to do was so chancy, so like being lost in your head. This makes it easier to tune. It's like cutting with a sharp knife instead of a dull one.''

''Right,'' Alec said. ''Now come on, we're burning daylight.''

''*Dark,*'' David amended. ''We're burning *dark.*''

''Which is what we need,'' Calvin chuckled. ''So let's get started.''

Liz nodded and stared at the crystal. David did likewise, trying to see what she saw—and did: the tower again, the surrounding sea once more, briefly Fionchadd in his prison. And then she drew back—slowly this time, searching for the World Walls she knew must lie close around, though below was only water.

And found them—passed through—and gazed not upon Atlanta, but on gray stone. She blinked, almost cried out, for David saw her lips part and her jaw stiffen. But she faltered only a moment, and drew further back. The stone vanished abruptly, and then David realized what had happened. The hidden country had shifted slightly. No longer did the tower lie beside the IBM Tower; now it was inside Stone Mountain.

David expected Liz to yank them out immediately, but instead she kept drawing back slowly, one part of her mind still trained on the landscape of the hidden country, the other on the World it overlaid. Further and further, until she found the borders of the one and passed beyond them.

''Jesus!'' David gasped at last. ''What happened?''

''It moved,'' Alec replied. ''—I think. I think it's sort of a free-floating World that kinda drifts above our own.''

''You mean the seas have no limit?'' Calvin asked.

''No, I think they've got limits, but there's nothing beyond them—*nothing,* Calvin. Which means that unless the ulunsuti can teleport us as well as open a gate, we've got to be closer, close enough for us to be inside the borders when we go over.''

''*How* close?''

''How far can you swim?''

''Far enough.''

"Well, looks like you're at least gonna have to be able to swim the radius of Stone Mountain."

"Or more," Alec appended. "We'll have to find a place to work outside."

"Right," said David. "Let's travel."

Chapter XVII: Diving In

(east of Atlanta, Georgia—
Monday, June 16—dawn)

David was becoming increasingly distrustful of the sky. It was pinkening far too rapidly, and traffic was picking up much faster than he liked as he urged the Mustang along the last scrap of rural four-lane east of Snellville. Once there, they'd be slowed considerably, Calvin had warned, so it was better to make tracks now. Not quite a suburb, more a series of overgrown strip-towns, half the workforce of Atlanta bedroomed in the burgeoning counties they were now traversing. David sighed, yawned, and tried to steel himself for the travail ahead.

Far too quickly, anticipation became reality, and he found his progress slowed to a nerve-wracking crawl. He eyed the patchwork of shopping centers, gas stations and fast-food joints wearily, fearing the day his own home county might take on that same tawdry veneer. A traffic light slowed him more, and his stomach growled as he found himself gazing wistfully at the I-Hop up ahead.

"Okay, Fargo," he prompted a couple of miles further on. "We're nearly there. Any idea where we do this deal?"

"Yeah," Calvin replied cryptically. "But we've gotta get closer, first."

David grunted and moved on with the traffic, giving a finger to the guy in the new red Camaro that honked at him from behind, then whooshed around him. The next several miles were more of the same, and then he crested a hill and caught first sight of their goal: the largest chunk of exposed granite in the world, according to the park brochures: Stone Mountain. Here, now, it resembled a beached whale, dark in the morning half-light except for a ruddiness to the east and the blink of light from the broadcast tower that marked its summit. He could not see the Confederate Memorial that was carved into its near side because of a stand of scraggly pines, but had seen it on plenty of other occasions, notably the Scottish Festival that was held there every October.

The road lost a lane as it narrowed into the feeder for the Stone Mountain Freeway, then widened again almost immediately as another highway merged in from the left. The mountain was a real landmark now, dominating most of the view on his side. And he could finally make out the memorial: Generals Robert E. Lee and Stonewall Jackson, and Confederate President Jefferson Davis preserved for all eternity in granite. David wondered what they would have thought about their carved visages standing sentinel to a sliver of Faerie.

"Left lane," Calvin noted.

"Got it." David started to swerve that way, but was cut off by a low-flying Nissan Maxima.

"Now!" Calvin supplied obligingly, gaze fixed over his shoulder.

A minute later they exited onto Mountain Industrial Boulevard, and a handful of turns after that, were enmired in the sprawl of subdivisions nearby. David wondered about that, doubting they'd ever find a place private enough for magic this close to Atlanta on the one hand, yet with easy access to the park on the other. Nevertheless, he followed Calvin's directions and turned into a narrow street marked by a DEAD END sign. Two blocks further, he turned left into the driveway of an unkempt-looking ranch house.

No lights burned, and the driveway was empty except for a patchwork of oil stains, none of them particularly fresh. The lawn could also have stood a good mowing.

"Home," Calvin stated simply. " 'Cept that Dad's probably not here—'least I hope he's not. Last I heard he was workin' on one of John Portman's new projects 'round on the other side, which means he's probably already taken off. No car here, anyway."

"Good enough," David muttered offhand. "But why here?"

"Show you in a minute," Calvin replied easily. "Let's get unloaded first."

Five minutes later they were ready, each hoisting a knapsack onto his or her back. Probably too much stuff, David thought, but then he had no sure way of knowing where they'd be going or when, so they'd crammed them full of food, cooking utensils, weaponry, bed rolls, and spare clothing—Sandy was just enough larger than Liz that her loaner togs merely looked stylish and Calvin had supplied David and Alec, both of whom were slimmer than he, though Alec was an inch or so taller.

David eyed the Mustang uncertainly. "Okay to park it here?"

Calvin shrugged. "We shouldn't be here long if we're lucky, and if we're not . . . well, we'll worry about that when it happens. I reckon I oughta leave a note, though, just in case, so Dad won't have your wheels towed."

"You don't get along, do you?" David inquired hesitantly.

Another shrug, then a long, awkward pause while Calvin contrived a quick message and stuck it under the wiper. "No great shakes," he replied finally. "He denied his heritage, which I don't approve of, but was his right. But then he tried to deny me mine, and that *wasn't* his right. We haven't spoken since."

"Whew!" David hadn't realized what a personal risk Calvin was taking here. *Daniel in the Lion's Den,* he wondered, *or The Prodigal Son?*

"This way." Calvin motioned them toward a locked gate in the hurricane fencing at the side. A second later, he had picked the lock and let them through. A brace of beagles raced up to him, leaping and hopping and raising their earnest brown-and-white muzzles to be cupped with two hands and fondled.

"Rabbit hounds," Calvin offered by way of explanation. "One thing Dad's *not* abandoned."

David squatted, obligingly petted a pup, and followed Calvin across the enclosed backyard, noting as they jogged along that the surrounding yards were similarly blockaded. The back of the lot fronted on trees, though: *lots* of trees, mostly oaks and maples.

"I'm afraid we'll have to climb over," Calvin apologized.

"No problem," David acknowledged, eyeing the fence, which was about as tall as he was. One smooth leap and he'd reached the metal pipe at the top; a twist of legs and torso, and he was over. Calvin did likewise, Liz and Alec followed more slowly. One of the numerous pockets that decorated Alec's jungle camos snagged and ripped, sending a shower of coins to the leaves on the other side. He scooped them up quickly and followed his friends.

Green enfolded them, and cool dimness, and suddenly they might have been miles from any city. Oaks grew close around, so full of thick undergrowth of dogwoods and rhododendron that it made David think of home. They were on a trail of sorts, and simply kept Calvin in sight, since he obviously had some destination in mind.

An instant later David knew they had reached it: a low, grassy knoll shielded by an arc of trees on one side and by a lower pile of dense underbrush on the other. A closer examination showed rooftops below. Evidently this was territory that had been abandoned and forgotten when the subdivision had been built: a scrap of wild trapped between backyards; the barrier below made of the remnants of these same woods simply bulldozed down and left to rot.

Only they hadn't exactly rotted. Bushes had claimed them, and then had come the kudzu. Now it was an island-kingdom of green in the heart of Atlanta's suburbs, giving an uninterrupted panorama of Stone Mountain to the left and unexpectedly close, and to the right of the not-so-distant sprawl of Atlanta. He could see the skyline clearly, a surprising number of lights still on (or left on) at the early hour, and a steady circulation of moving lights within it, as the South's largest city came slowly awake.

"This do?" Calvin inquired, grinning with so much self-satisfaction it was almost infectious. "I found it when I was a kid. Spent a good five years worth of afternoons here just daydreamin'. Lost my virginity right over there, saw a UFO one time."

"Neat," David exclaimed, thinking of Lookout Rock back home, his Place of Power.

"It borders the park on the left," Calvin pointed out. "And there're backyard fences 'round most of it. I doubt anybody'll ever find it."

"They will, though," Alec sighed wistfully. "Nothing ever stays the same."

"But maybe not in my lifetime," Calvin replied. "That's all I care about—all I *can* care about." He motioned them to a spot on the ground where a slab of mossy granite usurped the weeds and grasses.

"Best we grab a snack and get to," David suggested, slinging down his pack. He reached inside and dragged out an assortment of candybars they'd bought earlier that morning at an all-night convenience store in Winder. He claimed a Butterfinger, handed Liz a Hershey's and Alec the Pay Day he always chose. Calvin did not take one (he was evidently on some kind of fast), but was already fumbling around in his pack. A moment later he pulled out a plastic bag.

"Earth of Galunlati," he volunteered. "I think it might help a little."

David watched as Calvin crossed to a small patch of bare ground a little to the right of the stone, opened the bag, and began to trickle the sand between his fingers in a pattern David soon recognized as the cross-in-circle of a Power Wheel. Calvin stared at it an instant longer, then nodded, and resealed the bag. "Not as round as I'd like, but it'll have to do." He glanced up at his companions. "Alec, my man, looks like you're gonna have to be a part of this, since you're the Lord of the Ulunsuti. So you better come with me and Dave and help us get ready." He paused, staring at Liz whose eyes had narrowed with either hurt or resentment. "Sorry, Liz, but this is boy stuff. Partly 'cause of modesty—yours *and* ours—and partly 'cause the ritual says that's how it's gotta be. Don't worry, though; you'll have plenty to do, I promise. I don't know how long the gate'll be open, though—if I can even *get* it open. So we'd best be primed to move quickly. Dave, you comin'?"

David started at the summons, having almost dozed off, then nodded, snagged his backpack, and followed his buddies into the shadows of the woods.

They went only far enough down the trail to shield themselves from the clearing and, imitating Calvin's example, stripped. Once bare, Calvin poured water from his canteen into his hands and swabbed it across as much of the other two boys as the quantity permitted. "No time to go to water," he explained. "Got this at the creek I bathed in last night, though it's mixed with a bit of water from Galunlati. Hope it'll be sufficient. From now on, just follow my lead as much as you can. I really shouldn't talk much, and I've got a bunch of chants to do, so just kinda go with the flow, okay?" He paused, looking at Alec, who was, in turn, looking very uncomfortable, and not just from being bare-assed naked. "Sorry, man, but the outfits are part of the ritual—just in case. I'll be dressed the same, and I'll do what I can for Liz, but since me and Dave are actually goin' through, we'll have to make allowances for that."

"Huh?" Alec replied, confused.

"Basically, a lot of this is gonna have to be your baby,

Alec, since I can't exactly stay here to supervise. Also, since it's your ulunsuti, you're gonna have to do the part of the ritual that involves it—which is most of it. Now, I need to shut up, and get the show rollin'. Like I said, just follow my example. I'll give you a quick run through once we're finished here.''

Alec grimaced, but nodded and folded his arms.

Calvin reached into his medicine bag and pulled out a lump of waxy red material somewhere between clay and crayon. With it he quickly sketched a series of designs on his forehead, cheeks, chest, arms, and thighs—mostly lightning bolts and stylized falcons. As he made the first stroke, he began to chant slowly: *"Sge! Ha-nagwa asti unega aksauntanu usinuli anetsa un-atsanuntselahi aktati adunniga . . ."*

The chant droned on as he marked Alec, then David with similar lightning bolt patterns, though he drew a caricature 'possum on David's chest and, after a moment's consideration, a horned serpent pierced by a staff on Alec's.

The rest went quickly: David resumed the cut-off jeans, white T-shirt, and sneakers Calvin had leant him before, while Calvin vested first himself, then Alec in makeshift loincloths (apparently he'd appropriated *two* of Sandy's woven scarves). A short while later he was ready. He paused, looking at David, eyes a-twinkle.

''Scared, Sullivan?''

''Shitless,'' he admitted. ''But I've done it before, and it's gotta be done.''

''Good man,'' Calvin said. ''We'll go through the gate together, but I'll need you to lay low during the ceremony. I wish I'd thought to bring gear for all three—shoot, all *four* of us, but I didn't. Anyway, you'll have to look after my mundane stuff while I open the gate. Once through, I'll change if I have to. This stuff''—he gestured down at the flimsy loincloth—''ain't exactly made for heavy duty action. I'd hate to fuck it up. 'Sides,'' he added wryly, ''Sandy made it.''

"You got it, man," David assured him, and retrieved Calvin's pack as well as his own, then followed the would-be shamans back to the clearing.

Liz met them there, rising from where she'd been munching sandwiches. David took a swig of the Gatorade she offered him, and Calvin and Alec helped themselves to long draughts as well.

Liz was staring at them speculatively, saying a lot more with her eyes than her mouth, and a lot of it related to sexism. Finally Calvin rolled his eyes and shrugged. "Oh, why the hell not?" he muttered. And with that, he emptied the last of the canteen into his hands and anointed as much of Liz as clothing and decorum allowed. Warpaint followed, lightning bolts on her cheeks and a stylized flame on her forehead. "Red-haired woman with lightning eyes," he murmured. "This I name you."

Liz simply smiled, but David could see that the ritual had meant a lot to her.

Finally Calvin drew Alec aside, spoke to him briefly, then motioned David and Liz to join them at the makeshift Power-Wheel. "Ready?"

"I guess," Liz whispered. "What'll we do?"

"What I tell you," Calvin replied softly. "I'll be master of the ritual, but Alec'll do the actual motions. As soon as the gate opens—*if* it opens—me and Dave'll jump through. Your job is to keep it open if you can. Don't ask me how. Since I don't know how this'll work, I can't offer any suggestions. If . . . if we *don't* come back, give my regards to Sandy and tell her I love her."

"I don't have to tell you that, do I?" David whispered to Liz in turn, as he enfolded her briefly in his arms. The kiss was the shortest but sweetest he could remember, and even when they broke apart the feel of her body burned against his own like the shadow of a flame. A rough hug for Alec, a high-five from Calvin, and they began.

Calvin had laid out the Power Wheel so that each quadrant encompassed a cardinal direction. Alec was already in the South, but he motioned David to the north. Liz took the west, and he the east. Calvin's fannypack, full of six return-trip scales, a spare T-shirt, and cut-offs, they left outside the circle but ready to hand. (The survival kit wouldn't fit with the rest of the stuff, and he thought he'd need clothes more—besides, David still had *his* kit and pack—to which the bolt-cutters had been firmly affixed with a generous application of duct tape.) The rest of the scales were in David's backpack (Calvin's was again too full), which would not be going.

Calvin took a deep breath, retrieved the mysterious bag Uki had given him from his knapsack, and withdrew a smaller pouch, which he handed to Alec, who untied it and emptied the contents onto the center of the Wheel. "Shavings from a blasted tree," Calvin explained softly. "Strong medicine." He glanced up at Alec. "From here on, say what I say, and if I hand you something, use it like I told you."

Another bag yielded several small twigs, which Alec shaped into a pyramid, naming the species of tree or shrub as he did: "Cedar . . . pine . . . spruce . . . holly . . . laurel."

"All the plants of vigilance," Calvin noted, "so as to see between the Worlds."

Alec poured various herbs around it then, but David could not identify their scents, nor did Calvin identify them.

Finally came a dribble of some thin, oily liquid—and fire from flint and pyrite expertly struck (one of the fruits of Alec's five years in the Boy Scouts). Nothing man-made, David noted. Nothing that was not part of the natural world.

The fire blazed up immediately, far brighter than the material that comprised it would have suggested, nor did it smoke much. And, David noted to his surprise, neither was the material quickly consumed.

"Ulunsuti," Calvin prompted. Alec nodded resignedly, took the jar, and removed the crystal slowly, almost reverently. He placed it on a circle of deerskin before him

and began to repeat the chants Calvin fed him a few at a
time. And as he did he sprinkled the crystal first with more
of the strange oil, then with a second mixture of herbs.
David was not surprised when it began to glow. A longer
chant, and then Calvin took a deep breath and looked up.
"All blood or bone from a beast that lives in two worlds.
All leaf and root from plants that haunt the edges."

David nodded, knowing of this prime rule of Cherokee
magic: that things that were of more than one category
were sacred: bats, that flew like birds but had fur; frogs
that lived in land *and* water—he supposed plants like cattails that likewise grew in both.

"And now the catalyst." He motioned for David to get
the thermos. David gave him a quick thumb's up and
reached outside the Wheel to snag the chrome-and-plastic
cylinder. At another sign, he unscrewed the cap and
poured its contents into a pottery bowl Alec took from
Calvin and held between his hands until the still-warm
deer blood lapped against the rim. David returned the not-
quite-empty thermos to his lap (fearing that it would not
do for so mundane an object to touch Calvin's sacred
sand), and folded his hands around it expectantly. Wind
brought him a flash of odor: herb-smoke and fresh blood.
Alec lowered the bowl and set it before him, then took the
ulunsuti and gradually submerged it in the blood, once
more repeating the chant as Calvin uttered it.

David craned his neck, squinting through the rising pall
of smoke to see the bowl. The ulunsuti was glowing more
brightly, of that there was no doubt. And the blood level
was dropping as if the crystal sucked it in. Finally, though,
the talisman seemed to be sated, and no more blood was
absorbed, though a small quantity still remained in the
bottom of the bowl. The ulunsuti's glow had shifted, however: was now as red as the solar disc that was finally
peeking around the edge of the woods to the east.

"Two things left, folks," Calvin whispered. "We vi-
sualize our destination, and when it's there, be prepared
to act. Oh, and one more thing. It oughta remain open as

long as there is warmth in the blood. After that, who can say?''

David sighed apprehensively and tried to stretch as much as he could without disturbing the ritual, then followed Calvin's instructions and stared at the ulunsuti. This was getting to be the easy part: gazing at a rock and willing it to show him what he wanted. And this time it was made easier by the arcane glow that drew his eye toward it almost against his will. Brighter and brighter, a silver-red glow. Silver—that made it easier. He tried to key onto Fionchadd, caught an image of him writhing on the bed. He tried to call out to him, to send him words of comfort, tell him that help was on the way—but could not. Liz's mind overruled his: *out*, it seemed to say. *You must appear outside and try to get in. There appears to be some kind of barrier with this technique.*

Abruptly Fionchadd's face vanished, to be replaced by the tower, the strip of rocky land—and the endless waves. The tower was closer than it had been before, he realized with considerable relief—and then it was as if he saw two things simultaneously: Stone Mountain and the tower, each overlapping the other. And the water—water flowing around them, under them, yet not touching them.

"Christ," he heard Alec whisper.

"Hold," Calvin ordered, and David was aware that Alec had lifted the ulunsuti from the bowl and was slowly easing it toward the flame. One part of him glimpsed the crystal, one part the fire between them, one part a tower, and one part the clearing and the faces of his friends. And then David finally realized what Alec was about. Before he knew it, his best friend had thrust the crystal barehanded into the flames. He held it there for a moment, and David could see the pain etching itself across his face. And then he saw nothing at all, as the flame leaped up to form an archway as tall as he was through which he saw the sea-girt tower that imprisoned Fionchadd.

Somehow Calvin was beside him. David reached down, checked his fannypack, the uktena scale at his throat, along with Liz's token, the knife that hung sheathed at his hip. Calvin quickly donned his own scale and pack and weapon. David stared ahead, saw the gate to the Otherworld widen, grabbed Calvin's hand, and leapt.

—Or was pulled, he never afterwards remembered.

Chapter XVIII: Rescue

(a tower—no date—morning)

David had been prepared for everything—he thought—
except for the possibility that the World which enclosed
Fionchadd's prison might be bitterly cold. As it was, icy
air bit at him before he was even aware of falling; and he
smashed flat into frigid water from something like six feet
up in the king of all belly-floppers. The air exploded from
his lungs, almost stunning him, and the unbelievable cold
made him gasp double and shocked him enough to send
him flailing wildly. It was like the polar sea must be, and
the tiny rational part of him that was still alert wondered
what the freezing point of salt water was. Or *was* it even
salt? He tasted the rime already frosting his lips . . . Salt
indeed, though strangely seasoned. But then the gravity of
his situation dawned on him. He *had* to move, and quickly,
or he'd freeze to death. Already he'd lost track of his fingers and toes, and his ankles and wrists were no great
shakes, either. "Help!" he yelled, thinking inanely that
Liz or Alec might be able to throw him a line, but then a
glance over his shoulder showed him the gateway: a fiery
shimmer in the air two yards above his head. He could not
see his friends.

And Calvin? Jesus, where *was* Calvin? David spun around, dog-paddling in place. There was the tower, not three hundred feet away, gleaming silver-pink in the morning light—but no grinning Amerindian. Yet they had come together! "Calv—" David began desperately, but the cry became a cough as a wave swamped his mouth. He ducked under, and when he rose again—sputtering and gasping, teeth chattering beyond control—Calvin's head rose with him. He dared a sigh of relief, but then he saw that the Indian's eyes were wild with shock, and didn't seem to be focusing quite right.

"Oh . . . God, Sullivan," Calvin choked between bouts of uncontrollable shivering. "Oh Jesus God, what've we got into? I—" His words were cut off by another wave, and this time David made a frantic grab for his friend and held him up. His flesh was cold as ice.

"Quick, Fargo," David gritted. "We gotta get movin', and get movin' fast. Swim as quick as you can. Hang onto me if you have to; holler if you can't, and don't be proud. Ain't no tellin' what might be in this water."

"You . . . g-got it," Calvin managed.

David caught him by the shoulder. "You okay? I mean for sure?"

The grimace that followed could have meant anything, but David thought Calvin's eyes looked a little less wild. "Any trouble at all, you let me know!"

"Right on." And with that he jackknifed forward and surged toward the tower.

David gave Calvin a few yards lead to see that he was in fact more or less competent, then started after him, wishing he didn't have an awful sick feeling in his stomach.

Fortunately, their goal was fairly close—much closer than it had appeared through the gate. And equally fortunate, they were both good swimmers, though David thought once about reaching for the uktena scale that hung around his throat, trying to imagine what sort of beast might be able to live in such frigid conditions, and finding himself unable to think of anything but narwhales, which he didn't want to be. But the cold bored into him again and all he could think about was swimming: urging his body onward, trying to fight the numbness that crept in at him, turning every breath to a tortured gasp.

Faster and faster, harder and harder, keeping Calvin always in sight to his right, searching for any signs of faltering.

Closer and closer, and the waves were becoming much choppier as they approached the tiny island. He found himself probing downward with his all-but-numb feet, hoping to find some trace of bottom, but having no luck. Apparently the rock that supported the tower rose sheer from some unfathomable seabed.

Another wave blurred his vision, its twin choked him, a third grabbed him and flung him abruptly forward, narrowly missing the sheer escarpment that suddenly reared before him, its lip more than a yard above his head.

A fourth wave drew him back, but the next hurled him onward again, and this time he was prepared, this time he managed to grab the top edge of the rock face and hang on. He remained there a moment, panting, before he was finally able to summon enough strength to mount the final effort that sent him scooting over the jagged stone onto solid ground.

"Calvin?" he shouted, and realized dumbly that he'd lost sight of his companion again.

"Calvin!"

"Dave . . ."

"Where . . . ?"

"Dave, I . . . I can't hold on much longer."

David followed the cries to a higher shore maybe five yards off to his right. He peered over the edge of the cliff and finally saw his friend. Evidently the last batch of waves had separated them and flung Calvin toward a slicker, steeper bit of coast. He had caught the upper edge, though

only with his fingertips, but could find no other holds and
lacked the strength to pull himself further. And meanwhile
the waves were pounding at him—not helping, not thrusting him up to a better hold, but dragging him down, their
crests like cold, cruel knives. "Hang on, man," David
yelled, as he flung himself flat on the shore and slid a
hand down the cliff to grasp Calvin's wrist. "Hang on guy,
I gotcha!"

"You think I might *not?*" Calvin somehow dared to
laugh, as he freed his other hand and grabbed David's
forearm, which in turn freed him to maneuver the other.
At first David wasn't sure he was going to be able to make
it, since Calvin outweighed him by a good fifteen or twenty
pounds—especially as he could barely feel his own fingers
and doubted his friend's were much better. But with Calvin's persistent struggles and one final shove from a co-
operative wave, he managed to haul his friend ashore. Only
then did they realize how dangerously chilled they were—
for though the air itself was warmer than the water by
some small fraction, there was a wind that flung around
the base of the tower and sucked even that embryonic
comfort from their bodies with shocking rapidity. David
tried to recall everything he knew about hypothermia.
There were various stages, he knew, each characterized by
certain effects and responses, including a euphoric stage
that was *really* dangerous because it gave you a sense of
well-being right before it zapped you. Cold was the one
thing they had not counted on.

"Quick, to the tower!" he cried, as soon as Calvin had
found his feet. "We've gotta get out of this wind and dry
off a little; gotta take a minute to think."

"That's about all we can spare, too," Calvin replied,
rubbing his body frantically. "My hair hurts," he added
with a solemn chuckle.

"Mine too," David assured him, and dragged him into
the shelter of a projecting buttress. The low morning sun
lanced in there, and it was noticeably warmer. A quick

check in Calvin's pack rendered relatively dry cut-offs and T-shirt which David envied. "Jesus," Calvin whispered, as he shucked the loincloth and donned them, "I had no idea I was *that* far gone. Damn near went into shock there."

David started to reply that he was pretty burned out too, but then remembered that Calvin had gotten even less sleep than he.

"So what next?" Calvin wondered, apparently back to normal—for a person covered with goose-bumps from head to foot and shivering like an epileptic. Not that he was any better.

David surveyed the section of tower beside him. It was even rougher than it had appeared through the ulunsuti; was fissured and snarled with patterns that might have been natural or might have been carved, all wrought of the silver stone that comprised it. "Don't remember there bein' a door, but I don't reckon it'd hurt to look."

"Right."

David glanced back at him—and froze with his reply on his lips. Something had moved out there in the choppy, frigid sea; he was sure of it. Calvin noted his frown and followed his line of sight, shading his narrowed eyes with a hand. "What's up?"

"I don't know," David whispered—just as a slick golden shape broke water, followed immediately by a smaller, more angular form he thought might have been a fin.

"Dolphins, maybe?" Calvin suggested, though something in his eyes told David he didn't believe it.

David backed further around the tower—maybe ten feet. "I don't think so," he said slowly, straining his eyes.

Nothing.

And then—so quickly it took his breath—a shape reared from the cold silver sea not twenty feet to their left. Up and up it rose, towering over their heads. Foot-long claws slapped like matching daggers onto the shore of their suddenly precarious refuge.

Claws, yes: long silver hooked ones—and paws to retract them into: webbed and covered with sleek golden fur like a seal's. But the head that gazed down on them was like nothing David had seen in all his forays into other Worlds. Like a lion, it was—but like a shark as well: longish muzzle, a cat's slitted nostrils, fangs like a sabretoothed tiger backed up by the more extravagant dentition of a shark—all beneath slitted eyes as big as baseballs and greenly glowing, and the whole at least four feet across.

David caught only the smallest glimpse of body before he grabbed Calvin and ran—but that glimpse showed him a form at once mammalian and piscean—as if a smilodon had been raped by a great white shark and born hideous offspring. For the monster, though forelegged like an enormous lion, had the scaly hindquarters of a fish.

And now it was coming after them, and they had, David realized grimly, nowhere to go. There was water on all sides, the tower was only fifty or so feet in diameter—and the beast itself was easily half that long. It'd get them, sure enough, or the water would—if not the icy wind.

Unless . . .

"Quick, Fargo, the scales!"

"Huh? We can't make *fire* here. There's no t—"

"Who's talkin' about fire?" David yelled, reeling frantically on the rawhide thong that secured his uktena scale. "I'm talkin' 'bout the *other* scales—the shapechangin' ones. Quick, think small and portable and quick. Maybe we can hide in one of these fissures."

"Huh?"

" *'Possum*, Calvin, think *'possum!*"

And with that David grabbed Calvin's hand and clamped it around the scale that hung at his throat. He thought desperately, sparing a moment to glance toward where the monster had subsided back into the sea, hoping against hope that the thing could not come fully ashore, could only make frantic, sea-based lunges.

"Possum . . . ?"

David squinted his eyes almost shut, not daring to close them entirely for fear of unseen attack. If only he could focus on one thing for just a minute, banish fear for a bare sixty seconds. *Come on now, Sullivan, you can do it,* he scolded himself. " 'Possum, 'possum, 'possum," he began to chant. White 'Possum, he added, and felt the first twinge in his stomach that heralded the change. He did close his eyes, then; though fear almost consumed him, and he prayed the sea-lion would not come at them again in the instant that remained. What was 'possum? It was small, it was quick, it was furtive, it had delicate feet that were sensitive and could climb, it had a long pointy nose that could sort out odors. It couldn't see well, but had good instincts. It was . . .

The change came over him so quickly he gasped. He had only time to force Calvin's hand hard enough over his own scale to bring forth blood and hope the change would work as well for the Indian, hope their mingled blood would do the trick, when he lost himself in the agony of the shift. One moment he stood, the next was arching forward as his spine and joints shrank and re-aligned. He felt his face stretch, his vision blur and alter to read a different part of the spectrum; was vaguely aware of a thrusting at the base of his spine, of a sudden blessed wash of warmth as fur sprouted all over him.

Abruptly he was on all fours and tangled in something—his clothes; they'd not shifted with him—not that he'd expected them to. And what of Calvin? Yeah, there he was—another 'possum, ruddier than that bit of himself he could see, and darker about the head.

But then he had no more time to watch, for a huge splash behind him made him switch around, and he saw the monster again, only this time it had dragged itself wholly out of the water at a point where the shoreline was lower, and was making deliberate haste toward them.

"Run!" he hissed, and then *was* running, sparing only a moment to grab the cumbersome fannypack with his

teeth. (The changing scale was still on a thong around his neck where he prayed it would stay, along with Liz's token; the knife was a no-go, as were his clothes). Calvin seemed to be loitering, though, and David had to zip back and urge him along with a sharp smack of naked tail against his furry russet rump. *That* got him going: pack, changing scale, and all.

Door? Where was the door?—as they scurried around the base of the tower. Sounds behind them, enhanced beyond human hearing: a fishy-catty smell that made him want to gag. Perception strange: movement quick, but so little ground covered, and the dratted fannypacks kept snagging as they dragged across rough rocks—and that wasn't even counting the added mass of the bolt-cutters, which suddenly seemed very heavy and awkward indeed.

Slap, slap, slap: webbed claws behind them, followed by a roar that might have been out of a grade-B Tarzan movie—except that it scared the shit of him. Onward they scurried, and the slurpy-scratchy sounds grew ever louder. Calvin was lagging, too; twisting around too often to gaze back. But then they rounded the edge of a second buttress, and David himself risked a glance back, and saw the creature—sea-lion, whatever it was—gaining on them, its shadow stretched long before it, threatening them with a dark that was pale to what would surely follow.

Another swat at the dawdling Calvin, and they were making tracks again, with the monster still behind. Around another buttress, still no door—but there *was* an opening, at the juncture of the buttress and the tower proper. No, not an opening so much as a slit: the bottom of a fissure that seemed to snake and twist right up the side of the tower, not much bigger than their own furry bodies. David hesitated there for a moment, but then the monster's shadow fell full upon them, and he decided. A final swat sent Calvin scurrying inside; he followed, finding himself at once engulfed in a stifling, smelly darkness. Probably a garderobe shaft, he thought, or something that intersected one—if the Sidhe used such primitive solutions to basic functions—if they even *had* basic functions. But then there was no more time for thought, for the slit of light behind was obscured by a mass of yellow fur, and the smell of fish and wet feline overwhelmed all others. Calvin hissed viciously and barred his needlelike teeth, though he did not let go of his pack. David tried to quiet him, but could not.

Which way now?

That was the question. Their shelter was small, no more than two feet on a side—except up.

So up it was. David started climbing, hoping Calvin would follow, and thanking a variety of deities for 'possum strength and balance. Fortunately, the shaft was not quite vertical, but seemed to describe a slow, steep spiral that made it possible to make reasonable progress. Straight up David thought he could have managed as a 'possum, but not with their equipment—and they had to have the equipment. Up then, into darkness, feeling rough stone beneath and occasionally bits of slicker material, all mixed with a brush of mold or fungus that sent spores into his nose when he slipped past them.

Up and up, and he suddenly realized he had no idea where this tunnel went, or if it even led to Fionchadd's prison. But just when he'd decided it might in fact have no openings, another crack snaked in from the left, and he could see light through it: a guard room, it looked like; he could make out a trestle table, a handful of squat, half-human figures standing around one, the other manned by an even dozen bored-looking Sidhe in the black-and-scarlet livery that marked them as Finvarra's warriors. Curious, he scooted closer, wondering what he could learn. *Too* close, and a paw struck a loose stone, sending it sliding back down the shaft.

The noise made one of the Faerys look up, but by then David had scuttled back into the darkness and was following Calvin further up the shaft. Good, the Indian seemed to be adapting to shape-shifting nicely.

Higher and higher, and he was starting to get tired:

three hundred feet, maybe, and little 'possum legs had to move back and forth a lot to mark that distance, especially in the spiral path they followed. Another series of curves, another juncture of broken stone, another shaft of light arrowing unexpectedly in—and then a breath of fresh air found them, mixed with the sound of sweat and stagnant bodily fluids and a slow, steady groaning.

Quicker, now; crowding around Calvin and climbing higher, faster. More light, and he was suddenly looking down—not through a cleft in the wall as he had expected, but from one in the joint where a piece of vaulting met the webbing that backed it, at the juncture of ceiling and vault and wall.

Below—fifteen feet maybe—was Fionchadd.

Beyond all luck, they had found their quarry.

He was not alone, though. One of the squat figures David had seen before was just withdrawing a glittering needle from an inch or so below his navel, but not without giving it an occasional flick or twist. David saw his friend's near-naked body tauten with each movement as he obviously fought back screams, then relax at last as the needle joined other, even more wicked-looking implements, on a round table by the door.

A second torturer jerked Fionchadd's breeches up, but left his chest uncovered—so that he could lay a dagger there. It must surely have been of iron, too, because the Faery boy immediately turned very pale, and David could see his jawline tighten as he bit back a scream. Tendrils of smoke—or steam—began to drift up from the flesh beside that blade.

The first guard frowned, then shrugged, and adjusted the chains tighter. And then—God be praised—headed for the door. His fellow followed, and sharp 'possum ears caught the sound of a key grating in a lock and of a bolt being thrown. Primitive, David thought, compared with some of Lugh's precautions. Finvarra must be very confident of this place's secrecy.

A moment only it took to scurry down the intricate carving of the column that supported the vaulting, and they stood on the floor.

The room swung, shifted; David was looking up at it, at the narrow bed that held Fionchadd—at the chains of iron that bound him. Their Faery friend was apparently unconscious.

David started to speak to him, to whisper that all was well, that help had come, but only produced a discordant squeak. Something about that infuriated him. He bared his teeth in anger, started to attack the other 'possum for lack of a better target, then stopped himself.

Had he been human, he would have blushed. He was still a beast. Almost without realizing it, he had let the 'possum mind take him, had once more nearly sublimated his intellect completely to bestial instinct.

He nudged Calvin with his pink nose, reached a paw under himself to grasp the scale that still hung from his throat and scratched across the floor. A quick squeeze, and he felt pain as the change came upon him, and an instant later had regained his own form. He winced, blinking dizzily as the world spun and twisted around him and brought him at last back to his full five-foot-seven. A final spasm, a quick breath, and he released the scale. A glance at his hand showed it already healing, and then for the first time he truly looked at his Faery friend.

Fionchadd was not a pretty sight, not any longer; for the wasted form on the bed was a too-cruel caricature of his former elegance. Now there was only gauntness, bruises, lines and scars that should not be there—and dirt and foulness. Chains led from the boy's slender arms and legs to the floor, the flesh beneath the barely-padded shackles raw and faintly smoking from proximity to the iron that ate away at it, even as the Faery constitution sought to restore it again. And the dagger—that awful dagger! He knocked it roughly aside. The whole thing reminded him far too much of another friend a year before: Alec dying from the poison of the uktena.

Fionchadd moaned gently, but David forced himself to ignore him. It was time for the matter at hand, and please, God, let it succeed.

The chains first, and it was time to rip the duct tape off the compact bolt-cutters Sandy had assured him would nip right through solid high-chrome steel, never mind djinn-forged iron.

A second quick glance around, just to be sure. *Damn!* The 'possum residue was making him muddle-headed. Another survey, noting absently that Calvin was still fumbling with his scale—but sparing him no more thought except perhaps a twinge of irritation; this was no time to be fiddling around.

The door: yeah, that was it: best to barricade the door just in case. A second later he realized there was not one thing in the room to wedge it with—not one thing to keep it from opening. And it was locked on the other side, and probably warded as well. Blind good luck that they'd come the way they had, though if the tower were warded, there was still a good chance some sort of intruder alert might have gone off already. Lord only knew they'd made enough noise downstairs, and that didn't even count the monster out in the ocean. No telling *what* it'd do—or say, if it was sentient.

Still, there was no helping it; he'd just have to chance leaving it unwedged. Maybe he could thwack the guards with the bolt cutters if it came to that.

"David?" Green eyes slitted open, then abruptly opened wider. *"David!"*

"You got it, Lizard-man," he whispered. "We've come to get you outta here."

"We . . . ?"

"Me and Calvin."

"C . . . Calvin?" Fionchadd craned his head, scanning the room, suddenly much more alert now that he was suddenly presented with hope.

"Yeah—if he ever changes back."

Fionchadd's eyes closed again. He felt back onto the bed. "Hurts, David, *hurts.*"

"I know, guy," David replied softly, as he attacked the bonds, trying hard not to brush against already tortured Faery flesh. Finno could endure it, he knew, could rebuild eventually from almost anything—but he didn't want him to have to.

And then the one thing David had most dreaded: sounds outside: heavy feet on the floor: running.

And he wasn't finished, hadn't freed his friend yet—and what was keeping Calvin . . . ?

"*Calvin?*" he called in a hoarse whisper. "Come on, Fargo, cut the crap."

He searched the room, finally found his accomplice— still in 'possum shape, happily batting his uktena scale across the floor like an extremely ugly cat, his pack and its precious cargo apparently having been abandoned. David started toward him, but Calvin hissed at him—and then a terrible thought struck him.

Calvin was stuck. Not only hadn't he changed back, he *couldn't* change back. In spite of David's warnings, the beast had claimed him.

And there was no more time.

Only one chance—one slim chance, if he only could manage it. There was a brazier burning nearby, probably to take the worst of the chill off the room, though he imagined it had other applications as well, if the burns that pocked Fionchadd's flesh were any indication. If he could just find Calvin's pack, it was barely possible. Yeah, there it was, over in the corner. He snagged it quickly, emptied out three uktena scales, and flipped the flap back closed.

Sounds on the threshold now, the lock being worked.

Calvin? Where had that damned 'possum got to? Oh there—by the head of the bed. Enough time wasted, and none left for hesitation. David snagged him by the scruff of the neck, grabbed his scale from the floor and their packs as well, wincing as the 'possum tried to bite him.

Finno now—one chance. He tugged on the iron links, but they would not move, abandoned caution and yanked at the chains, felt one of them grate but not break. Only one other option, then: He grabbed the brazier, poured the coals on the floor, thrust in the three scales, and—as smoke and flame erupted from them as if they'd been made of magnesium—cried out as loudly as he could, "Alec, Liz—God in Heaven, please be there."

And then, as the familiar agony enfolded him, he clutched Calvin to his chest, grabbed Fionchadd's smoking wrist, and hoped his plan would succeed.

Heat, like superheated steam, like evaporation . . . For an instant his only thought was the pain of the transition between the Worlds, but it was not so severe this time, nor so long in duration. In fact—

Abruptly he was tumbling to the soft, warm earth of Calvin's make-do Power Wheel.

"Jesus," he gasped, as Alec and Liz reached toward him, and it took until then to dawn on him that he had succeeded, at least in part: Calvin was still with him, though in 'possum shape. And wonder of wonders, he'd actually managed to bring Finno through as well—without his chains. He heaved a sign of relief and sank down on the grass, oblivious to his state of undress: "We made it," he laughed, almost hysterically. "I don't believe it: we *made* it! I was so afraid I was gonna have to swim again—"

"Must have been the gate," Alec mused softly, as he handed David a bundle of clothes. "That would have been the simplest way between the Worlds, so when you burned the scale, it brought you here. We saw you earlier, but couldn't help—saw the monster, but had no idea what was going on inside the tower, since Liz couldn't scry 'cause she had to help keep the gate open."

David suddenly froze in the act of slipping on his cutoffs. "The gate—oh my God, Alec—the gate! We've gotta close it!"

He whirled around, saw the arc of fire that still burned

in the pink light of Georgia sunrise. And through it saw half a dozen shapes take wing from the top of the tower: enormous eagles. But each one, David knew, bore the mind and soul of a Faery warrior. And they were gliding straight toward them.

PART III

DELUGE

Chapter XIX: Panic City

(Stone Mountain, Georgia— Monday, June 16—morning)

"Close the friggin' *gate!*" David shouted, his eyes ablaze. A glance over his friends' heads showed him the flame-edged hole, six black eagles coming in fast.

"How . . . ?" Alec began, then: "But where's *Calvin?*"

"There," David gasped, pointing to the 'possum that had slipped his grip as soon as he'd tumbled to earth in the clearing and was now calmly nosing around the ice chest. Alec's eyes grew wide, and David noticed then that they were clouded with pain. His mouth was grim. Liz was already tending to Fionchadd, who was unconscious again. But David's concern was momentarily elsewhere.

"The gate, Alec! What did Calvin say about the gate?"

"*Nothing!*" Alec shot back miserably, staring at the eagles that had now covered half the distance from the tower.

"You're *sure?*"

A nod.

David glanced one last time at the birds—and acted. He shouldered past his best friend and flung himself on the ground before the glimmering hole in space, afraid to stand for fear he might be sucked in again.

Come to us, a voice whispered in his head. *You cannot defy us.*

There was no more time. The window into the Other-world had its origin in the ulunsuti that still blazed atop the remnants of the heap of twigs, its lower third embedded in glowing embers. David grabbed it—felt fiery agony burn into his hands like the king of all electric shocks as he jerked the crystal from its bed and hurled it aside.

Alec dived for it, caught it as it rolled, thrust it unthinking into the ice chest where a little water yet remained, then set about re-securing it in its pouch and jar.

David held his breath—the gate was still there, fading at last but not gone; and the Faery warriors had almost reached them now; he could see their vast wings filling half the circle.

Abruptly Liz grabbed the thermos that still lay at the edge of the Power Wheel. A deft twist of wrist unscrewed it and she emptied its contents into the soil.

"Liz! What . . . ?"

"It's what Calvin said," she shouted. "The gate'll stand as long as there's warmth in the blood. Maybe he meant *all* the blood."

There was time for only the quickest reconnoiter. A glimpse of the fading gate showed the eagles impossibly close. David lunged sideways to scoop Calvin-'possum from the glob of venison gristle he'd been nibbling and thrust him at a startled Liz. "Here, we'll worry 'bout changin' him back later. We gotta move!"

Liz took the struggling animal, clutched him close to her chest in spite of his protests, while David grabbed for the closest knapsacks. "He still got a scale 'round his neck?" he asked quickly.

Liz checked with her fingers, nodded.

David leapt over to where Alec was frantically tugging on his clothes beside the still-unconscious Faery.

"He's still out of it!" Alec cried. "We can't . . ."

"We've *got* to. Come on, I'll help you."

"But where . . . ?"

David shrugged helplessly. "Anywhere there's people. Those things won't dare show themselves, if we can just get back to Calvin's place. They can't enter a dwelling unasked either."

"You hope!"

"It's all I got. Now let's *move!*"

David reached down, snagged Fionchadd under an arm, lifted until Alec could work in under the other side. As one they stood, started across the clearing at an awkward half-jog, while Liz ran on ahead with Calvin and her knapsack. David was grateful for exactly one thing: Fionchadd's ordeal had evidently cost him a lot of weight, for he was unexpectedly easy to tote along. Occasionally he'd come to himself, too, and stumble a few steps, but then the weight would come back onto their shoulders again, and David would know he was gone once more.

Almost to the woods now, and David looked back: the World gate was still there, though rapidly disappearing. But it didn't matter anymore, because even as he stared, an eagle burst through the rift. Another followed, then a third.

Into the woods then, onto the trail, and he prayed the huge raptors would not follow them there. Against his will he found himself recalling another pursuit: Ailill in eagle shape chasing him through the woods near Lookout Rock. Nuada had saved him then, in the guise of a huge white swan. But this time there could be no Nuada. And he didn't even have his runestaff.

And what was to keep his pursuers from changing to some other form?

A cry from Liz meant that she'd stumbled. The irate "Dammit! Ouch!" that followed doubtless meant that Calvin-'possum had done something he shouldn't.

"Watch it," Alec hollered, as a branch snapped back into them. David dodged sideways, dragging Fionchadd with him, almost out of Alec's grip. Four steps to recovery, and they stumbled on. Fortunately, Fionchadd seemed to be coming to a bit more now; David could feel his muscles twitching.

No sign of the eagles, but he thought he heard vast wings flapping—hard to tell though, over the sound of Liz crashing on ahead, of their own hurried breathing, of Finno's occasional grunts and moans.

On and on—and Fionchadd tore free and staggered with them. Liz was nearly out of sight, and David hoped desperately that she, at least, would get away. Maybe she could bring help, though God only knew what kind.

Another dozen yards—and hope suddenly bloomed in David. He could see daylight ahead, which meant they were almost out of the woods. Light sparkled suddenly on Liz's hair, and he redoubled his efforts. Alec was halfway between Fionchadd and Liz but looking back frequently, and David was hanging back, keeping one eye on the Faery, and the other on the rapidly thinning tree canopy.

Light then: the narrow open strip between the fence and the forest. Liz fell against it, panting and breathless, still clutching the squirming, hissing Calvin.

Alec made it then, and David stumbled up behind. The Faery looked almost coherent now, but as they approached the fence, his face contorted in a terrified scream, and he fell to the ground in a whimpering heap.

"Finno, what . . . ?" David began, then stared at the fence in horror. "Oh, my God!" he exclaimed wretchedly, "the damned thing's steel! How in the world could we have been such fools?"

Fools! Fools! Fools!—the insidious accusations in his head again. *Fools, a thousand times, to toy with Finvarra!*

An exchange of glances with Alec and Liz proved they also had heard. Another glimpse of the sky showed the eagles slowly circling, as if gathering momentum to dive.

"Maybe it'll hold them off too," Alec suggested, but his face belied his optimism.

"Maybe so," David panted doubtfully. "But what now? Calvin's out of it, and we've still gotta get Finno over this bloody fence to get to either the house or—"

"What?"

"The car!" David exclaimed, thrusting assorted bits of gear in Alec's direction. "Quick, do what you can for just a second."

"What?"

"Just do it! Fight 'em with your bare hands if you have to. You've got knives. Just hold on!"

"David, I—" Liz began.

But he was gone: leaping over the fence in one fluid motion, sprinting across the yard as if his cut-offs were on fire.

The beagles came out to bark, but he outran them, so they turned their attention skyward and back, bounding as a body to the fence against which Liz was pressed, while Alec tried to shield Fionchadd with his own body, and the Faery writhed and screamed in helpless anguish, crumpled to a small heap on the grassy ground.

The second fence loomed ahead, and David was over it too, though he heard fabric rip and felt pain lance into his hand where he snagged it on a point of rough-cut metal.

The car, now: the Mustang-of-Death—if he had the blessed keys.

The keys! Pockets slapped fore and aft, no luck. Must have fallen out when he'd dressed so quickly back at the clearing.

However . . .

He popped the hood, snaked a hand under the edge of the fender cap and snagged his spare set, then slammed the panel closed again.

In a instant he was inside and praying the mother would start. He had to force himself to be calm; no good if he flooded the thing. Two long pats on the gas, then two short ones, clutch in, stick it in gear, turn the key and pray even more fervently to the God he suddenly wanted very much to believe in.

Vrooommmmm!

David could feel himself relax, feel the tension go out

of him as one small thing went right. A check through the opposite window showed the eagles still circling, but coming lower.

And with that he used the last fragment of his time.

Gear in reverse, stomp on the gas—and tires shrieked as he slid the car around in the road.

First gear now, feet on clutch and brakes and gas as one to build up the revs, hearing the motor scream—and scream louder in company with his tires as he popped the clutch, floored the gas, and accelerated.

—Straight toward the line of fencing.

A crash laid the gate section flat and sent beagles scurrying. He hoped he wouldn't hit one.

Hand on the horn and he jerked the wheel left, toward a section of fence a little way off from his friends. Faster, then hit it and jam on the brakes and hope this time that he didn't collect a tree.

He didn't, looked right, saw thirty feet of fence tilt at an angle and his friends dodge away as the car came to rest atop the section it had just knocked down.

He leaned over, unlocked the passenger door, shoved the car into neutral, set the brake, and jumped out.

"Quick," he yelled. "Hurry!"

Alec saw him, understood what he was about. He nudged Liz. She turned, gazed skyward—and ran.

David ran too—toward his friends. He met Liz on the way. "You drive!" he told her in passing and pounded on.

He was at Alec now, and grabbed Fionchadd's other arm. "The Fire!" the boy was screaming. "I can't stand it! Just let me die."

Let him and you die: a voice in his mind. *Give him to us and live.*

"NO!" David shouted back violently, as he and Alec hustled Fionchadd along.

A glance ahead showed him that Liz had reached the car, was in the driver's seat and frantically trying to disentangle the 'possum from her T-shirt.

—And then David saw the eagles dive. Six, in formation, arrowing earthward as one, growing huger as they came until their wings seemed to fill the sky.

David ran faster, dragging Fionchadd with him in spite of his screams, in spite of the fencing they were now traversing. Alec helped as much as he could, but David could see that he was crying.

"Flip the seat!" David yelled, as they got within ten feet.

Liz did, and David put all his flagging energy into one last effort.

Beside him Alec screamed, and then they were to the car.

"Oh, God," Liz moaned. "No, we can't do this!"

"Huh?" David shouted back, as they crammed the hysterical Fionchadd into the back seat, and David flopped in beside him. Alec slid into the front and slammed the door. Abruptly the mental harassment ended.

A thump on the roof, a dry rustle across the metal, and David heard an avian shriek and caught the odor of burning feathers. Another thump, and then something large and solid slammed into the backlight hard enough to crack the safety glass. A long, narrow gash opened right above his head.

"Gun it!"

Liz did, jamming the car into reverse and flooring the gas as she launched the car backwards across Papa MacIntosh's dog lot, once more traumatizing his hounds.

A thump was the other gate, another was the curb. A scream on the roof was one of the eagles being flung loose.

Suddenly it was there before them, on the road, big as a man, and half-changed into one.

Liz stuffed the car into first, floored it again, and David saw the creature leap out of the way at the last possible instant as she tore off down the road.

Suddenly the only sound was the wailing of Ford horsepower and the wild shrieks coming from Fionchadd.

"Finno, what . . . ?" And then David knew—*iron!* The car was iron—steel, anyway, which was just as bad—proof against folk of Faerie when in the flesh of that World, and thus also some proof against their pursuers. But likewise bane to Fionchadd. David could have kicked himself for making the same mistake twice in as many minutes. Of course in his more recent extended adventures with the Faery boy, Finno *had* worn the substance of man's world, which did allow him to touch the dreaded metal. Even in Faery shape he could endure a little, as a man could quench a candle with his fingers and not be burned. But not when he was in pain and half unconscious.

"This won't work," David groaned. "We're gonna kill Finno if we don't get him out of here right now!" And as he looked, he saw the Faery boy's face start to blister.

"Oh, Christ, no!" from Alec, who was trying to keep tabs on the 'possum by stuffing it into one of the knapsacks.

"Stop, Liz, *now!*"

"What? And give him up? No way?"

"You'll *kill* him, girl, I said *stop!*"

"No, not yet, not till we get somewhere safe. If he can hang on just a little longer, we'll be to the strip. No way those folks'll come at us there."

"Unless they put on men's shape and men's substance, which they can do."

"I'm driving, David! Just hang on—and trust me!"

"Wait," Alec interrupted. "I've got an idea. Look, Calvin's not changed back, so he's probably stuck in that shape. Finno can't stay in here much longer—just look at him—and you've gotta get him to the coast. We obviously can't go in the car, with or without those nice folks after us, so I think you guys should get the hell to Galunlati, and me and Liz . . . well, we'll take care of ourselves."

"Right," Liz chimed in.

David stared at the Faery. Fionchadd's whole face was red, and there were huge running blisters on his cheeks and brow. The unmistakable smell of burning was beginning to fill the car.

"We've still gotta stop to do the ritual."

"No we don't," Alec shot back smugly. And with that he grabbed a handful of the paper that littered the Mustang's carpet, crumpled it up, and stuck it on the flat rear part of the pot-metal console. An instant later, he'd pushed in the car's cigarette lighter, and when it popped out, thrust it into the wad.

"We'll have to act fast," he told them. "Soon as it flames, in go the scales; soon as you're gone, out it goes."

"But . . ."

"Here!" Alec cried, thrusting the startled 'possum into David's lap. "Hang onto this—you got your scales?"

David managed to fumble out the last three from Calvin's stash and resecured the pack while Alec fanned the smoldering flame. Liz rolled down her window—and as soon as she did, the shriek of the eagles came to them, that and the insidious threats: *no good, no good, no good.*

"Hey, why don't we all go?" David asked suddenly. "Just stop the car and we'll all go."

" 'Fraid not," Alec replied heavily, stuffing Calvin's knapsack into the space beside the 'possum. "We, uh . . . well, they were in your backpack, and . . . well, I'm afraid we left it back at the clearing. Not enough scales to get everybody where we need to go and back again, anyway. Besides—*you* guys are the ones the folks're after. Liz and I can always go back and get 'em if we get a chance."

And then there was no more time for discussion. Smoke filled the car, making them cough. They rolled down the rest of the windows—which had the fortunate effect of fanning the creeping brown edges of the slowly heating paper.

The parcel erupted.

"Now!" Alec shouted.

David took a deep breath, closed his eyes, and somehow thrust in three scales.

As the car filled with light, he hugged the 'possum to

his chest with one hand, and clasped Fionchadd around the waist with the other. *"Hyuntikwala Usun—"* he started to shout, and then the car swerved, light and pain filled the world, and he could not finish.

Chapter XX: Running on Empty

(Stone Mountain, Georgia—Monday, June 16—mid-morning)

For one horrifying moment, Liz was certain she was about to commit the ultimate sin, at least as far as David was concerned: she was going to wreck his car. The Cadillac simply appeared out of nowhere: an aging Fleetwood Brougham driven by a little old lady who could barely see above the steering wheel. One second there were two clear lanes ahead, the next there were fenders everywhere. Liz had only an instant to stab the brakes, to swerve, and to floor the gas, and she was somehow around. She heard tires scream and metal scrape but did not look back, because she was crossways in front of three lanes of oncoming traffic, there were monster eagles clawing at her roof, she thought she'd just run a red-light—and the car was full of smoke from the pile of paper Alec had just ignited. And that didn't even count the fact that her main man had just vanished in a puff of that same smoke, or that Alec had that minute gone half hysterical. No, all she could think of was that if she bent David's car he'd never speak to her again.

Horns blew, she swore loudly and proficiently enough to make Alec look up; gave the woman the finger—and sped on, catching the car on its second tail-wag and stuffing it neatly into the right hand lane between a Toyota Camry and a Dodge minivan full of Borzoi. There was only one thing she knew to do: stay where people were, stay in traffic, and hope the eagles grew tired of the chase and went away. Surely with all this iron, all the confusion of civilization, they wouldn't risk betraying themselves further. She didn't know all the rules of Faerie, not by a long shot. But she did know that the Sidhe didn't like to reveal themselves in public—and there was almost nothing in the world more public than Atlanta rush hour.

"Shit! Damn! Hell," Alec was shouting in staccato bursts as he tried to grab the flaming paper and fling it out the window. He succeeded on the fourth try, and Liz saw the fragment flop into the sidewalk, where it remained.

Another horn blew.

"Got it," Alec sighed triumphantly. "Least now we won't go up in flames."

"Not *those* flames, anyway," Liz agreed.

"They're gone," Alec interrupted, and there was a catch in his voice. "Now all we gotta do is hope they made it."

"I know," Liz replied sadly. "I saw 'em go—felt 'em, rather. Suddenly a hole in the car with nobody in it, and fresh air rushing in. Almost like a tiny thunderclap."

"Storms in the car," Alec chuckled half hysterically. "I like that."

They were silent, then, as they sped through the heavy traffic of Mountain Industrial Boulevard—a patchwork of shopping centers and fast-foot joints, warehouses, and small businesses. The eagles seemed to have abandoned them, at least for the moment. A mile they covered, half-a-dozen stoplights. "I . . . I think they're gone," Liz said at last, "but . . . Alec, I hate to ask you, but could you look out and—you know, make sure?"

"Sure thing, ma'am," Alec replied, and craned his head

out the window. "Can't tell for certain, but I don't see anything suspicious."

"That's a relief."

"Unless they can turn into Toyotas, or something. But there's a couple of things that still bother me." He took a deep breath and looked at her. "We can't hide out in traffic forever, Liz. We've gotta get to the coast somehow, just in case."

"But what can we do?"

"Nothing, maybe, but we both know we've gotta be there."

She nodded reluctantly. "Yeah, and to get there, we gotta drive. I know."

"Like the bird of paradise?"

"Huh?"

"Bird of paradise. The first skins they sent back to Europe from New Guinea or wherever didn't have legs attached, so the early scientists thought they never came to earth—just flew all the time."

"Neat story. Too bad we *do* have to light."

"Yeah. I keep thinking of that song about the guy doomed to ride the train forever."

"What? Oh, the MTA."

"Yeah."

"You know what we're doing, don't you?"

"What?"

"Talking about nothing to keep from going crazy."

"Yeah."

Another silence, then: "Did we do the right thing, Liz? It was so quick, but all I could think of was poor Finno cooking alive. And Lord knows I've never seen anybody look as bad as he did. One thing, though," he added slowly.

"I'm listening."

Alec's eyes filled with tears, and he almost broke down. "I hurt, Liz; oh God Almighty, I hurt."

Liz glanced sideways. What she saw almost brought tears from her own eyes. How could she have been so insensitive, so damned *unaware?* Alec was sitting in the other bucket, staring at his hands. They were blistered, red; parts were even blackened. He was simply looking at them and crying uncontrollably.

"Good God, boy!" she cried. "What hap—" but then she knew. Alec had stuck the ulunsuti into the fire with his bare hands. He'd had to, to get it seated right, and she bet anything it had something to do with the magic: the magic had to cost the wielder pain. Calvin had mentioned something like that when he'd told them a bit about the ritual used to prepare the scales to teleport. Blood too was involved, but she wasn't certain how. Nothing was ever free, though; that was a basic tenet of magic; and Alec had paid a high price without complaint. Worse, he'd stuck his hands back into the fire when he'd tried to put it out, and then used them to carry Fionchadd cross country, and to light another fire in the car, and then grabbed the burning papers to throw them out the window. How much pain could one man endure?

"I'm sorry," Alec sniffed, trying to regain control. "I shouldn't have said anything. A little burn salve, some bandages, and I'll be fine."

"No you *won't!*" Liz told him firmly. "You've got second-degree burns all over your hands. I've gotta get you to a hospital."

"No, Liz, *we've* gotta get to the coast!"

Liz braked suddenly, swung the car into the parking lot of a convenient McDonald's. She stuffed the car in neutral and turned to stare at him.

"I'll be *okay,*" he repeated. "I'll put some ice on 'em."

"*Alec!*"

"No, listen. It's only pain. I can live with it. God knows if I hadn't been so wimpy earlier, when David wanted me to use the ulunsuti and I wouldn't, maybe we could have avoided this. Certainly we'd have had more time to plan, 'stead of making it up on the fly. But we've got to be on the coast as quick as we can—tomorrow morning at the latest. I can stand it till then. It'll hurt like hell, maybe I'll get sick—but I'll be okay."

"You could get an infection, Alec. You could lose the use of your hands!"

"I nearly lost 'em last year, trying to impress David; but he saved me from something much worse. Can I do any less for him?"

"Oh, Christ, McLean, don't ask me to do this. I can't help David right now, but I *can* help you, and to do that I've gotta get you to a doctor."

Alec shook his head. "There's no time. Just think. David's gone. Calvin's gone. Finno's gone. It's you and me, now. We're the only ones 'cept Dale and Sandy that have any idea what's up. And we're the *only* ones with access to magic. And that's what David may need to get him back. I can't be in the hospital when I need to be down on the coast with the ulunsuti."

"The ulunsuti? Why?"

"To open another gate, if we have to. I mean, hasn't that occurred to you yet? I may have to open another gate."

"It could cripple you for life."

He shrugged. "That's a risk. So is driving in rush-hour traffic."

A glance at the steady stream of cars told Liz the truth of that. "Touché."

"Besides," he added, "if we don't move, we're never gonna get outta here. I'll look for the first-aid kit. Now, let's travel."

"Which way?"

"East," he said. "And south. Now what did we do with that altas?"

She sighed and pulled back into the traffic, heading against the heaviest flow. Almost she relaxed—until she heard the distant cry of an eagle, then heard it echoed twice more.

* * *

An hour and a half later they were running on straight caffeine and adrenalin—the former from the last of the two six-packs of Jolt Cola they'd bought at the same Winder convenience store as they'd got their morning candy bars; the latter from tension that would not go away. God knew they should be absolutely fried, given that only Alec had had a reasonable night's sleep in the last two, but Liz was wide awake: perhaps *too* wide awake, since she was so wired she was about to scream. She kept finding herself scrooching up under the steering wheel, peering forward with feverish intensity, straining her back as if that tension would grant the Mustang extra speed beyond the seventy-five she'd been averaging since they'd finally escaped Atlanta's urban sprawl somewhere around Monroe. They'd taken Georgia 11 south to I-20, and were still heading east, coming up on the thriving metropolis of Crawfordville—all 594 souls, according to Rand McNally.

A bump in the road, not major, but Liz started, almost cried out. Every sound she heard seemed to herald pursuit: death from above in some form she dared not even imagine. Worse, every sound the car made hinted at imminent disaster. She'd never realized how many sounds a car—especially an old one like David's—could make: squeaks, rattles, howls from the tires, the rear end, the transmission. Suppose something happened to the car: suppose they found themselves stranded in the wilds of Taliaferro County with a dead '66 Mustang?

One more thing to fret over.

Another thing was gas. It was one thing to get by on caffeine and adrenalin herself, but the car was something else again. The gauge had dipped past the last mark just beyond Madison, and now they were running on what David liked to call "air and imagination."

"I'm gonna have to stop," Liz told Alec, who'd been leaning against the passenger door with his head half out the window and his eyes closed, rousing only when he delicately fumbled with the radio every now and then. At least his hands looked a little better. He'd found burn oint-

ment in one of the surviving packs and had slathered the
damage with it, resisting the temptation to bandage them
as well, since what burns needed most was air, not con-
finement.

"Alec?" Liz prompted, somewhat louder. "I've *gotta*
stop. We've gotta get gas."

A slow nod. "Got any money?"

Got twenty bucks, that be enough?"

"To get us there, probably. To get us back? Who
knows?"

"Another thing," Liz added. "I think we need to find
a phone, we've gotta let some folks know where we are.
I know Mom's probably going crazy about now. Shoot,
she's probably already called the cops."

"Damn!" Alec exclaimed suddenly.

"Huh?"

"Your exams! Don't you have a big one coming up?"

She nodded sadly. "Yeah, gotta killer chemistry on
Wednesday, but—well, some things are just more important."

A sign caught Liz's attention up ahead: not the expected
Crawfordville, but simply a Chevron logo on a neat blue
background, with the legend: NEXT EXIT.

She slipped into the right hand lane and followed the
arrow up into the oil-stained forecourt of a small self-
service station that seemed to be standing guard at the
intersection of the interstate and some nameless secondary
road. Woods grew close around. A sign pointed south to
Orton Carlton State Park.

"I'll fill 'er," Alec volunteered, as Liz eased in between the pumps. "You be ready to fly if anything happens."

"I'll go look for a phone."

"Good idea, but stay close if you can."

"I've, uh, also gotta go to the restroom."

"Me too, soon as I get done here, but we'll go in shifts,
never desert the car."

"Okay."

Alec patted her arm awkwardly and almost as awkwardly got out of the car and trotted around back to void
the previous sale and stick the gas nozzle into the filler
between taillights. Liz could see him there, keeping a wary
eye out. She also saw his face blanch every time he ma-
nipulated the equipment.

She wished she hadn't said that about the restroom, too,
because all of a sudden she really did have to go about as
bad as she ever had in her life. If Alec would only hurry
. . . she squirmed around in place, stared out the window.
Alec was still vigilant, she could see his eyes shifting back
and forth as the numbers slowly rolled up.

Eventually the dollar amount reached fifteen, though the
gauge didn't seem to be registering, probably due to the
car's recent abuse. She saw Alec fish into his pocket and
pull out a twenty. He held it delicately between his fingertips. Probably the only way it didn't hurt.

A scraping sound was the gas cap being resecured, and
then Alec was trotting into the station.

Suddenly she couldn't wait any longer. She didn't *want*
to leave the car, but Alec was taking his own sweet time,
and she wondered if he'd decided to take advantage of
being out to do a little freshening up while he was at it.
She doubted he meant any harm, but *Jesus,* why now,
when she *really* had to go?

There was no helping it. She simply had to risk it. A
quick dash out back would probably be okay.

She got out of the car and trotted as quickly as she could
without being obvious around the side of the station, hoping the sign she saw was accurate.

As she walked in, she glimpsed Alec coming out again.
Good, that meant the car wouldn't be unguarded.

Five minutes later she felt remarkably better, though
mostly because of the water she'd splashed on her face
(she was still in warpaint, she realized), and the quick
toweling-down she'd given herself.

After the gloom of the restroom, the sunlight outside
made her blink, and she spared a glance toward Alec, who

was waiting patiently beside the car, then started toward the pay phone she'd noticed at the edge of the parking lot. She pointed; he nodded. She brandished a handful of change, and he nodded again and made shooing motions.

She went in, shut the glass door behind her. The receiver was working—fortunately. She listened for the dial tone, got it, punched up the operator and asked her to dial Uncle Dale, figuring he was the one person most adept at the various levels of diplomacy needed to bring half a dozen people of varying degrees of interest or involvement up to date on what was happening.

Behind her she saw Alec slowly walking toward her. He'd probably thought of something he needed to say.

The phone rang twice, and then someone picked up. "Hello?"

She deposited the requisite change, then: "Uh—oh, hi, Uncle Dale; it's me, Liz. I'm—"

"Miss Lizzy! Good God A-mighty, where *are* you? Yore folk've been worried sick about you, ever since you didn't call last night—I had to do a heap of explain' there, let me tell you!" A pause. "Hey, you okay? And what about Davy? How's he doin'?"

"I don't know," she replied, and caught herself on the ragged edge of tears. "We've got Finno, but . . . but we've lost Davy. He's somewhere in Galunlati."

Another pause. "I 'uz afraid of that, from what Calvin's lady told me 'bout y'all's plans. But where are *you?*"

"We're in—"

And then the phone went dead.

"Hello? Hello?" she called, low at first and then suddenly louder as panic took her. *"Hello?"* A subtlety of sound made her look around and when she did, every hair on her body stood on end, for she saw Alec leaning against the phone booth with a length of ragged telephone cable in his hand.

Reflexively, she jerked open the door, started to run— and saw *another* Alec start toward her from inside the station. He was walking by himself, but there was something odd about his gait, as if he were not quite in control.

He cleared the corner, but another figure was behind him: one of Finvarra's black-liveried guards. A *Word* pulsed in her head, freezing both her will and her body. Hands brushed her as the bogus Alec came up behind, and she saw four other black-cloaked shapes wander from the woods. "The metal steeds of this World are swift," someone said in strangely accented English, "but not as swift as the winds of the upper sky—not when one wears the shape of a dragon. Come, now, and join your friend." It was then that she saw the gas station dissolve back into the deserted block shell that had actually been there. "One sometimes sees what one desires to see," that voice told her. "And if there are those who can read desires, almost anything can happen—and often does."

And with that her legs took her against her will towards the woods.

Chapter XXI: In the Dark About Things

(Galunlati—night)

The first thing David noticed when he came to himself was the cessation of the searing pain of intra-World transition. It had been awful that time—much worse than any time before, and he still wasn't absolutely certain he was completely intact, either in body or soul; though in part that was due to the *second* thing he noticed, which was that wherever he had wound up was dark, and he was lying on his face in it. That was strange, too: zapping from a bright Georgia dawn complete with the distant hoot-and-holler of rush hour to the silence and dark of . . . wherever here was.

The third thing that entered his reality was that his left ear was being quite vigorously nibbled by a 'possum.

"Uhhhmmm," he half-groaned, half-sighed. He closed his eyes against the dark, feeling grateful to be alive—and thinking he'd be even more grateful if not for the insistent machinations of the blessed marsupial. If it'd only leave him alone for a minute, he'd get up and see what it wanted. For the time being all he wanted to do was lie here on whatever soft surface this was until his brain-cells got their act together again.

Tiny sharp teeth nipped his nose with exquisite precision.

"Shit!" he yipped, jerking himself to an awkward squat, arms flailing automatically. One connected with something small and furry and sent it tumbling head-over-heels. The other hit something larger and prompted a vaguely human groan out of it.

He blinked, shook his head, trying to clear his vision and finally figured out that the reason he couldn't see worth a damn was because he was being overhung by a handsome rhododendron and there was about a foot of wet hair in his eyes. He slapped both back, and took inventory of his surroundings. It was night: that hadn't changed. He was in the woods, though. And then the reality of his situation dawned on him. He was—or was supposed to be—in Galunlati.

Except that it didn't look like any part of Galunlati he'd been in before—not that he'd seen very much. He leapt to his feet (bare, he discovered to his dismay), glanced around—and saw trees. Oaks and beeches, to judge by their style of growth and bark, laced with a regular underforest of dogwoods, a few of which were still in bloom—but nothing else familiar. He stood on tip-toes, turned around in place—and made out only more of the same. A glance skyward showed him sky tinted with the hint of impending moonlight. Stars were everywhere, but not the ones he was used to. It was also rather remarkably warm.

There was a clear patch in the forest canopy a couple of yards from where he stood, and he staggered over there and gazed up at it. Three stars in a row, and a fourth and fifth right below it: almost like the belt of Orion, except it wasn't. But it was one of the constellations he'd found and named last time he was in Galunlati, so that must be where he was.

But where in Galunlati?

And what was he gonna do?

All at once the events of the last twelve hours came sneaking up on him and pounced, and he had to sit down again to keep himself from reeling.

Then it struck him that the particularly brave and obnoxious marsupial was without a doubt his old friend Calvin.

And finally that the groan had been Fionchadd who was in serious bad shape and probably ought to be looked at immediately.

He scanned the clearing in search of the 'possum, saw it absently nosing about the base of a tree. Good, let it stay there, he couldn't do anything else for the time being. Meanwhile . . .

A half-leap brought him back to his other companion. The Faery boy was lying on his back, and the moon had begun to peek through the trees enough for David to be able to assess his condition.

He was almost as ill-clad as David, except that David's cut-offs and T-shirt were relatively clean, if sweaty-damp, while Finno's ragged tunic and breeches were filthy. Gently he smoothed the tangled, matted hair out of the Faery's face, peered close, shifting his position to get out of his own light. His fingers brushed something soft and raised, something that split and oozed clear liquid when he touched it, and David remembered to his horror that the entirety of the Faery boy's face was blistered. Ditto his neck, his bare arms, his feet, even a section of belly. No charring, but it was as if the whole skin had bubbled loose.

It was awful. Almost he wept again, this time not from relief, but from the futility of it all: alone, almost naked in a strange land, with an itinerate 'possum and a deathly-ill Faery, and himself no great shakes either.

"Okay, Sullivan, get it together," he told himself aloud. The sound echoed loud in the night, made the 'possum look his way before going back to its rooting. Fionchadd groaned. David took quick inventory of his equipment. Clothes like he'd noted, his uktena scale still on its thong, Liz's medallion, and his fannypack. Another search of the clearing showed him that he also had Calvin's largely empty fannypack and knapsack, and—wonder of wonders—even the 'possum's uktena scale. Evidently the critter had scooted out of it upon . . . landing, or whatever they'd done. Okay, then, check the packs. He snapped his open, found tightly-wrapped plastic with his fingers, and dragged out the mixed-nuts can it contained—the one that housed Sandy's survival kit.

A quick flip undid the lid, and the next few moments proved sometimes enlightening, sometimes perplexing. There was everything from aluminum foil, string, and fishline, through a Swiss Army Knife, razorblades, and fishhooks, to instant coffee, water purification tablets, and a couple of batteries. There was also a tube of what might be burn ointment and a sheet of paper about the size of his hand covered with tiny black lines that might have been printed. He squinted at it in the moonlight, but could not tell what was on it, though he suspected it was instructions—probably everything in the can had at least two functions. But Sandy (presumably) had saved space even more by reducing it on a photocopier until the lettering was barely legible. He guessed she didn't plan on having trouble at night.

So what did he do with Finno?

Make him comfortable, he supposed, get him warm, dry, clean, treat his burns as best he could, and hope he'd come to and have further suggestions.

And to do anything else useful, he needed to get some water. A final check of the Faery showed him lying on soft, mossy ground. It was not cold, so there was no real chance of chill, and anything that could eat him would doubtless make short work of David as well.

He rose again, tuned his ears, suddenly aware of the night sounds unnaturally loud: owls, birds he didn't know, the distant yowl of a cougar that sent shivers up his spine. Unconsciously he gripped the uktena scale, knowing that—if he had to—he would do the dreaded thing and change shape again. He'd had no trouble last time, except mastering his own fear. Maybe that mental block was over. *Maybe.* Moving as softly as he could, he once more turned in place, now catching the soft rustling of smaller animals. And as he faced downhill, distantly, but distinctly, he heard running water.

He went that way, picking his route slowly because he was barefoot. A moment later he found what he was look- ing for: a small stream no more than a yard or so wide that tinkled down from the left. He knelt by it, drank from it (one of the good things about Galunlati was that you never had to worry about the water), and felt instantly refreshed. Acting quickly, he opened the plastic garbage bag from Sandy's kit, crossed his fingers, and let water run in. It was still only half full before he cinched it—no sense overstressing it. Now if he could just get back to Finno without rupturing it on some wayward branch . . .

A final long draught, and he was on his way back up hill. By the time he returned to his "camp" Fionchadd was stirring.

"Finno!" he cried, and would have leapt across the clearing had he not feared damage to the water bag.

It was true, though: the Faery was moving, twitching slowly back and forth, and working his lips. His eyes were crusted with blister-ooze that had pooled there and dried. David took off his T-shirt and carefully let a little of the water trickle from the bag onto it. With it, he rubbed Fion- chadd's eyes, trying to stay clear of the pervasive blisters while yet attempting to get off as much of the gunk as possible. One done, and the moaning got louder, but he thought it hid a hint of relief, and then the other done, and he went on as carefully as he could trying to clean off his friend's face. That accomplished, he moved on to the arms, finally the feet. When he started on the left sole, the whole foot flinched out of his grip. He giggled at that. The Faery was evidently ticklish. He'd had no idea.

A stronger groan brought him back to the head—that had sounded almost like words.

Another *was* words—sort of.

"D . . . d'v . . . d?"

David dabbed the cracked lips, the eyes once more, grateful they, at least, weren't blistered. "I'm here, Lizardman, I gotcha."

"David?" Much stronger this time.

"That's me."

"David!" And with that, beyond all hope, Fionchadd sat up.

David tried to ease him back down, though it was difficult because of his fear of popping one of the blisters, but the Faery was having none of it. Instead, he stretched, looked around, squinting into the gloom. "Is there any water?"

"All you need," David told him and resisted the urge to hug him. He started to hand him the bag, but thought better of it, and poured a little into the can (after removing its precious contents *very* carefully), and passed him that instead.

Fionchadd drank greedily, the slurps and gulps certainly dispelling any notions he had about Faery fastidiousness. When he had consumed three refills, he made it to his feet.

"Dana, I stink," he said; then, "Where are we and how did we get here?"

"Galunlati, I think," David told him. "We got here by uktena scale after I saved you."

"After you almost cooked me, you mean," Fionchadd retorted, but David knew he was only half-serious.

"Would you rather've stayed where you were?"

"Now that you mention it, no."

"We've got an expression about that, you know," David told him. "We call it out of the fryin' pan, into the fire."

Fionchadd chuckled, and David thought he had never heard so welcome a sound. "So what do we do, then?"

David sighed. "Yeah, well, that's a real good question."

"Perhaps if I knew how I came here, I could provide

some answers. But first, I must get clean. I have very little time."

"Time? Time for what?"

"To stay awake. I have been gravely injured, David, I must heal. But my kind are not as yours. I can conserve or spend my strength at will. Thus, I choose to be aware now, but I cannot remain so for long. For my body to recover, my mind must aid it, and I cannot do that awake."

"But . . ."

"Never fear. I will not hold you back from whatever errand has brought us here, and I doubt not it is a grave one. I can still travel, if I have to; my body can run itself. I simply will not be able to do anything that requires conscious thought, for I will be . . . inside."

The explanation made David even more dubious of the idea of Fionchadd expending precious energy on something as frivolous as bathing, but the Faery boy would not be dissuaded. So David finally had to lead him back to the stream he had visited earlier. But before he did, he managed to snag the 'possum and confine it in a make-do bag of T-shirt, where it promptly went to sleep. As for Fionchadd, he did not seem to mind if twigs snagged and ruptured blisters, and David wondered if his Faery metabolism was already kicking in, or whether it was simply massive self-control.

While Fionchadd bathed and washed his clothes, David told him the bare bones of what had happened, but long before he had finished, the Faery had climbed back onto the bank and stretched out on a rock to dry. By the time David had got to the actual rescue, his friend was snoring.

That wouldn't do either, because it more or less contradicted what he had just said, and also because their gear was back up at the camp, and David was suddenly getting a little bit paranoid. He was hearing more animal noises now, bigger-sounding ones, and closer. He had heard the cougar twice more, too; and that convinced him they either had to move on or make a fire—preferably both.

A nudge with his foot roused Fionchadd enough to get him to dress and drag himself up slope, but that bothered him: one minute out of it, the next lively and rarin' to go, the next copping Zs again. Still, by the time they'd returned to the camp, the Faery was trotting along famously, though his eyes looked strange and unfocused.

It was time for decision: did he move on (Finno's suggestion), or stay for the night? This wasn't a very protected place, and he still had a fair bit of energy. On the other hand, roaming around in unknown woods at night wasn't very wise, especially when some of the inhabitants might *look* like critters but had humanlike minds—and might not be friendly.

Eventually Fionchadd solved the problem for him, by simply standing and starting to walk.

"Finno, no, not yet!" David protested, but to no avail. In the end, he was left with no choice but to gather up gear (bagged 'possum included) as quickly as he could and follow at a rapid trot.

"Finno, goddamn it, wait!" he panted, when he finally caught up with his friend. "How do you know you're even going the right way?"

"South," Fionchadd said without emotion, and kept on walking.

David never knew how long they hiked through the moonlit forests of Galunlati, but by the end even Fionchadd was flagging. He was helping the Faery along again, and wishing he'd asserted himself sooner. They needed to stop soon; there were sounds all around them; and he couldn't find a good place to camp. 'Course a tree at his back would do at a pinch, even a good-sized boulder; and he could always make a fire, but he'd really hoped to find something better.

Another hill trudged up, another valley navigated, but more or less trying to stay by the creek, which ought to eventually run into the sea somewhere near where he

wanted to go if the geography was at all similar to his
World. And then his luck kicked in.

There was something about the place he came to that
told David he should stop there—spend the rest of the
night if he had to, for he was suddenly tired beyond belief.
"Things have Power because you give them Power," Oisin
had once told him, and so he had come to believe. There
was simply a resonance certain places had—a feeling of
primal *rightness*. Usually it was aesthetic, some conflu-
ence of images that spoke to one's very soul. Sometimes
it was more: a hint of strangeness, or something that dared
to be just a little skewed from the norm. Lookout Rock
was one of those—an excrescence thrust from the moun-
tainside to gaze out at the world and yet remain hidden
from it. This was a little like that.

It was not remarkable, really, merely a pile of boulders
that gradually lifted from the leafy slope in a narrow,
pointed ridge like the prow of a vessel, rising a little above
the surrounding valley. Not far to the land on either side,
though: an easy leap down if he had to, but a hard one to
scramble up. The stream gurgled right below the point,
strangely loud in the night, its margins clear save for leaves
and moss and a few quartzite boulders. There were scattered trees, too, mostly oaks and beeches—but only
enough to preserve the illusion of woods, for he could see
sky between the branches. It was maybe a little too exposed, but something told him to choose it anyway. And
there *was* shelter of a sort, because the point of the ridge
was a step down from the main body, and at that juncture
there was a sort of half-wall which would serve to protect
their backs.

Which was fortunate, because Fionchadd suddenly muttered, "Rest," and sagged against him. David eased his
friend down close to the wall. And decided it was time
for a fire.

Fingers dug through dry moss and found moist earth in
a spot big enough not to be risky, given that the woods
appeared to be almost brittle-dry. A handful of rocks made

a border, and dry moss acted as tinder to the flame he brought from a twisted strand of steel wool stretched between battery terminals. An instant later he had a merry blaze, and a very short while after that had poured water in his peanut can and set it on to boil. Tomorrow, he might even go hunting.

It was probably approaching morning, he realized dimly, though logic and his bioclock said it should only be around six P.M. if they'd gone through the gate at dawn, but he was as tired as if he'd never rested—which really he hadn't. Besides, it was dark, and he felt like sleeping, and he was pretty sure there was nothing more he could do now.

The last thing he did before he went to sleep was allow himself the luxury of one third of the pack of coffee, and to once more free the 'possum. To his relief, it did not run off, but snuggled by his side and slept. Before David finished his bare taste of home, he too was dreaming.

Chapter XXII: Trouble in the Woods

(Orton Carlton State Park, Georgia—Monday, June 16 —mid-day)

Liz had about decided she had spent her whole life in the woods—either that, or in cars. Looking back, it had been less than a day since they'd left Sandy's cabin. But that time had been spent first zipping around the tree-lined curves of Carolina mountains, then navigating the deep valleys of the Chattahoochee National Forest, to wind up first in yet another set of woods south of Jefferson, then in a fourth at Stone Mountain.

And now she was in another—and was getting insanely tired of looking at trees. Still, captive as she was, it was either look at the ones that surrounded them, or at her captors—and she sure didn't want to look at them, 'cause they gave her a monstrous case of the willies.

The whole situation was bloody curious, too. From what she'd been able to piece together from what the Sidhe had told her, and other scraps of information she'd gleaned from their careless conversation, it appeared that Fion-

chadd's guards had given up their chase fairly early in
Atlanta, thinking rightly that there was no point in attacking there with so many people around, and so much iron
and steel. They had simply retired to some refuge or
other—the forests of the Lands of Men offered Faery-kind
no threat and were an obvious choice. From there they'd
simply scryed for her and Alec, doubtless focusing through
any one of the several artifacts they'd abandoned at Calvin's Power Wheel. Lord knew they'd left enough there for
everybody in Erenn to have their own private "let's spy
on Liz and Alec" party. Once the Faeries had ascertained
that their quarry were no longer within the protective con-
fines of civilization, the plan that had led to their capture
had been no problem. (This she had learned simply by
asking, rightly trusting to Faery arrogance to ferret out the
truth.)

Their route to the coast was clear: east and south, and
the guards knew enough of Men's civilization to understand the rudiments of automotive needs. Thus, it had been
simple enough to ride the fast-moving winds of the upper
atmosphere faster than the car, and just as simple to find
the abandoned gas station, selectively englamour it, and
then plant subliminal needs in Liz and Alec's heads
when they'd made themselves vulnerable by rolling down the
windows. Liz doubted they could have maintained complete control; otherwise, they could simply have made her
drive where they wanted—or even wrecked them. But she
suspected that once they keyed into an urge or need (for
gas, for bladder relief, etc.), it was a simple matter to
make it the stuff of diremost necessity.

That was all it had taken. As soon as they'd got out of
the car and split up, the trap had been sprung. Alec had
succumbed as soon as he'd walked into the station, and
she immediately after. Apparently physical proximity gave
the Sidhe greater control. Evidently, too, at least a couple
were wearing the substance of the Lands of Men, because
they had emptied the car quite thoroughly of gear and
pushed it out of the way behind the ruins. All she needed

was to let David's treasured wheels be stripped or hauled off to a chop-shop.

So she sat on the ground and waited and contemplated her surroundings and everything she'd done wrong since that morning.

But at least she was fairly comfortable. The Sidhe had chained her wrists together, but not closely, and her legs were also linked to Alec's, which were in turn bound around the trunk of the immense live-oak they were leaning against, its girth more than sufficient for both of them, and its gnarled roots making surprisingly comfortable seats. She could not see far behind her because of the knobby bark, but she could see Alec. And lord knew she could see the woods. She'd already counted every tree in the small depression that housed them; not to mention catalogued their common names, genus, and species (trees had got to be one of her "things" the last year or so, and she was now considering a career in landscape architecture). She'd also examined each of the three man-high boulders that shielded part of their hidey-hole, and was pretty certain she could now draw the lichen patterns on them from memory.

But she absolutely could not stand to watch her captors.

There were four of them at the moment. One had gone off on foot fairly quickly, heading back the way they had come. He'd been sort of blurry to look at then, but she thought he might have been putting on human shape. If she had to guess, she'd say he was back at the bogus station looking out for intruders.

The other—she thought it was the one who had worn Alec's shape, and so surprised her—had departed right after she and Alec had been secured. One instant a tall, handsome man; the next a vast black-winged eagle.

He'd flown south then—she thought; at least that's what it had looked like when she caught one final glimpse of him gliding away above the trees.

Since then, she'd been watching, thinking, and—she had to admit—grabbing a few winks on the sly.

As if in response to that thought, her eyes grew heavy again, and once more she slept.

Liz didn't know what time it was when she awoke, as her watch had stopped running. But she thought it was a little after noon, judging by the position of the sun, which was now feeding harsh yellow light into the clearing, making everything go stark and threatening.

So too, were the Sidhe. They sat apart, now playing some kind of game that involved small bones, piles of tokens, and an intricate design sketched in the sand. In their long black velvet surcotes (intricately dagged along the edges), and with the collars of their similarly ornamented black satin cloaks drawn up high and pointy, they looked less like mighty men of Faery than a gaggle of roosting buzzards—an image made even more striking by the fact that three of the four had flaming red hair, and that two had on yellow boots. *Conjured stuff,* she imagined, for as far as she knew Faery clothes didn't change shape when their owners did. She thought David had mentioned that once: that they sometimes had to garb themselves in illusion or go naked. A minor inconvenience, she acknowledged, but it just went to prove that not even the Sidhe were perfect.

One of the men tossed three bones. Another looked at him and swore. A third chuckled merrily.

The fourth peered uneasily at the sky.

"What is it?" she heard one of them say—or read his thoughts, she was never certain.

"Y'Alvar comes," Shorter Yellow Boot said.

"Which makes me winner," Taller Yellow Boot replied, scooping up a handful of tokens.

Short Yellow stopped him. "Says who? We were to play until he returns. He is not back yet, not technically."

"Dana! You sound like a blasted mortal! So when *is* he back—*technically?*"

"When he touches ground and resumes his own shape."

"Bloody bones!" the other swore.

"Hark! Now!"

Liz followed Tall Yellow's gaze skyward, and saw a winged shape returning. A whoosh of wings, a coolness of displaced air, and he stood once more in the clearing: an eagle as big as a man. What followed confused Liz so much she was not certain what she saw. For an instant there was a bird, then it seemed to shrink into itself rather like one of those old Dracula movies when the Count changed himself into a bat, only this was the opposite, and then for a fraction of a second she thought she saw a tall naked man, but then a small whirlwind arose around him and when the visual chaos clarified, there stood the fifth guardsman, liveried more or less as the others, except that *his* boots were red.

"You are back, Y'Alvar," the biggest red-head said. "Tell us what you have learned."

Y'Alvar flopped against one of the boulders. "I have flown south, as you ordered. It is as we have heard: Finvarra's fleet sails this way and quickly—but Lugh sneaks around the southern coast to meet him, and I suspect a third force approaches as well, if the storm clouds I saw to the east are more than they appear."

"So it will be battle then?"

"Aye, and uneven against us, unless our Lord has hidden allies."

"Did you deliver the message?"

"Aye," Y'Alvar replied. "Though our own kinsmen almost shot me before I could declare myself. Rumors are everywhere: Lugh has boats that sail underwater; the Powersmiths have withdrawn; the boy has finally revealed what Finvarra wishes—though we know the truth of that one, curse him."

"No mention of the Mortals who stole him?"

"None. I was the one to bring word of that to Finvarra, where he stood on the deck of his flagship. It is a good thing I was warded, or I might have come back to you without my head."

"He might yet," Short Yellow chuckled, pulling out a wicked-looking dagger, which he began to sharpen. "If he learns it was you who could not find the key."

"You set the wards, though. Thus, the fault is equal."

"Aye," Tall Yellow replied. "A moment sooner, and we'd have caught the Mortal at it."

"What about *these* prisoners?" Big Red asked, lifting a shoulder toward Alec and Liz. "I trust you inquired of them as well?"

"Truly," Y'Alvar told him. "And the word of the Ard Rhi is this: we are to wait here until he can send someone to retrieve them, and take no further action. He does not dare risk further exposure in the Lands of Men. Once he has them, he will use them to force Lugh to bargain: their lives for the return of Fionchadd."

"But Lugh does not *have* Fionchadd."

"Finvarra knows this, but also knows that Lugh will probably not know anything about his escape at all, the borders twixt Tir-Nan-Og and this World being closed."

"Closed? I had not heard this."

"They are not physically sealed, but that might as well be so; it was a vow—a kind of ban, with some complex bit of extra glamour thrown in the bargain, which almost amounts to a sealing. But in any event, we did not come here through Tir-Nan-Og, thus we would have to pass through too many sets of World Walls to get home, and that we cannot do."

Short Yellow shook his head. "I have never understood all this about the Worlds and how they overlap in time. Not in a thousand years has it become clear to me."

Liz found herself snickering at that. So she wasn't the only one who found the multiplicity of worlds exasperating.

"The point is," Big Red said finally, "that we cannot return to Faerie from here unless we go by sea, for we did not come here from there—precisely."

"Never mind that to do so would also put us at large in

Lugh's land, which is not a thought I relish, not with the Morrigu searching every rock and stream for spies.''

"And the King himself, so I hear.''

"Curse him, too,'' Big Red snorted. "Had Lugh not . . .''

Y'Alvar cleared his throat ominously. "I had not yet finished speaking.''

Chastened, they listened to him.

"The fact that Lugh does not have Fionchadd, though Finvarra demands him, will doubtless be an excuse for attack,'' Y'Alvar went on. "Lugh will lose, for this close to his land he surely would no longer dare use the full power of Spear, it being harder to control the more Power lies in it, and it waxes every day, so I have heard. When Lugh falls, Erenn will claim Tir-Nan-Og. Then we can take our leisure to look for the boy—both boys.''

"Three boys, apparently. There was a third.''

"I saw only a small animal?''

"Which was also a boy. Did you not smell Power about it, though of an unfamiliar kind?''

"So humans shapeshift now?'' Big Red mused. "This is a new thing in the world. I trust you told Finvarra this as well?''

"I told him all—or had it taken from me. My head still aches from it.''

"You have not told us what to do,'' Big Yellow prompted, "nor how long we must remain in this noisome place.''

Y'Alvar glared at him. "Until Finvarra can send someone to fetch them; I thought I made that clear. It will probably be night, when there is less chance of being seen—and it will take less glamour to hide the ship.''

"Ship?''

"Ship. Morgalin has captured one of Lugh's flying craft. He will bring it here with him.''

"Ah, now I understand.''

"It is time you did,'' Y'Alvar sighed wearily. "And now, let us examine this curious crystal you had from the boy.''

Chapter XXIII: Playing 'Possum

(Galunlati—day two—morning)

A shaft of morning sunlight shining straight into his eyes woke David—either that, or the cursed 'possum rooting in his armpit, or Fionchadd's incessant moans. He blinked, scratched his nose, and squinted up through the froth of brown-edged leaves, then closed his eyes again and started to turn over. It was too damned early for this.

And then the 'possum licked his ear.

"Dammit, Fargo, stop that!"

Another lick, this time accented with a nip.

He sat up abruptly, if more than a little stiff around the back from having slept on solid rock. The sun was just slanting over the horizon, casting golden shafts of light among the trees. And he was turned just so he could see an infinity of tiny spider webs joining every bush and twig along a wide arc of horizon. There were long ones higher up, and short ones lower down, not webbed together in patterns, simply joining. And here, now, the sun transfigured them with subtle color, so that they glimmered red and gold and green in the morning light.

If only his back were better. He stood reluctantly, feel-

ing his joints protest, and actually hearing one pop as he
staggered over to the fire and checked it for coals. Fortunately, there was one. Dry moss made it a small fire, and
he put a tin of water on to boil before trotting off to tend
to necessary, if unheroic, business which suddenly would
not wait. That done, it was down to the stream where
water in his face refreshed him remarkably. Now almost
awake, he turned his attention to Fionchadd.

The Faery was still moaning, but he didn't appear to be
any worse. As a matter of fact, he looked considerably
better. Certainly those parts of his skin that had been red
as a five-hour sunburn were now somewhere between gold
and pink, which was basically their normal shade. And
the awful blisters seemed to have gone down some as well,
or at least those that had popped looked to be slowly
merging back with the surrounding skin. Oh, he was thin,
and it was true his eyes were swollen and his lips were
puffy, but David was beginning to believe in Faery powers
of regeneration. He wondered, suddenly, how the rest of
him was doing—and, if they could still make their goal in
time.

That brought him back to the hard side of reality: He
had no idea where he was, whether north or south of Uki.
He'd had no real goal in mind when he'd made the transition, either, and you were supposed to have one, or else
it would take you to whomever you'd called upon—except
that he hadn't actually finished even that and hadn't Calvin
said something about reaching the wrong destination by
accident last time they'd visited Uki because of some of
that foolishness with the sun? All he'd really had in his
head when they'd transited was an image of forest and a
general desire to get south. So the scale had probably simply deposited him in the analog of where he'd been. Since
then he'd been walking south, or so Finno said. But where
now? Suddenly he wished very badly he'd paid a lot more
attention to the geography of middle Georgia as it per-
tained to streams and rivers.

A check of the survival kit produced a bouillon cube.

He hated to risk sure food so early on, but still, the sooner he got fed, the sooner he could think clearly, and the sooner he could do that, the sooner he'd be able to search for edibles along the way.

And while the water boiled, maybe he'd relax a minute more. Wearily, he slumped down beside the Faery, folded his arms behind his head, and closed his eyes, but kept his ears open for the sound of water boiling.

What he heard was the 'possum hissing furiously at him as it thumped from a nearby tree onto his chest.

"What th—?" Then, "Calvin, you asshole!" And then he stopped himself. *Calvin.* He'd been so damned concerned about Finno he'd almost forgotten about his other companion! Well, it was about time he did something about it.

Which was a lot harder than it sounded.

Best to think logically. Item one: shape-shifting was risky at best; the beast brain tried to take over, and the longer you wore that shape, the stronger it got; and Calvin had been in this one much longer already than David had ever worn another skin. Item two: he'd sort of helped Calvin along when they'd begun, basically in the interest of time, so the guy might not have had time to prepare for it. Having both David's will and the sudden acquisition of 'possum-ness thrust upon you at the same time was bound to be more than a little traumatic.

Still, evidently the 'possum liked him, 'cause it hadn't run off yet. So there was probably some part of Calvin hanging around in there. The trick was to get it out.

But how?

Maybe the way he got him in?

It was worth a try, he supposed.

Very slowly he slid to a sitting position, keeping the 'possum on his stomach. With equal care he extended his right hand and gently touched its head, then, when it did not resist, first patted, then stroked, then scratched it. It seemed to enjoy the experience; or at least it grinned in that toothily winsome way only 'possums can do. Very slowly he increased his grip on it, holding it behind the forelegs, feeling its tiny heart suddenly accelerate. With his other hand he dragged out his uktena scale, still on its thong around his neck. Then, very gently, he slid his scale over until he could set one of the 'possum's surprisingly human-looking paws atop one of the points, and his hand over both it and the other.

"Okay, Fargo," he said. "I don't know if you're in there or not, but I'm gonna try real hard to change you back, and I'd appreciate it if you'd help if you can. I don't know if you're *able* to think but if you can, I want you to think human too."

The 'possum blinked its beady eyes at him, twitched its pointy nose—and yawned.

"Calvin!"

That got its attention, but it bristled, started to try to twist away.

"Okay, then, kid—if that's the way you want it."

And with that he pressed the 'possum's paw into the razor-sharp edge of the uktena scale, and closed his eyes against the pain as it likewise sliced his own hand. He tried not to think of the pain, focused on only one thing: Calvin. Dark hair, dark eyes, atypically stubby nose for one of his kind, wide cheekbones, ruddy skin on a strong, muscular body.

The 'possum hissed, wriggled, turned to bite him—and then he could no longer hold it, though he kept his eyes closed, trying vainly to maintain the image. It hissed again, and then that hiss became a trill, which became a scream. He felt a sudden weight on his chest, and when his eyes popped open by reflex, he found himself eye to chin with a genuine naked Cherokee Indian.

David blushed and scooted back, but Calvin stayed where he was, his eyes half-wild.

"Calvin?" David dared. "Fargo? *Edahi?*"

The last evidently triggered some hidden key, and David could practically see the memories flooding back.

And then it was Calvin's turn to blush, and very carefully stand and back away.

"Th . . . thanks, man," he stammered, and David could see his eyes sort of half-way crossing, almost as if he were trying to look at his own tongue in wonder. He noticed his hands, then, and then the rest. Eventually he squatted down.

David nodded toward Calvin's knapsack. "Think you've got some clothes in there. Finno's here but out of it. Breakfast is on. Welcome to Galunlati."

Calvin shook his head, then noticed the boiling bouillon and wrinkled his nose in disgust. "You're gonna drink *that?*"

"It'll do till I get something better. Besides, I've noticed what you've been eatin' lately."

"A lot better, probably."

"Spiders? And roaches?"

Calvin looked horrified at David's straight face, but then the facade cracked, and David giggled, and then they were both laughing like fools.

"Jesus, man, it's good to have you back," David panted when he finally regained control.

"Not as good as it is to *be* back, I'll wager," Calvin replied. "Now what's the deal? Last time I knew anything we were in a high hurry to rescue Finno. Obviously that worked. Last thing I remember clearly was something about a lion-faced fish—that and bein' cold as a witch's titty."

"In a brass bra, after being dead twenty years in Antarctica."

"Etcetera, etcetera, etcetera."

"But seriously, man; I guess I'd better brief you."

"Do," Calvin urged. "And while you're at it, why don't you pick us some of those blueberries?"

David looked puzzled for a moment, then glanced over his shoulder to see a low bush crammed full of the largest ones he'd ever seen, sprouting from the stones behind him.

He needed no second prompting and filled his mouth

with them at roughly the same rate he filled Calvin in on the facts.

"Yeah," Calvin said, as David inspected the suddenly inadequate-looking broth an instant later while Calvin was dressing in the shorts and T-shirt he'd found in his knapsack. "Sounds like you did all you could, considerin' the circumstances. Dad'll probably be pissed to find the fence down and the pups out, but it won't be the first time he's been that way. Besides, just imagine the alternative."

"What alternative?"

"Suppose you guys had taken shelter in the house and claimed sanctuary, and then the parental unit had come home and found the Sidhe outside masqueradin' as Hari Krishnas or something. Can you imagine that? Like what happened last year at your Uncle's house, only with nosy neighbors in the loop. I almost wish we'd done it."

"Give me a break, guy, we've got serious problems."

"Two, I make it—besides reconnecting with our folks: Gettin' old Finno where he's supposed to go, and somehow meetin' up with the Powersmiths. We never did really work any of it out, beyond a few vague ideas."

"As I recall we had a lot of other things on our minds," David said dryly. "The thinking was we'd work on that as we travelled; thereby, to quote Mr. McLean, 'making maximum effective use of available temporal resources.' "

Calvin giggled. "And you sound like him too."

"But seriously. Any suggestions?"

Not with Finno like he is. I suppose the only reasonable thing is for us to go on like we have been, if Finno's ambulatory. See if we can find water and make a raft or canoe, or simply float."

"To *Savannah?* That's five hours by car from Atlanta!"

"It's faster'n walkin', though, and not as tirin'. Remember, we've only got a couple of days, max, and probably a lot less. It'd take weeks to walk to there."

David's heart sank. "If only we could teleport or something. I still can't believe we lost the rest of the blasted scales.''

''*I* can't believe it either,'' Calvin replied pointedly.

David paused thoughtfully. ''What about this?'' He indicated the scale that had worked the change.

Calvin shook his head. ''No go. Like I said, they haven't been activated. Also we've only got two and there's three of us, and they require the blood of a sorcerer—that business with the deer was unique to the ulunsuti, and even then we had Alec helpin' out—who *is* a sorcerer, kinda, though he won't admit it. And anyway,'' he added, ''we don't have enough to do the amount of World hoppin' we'd need to do.''

''There's an easier solution, of course,'' David noted carefully. ''If you're willin' to risk it.''

Calvin raised an eyebrow. ''What?''

''You're not gonna like it. And I promise I won't blame you if you say no.''

''I'm better at listenin' than readin' minds.''

David took a deep breath. ''Okay, then: You use your scale to change shape to something that's fast, a bird maybe; and fly north, and try to find Uki and get him to help us. We know he's got more scales, maybe he'll lend us some.''

Calvin's eyes widened in horror. ''Uh uh, no way man. I just did that and it scared the hell out of me. I'm not about to change again so soon. I might never come back.''

David shrugged and looked away.

''Why don't *you* go?'' Calvin said finally. ''You're better at it than I am.''

''Maybe so,'' David replied. ''But it scares hell out of me too. Besides—and I'm tryin' to play Alec and be logical here—I need to go with Finno in case we have to deal with Faerie. I mean, this is your World, the one you know most about. That's mine, I'm therefore the logical choice.''

''*Damn* logic!''

''I'd have said that once too,'' David replied. ''But then Liz gave me this.'' He reached into his neckband and pulled out the medallion. " 'Head and heart,' it means. Logic and emotion. Right brain and left brain, or whatever. Everything you do's a conflict between 'em."

"And this is another, right?"

"Right. Heart says you don't wanta, says you're scared, and with good reason. Head says you oughta, says you can do it if you try, says you can always stand one more thing."

"Yeah, sure."

"You can stand *anything*, Calvin—long as you know for how long."

"Your philosophy?"

He shook his head. "Myra Jane Buchanan. You know, Runnerman's sis?"

"Good lookin' blonde in the picture on his dresser?"

"Calvin!"

"Right." He frowned then, fell silent, stared at the ground a long time. Finally he looked back up at David. "I'll do it," he said. "If I didn't, and things go wrong, I'll always wonder if they'd have gone better if I'd done something else. This way I won't have to worry."

David rose, embraced him impulsively. "Good man."

Calvin shrugged. "Yeah, well, I guess I decided you had a point, too. You go south and try to cover as much territory as you can. I go north and try to bring help. That way we're both workin' on different facets of the problem, and one or the other of us is more likely to have some luck. So . . . when do I fly?"

"How 'bout as soon as we've choked down this blessed broth. Probably need your help to feed Finno anyway."

Calvin's grin was almost rival to the sun. "I'm afraid you're right."

The broth was awful, thin and weak, but with Calvin's help David managed to get a fair bit of it where it would do the most good: inside their Faery friend. David tried once or twice to wake the boy, but had no luck.

An hour passed, maybe, though it was still long before noon, but David was starting to get antsy. He put out the fire, started gathering gear. "You ready, Fargo? I mean it's not like I'm tryin' to get rid of you or anything, but we probably really do need to get goin'."

Another shrug. "No, I'm not ready—but I never will be. Any messages for old Mister Darkthunder?"

"Yeah," David replied. "Tell him I said, *help!*"

"Will do," Calvin replied, and started stripping.

He fell silent then, and David could tell he was psyching. Calvin had reclaimed his scale necklace sometime before, and was now wearing it around his neck. He turned and mounted the boulder behind him, stood clear in open air.

"Good luck . . . *Edahi*," David whispered.

"Good luck to you too, Sikwa Unega."

And with that Calvin closed his eyes and clamped his fist hard on the scale.

David did not watch; something told him he did not want to see. But he saw the Indian's shadow, saw it spread and twist, and change. Not until he heard the harsh, shrill cry did he dare look again.

He wasn't certain what kind of bird Calvin had become, except that it was some kind of raptor. But he'd have bet anything it was fast. Probably a peregrine falcon.

"Take care," David called—and then the falcon flapped its wings and was rising into the sky. It circled twice, and turned north. David was once more alone.

He gathered up his meager gear, and knelt beside Fionchadd (who had stopped moaning once he was fed). "Come on, Finno," he sighed. "Best we travel."

Fionchadd's eyes suddenly popped open. "No," he said. "I think we ought to fly too."

Chapter XXIV: Wooden Ships

(Orton Carlton State Park, Georgia—Monday, June 16 —evening)

Somewhere around sunset Alec McLean stared down at his hands and realized they were no longer hurting. Oh, they were still chained together, of course, but the awful, burning pain was gone. He breathed a sign of relief—and immediately regretted it, fearful one of the guards might hear him and investigate. He didn't know what they knew, but he certainly didn't want to have to answer any awkward questions—not when he hardly dared believe how the healing had been accomplished himself.

It had all been blind good luck. He'd spent most of the time since their capture combating pain, trying to conserve energy, and attempting to think, none of which worked very well. At some point he'd faded out entirely, only to come to again about the time that Y'Alvar fellow flew in and started going on about fleets, and ships, and rendezvous, and stuff.

And then they'd started talking about the ulunsuti.

They'd got it out, naturally, passed it around, examined it from every angle, poked it and prodded it and tried to scratch it with knives. It was magic, they all agreed, but of a kind they did not know. It would make a fine curiosity for Finvarra, might even get them off the hook for the loss of the prisoner.

Eventually, though, they'd tired of trying to figure out how to work it and put it aside.

And then had begun Alec's good fortune. They had not heeded precaution, had not returned it to its deerskin pouch or the pottery jar. Rather, Y'Alvar had simply stuffed it back in one of the packs—and left the flap open so that Alec had a clear view of most of it.

Now being the rational sort that he was, Alec had not intended to try any magic just then; his mind simply did not work in a way that considered that a prime option. But he nevertheless found his eye constantly drawn back to the ulunsuti. And as the sunlight waned, the desire to stare at it became ever more compulsive. Perhaps it was the way it had of gathering light—almost attracting it, so that as evening gloomed the land, the crystal continued to grow brighter. In any event, he soon could not tear his eyes away from it. It seemed to be trying to tell him something, too, but every time he thought he understood the vague tickling in his mind, his hands would throb again and he'd get distracted. Eventually he'd gotten so frustrated that the passive desire for relief became an active obsession.

And with that, the pain began to vanish. That was all it took: desire focused on the ulunsuti by its master. The more Alec wished the pain away, the faster it fled. Eventually he gained a fair bit of control. It helped to be quite specific, he found: concentrate on this joint of this finger, then the next, and so on. It took nearly an hour, but eventually he was healed.

He was just trying to figure out some way to indicate this to Liz when the ship arrived.

The sight fair took Alec's breath away. One moment there was clear sky to the southeast, its eastern fringe still

fading scarlet between the tree trunks, but its higher
reaches already a glorious midnight blue quickly awaken-
ing with stars. The next instant there was a spark of silver
that he first thought was a meteor, except that it continued
to grow brighter—and larger—and clearer—as it flashed
and glimmered in and out of sight, until a very short while
later a ship hove into view in the air above their tiny clearing.

Their captors rose as one, gathering possessions,
straightening garments. An unintelligible order sent two
striding toward him and Liz.

But he was not looking, for he was too caught up in the
wonder of the Faery vessel. It was silver, though whether
that was metal, paint, or simply "glow," he could not
tell. In shape, it was long and slender and low of draft
like a Viking ship. Like one of them, too, it had a dragon
prow and a mast and sails. These last were a little strange,
for they were black emblazoned with red eagles that did
not quite fit the color scheme of the rest of the vessel. He
supposed, though, that if it were a ship Finvarra had captured from Lugh, those might well be sails the captors had
added. There were oars, too: ten at least to a side, all
stirring empty air. As he watched, they ceased their action.

Buzzing filled his head, making him blink and squint
with a sensation that was not quite pain. It was an echo
of the mind talk the Sidhe sometimes used among themselves, he knew. But he didn't like it because this way,
when it was not directed at him, it was sort of the mental
equivalent of white noise, disrupting all other language
processes, as if those parts of his brain that made sense
out of speech were receiving two sets of inputs at once
and producing gibberish.

The upshot was that he was staring stupidly when Y'Alvar came up to him, gripped him under the shoulder, and
with the aid of another guard simply rose with him into
the sky.

He almost lost it at that, and would have cried out except

that a sudden paralysis gripped his throat. More Faery magic, probably, but that didn't stop the gag reflex—with the result that the first thing he did when he arrived aboard the beautiful silver airship was to toss his cookies all over the gleaming deck—and one of the guards.

He got a forearm in his face for that, and a quick, if unpleasant, interface between the deck, his butt, and his elbows. But he also got a small twinge of satisfaction. He was just starting to gather himself up again when he saw Liz likewise levitated on board. She seemed to be behaving with better grace than he had, but her eyes, visible in the reflected glow of the twenty-odd torches that ringed the long narrow railing, were ablaze with indignation and fury.

More voices buzzed in his head, hands hauled him up and brought him over to where Liz was standing. The chains went around their legs again, and another set joined them to the mast—closer than they'd been to the oak tree. Obviously the commander of this vessel did not want them roaming around.

A final set of barked orders, a thrum through the hull, and they were moving.

He saw the dragon prow come around, saw the constellations of Georgia summer slowly swing past it, and then they were pointing south and gathering speed. Speed, yes, but there was no sensation of movement. He only knew that the bits of landscape he could make out beyond the railing were sweeping by with unnatural haste. Yet the sails, though swollen, were not straining, and the torches did not seem to be aware of any wind.

The transition to Faery came suddenly. As soon as they were no longer over land, and thus no longer over mortal territories that overlapped Tir-Nan-Og, there was an abrupt, awful, twisting sensation; the world sort of turned in on itself; and suddenly they were sailing above the choppy seas of Faerie.

Alec had never seen them before, and though he was

scared, and pissed, and had the taste of stomach acid in his mouth, he nevertheless could not help but appreciate them. It was as if blue velvet had been overlaid with emerald green glass, and the whole sprinkled with dancing diamonds. The air was perfect: warm but soothing, with maybe the merest hint of some distant storm to give it passion; and there was a smell of both salt and cinnamon. A flock of seagulls was still quarrelling and protesting and insulting them from when the ship had emerged from nothing in their midst.

And the sky: more velvet, but a different shade of blue, and without the glass—but with jewels that were the stars, all far brighter and with far more clarity of color than he had ever seen on the skies of earth. There was an aurora to the north, too; and now he looked more closely, both earth and sky were alive with the pale, golden glitter of Straight Tracks.

With absolutely no warning, the deck tilted and he found himself flung shoulder-long into Liz. The impact jerked a grunt from her, and he felt the paralysis on this throat relax. "Liz," he managed in a sort of half croak, half whisper.

"Yeah," she told him. Then: "Hey, I can talk again!"

"Good thing, too, 'cause—"

The deck tilted again, even more steeply, and the air filled with shouts. Some of the crew had already fallen overboard, but a fair number more were shifting shape and taking wing into the dark skies of the east. He and Liz seemed to have been forgotten.

"Dana!" someone swore. *"Ambush!"*

"It's Lugh!"

"Curse his luck forever!" That from another.

"Lugh?" Alec shouted, glancing at Liz. They were almost on their side, keeling over on an ocean of air a hundred yards or more above the water. But this time when the ship jerked and twitched they could see what caused it.

There was another vessel there—no, an endless file of

them, all rowing in the empty air, while an even greater fleet darkened the seas below it. Alec wondered that he had not seen them before, but then he had no more time for thought because a light blazed out from that first ship and arrowed straight toward them. It caught the sail above them and set it aflame. A second bolt wrapped the dragon-prow with fire.

The third blast of flame struck the hull even with the mast—which meant it was even with them. Alec felt it lick at him, heard Liz's scream, even as he surpassed it with his own, which was born both of surprise and his new dread of fire. He felt his eyebrows crisped away and caught the stench of burning hair. This was it then: Mama McLean's only boy, would-be rocket scientist, hacker extraordinaire, was gonna buy it by being cooked alive in a flying boat over the seas of an unreal ocean. Poetic injustice for certain!

A fourth bolt flowered where the other had, and with that, the boat tipped over.

Alec closed his eyes and prayed. They were gonna die, were gonna die, were gonna die. From impact, from drowning, from flame, from monsters that lived in the sea.

"Shiiiiiittttt!" he heard himself yell as he started to slide. They would have smashed into the railing, had they not been chained to the mast, but just as they were yanked up short, he heard a crack, saw one final bolt lance out from the fleet, and center the mast.

It shattered, blasting them with shrapnel. They were upside down now, hanging by the chains that wrapped their feet. Liz seemed to be unconscious, but then she'd been closer to the impact. He hoped that was all she was. He snagged her awkwardly as she flopped into him again. If they went down, at least they'd do it together.

And then something snapped and they were falling.

Alec flailed out—felt—*heard*—air rushing past his ears, saw glittering blue darkness rushing up at him, and had only time to duck his head and grab one final breath before impact.

Warm water enclosed him, and he found himself bul-
leting far down before friction slowed him and survival
instincts took over. Something dragged against his arm,
though: Liz—a dead weight there—maybe dead in the most
literal sense. He hoped not, but then the need for air became uppermost, and he was swimming for all he was
worth, fighting the pull of the water against his clothes,
the stronger tug of the chains, the fire in his lungs as he
made them wait a little longer.

Abruptly he broke surface, almost brained himself on a
bit of shimmering timber. He grabbed for it, slipped,
grabbed another and held, managed to get Liz's head out
of the water. Good, she was still breathing. Water slapped
into his mouth and he sputtered. "Liz?" he called softly.
"Liz?"

Her eyelids fluttered, and he breathed a sigh of relief.
"Liz, oh thank God!"

"Where are we?" she gasped between fits of coughing.

"The ship crashed. I think Lugh ambushed it."

"Lugh!" she cried. "We've gotta get hold of him, gotta
signal!"

Alec felt his heart flip-flop, for that really was a good
idea. But then he gazed skyward—and saw to his dismay
the vast airy armada already almost out of sight to the east.

"No!" Liz groaned hopelessly, and sagged against him,
her eyes awash with tears.

"But at least *we're* still alive," Alec tried to reassure
her, though he took small comfort from the fact. "That's
more than a lot of these guys are." He nodded at a corpse
that was bobbing past—one of the yellow-booted guards.
The Faery was floating face down. His tunic had been
flamed away on one side, leaving his back and one arm
exposed, and they were covered with blistered and crisped
flesh. But the other hand—Alec could not believe his luck.
The other hand still clutched the bag that held the ulunsuti.

"Oh, Christ, Liz—I've gotta get that!" Alec cried, already starting to paddle toward it.

The words were scarcely out of his mouth, though,

before his elation faded. For even as his fingers brushed the tattered remains of the Faery's cloak, the pouch slipped free and sank beneath the waves.

"Damn!" Alec spat helplessly, his eyes also welling with tears. "Christ, it was so close! So goddamn close—and now we're stuck here!" He sank back against the float, not caring whether he held on or not.

Liz stared at him, her face suddenly hard. "Snap out of it, Alec! It's gone, there's nothing you can do about it. We've got more important things to deal with now!"

"Yeah, but it's our way outta here. I've blown it!"

"No you haven't," Liz told him sharply. "None of this is your fault."

"Yes it is," he retorted. "It's *all* my fault—from the moment I didn't believe David when he told me about meeting the Sidhe. I—"

"Well then *do* something about it!" Liz interrupted. "We've always gotten through these messes somehow, we'll get through this one too! Use your famous brain to think, not feel sorry for yourself! Shoot—use the goddamn ulunsuti!"

"It's lost!"

"*Is* it?" she asked suddenly. "It's under water, but that's not the same. If . . . we were in the desert and you'd seen it roll down a sand dune and out of sight, would that be lost? Besides, you're its master—*master* it!"

"But . . ." Alec began, and then his face brightened. Perhaps she had a point. "You're right, Liz, maybe there *is* something I can do."

And with that he began fumbling with the mess of chain and broken mast. There was an angle of ragged metal there—one that kept poking him in the back, but maybe . . . The ulunsuti responded to blood, so it was just possible . . .

He twisted around in the water, gulped a mouthful of the stuff, and brought the heel of his right hand against the brass projection. Once, twice, and he closed his eyes and gritted his teeth, and slashed his hand across it really hard—and felt a warm trickle of blood. This was it then—

the experiment to end all experiments. He closed his eyes,
tried to envision the ulunsuti somewhere at the bottom of
the sea, then tried to imagine his blood wending its way
there—and tried *not* to think about sharks and such like.

A deep breath, and he began his call: *Come . . .
come . . .* Over and over, endlessly repeated, while he
tried to think only of one thing: the ulunsuti on the bottom
of the sea, slowly absorbing his blood, wakening to it with
that bright light it held—*responding!*

He never knew how to describe it afterwards, but he
somehow became aware that he *had* connected. *Come . . .
come . . .* he continued his litany.

And the ulunsuti came. One moment Alec felt his
thoughts stretched taut through the darkness of the Faery
ocean; an instant later, warm wet leather brushed his hand.
He grabbed for it awkwardly, almost lost it again, but then
managed to cup it in his hand and slowly work the pouch
into a pocket.

"I did it!" he shouted. "Liz, I did it!"

But an hour later they were still floating.

Chapter XXV: Wingin' It

(Galunlati—day two—mid-day)

David stared at Fionchadd incredulously. "You're *not* serious," he whispered. Then, when the Faery's expression did not change, "No, I reckon you are."

Fionchadd regarded him calmly, and David could see that his face, at least, had almost completely healed in the little while since David had first awakened. "Certainly," the Faery affirmed. "I would never jest about anything as important as this."

David sat down abruptly and drained the last of the bouillon, grimacing at the taste. "So what'd you have in mind?" he asked carefully, not looking at his friend. To keep his trepidation at reasonable bay, he began half-heartedly scouring the peanut-can pot with sand and a little of the water that remained in the bag.

"It is as I suggested," Fionchadd told him. "You have changed shape before, have you not? You can therefore do so again. I know of no other way to cross the distance we must in the time that remains."

David put down the can and looked away. "What about you? You can't shapeshift . . . can you?"

Fionchadd gave a gentle half-snort of surprise. "Of course I can—all the Sidhe have that art, though some are stronger than others. Like many other talents: it improves with practice.''

"And you feel up to it? I mean, a day ago you looked like somebody's thrown-out scrambled eggs—and I've got a feelin' you were more than a little fried inside too!''

The Faery took David gently by the arm and eased him around to face him. "Look at me, David Sullivan.''

David did, though he didn't want to. Green eyes flashed before him—not with anger or fear, but with concern.

"I do not understand this fear I see, David. You have done this thing before—surely you do not fear it now!''

David stared back up at him, and felt his eyes suddenly a-brim with tears, which embarrassed him considerably. "Don't I?'' I'm fine if I don't think about it, but if I do . . .''

"Fionchadd frowned in perplexity. "But those other times you acted in haste, from strong emotion; you did not have time to mark that which makes you human. This time we can change more slowly, then fly. Flight is a—what is your word?—*reflex*. You can still be you. We can even talk as we travel—mind to mind. That should keep you sure of who you are.''

"I . . . just don't know,'' David said.

Fionchadd shook his head. "Yes you do. You knew as soon as I first mentioned it; I saw it in your eyes.''

"I guess it's like Calvin said,'' David sighed. "I guess sometimes you really do have to just grab yourself by the balls and jump.''

"I guess,'' Fionchadd chuckled, "you do.''

It took them but a short while to make ready. David cleaned up the campsite and repacked the survival kit, though he did allow himself the luxury of a cup of coffee. The main problem was in deciding what form to take. It had to be fast, it had to have endurance, it had to be strong enough to fly with a bit of extra weight because David was not going to abandon the survival kit, and had to have the uktena scale to change back.

"So many choices, it if were me," Fionchadd mused. "All the flying things of Faerie. But you have *not* so many options, you are limited to the beasts you know: birds and bats."

"Bats," David said thoughtfully. "Now *there's* an idea! I never would've thought of them, but that might be kinda neat. Think it'd work?"

"It would be fine with me," the Faery replied with a shrug. "Any time you are ready."

But still David hesitated.

"There is a strange thing about anticipation," Fionchadd told him. "It is generally both more and less than the actuality that follows. A thing desired is rarely as pleasant to possess as it is to anticipate; a thing dreaded is rarely so foul."

"And this is both, I reckon," David replied. "All my kind dream of flyin'."

"Mine too," Fionchadd acknowledged. "It seems to be a common ambition."

"Yeah, but we're also scared shitless of fallin'," David added, laughing softly.

Fionchadd returned his uncertain smile more vividly. "Come now, foolish Mortal, let us begin."

David rolled his eyes and joined his friend on the ledge above their campsite. Fionchadd had insisted on taking the fannypack containing the survival kit, and now wore it strapped around his scrawny hips—in spite of the fair bit of steel it contained, though the denim would offer some insulation. They had also, at David's prompting, managed to fold David's cut-offs and the Faery's breeches small enough to fill the remaining space.

"I have my reasons," Fionchadd assured him, when David would have protested the Faery's decision. "It is enough that you carry the scale."

David grimaced in resignation and squared his shoulders. "Now?"

"Whenever it pleases you."

David took a deep breath and closed his eyes. Another,

and he raised his right hand to the scale, which was still on its thong around his throat—right beside Liz's token. A third breath, and he grabbed it, felt the glassy edges bite into his flesh, and the familiar warm, sticky ooze of blood.

Think bat!

Bat: small, light, but not *too* small, because he needed to be strong; wings stretching taut and leathery no tail, short legs—head . . . A moment's panic. What *kind* of head, surely not the ugly faces the local kind had, and then he thought better: what were those neat fruit-eating bats called? Flying foxes. They were big too, and therefore strong. He'd become one of them. And as he chose, the image clarified.

Of what followed the only things David could recall clearly were the moment his arms demanded to be raised from his side, and the instant his major sense shifted from sight to hearing and it seemed that the whole world had suddenly become as rich with sound as before it had been with color. The air was awash with it: the buzz of bees, the dry rustle of over-heated leaves, the click of beetle-bodies as they clambered over the rocks and moss, the tinkle of the stream, the sussuration of a more distant river.

The wonder of it made him gasp, lifted his heart, made him wish for the air so he could gather in more of this strange new sensation. Before he knew it, he was flying.

Pleasant, is it not? came Fionchadd's thought into his mind, tickling certain parts of him awake.

Yeah, real neat. I could get to like this, David replied, and then he shifted attention to his senses. He could see very well—which surprised him. But he could see with his ears almost as well: yell a little (sheer exultation made that easy), and read the shape of the land in the resulting echoes. He read Fionchadd's shape, too, and found something strange there, something he confirmed with his eyes—a thing that made his heart skip a beat.

It was the fannypack. The Faery still wore it around where his hips would have been. (He had chosen to become a *very* large bat of unfamiliar species.) But what gave David pause was the fact that flesh had grown out over parts of the alien substance: wing membrane that joined his fingers to his side sandwiching denim between. No way that thing would fall now.

Yes, it pains me, the Faery said in response to David's unasked question. *But pain is a thing I now know very well—and I know that this one is temporary.*

But . . .

Enough. There are other things both of us need to discuss.

They exchanged thoughts for a long time then. Eventually it reached the stage where David had only to brush his mind across an image or an idea or an emotion, and Fionchadd would understand. Reciprocating was harder for him, who was used to thinking in words; but by and by he got the hang of it, though Fionchadd had to assist him. In this way he was able to pass on to this friend a much more detailed account of what had transpired from the time Fionchadd had set sail on his ill-fated voyage to the Land of the Powersmiths through Alec's healing and the revelation of Eva's betrayal to the aberrant weather that had precipitated the current crisis.

I think it would help if I understood the nature of this war, David told him. *I only know bits now: that Alec was fooled into switching the dagger that was supposed to guide the ship to the Land of the Powersmiths for one that took you to Finvarra. That he promptly captured you and held you for ransom, and that your mother was prepared to give herself up to save you from the Death of Iron. Evidently that didn't happen.*

Alas, no, Fionchadd responded, *though I would not know this had my captors not spoken carelessly around me.* He went on then, recounting the whole tale of the war from Morwyn's aborted surrender through his speculations about the reasons for his torture, to his assumption that the Powersmiths had now broken the siege that had held them in stalemate all winter.

Interesting, David thought back to him. And then they simply flew, propelled by a particularly strong, steady wind from the north.

Hours passed, always at wing, seeking into the higher air where the north wind skimmed them even faster, if more treacherously. Feeding sometimes on things they caught on the wing (David was slowly mastering the art of letting the animal take control at times of need like these, though he balked at sampling the many high-blown spiders). As for the landscape below, it slowly began to change. At first, it was trees, meadows, slowly meandering rivers, occasional lakes. Sometimes herds of game (bison and pronghorn mostly, though he was certain he once saw a giant ground sloth and a small herd of mammoth). Once they met a flock of passenger pigeons winging north—their numbers so vast they shadowed an entire forest. But as they continued to beat their way south, the terrain began to alter: the mountains shrank, became rolling hills, then sandy flatland. The last hour they'd begun to see marshes, and the rivers were wider but much, much slower, and David guessed they were approaching the coast. He hoped his friend knew where he was going. And wondered suddenly about Calvin, wondered if his other partner-in-chaos was enjoying his part of the mission as much as he.

The sun was beginning to warm the horizon when Fionchadd finally tipped a wing and slipped into a slow dive. A squeak brought back new images: flat land and shallow water, and at the edge, even more water—probably the sea.

Half an hour later, they were swooping low over live-oaks, interspersed with wide coastal marshes full of cattails and marsh grass. There was increasingly less solid ground, and many more small, unsteady islands—most overgrown with more live-oaks, scrubby slash pines, occasional palms, and palmettos. The smell of salt, methane, and dead fish was strong in his nostrils: the slap of waves was a steady thunder in his sensitive ears.

David held back a little, let Fionchadd take the lead, watched as his friend swooped so low the downstroke of his wings brushed the top twigs of an oak and brought away a shimmer of Spanish moss.

Another dip, lower yet, and the instinct took over and he was fanning his wings to land.

A thump, a flip head over heels, and he was lying on his back in pale, dry sand. It was also hot, for it had been baking in the too-near sun of Galunlati for hours. His cry of surprise came out as a chirp and brought back the most amazing echoes. And then he was levering himself over and reaching awkwardly for the scale that had been a burden around his neck. He found it—barely—pressed his hand into it, and called his own face to mind.

A sick feeling, a swirl of pain, joints popping and wiggling, an outward rush, and he was himself again—lying on his back on an unfamiliar coast. Before him was an endless shimmer of waves; behind him the sun was a hand's width above the horizon. He blinked—vision was strong again, and the color range had shifted, but he thought for a moment he had gone deaf until his ears readjusted. The effect was a great deal like the way his ears had seemed stuffed with cotton after the one rock concert he'd seen: U-2 at the Omni in Atlanta a couple of years before. But this was his normal hearing. Only the contrast made it seem odd.

"Whew," a voice breathed beside him, "I'm glad *that* is over." He glanced to the right, saw Fionchadd stand, and with great relish disengage the fannypack. He handed it to David, who immediately set about reclaiming his cutoffs.

"Sorry 'bout that," David told him ruefully. "If I'd known you were gonna carry it like that, I'd have volunteered."

"You could not have," Fionchadd replied. "You have not the control."

David regarded him doubtfully for a moment, then shrugged.

"Oh well—thanks. If I hadn't been scared I'd lose you, I'd have done without, but I just can't risk losin' everything. Living's just too perilous right now."

"How so?" Fionchadd wondered, calmly digging in the sand until he produced a shell, which he flipped open with a deft bit of pressure—and probably a touch of Power. The mollusk inside disappeared raw down his throat. He licked his lips.

"So," David sighed. "We're here—wherever here is. Now all we've gotta do is get one World over, is that right?"

"Correct," Fionchadd acknowledged. "And I have an idea about that—but it must wait until sunset."

"But that's still an hour or so off, so I make it."

"You do not need to rest and eat?"

"More than anything in the world, but I don't dare. I'm scared that if I go to sleep I'll never wake up—and as for food . . . well . . . I'm not really into raw clams."

"I can call some fish," Fionchadd volunteered quickly. "I think they will come to my call even here. After all, I am in my own body now, not so limited in Power."

"I'll wait," David said quickly. "I'm not into sushi either."

"You can cook," Fionchadd pointed out a little irritably. "Else why bring that ridiculous can?"

David sighed. "All right, you win. You call the fish, I'll fix 'em—and meanwhile you can tell me about that place you were captive in. I still haven't figured that out."

Fionchadd sighed in turn. "Nor have I, completely. As best I can determine from what you have told me and things read between words, the place I was is a thing that is almost a legend in Faerie. Tir-Gat, we called it: the Stolen Country. It seems that once a minor Druid from the Faery realm of Alban discovered some silver Tracks and followed them to a World that was still a-forming— you have told me a little of this: how matter attracts matter and so creates the Worlds. But however it may be, this Druid wished to be mightier than he was, and so in secret moved to this place and set up his own kingdom. But it was slow in forming, so he thought to speed it along, and thus began using the Tracks to draw substance from other realms—Alban, mostly, though he also pillaged Erenn and even, I am told, your own World. Eventually he was found out and executed—the Death of Iron, so it happens. But that did not destroy him, and he escaped by hiding his soul in the hilt of a certain sword which he then caused to be secreted in the Lands of Men. There he waited until time came right for him to try to escape again. Meanwhile, no way could be found to recover the land this Druid had stolen, for he had cleverly sealed its borders, and Alberon, who was king of Alban, was too ashamed at being made a fool of to ask aid of his fellow princes. Finally the Druid acted; this I heard in Faerie before we set sail. His plan was thwarted, though, and his realm destroyed—so it was thought. Apparently, however—and here I begin conjecture—Finvarra felt the disturbance in the rhythm of the Worlds, investigated, and found a small bit of Tir-Gat remaining. This he warded for himself, and claimed, and swore Alberon of Alban to absolute secrecy. That is where he put me. That is the place from which you rescued me."

"Jesus," David sighed, flopping back on the sand. "Yet more Worlds—and another kind of Straight Track!"

"It never becomes any simpler," Fionchadd informed him. "Nothing ever does." He rose suddenly, strode to the edge of the tide. "Now, let us see about those fish— we should be just about be finished by sunset."

"Sunset?"

"A between time, when Power is strongest."

Chapter XXVI: Changing Places

(Galunlati—day two—sunset)

By the time David had finished boiling the two fish Fionchadd had lured to shore, the sun had touched the horizon.

"So what do you intend to do?" he asked, settling back into the depression he'd scooped in the sand and licking his fingers appreciatively. He aimed an absent salute toward the waves, since he'd forgotten to ask thanks of the fish earlier, as was the custom for anything killed in Galunlati. "How do we get our asses outta here?"

Fionchadd tongued his lips with similar relish. "I have been thinking about this," he said. "You came here by burning a scale of the great uktena, correct? You can use it to transfer one World at a time if the scale is properly treated, but the transfer destroys the scale. However, it is also possible to treat the ulunsuti so that it can open a gate between many Worlds—and it does *not* perish in flame. Therefore in order to complete your plan, which I believe is the right one, we can use the remaining scale to return to the Lands of Men, meet your friends, and have them take us to Faerie—and the Powersmiths—using the ulun-suti.''

''You're forgettin' one thing, though,'' David noted, scowling. ''We've only *got* one scale, and it's not acti-vated.'' Unconsciously he fingered the thong at his throat.

''You are correct, of course,'' Fionchadd admitted. ''But *you* forget that I have Power in my own right, Power that can take me between Worlds once I know the way. Also, I think I know how the scale can be made to tele-port.''

''You *what?* How?''

''You yourself told me, in a way. You showed me your memory of the opening of the gate, and I have now locked it in mine. But I remember more perfectly than you and I can recall the ritual your friend used to charge the ulun-suti—and I believe I can collect most of the ingredients in the remaining time we have.''

''Oh, Lord, *yes!*'' David cried. ''It might just work— but you need the blood of a sorcerer, don't you?''

''And what do you suppose I am? Or yourself, for that matter.''

''*Right!*'' David exclaimed. ''Oh Jesus, I think you've got something.'' He hesitated then, frozen by a sudden misgiving. ''But wait a minute,'' he added, disappoint-ment weighting his voice. ''We've still got a problem. There's only one scale, there's two of us.'' He shook his head. ''No, maybe that's okay. You can go, and then send somebody back here when you can.''

''No,'' Fionchadd chuckled. ''We *both* go.''

''But how . . . ?''

''Shapechange. I become a flea or a louse. I ride in your mouth, in your ear. Thus, when you go, I go; for I am a part of you.''

David stared at him doubtfully, then laughed loudly and slapped him on the back. ''Oh, hell, Finno, why not. I mean what's one more impossible thing?''

Fionchadd peered at the pulsating sun. ''One impossi-

ble thing is to stop the sun from moving—unless," he
added ruefully, "one is Lugh, or has control of his spear."

"Yeah," David sighed. "As Alec's fond of sayin', we're
burnin' daylight."

"Right. You lay out the Power Wheel, I will seek for
the ingredients and review my memory."

David nodded, then found himself still at a bit of a loss
for how to proceed. He considered simply incising the
cross-in-circle in the sand with a stick, but something
stopped him. Finally he decided. The tide was going out,
leaving a wide flat shelf of sand that was still damp and
therefore darker than that on which they sat. He thus simply marked the pattern by filling his hands with the dry
white sand from higher up and letting it sift through his
fingers. It took several trips, and the Wheel was a small
one, but he thought it would suffice, even if it was white
against gray. As an afterthought, he found shells in the
colors of the cardinal directions and set them in the ap-
propriate places. The sun was down when he finished, and
both sea and sand had turned the color of blood. He was
beginning to sunburn, he noticed absently.

Fionchadd returned at that moment, his hands full of
various herbs and other, less obvious, items. "I will take
the east, you the west, if you will," the Faery told him.
"The scale, I believe, goes between."

David nodded and slipped the thong from around his
neck, then freed the scale from the intricate wirework that
bound it. He was a little sad to see it go . . . They had
been through so much together.

Fionchadd took it reverently, held it in his palm, and
began.

David had seen much of the ritual before, and heard the
same chants. But this time they were on the beach, this
time it was Fionchadd repeating the strange phrases; and
when the time came for the scale to be dipped in blood,
Fionchadd suddenly reached to the sand beside him and
snatched up a razor-sharp shell. Before David realized
what had happened, the Faery had whipped the scale first

across his own cheek, then across David's, deftly missing nerves and major vessels, but bringing forth a great deal of blood: David could feel it trickle over his chin.

The blood did not drip onto his bare chest, though, but onto the scale Fionchadd held below it. He stared at it in fascination, realized they had their heads close together, that blood was running down both their faces in almost equal amounts, and that the scale was greedily absorbing it.

A touch of Fionchadd's hand made the pain grow less. "Now," the Faery whispered, "I think we are ready."

David nodded and commenced preparations for the small fire Fionchadd had told him to build—Lord knew there'd been enough dry material around. Practically all you had to do was reach down, even here on the beach of Galunlati. It blazed up quickly.

He stood, took the scale from Fionchadd's fingers. "That should do it," the Faery said finally. "If not—it was a valiant effort."

David shrugged. "We'll see. Now—what're you gonna do? How're you gonna come with me?"

Fionchadd grinned. "I would like to surprise you."

David frowned at him. "Whatever you say."

A hand brushed his shoulder, and when he looked down, the Faery was nowhere in sight.

Now! a voice echoed in his mind.

David nodded and cast the scale in the fire. He closed his eyes and thought very hard about home, about Liz and Alec. *"Alec McLean!"* he shouted when the scale flared up, since Alec was Master of the Ulunsuti, and the closest to a man of Power they had in their home World; then, just to be safe, "Elizabeth Hughes"—and to keep the bases covered, Alec's name in Cherokee: "Tsulehisanunhe!"

And then flame reached out and engulfed him.

It was different this time—less pain, or perhaps he was getting used to it, and there was more of a sensation of actually moving, of transiting somewhere. He was somehow aware of every cell of his body, could feel each bone and fiber, separate and distinct.

And then his disparate parts smashed back together, and for the second time in twenty-four hours, he found himself precipitated into water.

—Except that it was blessedly warm this time, almost warm as blood. They had arrived at night, too, and a storm seemed to be brewing, for the sky was wild with scudding black clouds sweeping unnaturally quick beneath a blue ablaze with indignant stars. The waves—black, accented with silver—were high and choppy; the sporadic rain that splattered his face felt like needles of ice.

He ducked his head, rose, gasped, and began treading water. "Finno!" he shouted. "Hey, Lizardman, where are you?"

A sound between a snap and a pop, a twinge of pain on his back, and then a sudden splash and a laugh.

He turned, furious—to see a wild-eyed Fionchadd grinning at him from a few yards away.

"So, how'd you get here?" David demanded.

"As a tick between your shoulders. Your blood is very good—thicker than ours, but sweet . . ."

David glared at him. "I oughta . . ."

"Kill me? If tonight's work goes aright, you may well be rid of me sooner than you think."

"Why's that?" David felt a vast uneasiness well up inside him.

"Have you not guessed? This is not your World, this is Faerie!"

"Faerie!" David gasped, only to have his mouth promptly filled with salt water. "But how? We can't teleport two Worlds away with the scale."

"No," Fionchadd acknowledged, "not normally—yet we obviously have, and the only thing that was different in the ritual was that we used your blood and mine to activate the scale. Also . . ."

"What . . . ?" David interrupted, then felt his eyes go

huge. "Oh no! We . . . we called on Alec and Liz to anchor us, and wound up here, which means . . ."

"That they are also here," Fionchadd nodded. "So I would think. And probably close by."

David tried to leap clear of the water but could not. One thing he did notice, though, was that there was a huge amount of storm wrack about: floating bits of wood. One nudged his back with a splintered edge, and he yipped and twisted around. It was a piece of very pale wood, polished to a high gloss, lightly gilded with silver, and with a bright metal fixture attached which he thought might once have held some rigging.

"Boat parts!" he cried; then, as dread caught him, he shouted, "Liz! Liz—Alec—can you hear me?"

Fionchadd added his voice then, pitching it carefully so that it pierced the night.

No answer.

David met Fionchadd's gaze, fear and dread and anger warring for priority there. "This is a shipwreck, Finno."

"We called on them and the scale responded. Were they not still alive, I imagine we would still be in Galunlati," the Faery replied simply.

David brightened at that. "Good point. Come on, then, let's see what we can find—check this drift—might be smart anyway, if a storm's comin' up. It'd be good to have something to hang onto."

"A wise suggestion. I have used much Power lately, and am very weary. I do not think I could last out a storm at sea unaided."

"Not even as a fish?"

"I have no more changes in me—not for a very long while."

David sighed, and struck out in the direction from which the greatest amount of debris seemed to be drifting.

He searched until his arms were tired to the point of cramping and his breaths were coming in gasps. He barely had strength enough to yell out his friends' names, yet he did—over and over.

The slap of waves, the cry of night-flying birds was his only answer until, faintly: "Here!"

"Liz?"

"Davy? Here, over *here!*" The cries became a whistle, long and drawn out: Liz's distinctive signal rising clear above the sound of waves and—increasingly—wind.

In less than a minute, he had found them.

They were a sorry sight, hanging from a floating shaft of what might once have been a mast. Their hair was plastered to their heads in limp, salt-laden tendrils; their eyes and lips were swollen. And there seemed to be a vast encumbrance of chains. David grabbed hold of the spar, felt it bob but keep its buoyancy. Fionchadd took the other end. It was all David could do to keep from trying to hug them both, and he wanted to kiss Liz so badly he could hardly stand it, to wipe away the fear and pain from her face. To kiss her happy again.

Instead, he asked, "What happened?"

"Finvarra's guys captured us in our World," Alec began. "And—"

"And Lugh ambushed them as soon as we wound up here," Liz finished. "I don't think he knew we were aboard, and he didn't stay to investigate. His fleet went east very quickly—on water, and above it."

"That would make sense," Fionchadd mused, "if the rumors I heard are true and Finvarra truly wishes to engage him far at sea."

"But what about the spear?" Alec asked. "I thought he was going to use it on Erenn on Midsummer's . . ."

"Fuck the friggin' spear," David gritted. "We've gotta get you guys outta here."

Fionchadd nodded in David's direction. "There is land that way, not far. The tide will take us there if we drift. It is coming in."

"Yeah, but we can get there faster if we all paddle."

And so they did.

It was still not midnight in Faerie (so Fionchadd informed them, having read the positions of the stars between the ever larger banks of tattered clouds) when David felt his kicking feet finally brush bottom. They dragged themselves ashore, and David and his mortal friends lay there grasping while Fionchadd made short work of the chains that still linked Alec and Liz. As soon as she was freed, Liz rolled into David's arms, and they clung together for a moment, then found each other's lips . . .

Eventually Alec cleared his throat. "Uh, I hate to tell you folks this, but I think a storm's brewing."

David disentangled himself and looked up. Sure enough, the sky was solid black now, and the wind was whipping through the trees nearby with a new fury. He gazed at those trees a moment, decided they were little different from the native Georgia live oaks, except that they were taller, thicker, and more extravagantly knobbed and whorled. Far to the right he could see a gleam of light on the shore and make out what might be white buildings.

"Lugh's southern fastness," Fionchadd observed, "where all the Tracks eastward converge. We cannot get there now, for it is further than it looks—at least, not and weather this storm."

Even as he spoke, there was a single crash of lightning, and the World went white. One instant the air felt quick and hesitant and smelled faintly of ozone; the next rain was pouring down.

As one they ran for the shelter of the trees, crouched there, huddled together and watching the storm.

It was not natural, they knew. And never had they seen such fury loose in the skies. The storm that had lashed around Uncle Dale's farm was as nothing to this, for here the whole World was involved. Clouds fought and shattered, waves rose and smashed the shore. Trees moaned and snapped and disintegrated, and lightning was everywhere, increasingly vying with a stab of yellow light far out to sea.

"The Spear," Fionchadd gasped. "Lugh uses the Spear of the Sun—and at night. Mighty indeed he must be!"

"Why's that?"

"Because it draws on the Power of the sun, or on the Power of the sun stored in something—in this case, Lugh himself, I would suppose. The Lord of Tir-Nan-Og must truly be hard pressed."

"I thought the plan was for him to attack Erenn."

"Not necessarily," Fionchadd informed them. "That could well have been a feint: send their attention that way, attack the smaller fleet instead, and so clear the southern sea of Finvarra's forces, then assail the north both from land and sea. And . . ."

But thunder overruled further conversation.

For roughly the next hour they lay on the sopping ground while the storm got worse and worse. Waves rose higher, taller than three men, and were slapping the shore closer and closer. Many of the trees beneath which they had sheltered had snapped, and once they had to relocate quickly to avoid being crushed when a limb splintered off above them.

"It's like a friggin' *hurricane!*" David shouted, and heard his voice taken away by the howling wind.

"No, it's worse," Alec yelled back. "Much worse. Look!"

He pointed seaward, and for a moment David saw only silver-lit darkness. But then he noticed it too, and felt the hair rise up on his body, in spite of being waterlogged. For he was no longer seeing one reality.

One moment it was the lightning-limned seas of Faerie; the next it was a morning sea in Galunlati, but with the sun glaring so hot the very waves were steaming. The one after that, it was coastal marshes of Georgia, bright beneath a glimmering moon, but with a fey wind stirring the cattails and reeds.

And then it was all a jumble, as the Walls between the Worlds, for brief instants, dissolved. One moment they were in sunlight, one moment back beneath the tree, a third they were lying up to their necks in stinking mud and marshgrass, and hearing the buzz of a seaplane. David wondered, suddenly, how the folk of the other Worlds were experiencing this. But then his attention was drawn to something nearby. Two ships had appeared, as if spun from the very substance of the storm. They were locked together, one a silver vessel floating in the air, the other a water-ship, both linked by grappling hooks and chains. David could not tell whether one was trying to draw the other up, or pull the other down. But then the yellow light flashed that way, and the lower ship erupted into flames.

"This has to stop," David announced suddenly. "This has gone on long enough!"

"*Stop?*" Liz cried. "And how do you stop something like this?"

"Like you said," he smiled, kissing her forehead, "one person at a time, and one side."

"You really *mean* that?"

"Absolutely. We're here; we have to do what we came for."

"You still think you can end this by giving Finno to his people?"

"No," David whispered. "But it's all I've got."

"Yes," Fionchadd spoke up. "He is right. It might succeed. If my folk were to regain me, Finvarra would have nothing with which to bargain."

"And how're we gonna do this?" Alec asked archly.

"Simple," David replied. "If we can just get out there. Have you still got the ulunsuti?"

Alec patted the pocket of his camos where he'd stashed it. "Sure thing, why?"

"I was thinkin' 'bout doing one final piece of magic— if we can get a fire goin'."

"Oh no," Liz protested, eyes wide. "You're not gonna try to build a gate again!"

"Sorry," David replied slowly, "but yeah, I am. I'm gonna try to get us to the Powersmiths—or Finno anyway. Since they won't come to us, we'll have to go to them."

"And how're you gonna build a fire in this mess, and do the rest of the ritual?"

Chapter XXVII: Blood Talks

(Faerie—high summer—night)

"What're you *talkin'* about?" David practically shouted at Alec. "There *aren't* any large animals here!"

"Except us," Alec replied calmly. "If Finno can heal me, I think I can spare enough blood."

"Alec, no!" Liz cried in turn. Her eyes reflected the pervasive lightning, but added their own intensity. "You're crazy! I mean, you're half dead already. You can't risk it!"

"Yes I can," Alec repeated, still in the same calm tones, but with an undercurrent of resolution that indicated further argument would do no good.

"No!" David and Liz protested as one.

"Maybe," Fionchadd chimed in. "No, actually, it *might* succeed. If Alec can provide enough blood, I believe I can heal the wound. I still have sufficient Power for that."

"It won't take much," Alec went on quickly. "I think there was maybe a quart in the thermos, but we didn't use nearly all of it to empower the ulunsuti—maybe just a pint or so. Shoot, I drop that much every time I give blood at school. No problem."

"I don't like this," David persisted. "You'd have to cut yourself really deeply to get enough. What if you hit a vein?"

"I'd be through quicker," Alec shot back almost giddily. "But seriously, we've never dealt with it, but . . . what happens if you just let the thing have all the blood it wants? I mean, it seems to sense what's demanded of it and absorb accordingly. So suppose I simply cut myself on the hand—not badly, you know; just enough to insure a steady flow, then slap that on. Wouldn't that do it?"

David shook his head, and Liz looked equally doubtful. "It's *not* your fight, bro."

"Yes it is," Alec maintained. And with that, he withdrew the scrap of ragged metal he'd been secreting in his pocket and very neatly slit the heel of his palm. Liz gasped, and David felt his balls make a twitch, but Alec simply sat there in the lee of the tree, face white with pain, hair and clothing plastered to his body. He looked awful—tired, sick, maybe a little crazy. But the gleam in his eyes was absolutely sane. He held the hand out into the wind and rain. Already blood was pooling there. "I can turn it over," he threatened. "I can waste this—or I can use it. What's it gonna be? Do I risk a little and maybe we end this thing, or do we risk nothing, and regret it forever?"

"Damn!" David gritted in frustration. "You're sick man, you could at least have let *me* do it!"

"But I'm Lord of the Ulunsuti," Alec replied with a return of the disarming calm. "It's my responsibility."

"Alec—" David began, all confusion. Then, "Oh hell, go ahead, I reckon."

Alec smiled grimly, and David watched with a mixture of fascination, horror, relief, and guilt as his best friend flung away his makeshift knife, then carefully maneuvered the ulunsuti from his pocket and deposited it in his bleeding palm. He held it there for a moment, then shifted position so that he could rest his arm on his knee. His already pale face had grown whiter yet, but the crystal had started to glow.

Lightning struck once, close by, and he almost lost his grip, but David's hand on his wrist steadied him, then slowly withdrew. For an instant there was only the flash of lightning and the sting of rain; the rumble of thunder and the howl of mage-born wind.

"How're you doin', bro?" David whispered when he could stand the wait no longer.

Alec shrugged minutely. "It doesn't hurt, though I can sorta feel the cut. It's just a kind of drawing. Really, it's not much different from giving blood, 'cept you don't have to worry about a needle wiggling around in your arm."

"Gross," said Liz, who had always had trouble with needles.

David felt utterly helpless, but finally acted on his frustrated need to do *something* by wrapping one arm around Alec's shoulders and hugging him close. Liz was already curled in the crook of his other arm.

"Let me know when you need fire," Fionchadd urged, squatting opposite, back to the wind.

Alec shrugged again and continued to gaze at the crystal. It was definitely glowing now, assuming an emberlike ruddiness. It was hard to tell more in the uncertain light, but maybe a minute later Alec took a deep breath and said, "I think it's done . . . I don't feel anything else. In fact, I think it's already closed the wound itself."

David stared at Alec's hand, trying to see the gash beneath the ulunsuti. As best he could tell the trickle that had dripped slowly from between his friend's fingers was gone. So was the small pool he was certain he had seen in the cupped palm before.

"Okay, Finno," Alec breathed a little shakily. "Do your stuff."

The Faery nodded and brought his hands together close before him. He shut his eyes, uttered a Word and brought fire from his living flesh: tiny sparks and flames that leapt and danced in the driving wind.

"Hurry," Fionchadd exhorted them. "This is difficult to maintain in this weather."

Alec wasted no time. He took the ulunsuti with both hands and set it into the fire in the Faery's palm.

"Now, quick, think of our goal—you've been there, Finno, you get to drive."

"But . . . *two* things to focus on! I cannot . . ."

"You can!" David insisted.

The Faery closed his eyes—and evidently succeeded, because one moment there was only the crystal kindling brightly in his hand, and the next an arch of crimson fire seared the storms of the Faery night.

David and Liz scooted backward in alarm. Alec stayed squatted where he was, letting the light bathe his face, staring at his hand where only a thin line now remained; while Fionchadd slowly lowered the ulunsuti—flame and all—to the ground and sidled around to crouch beside them.

Through the gate—where before there had been wind-whipped forest—was now only night and storm; war; and ships blazing in the heavens and on the sea. Except that exactly in the middle a vast airship gleamed orange-yellow, as if it were wrought of copper or gold. Immediately behind its dragon-beaked prow a woman stood, wrapped in a billowing cloak of the same shimmering gold as the thrashing sail behind her. She was staring straight at them, and as they watched, her face expanded to fill the entire arch, like a long-shot panning to a close-up in a film. Her eyes were aflame with fury.

"Ilionin!" Fionchadd shouted, his voice rising clear above the thunder.

"Ilionin!" came Alec's half-screamed echo—and suddenly the gate collapsed upon them, and they were in a storm of a different kind.

Perhaps because they had teleported within the same World, David was aware of far less pain of transition this time. It wrapped him, ripped him apart, but before he could cry out, it had ended.

The first thing he noticed was the cessation of cold rain

and noise, replaced with dry warmth and a distant sussuration that might be the muffled storm. The second was that everywhere he looked—at deck, or rail, or sail, or at the warriors that surrounded him—he saw gold or yellow or orange. It reminded him of when he had awakened in Morwyn's Room Made of Fire, except here the color scheme had shifted down the spectrum.

Even the woman who was glaring at him reminded him of Morwyn. She was tall—at least as tall as most of the orange-liveried spearmen—and very beautiful, though rather hard-faced, which did not surprise him. She looked even more competent than Morwyn too, and that was saying a great deal. Her eyes were green, her short-clipped hair red-gold; her nose was strong and straight and her chin narrow but square. Almost a masculine face, were it not for the curves of lips and cheeks.

Beneath the golden cloak she wore a long, open robe of orange brocaded in yellow, over scale armor that looked to be made of gold inlaid with copper and bronze. She wore no helm and carried no weapons, but a pair of the spearmen held what were probably them, if the design, workmanship, and material of the crowned cap-helm, broadsword, and shield were any indication.

The woman barked an order and turned without ceremony, ducking the boom, and striding toward the low cabin aft. *Follow!* prodded David's mind as the guards encircled them, spears at ready.

An instant later, they made their way down a short flight of cedar wood steps and entered what was probably the captain's cabin, to judge by the rich orange carpet, gold-figured tapestries, tawny furs, and carved ruddy wood with which it was decorated—none of which were a match for the woman who now glowered from a gilded copper chair before them, obviously highly irritated and perplexed.

Equally obvious, war was still raging, for there were shouts above deck, and odd thumps, and every now and then a sudden abrupt movement hastily compensated for, though if it bothered the guards that now flanked the woman, they gave no sign.

"Speak quickly," the woman barked. "Who are you? Why have you come here?"

"To end this war," Fionchadd replied simply, stepping out where he'd been standing rather unobtrusively behind David.

"And who are *you* to propose such a thing, Faery boy? Who are you who consorts so freely with mortals?"

"Mortals who use *Power,* if you had not noticed," Fionchadd gave her back, not in the least cowed. "Also, I am the cause of all this."

The woman stared at him incredulously. *"You?* A sorry-looking thing like yourself?"

Fionchadd drew himself up to his full height, suddenly every inch the elven prince in spite of the tattered gray wool breeches that were his only garment. "You would not look well either . . . *Aunt* Ilionin, had you been tortured with Iron for half a year's seasons, nearly cooked alive in a Mortal chariot, then almost drowned—and finally thrashed about by ill-wrought weather. And let me add that *surely* you could have ordered the lightning better."

"The intent is to destroy vessels, not soldiers," the woman shot back. And then froze, and peered at him intently. "Aunt," she whispered suddenly, as if the word were new to her. "Yet . . . yet . . . *yes!* You *are* Fionchadd!" With a smile like sunlight dispelling morning fog, the woman rushed forward to embrace her nephew.

"So my mother, your sister's daughter named me," Fionchadd replied dryly, when he had disentangled himself from the mass of armor and silk. "I generally manage a better appearance than this," he added with a chuckle.

"That can be remedied easily enough," Ilionin shot back airily, returning to her seat. "Arnor, Astrid, fetch clothing, and food—wine too, for our . . ."

"Guests," Fionchadd finished for her. "Mortals, aye,

but they are the ones who rescued me from Finvarra and brought me here.''

Ilionin's eyes narrowed again. "Sit," she commanded brusquely, indicating a series of low, cushioned benches built into the walls. "Now what is this about Mortals bringing you here? Some Power of which we are unaware?''

"Aye," Fionchadd replied quickly. "A Power Uncle Finvarra would pay dearly for, since it holds the secret of travel without Tracks.''

"This we know as well," Ilionin said. "Long have our ships passed at will between the World Walls.''

"But *not* instantaneously from place to place," Fionchadd noted carefully.

"Hold on here a minute," Alec inserted. "I hate to say this Finno, but . . . well, it sounds to me like you're bargaining with the ulunsuti—and it's not yours to bargain with. I mean you ought to *ask,* at least," he added.

"I am set straight," Fionchadd replied, grinning both at his friend and his wary aunt.

"As well you should be," Ilionin told him sharply. "If it is not yours to give, it certainly is *not* yours to bargain with. And yet," she added, "I am curious. Might I see this thing?''

Alec shook his head. " 'Fraid not. It's back on shore. We kinda left—''

"There you are wrong, my friend," Fionchadd interrupted, unfolding his hand to reveal the ulunsuti. "I retrieved it as the gate collapsed.''

"Finno!" Alec spat in exasperation, snatching away the crystal.

David could contain himself no longer. "Never mind the damned ulunsuti, lady," he cried, rising and striding forward until scarcely a yard lay between them. "What about the bloody *war?* I mean we . . . well, we went to a lot of trouble to try to free Finno, partly 'cause he's our friend, but partly 'cause we've got to end this blessed war somehow! It's sloppin' over into our World bad, hurtin' lots of people; and it's threatenin' another World—one closer to your own, I think. The one . . . the one on the other side of the Burning Sea.''

"The Burning Sea?'' Ilionin's expression was suddenly intense. ''You mean the land where the red folk dwell?''

David's nodded. ''Galunlati. It's bad there, *real* bad. Not your doing, not really—mostly Lugh's, I think. He's drawin' on a lot of Power to protect his borders and keep off Finvarra's storms—least I suspect that's what started it. But he's been usin' some kinda magic spear as well, and that's when all hell really started breakin' loose, 'cause every time he uses it, I'm afraid''—he paused, swallowed—''that is, *we're* afraid it kinda overstresses the sun of that adjoining world we just told you about. And—''

"We intend to speak to him about that spear,'' Ilionin interrupted, ''when he has finished doing our work with it. Still, he does not seem remarkably responsible with his . . . toys.''

"*Speak* to him?'' David spat, suddenly feeling weeks of frustration, anger, impatience—and three days with very little sleep suddenly strip aside all sense of propriety. ''You *need* to stop him right now! He's your ally, isn't he? And you're the big mojambo heavy hitters over here, aren't you? 'Could rule the Worlds if you chose,' and all that—accordin' to Morwyn. Right? So do it then: *Stop* him!''

"Why? He is doing a splendid job of decimating Finvarra's hosts. If he did not, we would have to. There will be time enough to put him in his place when he has finished.''

"Dammit, woman, if I could show you I would.''

"You could!'' she snapped. ''If it is as you say, perhaps I *will* intercede. The fate of the Worlds is related, this we freely acknowledge.''

"Huh?'' David replied, taken aback at her sudden change of demeanor.

She stared at him, anger and wonder ablaze in her eyes. ''I could read your memory,'' she said simply. ''Everything you have seen, everything you have thought or felt would be laid bare. Then I will know the truth of what you say.''

David exchanged glances with Fionchadd, with Alec and Liz. ''You won't like it,'' the Faery muttered. ''But it *would* be the wisest thing. Ilionin is wise even among the Powersmiths, even Lugh and Finvarra know this. She will be able to understand things you have seen that even you do not. Everything Uki showed you, all he told you, she will also know.''

David sighed, took a deep breath. ''Oh, why the hell not? At this point I'm too tired to care. Just look, and lock me up or toss me overboard, or whatever.''

''I do not think so,'' Ilionin told him with unexpected gentleness. ''I have heard of you, *David Sullivan*. And I do not think the rumors were short of the truth. I—''

A knock on the door was a guardsman bringing wine and food—bread, soft cheese, fruit, along with orange robes for the scantily clad Fionchadd and David. The boys donned them quickly, and all dived in greedily—except for David, who was almost consumed with impatience.

''You are not hungry?'' Ilionin inquired.

''Not when we've still got a goddam war to stop! Let's get to it, lady: Do it and get it over with!''

Ilionin sighed and set her mouth. ''Perhaps you are correct. It would be best if you closed your eyes. And truly, it may not be as bad as my kinsman suggests—you are weary, that will make it easier. Try not to resist. Think of the time when this began, and I will read it with you.''

David nodded, sat down, and flopped back against the wall. Ilionin knelt before him, resting her fingers on his wrists, which he had simply laid in his lap. Her touch was light but firm. He could feel the delicate prickle of her nails. ''Now,'' she whispered. ''Begin.''

He swallowed, tried to recall. It was difficult, he discovered, to *find* the beginning, for so much had happened in between, but somehow he managed to make order from the chaos. He suspected Ilionin was helping there, establishing order among the whirling, disjointed impressions.

Sometimes it seemed she glossed over things. Other times, as when she relived with him his memory of Lugh's unveiling of the spear or Sandy's description of her unified-field-theory of Worlds or Uki's despair at the status of his own land, she went far more slowly, and it was almost as if David experienced them again in real time.

And then, quite without warning, it was over.

David blinked, gazed into her eyes. Her face was grim and thoughtful. "I think," she said finally, "that you are correct. I think it is time things changed."

David heaved a sigh of relief.

"And what will happen now, Aunt?" Fionchadd asked, looking far better already. "I thought simply bringing me here would be enough. The war was over me, after all. Or has my mother . . . ?"

"She is safe and well," Ilionin told him absently. "You will see her shortly. As for the other, it was jealousy and greed that began this war—and the everlasting boredom that affects even our kin. It always is. You were an excuse, nothing more: tinder, but not the spark. Still, that does not change the situation now. I have learned more in the few moments I spent exploring your friend's mind than I have in many years, and it troubles me. It should trouble Lugh, too—and Finvarra."

"So all you have to do now is get them to listen," Fionchadd said with a touch of sarcasm. "Neat trick, if you can manage."

"You speak with the tones of a mortal," Ilionin told him sharply. "And you are incorrect as well. They will not listen now, not in the heat of battle. I must therefore end the battle."

"Which you cannot accomplish, or you would have done so long before now," Fionchadd gave her back, "no matter what you told us earlier."

"Which I could not do, but now can—with Alec McLean's assistance. And permission," she added wryly.

"Me?" Alec cried, starting from his place and upsetting a glass of wine in his lap. "Me?"

"You are lord of the magic crystal, are you not? And such Power I have seldom seen before. Already in David's mind I have witnessed it in use, and from that surmised much more. And already I have a plan."

Alec stared at her curiously.

"I will bring them here," she announced. "I will explain this thing—better, I will let David do it, if he will. I will have others know what I now know: that the fate of all the Worlds is one."

David exchanged glances with Alec, gave him a quick high-five. "Come on bro, let's get at it."

Five minutes later the plan was in place. Though David wasn't certain they would need it, he constructed a makeshift Power Wheel, using a few grains of Galunlati earth Alec had managed to salvage when they'd fled Stone Mountain. Once again, Alec would occupy the south and risk his own blood on promise of Powersmith healing if the crystal failed to perform that function. Once more Liz would act as anchor in the west, while David represented the north. Fionchadd, in the east—the direction of his homeland—would be the one to invoke the names. There was one change though: Ilionin stood behind her nephew, proud in her power, ready to do the one thing that would be different.

Flame rose up from a brazier in the center of the Wheel. Alec bit his lip, slit his unwounded palm, and let the ulunsuti drink deep of the Power that was in his blood. Rituals were repeated from Fionchadd's memory. The crystal was thrust into the flame—and a gate opened: an arch of baleful red in the orange room.

This time, though, it showed *two* places at once. In one red-clad Lugh, Ard Rhi of Tir-Nan-Og, stood proud if a little harried in the prow of his flying silver flagship, long mustache beating against his golden cheek-guards, yellow embroidered sun-disc rippling upon the crimson silk sail behind him as he held the spear aloft and scanned the skies and the waters with eyes grown narrow and wary.

The other place revealed Finvarra. A dour prince in black and gold, standing aloof from his men and shouting orders from the bow of his jet-black vessel while behind him warriors took on the shape of wyverns and winged aloft to harry the gryphons Lugh's forces had sent there to reconnoiter. His face was rather gaunt, his hair black, and there was a familiar hint of madness in his eyes.

The ritual was different this time, though: For the first time no one leapt through the gate. Instead, Ilionin simply gestured and uttered a Word, and before David had time to know what was happening, the gate faded, and two more figures suddenly appeared in the cabin—and were immediately surrounded by bristling spears.

"You!" Lugh shouted, upon first seeing Finvarra. "What folly is this?"

"*You,* I should say," Finvarra interrupted with a sneer—and then fell silent as his gaze slid sideways past the guards to Ilionin. "Dana! What treachery has befallen us?"

"I am not Dana," Ilionin replied calmly. "But I sometimes speak in her name. You are on my vessel, and I am captain of this fleet, therefore I could claim both of you as prisoners—if I sought to precipitate another war. Or we could stay here and watch this one a while longer, and see how many more people suffer needless pain. *Or* we could talk about peace—and perhaps an even more serious thing."

"Such as?" Finvarra spat, eyeing Lugh with even more distrust than he eyed the guards whose spears ringed them at chest level.

"Such as the fate of all the Worlds here about."

Lugh suddenly seemed to notice David and lifted a slanted eyebrow. "Well, David Sullivan," he chuckled, oblivious to the glowering Ilionin, much less his adversary. "I had not expected to see you again, and certainly not here—though now I think on it, I am not surprised."

"You *shouldn't* be," David told him with more sarcasm than he'd intended, given the delicate situation. "You hinted enough about the war sloppin' over into our World.''

Lugh looked genuinely concerned. "And has it?"

"You could say that."

"Enough," Ilionin commanded. "It is time we spoke of certain things." She turned her gaze to David. "David Kevin Sullivan, would you like to begin?"

David took a deep breath. "Maybe if we all sat down . . . ? I mean, this is gonna take a long time, and I *know* you folks know each other"—he eyed Lugh and Finvarra—"so you might as well forget about puffin' up and posturing and listen to what I've gotta tell you."

"Upstart Mortal!" Finvarra shouted. "I will—"

Ilionin cut him off. "You will do *nothing*, King of Erenn—except listen." Her tone left no room for discussion.

David glanced at her, shrugged, and as soon as the guards had prodded the two unwilling guests to low cushions on the floor, began again. "Well, to start with, how much do you know about the Worlds? *Really* know, I mean?"

"There is Faerie," Finvarra said promptly. "There are the Lands of Men—and the Country of the Powersmiths, I suppose," he added sourly. "If one can truly consider that a realm. And of course there is the place we came from."

"There are others, too," Lugh took up. "The Lands of Fire that lie below Tir-Nan-Og . . ."

"And many others," Ilionin finished for him. "But it is of three, in particular David must speak."

"I do not wish to listen to this," Finvarra spat. "No Worlds matter but our own—and certainly not the Lands of Men!"

"*That's* where you're wrong!" David shouted, then regained control of himself. "Without the Lands of Men, there'd probably *be* no Faerie!"

He went on then, explaining as much as he could about the multiplicity of Worlds, about the Tracks that linked them and sometimes created them, about how the

suns of three worlds were intimately connected so that a
threat to one was a threat to all.

Sometimes the concepts were almost beyond him, and
at those times he vainly wished Calvin was there, then
found himself wondering if the Indian had succeeded in
his quest to find Uki. At other times, fatigue—and nerves—
and Finvarra's constant glower—nearly overpowered his
adrenaline rush and made him forget something important
or lose his train of thought, so that even the wine Ilionin
had offered him perked him up but little.

"So," Finvarra snorted, when David had completed his
discourse on cosmology, "but what has this to do with our
war?"

"A lot," David said, taking a long draught of wine to
fortify himself. "If one of those Worlds ceases to exist, it
could endanger all the others."

"And what is that," Finvarra wondered, "to we, who
are immortal?"

"Because . . . because you're not *alone* in this!" David
stammered furiously. "Because there're other sentient
creatures who don't have it so lucky! Because . . . it's just
not your *right* to make decisions that big. You're a goddamn *king*, Finvarra! You're supposed to govern your
country, do what's best for your folks! Do you *imagine*
there's one of 'em that'd choose to die if he didn't have to,
even if he was gonna be reborn? And what if you can't
be? What if there's no substance for you to rebuild bodies
from? What if there're no wombs to re-quicken in? How'd
you like that, huh?" He paused for breath. "I mean, *we*
deal with it all the time, us 'foolish Mortals,' as you guys
like to call us. We *know* we're gonna die, and we *don't*
know what comes after and it scares the shit out of us.
And now you're lookin' at the same thing if you don't stop
this goddam war! Think about *that*, Finvarra—you too
Lugh, though I think you've got a little more sense—you
guys might *really* die. And even if you did come back,
who's to say you'd be lucky again and find a World where
you could be immortal? Wouldn't *that* be fun? Maybe then

you'd gain some respect for Mortals. Maybe then," he added, "you'd really know something about fear."

He went on, did not know how long he spoke, only that by the time he had finished stating his case a strange sort of eloquence had set in, and he found himself speaking in ringing phrases and catchy lines, rather like he had felt when composing the graduation speech he had delivered such a few days before. Lugh nodded from time to time, and eventually even the dour Finvarra began to look troubled.

Finally Lugh broke the silence. "This is a dire thing, Lady," he said to Ilionin, "and war or no, motivation or no, the boy is correct: it is not a thing that can continue. War itself may be entertainment, often it is, though not always for those who fall by the way. But when that war threatens existence itself—who can say what might happen? Oh, aye, we are immortal. But if there is no Galunlati, there might soon be no Lands of Men, and if no Lands of Men, then no Faerie. What would happen then? Would we be souls adrift with no bodies? That is not a thing I like to think on. Is it for you, brother prince?"

Finvarra shook his dark head grimly. "I am not convinced."

"Not convinced!" David threw up his hands in exasperation and flopped backward on the thick gold-and-crimson rug, his mind completely blank of responses. "I give up!"

Alec and Liz were instantly beside him, offering wine, and urging him back upright.

He took a sip, then set it aside and glanced sheepishly at Ilionin. "Sorry, Lady, I've given it my best shot and this . . . this arrogant *fool* won't listen. That's it, I'm done. The ball's in your court now."

Ilionin started to speak, though her face too was dark with anger, but Alec interrupted.

"No, it's still in our court," he said quietly. "There's still one thing we can do: we can show this S.O.B. the future!"

David looked up, his face suddenly bright with cautious

hope. "Good God—you're right! We've still got the ulunsuti—if we can get 'em to use it. And *they'll* have to do it too—we can't show it to 'em, they'd never trust us!"

"A notion of excellent merit," Ilionin acknowledged, then turned her gaze to her unwilling guests. "I could hold you for ransom if I wished, and perhaps end the war that way—or perhaps only relocate it. Or I could send you back and let you discover your own folly—and the folk of three Worlds with you. Or you can mix a bit of your blood with mine and see what we shall see."

"I am willing," Lugh said slowly.

"I am not," Finvarra snapped. "Who is to say there is not some treachery afoot to confound me?"

"Yourself will tell you," Ilionin informed him. "You know something of augury, else you would not wear your crown. Surely you can distinguish false from true."

"Or are you just scared?" David asked from the floor. "I've conquered my fears about this stuff—about shapeshifting and all. Alec has too, he's been scared shitless of magic, and yet he's the one who's come up with the best suggestions lately."

"And scrying usually tells me things I don't really want to know," Liz added, taking David's hand.

"I fear nothing!" Finvarra cried.

"Then you will agree," Ilionin told him sweetly. "Come, we will even use that little dagger you think I have not seen you fondling."

What followed was the familiar ritual, except that the participants, save Alec who had to take part, were all immortals.

Alec took the west, Ilionin the east, Finvarra the north, and Lugh the south. Blood was spilled, the ulunsuti was fed, and to David, who sat on the sidelines and watched, very little happened, except that the Sidhe closed their eyes and breathed very, very little—until suddenly Finvarra began gasping and collapsed forward across the crystal, breaking the bond that had linked them. Lugh blinked, then Alec and Ilionin. The Powersmith scooted around to examine her fallen foe.

Finvarra's face was very pale indeed, but he opened his eyes. "Death," he whispered, "and nothing beyond it. All roads lead to that but one."

"Is it peace then?" Ilionin prompted, as she helped him to his feet and returned to her throne.

"It is," the Ard Rhi of Erenn acknowledged sourly, "though my tongue chokes me to admit it." No more would he say.

"Will you call off your fleets, then?" Ilionin asked calmly, though her tone indicated there was only one proper answer. "I will call off mine at your word."

"Aye," Lugh replied quickly. "I will do this thing."

"I also," Finvarra grunted. "I have no choice any longer, and truly I am weary of all this contention."

David heaved a sigh of relief. "Then it's over?"

Lugh shook his head sadly. "Not over, David. There is still the matter of your World encroaching on Faerie, that neither of us can control. There is still a threat, we have merely removed one. The responsibility is now on you and your kind."

"I can't do anything about *that*, though," David protested wearily.

"Can you not?" Lugh asked him. "All things are possible in time."

"I'm mortal, though. Time's the one thing I don't have."

"Then you will have to hurry, won't you?" Lugh chuckled.

"But the war's over, really? You promise?"

"I promise," said Lugh, casting a wary eye toward Finvarra before turning his gaze back to David. "Do you?"

"I can't speak for my kind," David sighed helplessly. "I wish I could." And with that he fell silent, as Liz took his hand and led him back to his seat.

* * *

The war that had begun with a storm ended with lightning. One last time Alec and Ilionin called upon the Power of the ulunsuti (of which it still had much, thus he had to provide no more blood) to open gates. This time Lugh and Finvarra passed through—as one, so that neither would feel himself slighted. The atmosphere was still edgy. A flash of light, and the Faery kings were gone.

The gate was still fading in the cabin when Ilionin ushered them on deck a good while later. It was morning—almost, or at least the sky was brightening in the east. David sprinted to the prow, for he had seen something there that intrigued him. Beyond the copper dragon he could see three armadas—both in the air and on the water—each slowly disengaging: Black sails to the north and gold to the east—and red sails southward. The kings must have passed their orders quickly. He hoped they were sufficient.

For a long time all he did was watch and ponder.

Eventually he spoke to Fionchadd, who had trotted up to prop his forearms on the rail beside him, "Well, Finno, as best I can tell, we've only got one more problem."

"*Only* one more? That is unusual for you."

"Only one more for now," he amended, then turned to Liz who stood at his other side—and paused for a moment, caught up by the sight of her: red hair twitching in the breeze, exactly complemented by the tawny fur robe Ilionin had lent her, all framed by the golden sail behind her and lit by torches and sunrise. But then practicality once more banished romanticism, and he poked her in the ribs. "Come on, lady," he sighed, "I reckon we better go butter up poor old Alec one more time."

"You don't need to," Fionchadd informed them promptly. "If it is returning home that concerns you, I have already spoken to my aunt about that. If you will wait but a little while, she will take you there. This vessel can sail between the Worlds, but cannot do it quickly. Meanwhile, there is time to rest, to eat—to heal."

"I wish there was time to *study,*" Liz groaned. "I've

got a major league test real soon, and Lord only knows what's going on in our World.''

"We can arrange that, too," Fionchadd told her.

"No," Liz replied with a vehement shake of her head. "No more magic, no more fooling with time—my brain couldn't stand it. I only wanta get back home."

"Where at home, by the way?" Fionchadd inquired.

"Oh, Christ, yeah: good question. I left David's car back in Crawfordville . . ."

"You *what?"* David screeched.

"It's not *like* I had any choice in the matter!" Liz informed him shortly.

Fionchadd chuckled wryly. "Do not worry about it, leave this part to me."

And with that he turned and left them.

Liz took David's hand. "They said we had time: food, sleep, and I think I heard something about a bath waiting below."

"Alec's already in it," David laughed, "or is if I know him."

"Think he'd mind sharing?"

"Probably, but we could always ask."

"Let's do."

And with that they went below decks, with Fionchadd close behind.

Epilogue: At Loose Ends

(Cumberland Island, Georgia— Tuesday, June 17—morning)

It was a much cleaner, happier, and better-fed David Sullivan who was standing on the deck of the Powersmith flagship when it burst through the World Walls and came once more into the Lands of Men. It was not a thing Ilionin had wanted to do, he knew, but she also knew obligation when she saw it, and so she had consented to deliver them to land. But even at that she had been careful. A certain sort of Sight had helped her choose her destination, making sure it was free of lurking humans that might be alarmed by a vast copper dragonship suddenly propping into existence in the shipping lanes. Thus she had chosen a stretch of deserted sea, and further insured her secrecy by wrapping the boat in a glamour *and* raising a fog. No Minniebelle Cokers would speak of close encounters with *her*.

As for the transition, David scarcely noticed it, though perhaps it was the fact that he had Liz to distract him at the time—and would have been letting her distract him even more had Alec not been talking to Fionchadd right behind him.

"This may truly be goodbye," the Faery was saying.

"Lugh says he will still keep the borders closed, and Finvarra has agreed to shut his as well, though I doubt he will be able to fulfill that, since the World Walls are so much thinner in Erenn that many cross by accident."

"It's kind of a shame, though," Alec mused, and fell silent as he noticed David listening.

"Yeah," David tossed over his shoulder. "But a year ago I said there was a lot of magic left in the World, even without Faerie, and there still is. I've decided a couple of things, Alec, whether you like 'em or not. One is that you and me are gonna work with that ulunsuti whether you like it or not, and the other thing is that I'm goin' to Galunlati and see if I can't put all of this together. I've seen so many hints of things, heard so much that almost makes sense, that I really think if I can sit down with the right folks, I can figure it all out. 'Course I'll have to clear it with Calvin," he added, and suddenly felt a twinge of guilt.

"Any word from him?" Alec inquired.

David shook his head. "None. I'm sure he's okay, and I've asked Lugh and Ilionin to keep an eye out for him if he pops in here, but that's one thing I guess I'll have to deal with when we get back."

"Actually," Alec began hesitantly, but with a bit of pride as well, "I suppose we *could* search for him with the ulunsuti."

"Good job!" David exclaimed, slapping him on the back. "We'll make a wizard out of you yet."

"But unnecessary," Liz chuckled, pointing past the dragon prow. "Look!"

Without them really being aware of it, Ilionin had let the boat slip to earth and now the figurehead was knifing through the last wisps of fog before making landfall. Waves were cavorting and frothing around the hull, and even as he followed Liz's extended finger, David felt the grate of the keel against the land, though the sea was so shallow there they were still a fair ways from shore.

"Calvin!" David shouted joyfully, for he had seen the

black-haired, bare-chested figure standing on the beach at the high-tide mark—the figure that was now running headlong into the waves.

"I cannot touch your land," Ilionin said behind him, her voice gentle as the rustling of her heavy silk cloak. "You will have to wade the rest of the way. I am sorry, but the Laws of Dana command it."

"You follow them *too?*" David asked incredulously, then remembered he'd heard her speak of them before.

"Aye, some. But there is no more time to speak."

"Except to me," Fionchadd laughed, slipping past her. "I need to tell you all goodbye—and I find that I cannot." And for the first time in his life David saw tears in the Faery's eyes.

He hugged him impulsively, hugged him long and hard, like a brother he might never see again. His own eyes misted. "Take care, Finno. Let me hear from you if you can. You know I'll be thinkin' 'bout you."

"And I you," Fionchadd replied, planting matching kisses on each of David's cheeks—kisses David gave back impulsively. "And thank you . . . brother. No real brothers have I, but you have become like one to me."

"You too, man!"

Fionchadd embraced Alec then, and Liz, thanked them both, and they could have stayed there half the morning wishing to go ashore, yet fearing to end what might truly be an ending. Eventually, though, a pounding on the hull drew their attention that way. "Hey," Calvin yelled, from where he stood waist deep in water. "You guys don't get your butts down here, I'm gonna have to come up there and drip all over that pretty boat—and I don't think the owner'd like that very much—least that's what Finno told me when he came flyin' up to me in bat shape a little while ago! Like to've scared the crap outta me," he added, with one of his famous grins.

"So *that's* where you went to so fast after breakfast," David said, lifting a wry eyebrow in Fionchadd's direction.

Fionchadd tried to look innocent, but then his face broke into a grin. *"Go,* foolish mortal," he intoned with obviously bogus arrogance. "I would not have my effort be in vain!"

David started to reply with some comment about vampire bats and *veins,* then caught himself. He'd never be able to say enough, he knew, there was always one more thing to be said to a friend upon parting. Finally he simply gave Fionchadd a high-five, and climbed over the side. Alec and Liz joined him—Liz on David's back.

"Don't look back!" Fionchadd called, and they followed his advice until they felt dry land under their feet. When they *did* look back, it was to see a pink mist slowly fading above the morning sea.

"So where are we?" David asked, surveying the land ahead. It was typical Georgia coast, or typical *deserted* Georgia coast, anyway, of which there was not a great deal. White sand marched into grassy dunes which in turn invaded stands of scrubby live oaks, the whole strewn with what looked like storm wrack. There were no obvious buildings. And then he saw the wooden sign driven into the ground nearby: CUMBERLAND ISLAND NATIONAL SEASHORE.

"Well, that answers that, I guess," David said with a grin, flopping an arm across Calvin's shoulders. "But how in the hell did you *get* here? Best I can figure, you oughta still be stuck in Galunlati!"

Calvin had already opened his mouth to answer when a familiar voice interrupted with an irrepressible cackle as its white-haired owner rose from where he had been sitting in the scanty shelter of a large chunk of driftwood. "Come the same way I did!"

"Uncle Dale!" David shouted joyfully. He slipped free of Liz and Calvin and dashed forward to embrace the old man. "Oh Jesus, Uncle Dale, how in the world . . . ?"

"Out of the world," the old man laughed. "Ask Mr. Calvin, I can't explain a word of it."

David turned back to his friend. "Okay, Fargo, spill it."

Calvin sighed. "Sure . . . but back in the trees, okay? I've had *enough* sunshine for a while."

David started to follow him, but froze. "How *is* Galunlati?" he asked carefully.

Calvin shrugged. "Don't know for sure, but I reckon it'll be fine now."

"You act like you know what's been goin' on."

"I do, as a matter of fact."

"Oh?"

"Yeah."

They had reached the shelter of the trees now, and David saw that a breakfast had been spread across a blanket on the ground: a selection of McDonald's biscuits, a thermos of coffee, hash browns, even orange juice.

"Not the best," Uncle Dale admitted. "But the most available."

"It's great," David assured him as he grabbed a ham-and-cheese. He glanced back at Calvin. "So *spill* it, man."

Calvin sighed again and leaned back against a convenient live oak. "Well," he began, "I flew north searchin' for Uki, like we'd agreed. But there was one thing we forgot, which was that he still had his ulunsuti. He'd been usin' it to spy on us—at least as far as the stuff in our World was concerned—and so was ready when we popped into Galunlati. Not as ready as he'd have liked, natch, since a couple of glitches kinda landed us in the wrong place—but ready. Unfortunately, the place we wound up was pretty remote, so even Uki couldn't get anyone there quickly, but I met his emissary—it was Awahili the Eagle, and he told me that Uki had decided the only fast way to get Finno to the coast was for you two to shapeshift—which was exactly what you had already done. He had only five scales left, and couldn't spare all of 'em, but he gave me one so I could reenter our world, and another so I could rejoin him some time down the line. But he told me to tell you to use Finny's blood to empower the scale you already had with you, since he thought Faery blood might be strong enough to get through two sets of World Walls, and he had a good idea Finny could figure out the ritual. He also sent a strong north wind to speed us both along, and I tried to catch up to you, but you were always ahead. I got to the beach just in time to see you guys burn your scale and vanish. And by then I was so tired that war or no war, I only wanted to sleep. I did for a little while—had no choice—but then I decided it was time I got the hell out of there. I figured you guys were back in our World, since that was the plan, and I thought you had to stop off there on your way to Faerie. So I aimed for there when I burned my scale. Called on all three of you," he added. "Got no answer. It was kinda the world's ultimate wrong number. Well, I thought this was a mess 'cause I only had one more scale. I couldn't think of who to try next, since it needs to be a person with Power. I thought of Sandy, but wasn't sure how 'powerful' she is, and I didn't really wanta wind up back in Carolina, and had no clear destination along the coast. So I settled on Uncle Dale, figurin' he was a better risk and was that much closer—at least in Georgia."

He paused, took a long draught of coffee. "Well," he continued, "imagine *my* surprise when I burn the last scale—and find myself somewhere in the wilds of middle Georgia watchin' an old man talkin' to the State Troopers 'bout a certain red '66 Mustang they'd found abandoned with suspicious damage around the front end. Trouble was, I didn't have any clothes on as a result of my latest round of skinchanging, so I couldn't come out until they'd left, but they finally made a couple of calls and evidently ended up pretty satisfied. Luckily, this was some time 'round midnight our time, so they didn't see me pop in. But anyway, I got with Uncle Dale, and we decided to come on south in the Mustang, it bein' in better shape than the truck. Weren't sure where to go, exactly, so we just sorta winged it. Figured there'd be some kind of manifestation in this world if the battle happened as planned, so we went lookin' for bad weather. Wound up at the Cumberland Island Ferry, and that was really a mess, since they're kinda picky about who goes over and when. Uncle Dale knew one of the rangers from when he'd been stationed up in Enotah County, though. He pulled some strings, got us over.''

"And that's it," Uncle Dale finished. "You guys ready to go home?"

"Lord yes," David sighed. "I'm so ready I'd even let Alec drive."

"Oh, no," Alec protested. "Not me, not with your clutch!"

"Liz?"

"I've had enough of the Mustang-of-Death, David. You need to get your front end aligned."

"I reckon I'd better drive, then," Uncle Dale grumbled theatrically, with a wink at David. "You guys can sleep, 'cept—" He eyed Calvin speculatively, then grimaced and snapped his fingers. "Dammit . . . I *knew* I shoulda brought the truck. It's gonna be a tight squeeze for all of us."

Calvin shook his head and smiled. "I'll walk," he said. "I need to get some things out of my system, and there's nothin' like a good road trip to do that."

"But you'll miss the wedding!" David protested.

"Nope," Calvin replied. "I figure I'll just about take that long to get this stuff worked out. Tell you what: I'll give you a call if it looks like I'm gonna be late. One of you guys can come and get me."

"One thing, though," David insisted.

"What's that?"

"You've gotta join us for lunch. Way I've got it figured, we oughta just about be hittin' the mainland 'round lunch time. And there ain't nothin' in the world I like better'n fresh seafood."

"You got any money?" Uncle Dale asked wryly, lifting an eyebrow.

David chuckled wickedly. "No, but I bet you do."

"Besides, we could always sell a couple of David's hub-caps," Alec ventured.

David aimed a kick at his bottom which he expertly avoided. "Fool-of-a-very-blind-Scotsman, I don't *have* hubcaps!"

"Got some clothes for you in the truck, though," Dale noted. "Picked 'em up on the way. Thought you might need 'em."

"Good job!" David laughed, giving him another quick hug. "Seems like I always end these things either naked or in rags."

"I vote for the former," Liz whispered in his ear before she nipped it.

"*I* vote we travel," Alec sighed. "The sooner I get home, the sooner I can get to work on the ulunsuti."

"And the sooner I can get to my chemistry," Liz groaned. "Lord, I hope I don't fail."

"You won't," Calvin grinned. "I know you."

Liz rolled her eyes. "But do I?"

"We could always *check*," Alec ventured, "now that we've got a pipeline to the future."

"We will *not!*" Liz said firmly. "And that's that!"

Uncle Dale's warning cough masked Alec's reply, and they turned and marched further into the woods.

Three hours later, in the white-sanded parking lot of Whidden's Steak and Seafood somewhere north of St. Mary's, they said goodbye to Calvin. It was not as tearful a parting as their leavetaking of Fionchadd had been, but it still hurt. They'd all been through so much lately that their minds were still reeling, their bodies pumping so much adrenaline they were almost giddy.

"*Sure* you won't come with us?" David asked the Indian. "I bet Alec'd let you sit in his lap."

"Thanks, but no thanks, Dave," Calvin replied, suddenly very serious. "I really do have some pretty heavy things I gotta think through. I've called Sandy and told her I'll be there when I get there.''

David flopped an arm around his shoulders and drew him close. "Just be sure you don't miss the wedding," David said. "Don't forget you're a member of the MacTyrie gang now."

"Always and forever," Calvin acknowledged. "Wonder what color the tuxes are this mornin'."

"Plaid, probably," Alec shot back deadpan.

"Well," Calvin chuckled, winking at David and grinning so wide David thought his head would split, "I doubt seriously it'll be my last one. I mean I'd *hate* to miss a wedding."

"Long as they don't get to be too stylish, if you get my drift," David laughed back, kicking at a stray oyster shell.

Liz pinched him.

"Looks like another war," Calvin confided to Alec, as he turned to go.

"Yeah," Alec replied, "and this is one I *really* don't wanta get involved in."

Uncle Dale opened the car door and motioned his charges forward. "Take care," he called to Calvin.

"Bye, y'all!" Calvin shouted, still backing away. David climbed into the back seat with Liz. Alec inherited the front shotgun.

Calvin was still waving as the Mustang grunted to life and rumbled away. The sun stood straight above him, highlighting his body against the surrounding tangle of trees, but wrapping his feet in a puddle of shadow. David stared at his friend, then at the sky, where the sun showed absolutely no sign of moving, then at his friend again. Finally he rolled down the window and raised his hand in salute.

RETURN TO AMBER...

THE ONE *REAL* WORLD, OF WHICH ALL OTHERS, INCLUDING EARTH, ARE BUT SHADOWS

ROGER ZELAZNY

The New Amber Novel

SIGN OF CHAOS 89637-0/$3.50 US/$4.50 Can
Merlin embarks on another marathon adventure, leading him back to the court of Amber and a final confrontation at the Keep of the Four Worlds.

BLOOD OF AMBER 89636-2/$3.95 US/$4.95 Can
Pursued by fiendish enemies, Merlin, son of Corwin, battles through an intricate web of vengeance and murder.

TRUMPS OF DOOM 89635-4/$3.50 US/$3.95 Can
Death stalks the son of Amber's vanished hero on a Shadow world called Earth.

The Classic Amber Series

NINE PRINCES IN AMBER 01430-0/$3.50 US/$4.50 Can
THE GUNS OF AVALON 00083-0/$3.50 US/$4.50 Can
SIGN OF THE UNICORN 00031-9/$3.50 US/$4.25 Can
THE HAND OF OBERON 01664-8/$3.50 US/$4.50 Can
THE COURTS OF CHAOS 47175-2/$3.50 US/$4.25 Can